Copyright 2016 Dana Fraedrich

Maps by Hannah Pickering and Dana Fraedrich

Cover digital scrapbook pieces courtesy Doudou's Design

Book cover by Dana Fraedrich

Chapter heading art by Dana Fraedrich

**Content Warning: This book contains violence, homelessness, sexism, imprisonment, torture, death, and brutality by law enforcement**

ISBN: 9780692909232

WordsByDana.com

BROKEN GEARS

# OUT
## OF
## THE
# SHADOWS

## DANA FRAEDRICH

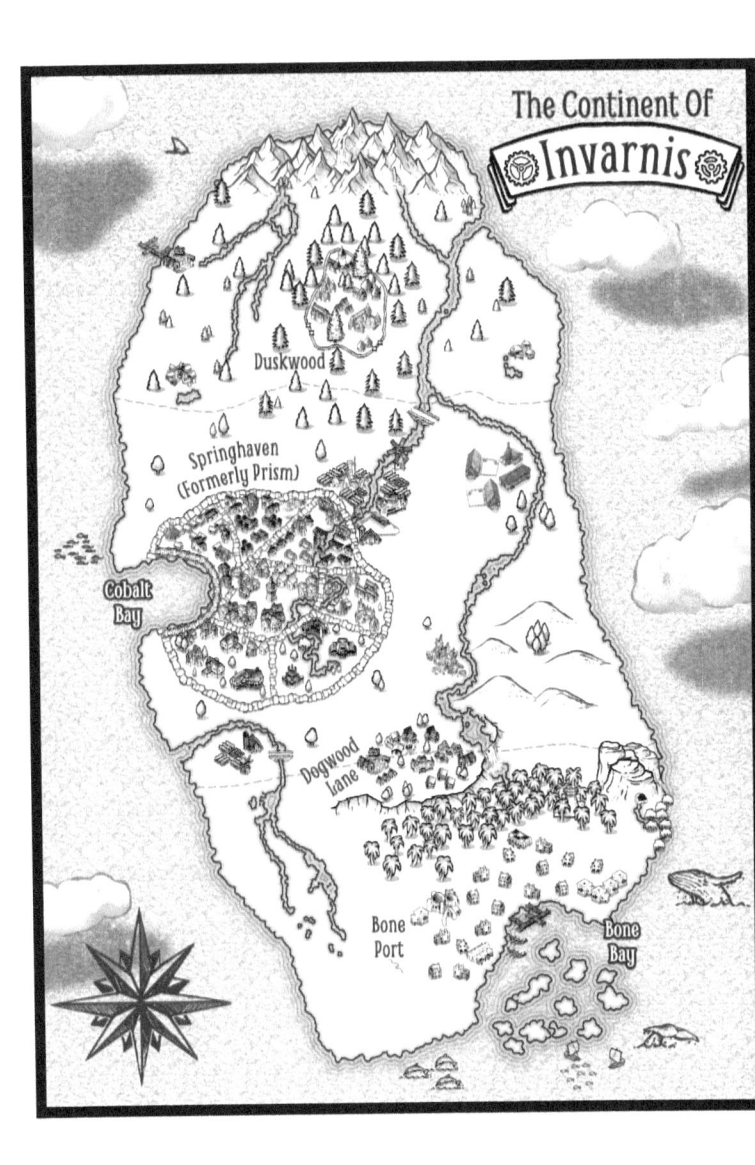

The Continent Of
Invarnis

Duskwood

Springhaven
(Formerly Prism)

Cobalt
Bay

Dogwood
Lane

Bone
Port

Bone
Bay

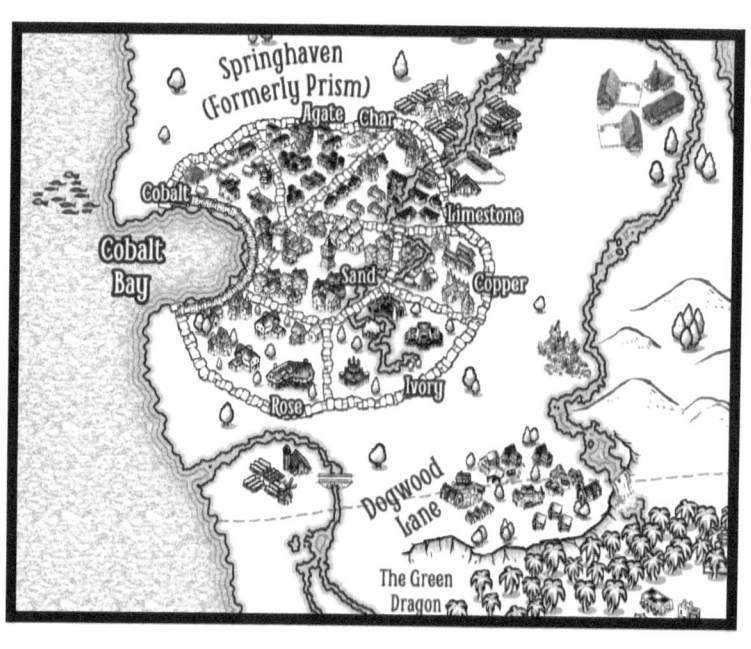

Springhaven
(Formerly Prism)

Agate    Char

Cobalt

Cobalt
Bay

Limestone

Sand

Copper

Rose

Ivory

Dogwood
Lane

The Green
Dragon

# 1

# STRANGE SAVIORS

L enore ran. She ran as fast as her legs would carry her. Her muscles felt like they were on fire, but burning alive was far better than the alternative. The Enforcers weren't known for their clemency or for doling out *quick* punishments. Lenore had one advantage: this was her turf. Well, not hers per se, but she knew it well enough for it to be hers. She dipped into alleys, scaled fences, double backed, and even released a few harried chickens from their little wooden cages, wincing and mouthing a few silent apologies to the owners as she did so. She had no choice, though. Despite everything she did, the Enforcers remained on her trail, getting inches closer with every stride. Lenore began to panic. What if she couldn't lose them? What if they caught her? How bad was it going to hurt? She pushed herself to go faster, but her body just couldn't obey. Lenore was counting off suicide options in her head when her midsection flew back, trailed closely by her head, arms, and legs.

*Calm down! Calm down! What's wrong? What's happening? Why did he feel this way? Was it Lenore? Sitting in his office, out of nowhere, panic had suddenly gripped him tight and was shaking his insides. His heart was racing, his mind desperately searching. But for what? There was the pain as well, like a repeated kicking to his back. It wouldn't stop. It was* angry*! It was pushing him to do something, to help her. His men were just outside… no. They couldn't see him like this. They couldn't know about her. No one could. He couldn't allow word of this, either the panic or her, to get out. It could ruin him. It could kill her. He sat back in his chair, willing the roiling in his stomach to settle. Closing his eyes, he tried to imagine something soothing, something that would calm his heart or distract his mind. Nothing worked, and he sat alone at his desk, riding out the waves of panic that swept through him and prayed that Lenore was safe.*

On the surface, it seemed a fairly quiet, content city. It was called Springhaven due to the freshwater spring in the southern part of the city, which fed a brook that gamboled merrily through the city. Its old name had been Prism, named for the different colors of stone that had been used to construct nearly everything in the Old World. Many of the buildings from that time were gone, save for the old palace, which was now the Parliament building, and a few others, but the walls and their distinct colors remained. Thus, the people still referred to each section of Springhaven by the old names.

Most people did well enough to feed their families and then some. The streets were kept in good repair, loose cobblestones being replaced within days, while education was provided for children until they came of age at sixteen. The farms around the city produced, medicine was competitively priced, and people had the freedom to learn new trades if they proved capable. There were, of course, those who had made more or less of themselves, but that was the responsibility of the individual. If one wanted to increase their station, they simply had to work for it. What the casual observer didn't see was the fear, the discontent that simmered barely beneath the mask of idyllic provinciality.

There were penalties for disrupting the system, severe penalties. Those that threatened to "bring chaos unto the public" were made examples of. Therefore, any activities that might be deemed as chaos-bringing had to be done in the darkest of shadows, away from any eyes that might know someone who knew someone who knew someone that might feel the need to inform the local law enforcement about those activities and their engagers. To be a criminal was to take one's life—perhaps one's sanity before that—into their own hands. To hide, aid, abet, or turn a blind eye to a criminal, though, was almost as bad.

It created an odd dichotomy in the public. Many understood the laws and followed them to the letter, staying as far from anyone remotely shady as possible and washing their hands of any blame when the need arose to report someone. And then there were those who decried the severity of the law, citing how ruthless the criminals that somehow evaded identification and capture were forced to be. After all, if a ne'er-do-well did ever decide to turn over a new leaf, he was forced to undergo the purging, grueling, torturous trials to prove his sincerity. Funny enough, almost no one ever came forward to repent. The other side would then claim that the fact that the career criminals were so terrible just proved why the laws were necessary. Just think of how bad it would be if the laws weren't as strict as they were. In addition to that, let no one forget that it was the criminal's choice in the first place to involve themselves in something everyone knew perfectly well carried a heavy price. And on and on the debate went.

It had been a normal evening for Lenore so far. Her marks strolled by unaware of her presence in the willow tree above them while she sat as silent as a cat stalking a mouse. The gardens were a good place to work. The visitors were almost all well-to-do, there were plenty of places to hide in the trees and bushes that were scattered about, and the babbling of the brook masked any noise she might make, as if the babbling of her marks didn't do that well enough for her. They were mostly empty-headed dolts that had nothing better to do than walk through the government-maintained giant flowerpot, also known as the city gardens. Oh, to have no financial worries whatsoever. Lenore wanted to kick each and every one of them in the teeth, but she'd settled for nicking their trinkets. Then she'd head back to the attic, maybe have a bite to eat, sleep, and do the whole thing all over again.

It wasn't Bitsy's fault that everything had gone wrong in the end, though he had been acting like the coast was clear, which was what Lenore usually used as a guide. Bitsy was Lenore's faithful little ringcat and partner-in-crime. She and Bitsy tag teamed on pickpocketing the patrons of the garden. The best was when they could detach the mark's coin purse—it was stupidly fashionable to display this prominently for everyone to see just how rich you were—as coins didn't require appraisal. She would take what she could get, though, and if that meant a bracelet or fob watch of unknown worth, well then, that was that. As soon as the mark was done staring into their paramour's eyes or up at the stars or down into the brook, as marks were wont to do while on a romantic stroll, and had decided to move on, Lenore would move on to a new spot. She never liked staying in one place too long, lest her victims come back to search for their lost items, which was why she liked the tipsy ones best. She often watched Bitsy for his body language and used that as her cue for when it was safe. Admittedly, though, she liked to prowl from under willow trees because of the excellent cover they provided.

The timing had just been all wrong this time. Lenore had just alighted to the ground to join Bitsy and see what goody he had managed to pluck from the gentleman's pocket. Hmm, it was a small, smooth stone, but it was too dark to make out much else. Oh well, maybe it would get her a few coppers. Suddenly, the wall of leaves parted and a new couple walked into Lenore's hunting ground.

"What in the world…" the man exclaimed.

Then there was a period of a silence for a few seconds wherein Lenore simply stared at the couple dumbly while they stared back at her. It was the hesitation that did her in. Lenore had wasted those precious few seconds debating whether or not to try and lie when she should have just run. It would have been fruitless anyway. Lenore did not fit the bill for the garden's usual clientele, not at all.

Issue number one, Lenore looked far too young to be out at that hour. She made herself look that way, though, because people were far less skeptical of someone that looked like they belonged in mid-level courses than of someone who had only recently come of age. Her dark hair was left down and had braids in a few places to mimic the style that most young girls were currently wearing. Issue number two, her clothes screamed criminal. She wore boy's clothing because they were simply easier, but they were all black to help conceal her. Issue number three, she was dirty and carried what looked like a skinny, stripey tailed cat with her. Although, Bitsy shot off into the darkness in that moment, so at least he was safe.

The next sound was the astonished gasp of a woman from behind her. Lenore spun around to see that the couple from before had returned, probably alerted by the first man's exclamation. The robbed couple was shouting for the Enforcers before Lenore was three strides away. Even worse, the garden was surrounded by gates, gates that couldn't be scaled. Lenore knew this for a fact; she had tried before. She made a beeline for the entrance as fast as she could, and thus ensued her mad dash through the city, whizzing by fine plaster-and-dark-beamed manors, shops, and upscale eateries with harried chickens in cages beside them.

When Lenore was pulled backwards, she was surprised because she thought she'd had at least a bit more of a lead than that. It didn't matter, though. She wasn't going down without a fight. Maybe by some miracle she'd catch a break and get free again. Lenore drove both elbows back as hard as she could, which may have just worked if it weren't for the fact that she and her captor were already falling backwards. She landed on something soft in complete darkness and was on her feet again in less than a second. There was that complete darkness thing, though. When she had been running a moment ago, her path had been lit by the soft glow of petrolsene lights and the moon. Where was she now? Lenore backed up until she hit a wall and remained ready to fight. She began inching her way to the side, thinking there might be a door somewhere. The sound of heavy boots running approached and then faded, followed a few moments later by a single match light. The match light became an oil lamp, and the area all around Lenore was suddenly bathed in a warm, yellow glow. She saw the man first, gingerly holding his arm across his abdomen. She was about to cry out, "You!" but a delicate hand clamped itself over her mouth with a determination that belied its delicacy.

"Shhhh!" a female voice hissed in her ear. "Do you want to get us all caught?"

Lenore did not try to speak, but shook her head earnestly. Of course she didn't, but what did her would-be accusers have to worry about?

"I'm going to let go of you now, but you must stay silent. Understand?" the woman said firmly.

Lenore nodded this time and was released. The woman joined the man and began to poke and prod him in a way that looked more like a medical examination than anything else. The man made no move to stop her, and Lenore watched them both warily. Finally, when the woman seemed satisfied, she kissed the man on the cheek and turned her attention back to Lenore. She glanced at what Lenore could now see as a cellar door and motioned for her to follow. Lenore had no desire to do any such thing, but couldn't think of a better idea. There were Enforcers outside looking for her, but these two could just be planning to turn her in later. That logic didn't really make sense, though. If they had any kind of sense, they wouldn't waste time that the Enforcers could use to accuse them of helping Lenore. Besides, there were no Enforcers inside… as far as Lenore knew, anyway. That being the case, she followed, but at a distance that kept her safe from the couple's reaching arms in case they tried to grab her again.

The three walked up a narrow staircase and up into a large kitchen replete with a potbelly stove large enough to cook an entire lamb in. From the kitchen they walked through a butler's closet—*closet my eye,* Lenore thought—and into a grand dining room. The woman motioned for Lenore to sit, which she refused to do with a defiant glare.

"Suit yourself," said the woman with a very unladylike shrug.

She then sat while the man stood behind her and put his

hands on her shoulders.

"First of all," the man said kindly, "let me apologize. I am deeply, deeply sorry for drawing attention to you. We did not mean for you to be discovered."

Lenore was very confused and intrigued by this, but still said nothing.

"Allow me to make the introductions," the man continued. "I am Sir Gwenael Allen and this is my lovely wife, Philomena."

"Mina will do just fine," the woman interjected suddenly, giving her husband's hand a squeeze.

He smiled and added, "You may call me Neal."

Lenore didn't call either of them anything. She simply remained silent, wondering whether or not she could make it out the cellar without being caught.

"We're not going to turn you in," Mina said after several moments.

"Why not?" were the first words Lenore said to the couple.

The two shared a smile that seemed to hold a great meaning for them and then turned back to Lenore.

"We do not… agree with the severity with which criminal punishment is exacted," Neal explained.

"Don't think that means we condone criminal behavior either, however," Mina added firmly, giving Lenore a hard glare.

"Well, I appreciate you hiding me and all. Trust me, I really do," Lenore said defensively, "but, seeing as how my criminal behavior is going to continue, I'll just be on my way."

Lenore turned to leave, but Mina spoke again with such force that Lenore stopped in her tracks.

"And just what is so important for you to get back to?"

Lenore narrowed her eyes at the woman there who was now standing tall and ramrod straight. She didn't like the woman. Who was this stuck up peacock to think she had any business asking Lenore such personal questions?

"Thank you both again," Lenore snipped. "Good night." With that she turned on her heel and left the way she came.

Bitsy was waiting for Lenore back at the attic when she arrived just before dawn. It wasn't really an attic so much as dead space between the attics of her parent's old house and the one attached next door. It grew almost unbearably hot in the summer and bone achingly cold in the winter, as simple wooden walls were all that separated Lenore from the outside. She'd discovered the space when she was little, having accidentally found the hidden latch to the small door and crawling through. She'd found a similar entrance on the neighbor's side and jammed the handle with some scrap metal. Thankfully, no one on the other side seemed to know about the space. At least, Lenore had never heard anyone try to get in. If they did, she didn't know what she'd do or where she would go.

Lenore had to move in her cramped little space carefully, always being as silent and stealthy as fog creeping over the earth, lest the neighbors or new occupants of her parent's old house heard her. She only ever came and went when it was properly dark outside, sneaking out via a window in the attic and the large tree growing just outside.

As for Bitsy, Lenore never worried about her little companion; it was easy for him to disappear when necessary. He was sitting on a rafter when she came in and leapt down to greet her ecstatically. The little creature nuzzled her neck and wrapped his long bushy tail around it as he chattered happily.

"I'm glad to see you too," Lenore sighed. "That was a close one tonight. Glad I caught a break for once…"

Lenore's mind drifted back to the couple that had saved her from certain torture. They were certainly different, odd maybe, but they had been kind, and Lenore had not experienced real kindness in a long time. Oh well, it was done now. Lenore took just enough time to fill her stomach with some stale bread and dodgy-looking cheese before falling asleep to the sounds of a waking city.

*Ninth Year of the New Age, Second Day of the Earth*
*Official report submitted by Fifths Campbell and Ellis:*

*We were alerted and gave chase to a thief this evening. The thief was preying on citizens visiting the gardens. Cries from the latest victims—a Mister Malachite Nichols and Miss Temperance Hester—alerted us to the trouble just after a quarter past twelve as we patrolled our usual route. Mister Nichols reported a prized piece of Old World Jade as stolen. See the end of this report for a record of the eyewitnesses' descriptions of the thief\*. As we began pursuit, the perpetrator made for the Rose quarter of the city. Visual contact was difficult to maintain through the alleys she took between the manors. She disappeared completely somewhere between the Chicory Lane and Anemone Green. We recommend working with local shopkeepers and residents to put up barriers and fences to block these types of escape paths.*

*Eyewitness Description Report: Female, small, probably about fourteen years of age. Most likely a vagrant, judging by the clothing, which was black, made for a boy, and very shabby. Very dark eyes and long, dark hair. Light skin.*

*\*We understand there were two other eyewitnesses, but they disappeared before we arrived, and neither Mister Nichols nor*

*Miss Hester could name them or remember anything about them.*

# 2

# A DEBT AND AN OFFER

hings were bad. They hadn't been this bad in a long time, but Lenore couldn't risk going back to the gardens. Enforcers were surely keeping an eye out there for suspicious characters after she had gotten away the previous month. She might be able to return one day, but not any time soon. It probably burned them up that their prey had evaded capture, and she wasn't stupid enough to test her luck. That was why she hadn't taken Bitsy out with her since that awful night. Much as she loved the little creature, she just couldn't risk him being seen. He was too recognizable. When she was really honest, she wasn't that great a thief, just a safe one. She always picked stupid and/or distracted targets. The gardens had really been an ideal spot, and Lenore cursed Neal and Mina for ruining it for her. Lenore had been forced to steal from the grocer in order to eat, something she actually despised herself for doing.

Lenore didn't like being a thief, but she had no choice—despite what the Enforcer supporters claimed—so she dealt with it the best way she knew how. The daughter of "criminals" couldn't get employed or apprenticed out to anyone. There

Dana Fraedrich

were poorhouses, which Lenore had considered, until she overheard Enforcers sniffing around the neighborhood and asking questions about where she might have gone. That was it. Lenore had to stay hidden, so this was the only option left to her. She generally only stole from those who could afford it. Grocers, farmers, bakers, and the like were often hurt to some extent by being robbed, though, and those that could afford to be robbed could also afford security. Once again, Lenore was left with no choice but to hurt others. Story of her life.

Before her discovery at the willow tree, she had simply bought food from the underground market, a grungy place in the basements of an abandoned warehouse in the Char district, the worst part of town. It was a well-kept secret—it had to be—and was strictly policed by thugs in the employ of the owner, whoever that was. Lenore had no desire or intention to find out and always visited covered in a long, black cloak to conceal herself. She wasn't the only one that dressed this way, as cloaks were helpful in concealing one in the dead of night, but she was only one of a few. The market was a quiet place due to the need for secrecy, and Lenore only stayed as long as it took to get the essentials. She hated that part of town.

It had actually once been part of the Agate quarter, which had been very sought after with its exotic orchid, lavender, and plum colored walls. Destruction from the War of Light, however, had permanently blackened the ground and walls, thus earning that section of the city the name the Char district. There had been a few attempts to revitalize the area in the last hundred years, but nothing would grow there, nothing would clear away the black, and anything built there seemed fraught with difficulties. Most people believed the area was cursed from the war, and it had been long abandoned.

Shopping for groceries was difficult with no money or trinkets, however. She was fairly sure she had been cheated when she took the green stone around to the few fences she knew. She had only gotten a silver for it, but the twitch at the corner of the man's mouth had made her uneasy. She knew she should have held out for more, but she was out of money and needed food soon. That had run out about two weeks ago. Most of her successes since the harrowing chase had taken place outside of pubs as patrons were drunkenly stumbling out to return home. These marks, however, had unsurprisingly little, if any, money in their coin purses after a night of carousing. That was where Lenore was now. Sure, she could try to go work for the anonymous crime lords that ran the underground market and engineered strikes against the Enforcers and whatnot, but Lenore was no cutthroat. She knew she didn't have what it took to be a proper criminal, nor did she want to. She also had no desire to become known… by anyone. Nevermind that there was no honor among thieves, so she remained a lonely shadow. She just wanted to survive.

A good mark appeared in the doorway of The Kicking Mule, bracing himself against the railing of the steps that led up into the pub. He turned to wave and yell at his mates that were still inside.

"A top night, gents, a top night!" he slurred. "Behave yourselves now. Don't go getting into trouble without me."

Lenore winced as the man almost fell backwards down the steps. It looked as if he was in danger of breaking his neck, which he probably was, but he pulled it together at the last minute. Toddling down the four or five stairs, the man grumbled to himself about them, citing a "ruddy fool thing to do, having steps to a pub." Lenore couldn't help but agree. Once he was down and had entered the gloom of the night, Lenore moved. She stepped out of the shadows and did her best drunken tumble into the man. Giggling like an idiot, she twittered at him.

"Oh, excuse me! Didn't see you there."

She put her hand on the man's hip as she spoke, feeling a few coins in his purse. If she was lucky, they'd be silver and not copper.

"Well, darling," the man breathed into her face—Lenore barely held her composure against the stench—"now that you have, would you mind escorting me home? I seem to have lost track of my feet a bit."

Lenore just giggled again. She needed that purse, so she let the man lean on her and began to teeter with him.

"Stop right there!" came a strong, commanding voice.

Lenore's heart froze inside of her. They found her! Someone recognized her! This was it! Her new friend swung her around with him before she could do anything, though, so she found herself watching an Enforcer stride towards them. She sized him up quickly. Young, probably just a few years older than she, which either made him overzealous or, more preferably, a bit of a pushover with the ladies. Too bad Lenore looked nothing like a lady at the moment.

"Do you know this… person, sir?" the Enforcer demanded, looking at Lenore suspiciously.

"Course!" Drunkie, as Lenore had named him in her head, blustered. "This here's me friend. She's walking me home."

"What's her name?" the Enforcer asked.

"What's it matter?"

Lenore was doing her best to look casual and unconcerned and inebriated, but she was pretty sure her pounding heart was giving her away.

"It's a matter of security," the Enforcer said sternly.

"You Enforcers and your security," the man said, suddenly angry. Lenore instinctively took a step away. Incriminating or no, angry drunks were dangerous. "We do just fine without your help," he spat. "Come on, love, he can't fight us both."

Lenore very much wanted to point out that the Enforcer could probably fight them both six times over, but there was no time. Drunkie suddenly pulled a knife on the Enforcer and lunged at him. She saw everything with an almost superhuman clarity. The Enforcer's eyes suddenly filled with fear as he was charged by a stinking, drunken force of senseless rage. Lenore may have overestimated his age. He now looked as if he hadn't been in a fight his whole life. Fear turned to shock as the knife penetrated his flesh and he turned his eyes onto Lenore... begging. Things sped up from there. Drunkie staggered back from his target looking incredibly smug for just a moment before violently puking onto his own feet. Without thinking, Lenore ran forward and caught the Enforcer before he fell.

"You need a doctor," she said stupidly.

The Enforcer made a terrible, strangled noise before saying, "Copper quarter... near Thyme's Apothecary."

Lenore briefly wondered if he realized that no physician would be open at this hour, but she said nothing. Instead, she steered the Enforcer around Drunkie, who was kneeling in his own vomit and heaving now, and began the long, terrifying walk.

What was she doing?! As soon as another Enforcer spotted them, she'd be discovered. Why was she even helping this one? He'd been ready to shackle and drag her away to the Halls of Justice not minutes ago. She knew why; it was her fault. She'd been the reason he'd even approached the drunkard. If it hadn't been for her, he never would have gotten stabbed. Still, that didn't excuse her current stupidity. Thankfully, the Enforcer said nothing as they walked the agonizingly slow path to Thyme's Apothecary. Under normal circumstances, Lenore could get there in just a few minutes. Now she wondered if her charge would bleed out before they even arrived. Arrive they did, however, and Lenore was elated when she saw light in the window of the building next to the apothecary. This part of town was near the gardens and therefore nice enough for the petrolsene lamps to still be lit. Lenore hung her head forward so that her face remained hidden behind her hair and planned to run as soon as the door opened. Surely no doctor would turn away an injured Enforcer. Her part in this would be done and she could go curl up in a safe, quiet, dark place… for a few days if need be. Lenore rapped on the door sharply, breathing fast until it opened.

The door did open, but Lenore stood frozen to her spot. There in the doorway before her was Mina in a doctor's coat.

"Good heavens!" Mina exclaimed at the sight before her.

The fugitive from last month was there with a badly bleeding Enforcer.

"Inside. On the table in the back." she said, taking command of the situation. She caught the hesitation in Lenore's eyes. The girl wanted to run and she would given the chance, so Mina didn't give it to her. "Now!" she said in a tone that brooked no argument.

Lenore staggered in with the Enforcer, squinting at the brightness of the room. Petrolsene sconces lined the walls here, outlining every detail of every object. This was very bad for Lenore. The Enforcer had been getting weaker during the journey and leaning on Lenore more and more, so she was only too glad to unload him onto the metal table as Mina had instructed.

"Camilla! Sutures! Room one!" Mina called into the building.

She then went about cutting the Enforcer's jacket off of him and examining the wound. Lenore was beginning to inch her way back towards the door when Mina snapped at her.

"You will go into the laboratory and help Camilla with anything she needs. You will *not* run off and you will stay. Out.

Of. Sight."

Lenore scowled at the woman. Again, who did she think she was? Lenore began to stomp out defiantly, when Mina snarled at her.

"You owe me a debt! I expect it to be paid!"

Lenore shook with rage. How *dare* she?! Everything in Lenore screamed at her to keep walking, to just leave. Nothing would happen. Words did nothing, but there was a dark fear in the back of Lenore's mind, a fear that told her she had to do as Mina said. If she didn't, the consequences would be worse than anything the Enforcers could do to her. Lenore turned and glared at Mina venomously. The woman paid her no mind as she continued her examination. Lenore then swept towards the back of the building to where she decided the laboratory must be.

Her assumption was correct. A girl a little older than she was there picking up a tray of silver medical tools, gauze, and suture thread.

"What do you need?" Lenore asked shortly.

"Distilled alcohol, please. Top shelf," the girl replied pleasantly, carrying the tray past Lenore into room one.

This must be Camilla. Lenore begrudgingly followed her instructions and climbed up to get the bottle of clear liquid from the top shelf. Camilla was back in a few minutes to fetch it, which she did with a smile that made Lenore even angrier. And so it went. Lenore fetched what Camilla needed, and Camilla took it out and assisted Mina. The injury was apparently pretty mild. No organs had been hit. It was just a matter of stopping the bleeding and stitching the flesh back together. Lenore turned a bit green at hearing this and even greener when Camilla carried the bloody gauzes back into the lab.

"You get used to it," Camilla chirped.

Mina appeared a few minutes after that, holding the blood-covered gloves she had been wearing gingerly by the corners. Camilla automatically took them from her to clean them along with the gauzes.

"Is he gone?" Lenore asked immediately.

"Yes," Mina replied evenly. "It was a clean cut, easy to repair. Camilla fetched a few of his comrades to help carry him out to a cab. I didn't charge them, of course, and they were so concerned for him that they didn't ask any questions. You're in the clear, as they say."

"Good, so what do you want?" Lenore demanded.

"I beg your pardon?"

"What do I have to do to pay my debt?"

Still speaking with that same steely, even tone that Lenore found very odd for a woman of Mina's position to have, she said, "Camilla, dear, could you leave us for a moment? I'll finish washing up here."

"Yes, ma'am," Camilla replied before disappearing out of the room and silently elsewhere.

As promised, Mina began to wash the gloves and gauzes. She donned a pair of heavy rubber gloves that reminded Lenore of the kind her father used to wear when he worked on his machines and began dipping everything into a foul-smelling bath.

"You are a foolish girl," Mina said matter-of-factly. "You just can't wait to rush back out there and endanger your life."

"Don't act like you know so much," Lenore spat. "What do you know about how hard it is on the streets? You've got money and a house and, for some reason, a surgery of your own."

Scrubbing the items against a washboard, Mina said, "I'm sure you don't like to hear it, but the fact is that you are condemning yourself to a painful, tortured life at the hands of the Enforcers. It may not come soon, but, at the rate you're going, it will be."

"Then that's my choice, isn't it? Now tell me how I can pay back my debt!" Lenore was shouting now. She was so angry she was shaking.

"I won't hold you," Mina said coldly, "but I will make you an offer. Stay with Neal and I. I'll need another apprentice soon. I'll teach you the skills of a physician."

Lenore didn't know what to say. She didn't know what to think. This was crazy. Then again, it wasn't the first time Mina and Neal had helped her. What if it was a trick? What if it *wasn't*? It came down to two things: they'd had the opportunity to let her get caught and turn her in and didn't do either, and Lenore just wasn't that stupid. She was being offered a job and a home. Sure, there was still some risk, but that risk seemed to be shrinking by the minute. It certainly seemed less risky than her current circumstances. She pounced on the opportunity.

"Fine. So now what?"

"Now, you can finish washing these things," Mina said, carefully removing the rubber gloves. "I have to go disinfect my tools. Mind you don't get any of the cleaner on your skin and step away if you begin to feel faint."

"How do I know when they're clean?" Lenore asked petulantly.

"When they're snowy white," Mina said simply and then left.

Lenore slipped her hands into the gloves and stepped up to the sink. She almost choked on the fumes; it smelled like burning metal and alcohol. It took her a moment to collect herself before she could get to the task of washing. Very carefully, she dipped her hands into the cleaner and felt around for the gauzes. Her fingers barely felt something soft through the thick rubber, and she picked it up. She began to rub the material over the washboard. The now brown blood had mostly come away from the material, but there were still disturbing large, tan splotches across it. Lenore fell into the steady rhythm of washboard-dip-check-washboard. Her attention snapped to the doorway every time she heard footsteps, however, but it was always just Camilla or Mina. Then, one time, it was Neal.

"Hello there," he said. "I was surprised to hear you had come back into our lives. I'm very glad for it. We were rather concerned after you left that night."

Lenore said nothing, not because she wasn't grateful but because she simply didn't know what to say.

"I don't think we even know your name," Neal continued as if the awkward silence between them didn't exist. "Do you think that might help?"

Lenore looked sideways at the man. He was leaning casually against the counter and smiling at her just like he would a friend. She furrowed her brow. What was wrong with these people?! Nevertheless, he had a point.

"Lenore," she said quietly. "And… thank you… very much… for taking me in."

She might not trust these people, they might even be a little mad, but she had not been raised to be ungrateful.

"Think nothing of it. It's the least we can do. From what I gather, we spoiled things for you a bit. Once again, I apologize for that. It's good to meet you, Lenore."

Then he bowed courteously to her, and Lenore felt something catch in her throat. Quick as a flash, she looked away and pushed the feeling down. There was no way she was going to cry! She was no simpering, pathetic waif. She suddenly wondered if she should have given a false name. Oh well, it wouldn't have made that much of a difference. Even if there were records on her, it wasn't like she was running for public office. There were enough Lenores out there, and she hadn't given a surname. Neal remained while she finished cleaning the gloves and gauze. He said nothing, but Lenore had the distinct feeling Mina had sent him to make sure she didn't disappear. Camilla reappeared later and helped Lenore finish. After everything was clean and rinsed and hanging up to dry, Mina and Neal locked everything up, and they all left together.

Lenore stuck to the shadows as they walked. She had begun wearing long skirts again to rob drunks—looking more feminine increased her success—so she didn't look like a complete ragamuffin, but she still wasn't far off. Neal asked Camilla how her day was and conversed with Mina about various things, but Lenore wasn't paying attention. She was watching their surroundings, waiting for Enforcers to appear from around every corner. Mina's shoes were tapping far too loudly on the street... Neal's voice was carrying too far... this was a terrible idea... she was going to get caught! Suddenly, the feel of someone touching her shoulder broke through her panicked thoughts.

Lenore jumped back, but knew better than to make a sound. It was Mina who had touched her and it was Mina who was smiling at her a little sadly now.

"We're here, dear," she said softly. "It's alright."

Lenore looked and saw Neal opening the door of a very fine manor home. It was large, though not ostentatiously so, with well-tended flowerbeds that ran all the way down the front of the house. The dark brown beams contrasted starkly against the clean white of the plaster walls. When Neal opened the door, golden light poured out onto the street, and Lenore could see the same type of expertly crafted furniture inside that she remembered from her first time here. She followed Camilla up the steps quickly, skipping those that she could, and slipped inside. The sooner she was in, the sooner she would be out of sight from the Enforcers.

As soon as the door closed behind them all, a great wave of

exhaustion broke over Lenore. She leaned again the wall, feeling like she could lie down and sleep for days right there on the floor.

"I think our guest could use a meal, don't you, dearest?" Neal said to Mina.

"Agreed, but a bath first."

Lenore looked to the two with narrowed eyes.

"I mean no offense," Mina said evenly, "but you must admit it's needed."

Lenore couldn't argue with that. It had been a very long time since she'd had a proper bath. The occasional dip in the brook in the gardens hardly counted, and she hadn't done that for more than a month.

"Lead on," Lenore finally said.

"I'll just be making sure dinner is all taken care of," Neal said, slipping out of the reception hall.

Mina then walked to a staircase, leading Lenore and Camilla, who had been obediently standing by. Up the stairs they went and down a hallway to a set of closed double doors, which Mina opened to a very fine bedroom.

"This will be your room, dear," Mina said. "Camilla is right next door. The washroom is there and the water closet is inside. Camilla, dear, will you please let Lenore borrow some of your things? We'll get replacements and new clothes tomorrow. Lenore, will you be alright on your own?"

Once again, Lenore suspected she was only being asked because Mina thought she would run off. Then again, maybe it was because she looked so young or maybe Mina thought she might have forgotten how to bathe after all this time.

"I'll be fine," Lenore said simply. Then, after a pause, added, "Thank you."

"Of course, dear," and Lenore was surprised to see Mina smile at her.

"I'll be back with some things for you," Camilla said.

The two women then left. Lenore slumped as soon as they did. She seriously hoped she wouldn't fall asleep in the tub and drown. She sighed inwardly at the potential irony. The washroom was pretty basic in its amenities, though there were numerous bottles of bath creams, lotions, soaps, salts, and oils. Each one was labeled with a particular fragrance, which reminded Lenore more of a spice cabinet than anything else.

*Poach one Lenore in hot water seasoned with lavender and vanilla...* she thought to herself with a smirk.

Maybe she'd try seasoning her bath another day. For now, she just needed to get clean. As soon as the tub was full, Lenore climbed in and practically melted. It had been so long since she'd had anything close to a hot bath. It was like heaven. Yes, the possibility of falling asleep was imminent, so Lenore quickly went about the business of bathing. As she did, she tried to focus on her surroundings to get her mind off of how tired she was.

The first thing she noticed was that Mina and Neal had left the copper pipes that led to the tub exposed. It had become fashionable to hide any exposed plumbing with various types of decorative covers, stools, curtains, and all manner of other things that Lenore found fairly ridiculous. She rather liked the look of the copper pipes; it was like working artwork to her. Lenore also saw a window there in the washroom. She automatically made a mental note of this as she always did wherever she was.

Lenore had emptied the tub once and refilled it by the time she was done washing. The water had turned cloudy and opaque before she had even gotten to her hair. The braids in her hair had kept some of it from tangling, but that was little help when compared to the rest of her snarled and occasionally matted tresses. She'd worry about that later. Exhaustion was really setting in, so Lenore quickly finished and wrapped up in a surprisingly fluffy robe. She peeked out into the bedroom to make sure… well, she didn't know what she was making sure of, but there was nothing there that worried her, so she headed out.

Lenore was out of her room within minutes. The smell of food had started wafting through the air, and Lenore's stomach was about to turn itself inside out. She immediately hated the dress Camilla had left for her. It was a black and pink beribboned travesty complete with corset and high-heeled boots. She left the corset and boots behind, but changed into the dress as fast as she could before heading downstairs in bare feet. Camilla, Mina, and Neal were all already there in the dining room. More importantly, a platter of food was already sitting on the table, calling to Lenore.

"There she is," Neal said jovially. "Are we ready to eat then?"

Lenore nodded, trying her best not to look too desperate. They all sat down at the dining table, and Mina served them.

"Neal was kind enough to prepare dinner for us tonight," she told Lenore. "He fancies himself a bit of a cook." The two exchanged playful smiles before Mina added, "He's actually quite good."

Lenore nodded and said simply, "Thank you very much."

She waited only a split second after her hosts had begun to eat to dig in herself. She imagined that she was practicing impressive self-restraint, but in reality she resembled a wildling of the Old World. No one said anything, however, and gladly obliged when she asked for more.

"Tell us, Lenore," Neal said after she had finished her

second plate. "Where's your furry friend?"

Lenore looked at the man sideways. Had he really seen Bitsy? They hadn't stared one another down for more than a few seconds, and that had been over a month ago.

"I didn't bring him with me," she said evasively. She then paused and said nervously, "Will he be allowed to live here too?"

"Of course, dear," Mina said. "I believe every young lady needs a little companion. My question for you is whether or not he can protect you?"

"What do you mean?"

"What I mean is that a lady's companion, should she choose to have one, is not just for show. He should be able to protect her should the need arise."

"Are we still talking about animals?" Lenore asked before she could stop herself. She did always have a big mouth.

Neal laughed, while Mina smiled appropriately.

"Yes, dear, I am."

"In that case… I don't know. Bitsy always just runs, and I prefer it that way. I don't want him getting hurt."

"Understandable," Neal said.

After that, Lenore felt as if she would pass out right then and there. Mina suggested she retire, and Camilla mentioned that a nightgown had been left on the bed for Lenore. Lenore nodded, thanked them all again, and headed upstairs to sleep.

*What the blazes was happening?! It had happened again, earlier that evening. He was calm again and could now focus on the problem properly. The panic had come upon him, though this time it had been a slower build… relatively speaking. "Think logically," he told himself. She couldn't be a prisoner,*

*could she? No, that didn't make sense. He'd be in constant agony if she was. Not that earlier had been particularly pleasant. He rubbed his lower back. It was still pulsing slightly, but it was nothing compared to the red hot pain from earlier. Then again, did it feel better now? Pain was such an odd, subjective thing. He'd felt for about a month now that she must be in some kind of trouble with the constant irking in his back, but he hadn't a clue as to what was wrong.*

*He had sent his feelers out, deftly poking here, prodding there, listening for any word of her. There was nothing, nothing definitive anyway. There were rumors that someone had escaped the Enforcers that night, but only by the skin of their teeth. How it had been done was a mystery. He had hidden it in the moment, but his heart skipped a beat at hearing the news. Had that been Lenore? Had she really been inches from being caught? If so, where was she now? He* needed *to find her, needed it unlike he had ever needed anything else in his entire life. Besides the rumors, however, there was nothing else. How could she disappear so completely? She was like a ghost. Then again, how did he even know she was still in the city? Was it possible she had gone elsewhere? Doubtful. The permits required to travel between the various independent city-states of Invarnis required resources he didn't think she possessed. Besides, he somehow felt that she was still here. He couldn't explain why, he just did. Not that it helped. He still had no idea where she was or why he was being assaulted by these feelings. He'd have to investigate again… carefully. He couldn't lean on anyone too hard, lest they figure out what he might really be after.*

# 3
# DAYLIGHT

Lenore awoke to a gentle shaking and immediately jumped up and out of bed... and right down onto the floor. She was not lying on her pallet back at the attic, but rather in a real bed in a real room. Her mind raced to figure out what was going on. Only when she saw Camilla did she remember.

"Are you alright?" the girl asked, her blue eyes wide with concern.

"I... ah... yes... I think so..." was Lenore's reply.

"Good," came Mina's voice then. "Then let's get you presentable. Come over here, please."

Lenore's surprise was quickly being overtaken by annoyance. She was good at waking up fast, but that didn't mean she was happy about it. Mina saw her reaction and responded simply.

"Now, please. This is a perfectly acceptable time to sleep till after a night like last night, but we do have things to do."

Lenore unhappily headed over to the vanity where Mina was standing and sat down on the stool. She eyed the hairbrush in Mina's hand like she would a poisonous snake.

"I'll try to be as gentle as possible," Mina promised.

Then the woman went about the tedious work of brushing through Lenore's snarls and tangles and snipping out mats when the brush simply wasn't up to the job. She really did try to be gentle, though there were moments wherein Lenore had to grit her teeth and bear it.

"Done!" Mina finally declared, after what seemed like an eternity. "And your hair is so lovely, Lenore."

Lenore looked in the mirror and saw her long, dark hair was indeed all brushed out for the first time in who knew how long, if not somewhat still disheveled.

"After you're dressed, we'll put it up so you can't see where it's been cut," Mina added. "Camilla's brought you some more clothes to wear today."

Lenore mentally cringed at the idea of another one of Camilla's outfits. Nevertheless, she turned to see what was waiting for her. Hanging there on the armoire was a less-than-tragic lilac colored dress. It still wasn't really Lenore's color, but at least it wasn't pink. It did, however, still have a corset and high-heeled boots.

"Do I have to wear the corset?" Lenore asked before she could stop herself. Then, very quickly, she added, "Not that I don't appreciate it and all, but it's just…" She trailed off as Mina raised her hand.

"Yes, you do have to wear the corset, but not too tightly. Honestly, it's really quite unhealthy to wear it as current fashion dictates. Bad for the ribs, bad for breathing, bad for lots of things really, but it is considered part of a lady's proper undergarments, so we wear them. Some of us just more wisely than others." Mina gave her a conspiratorial smile and then offered, "Here, I'll help you dress."

Lenore allowed herself to smile back for the first time. Maybe the woman wasn't a complete harpy. Mina had Lenore take in a breath rather than let one out when putting on the corset, for which Lenore was very thankful, and Lenore decided to ask something that had been bothering her since the night before.

"Mina, how is it that you're a doctor? Isn't it an awfully... odd occupation for a woman of your standing?"

Mina laughed a little and said, "Of course, by 'odd' you mean 'inappropriate'." Lenore opened her mouth to object, but Mina beat her to it. "Yes, it is looked down upon, especially in the circles Neal and I travel in. It's too gruesome, too taxing, a profession for a woman. Well, women have been carrying, birthing, and even delivering babies since the beginning of time, so I think a little healing and stitching up of the human body is nothing compared to that."

"How were you even able to get schooling for it, though?"

"Anything is possible when you or your parents have enough money."

Lenore involuntarily rolled her eyes. Of course it was an issue of money. Mina caught her expression, and her gaze turned steely for a moment.

"Now, don't go thinking I'm just a spoiled, rich daughter. My parents taught me the value of hard work. They allowed me to choose my own path, but always warned me that they would cut me off three months after my schooling was done and that's just what they did. You'd better believe I had a hard time finding someone to apprentice me, and an even harder time making it through school. Imagine being practically the only woman in your whole field."

Lenore believed her. She had never heard of such a thing as a female doctor before, and people, even those from the higher classes, were immature at the best of times and downright cruel at the worst.

"I think it's very brave of you," Lenore said simply.

Mina chuckled mirthlessly. "That's what I have to tell

myself some days."

Lenore decided it was time to change the subject. "So… how does Camilla fit into all of this? She's not your daughter is she?"

"Very astute," Mina said, the softness in her personality now back. "No, Camilla is my niece. She lost… we took her in when she was ten."

Lenore said nothing. She could figure out easily enough what happened to Camilla's parents. It was too common a story.

"Her parents were taken by the Enforcers weren't they?" Lenore said softly.

"It is not my story to tell," Mina replied, "but that is *not* the sum of it."

Lenore said nothing more. The conversation had hit too close to home, and she was already weary of speaking. Mina continued in her ministrations until Lenore was dressed and looked, incredibly, like a proper lady. Her hair was pinned up in loops that looked like a complicated maze of tresses, but Mina had only spent about ten minutes on it in total. They then went down for breakfast where Camilla and Neal were waiting.

"Good morning, ladies," Neal said jovially. "Esther has whipped up a very special treat this morning."

"Oh, don't spoil my surprise, Master Neal," said a stout, older woman as she came in carrying a huge covered platter. "And this must be the young lady you told me about." Esther set her platter down and circled round to Lenore more quickly than the younger woman would have thought possible, all while continuing to talk. "It's Lenore, isn't it, miss? Lovely name, just lovely. And how do you take your tea, dear? Very important detail, you know. Tea fortifies you for the day, cures your ills, and helps you sleep. Any specialties you'd like me to fix up for you? Miss Camilla particularly likes candied dates."

Lenore gaped like a fish for several moments before she

finally said, "Honey with just a touch of cream... for my tea that is."

"Straight away, Miss Lenore, straight away," and with that she scuttled off, presumably to get the tea.

"Isn't she wonderful?" Camilla giggled, watching the older woman leave.

"She's lovely," Lenore said smiling. Esther had made her feel rather warm and fuzzy in that short amount of time.

The special treat that morning turned out to be steak and eggs, which Lenore had a feeling was a favorite of Neal's. Neal, Mina, and Camilla all chatted amiably during breakfast, while Lenore sat silently and ate far more slowly than she had the night before. Things were beginning to sink in.

Lenore was a criminal, one who would be tortured and made an example of if she was caught. Though she would argue that she'd had no choice, she had written her own warrant by her actions. Then there was the Allen family. They had saved her from certain doom. Yes, they had caused her to get caught, but, in her heart of hearts, Lenore knew that it would have happened eventually, though she never would have said so out loud. Then they had taken her in, fed her, and clothed her, all at great personal risk to themselves. She suddenly felt inadequate and a little overwhelmed. She wouldn't fall apart here, though. No, she stared down into her plate and took deep, calming breaths.

"...and we'll go to Tilly's and have her put together a few basic ensembles for Lenore," Mina could be heard saying through Lenore's ruminations.

"What?!" Lenore exclaimed. "We're going out? I can't... I'll be seen... I-I-I..."

Lenore's whole body filled with fear, proper blind panic. Her heart began to race, and she began to sweat. She got up from her seat and backed away from the table. Mina was beside her in a moment.

"Lenore, dear, calm down. You need to relax." Mina was a doctor now, an excellent one, mixing just enough coddling with a sterile firmness. She took Lenore's face in her hands and said, "Look at me. There now, breathe... slowly... a little more in. Now let it out slowly... five... four... three... two... one. Again."

They repeated that process several times, all while Lenore looked into Mina's clear, blue eyes.

"Now, slowly, tell me why you're so afraid," Mina said at last.

"I'll be recognized if we go out. The Enforcers will arrest me. It's *daylight* out."

"I see. Lenore, come with me." Mina led Lenore into the next room where a large mirror graced one wall. "Look in the mirror, dear."

Lenore obeyed, but wasn't sure what she was looking for. She looked to Mina for help.

"Notice anything different?" Mina asked gently. Lenore shook her head, and Mina said, "You're clean. Your hair's brushed and arranged and you're wearing proper clothes. You look your age. Lenore, you look like a completely different person than you did last night. You'll be perfectly safe."

Lenore looked in the mirror again, more closely this time. She did look different, like a proper lady now. Now that she was really thinking about it, even she had a hard time believing the Enforcers would connect her to the ragamuffin that had been haunting the streets by night all this time.

"Alright," Lenore said finally, "but, please, I want us to be careful."

"Always," Mina said touching the girl's nose affectionately. "Now, let's go finish up."

✿

The ladies left within the hour. After breakfast they finished getting ready and headed out.

"We're not going to take a hansom cab?" Lenore whispered to Mina as they began to walk."

"Not today. It's lovely out, and exercise is good for you."

It was a longer walk than Lenore liked, as they were heading to the Copper district, and she couldn't help but glance sideways past the few tresses that hung round her face at the Enforcers who patrolled the streets. Most nodded to the ladies in greeting, to which Mina would smile prettily in return but nothing more. Lenore began to feel afraid again a few times, but she thought back to her reflection in the mirror each time to calm herself. They finally arrived at a ladies' shop called Tilly's Tailoring for the Fine Woman and went in.

"Mina!" a woman behind the counter trilled when she entered. "So lovely to see you, my dear!"

The two women embraced and shared a kiss on each cheek. Lenore immediately began to size up the woman. She was about Mina's age, and plump with a pleasant, open face. Her attire was immaculate, as would be expected of someone in her line of work, and she apparently went in for the—to Lenore, somewhat silly—current trend of expressing her passion via her attire. The woman's shoes and hat were decorated with rosettes made of tape measures. For a moment, Lenore tried to imagine what Mina's accessories would look like if she did the same— scalpels and ribbons of gauze and some kind of macabre coloration.

"How are you, Tilly?" Mina asked the woman. "Your little ones, are they doing well?"

"Oh, very well. Millicent got herself into a spot of trouble at school the other day—talking during class… again—but she comes by it honest, so I couldn't be too cross with her. Ah, your sweet Camilla is here too. How are you, love?"

"Very well, ma'am," Camilla said politely. "Thank you."

"And who's this?" Tilly asked, looking to Lenore. "Oh, I'll bet you're from Neal's side. She has his coloring. A winter, I think."

"Yes, this is Lenore, a cousin of Neal's," Mina said easily. "She's come to stay with us. Not very good prospects in her area, you understand."

"Oh, I do indeed," Tilly agreed. "Never settle when you know you can do better, dear."

Lenore didn't know what to say. All of this ridiculous fluff-talk was beginning to make her want to hit something. It was Camilla who saved her from having to make a very awkward apology later.

"All of Lenore's things were lost during her journey here. The cargo men on the train just misplaced them!"

"My goodness! You poor thing!" Tilly squeaked.

"Yes," Mina added, "the station manager compensated us, but it doesn't put clothes on her back, now does it? Lenore's actually wearing one of Camilla's outfits today."

"Awful, just awful," Tilly tut-tutted. "Well, don't you worry, love. Tilly's going to make things right as rain before you can say backstitch chevron."

Lenore didn't make the attempt; she was dumbstruck. Camilla, who she had chalked up as a bit empty-headed, had delivered a lie—a rather good one—without batting an eyelash, and Mina had followed without missing a beat. The way the two had interwoven truth and fiction was almost artful. Lenore felt a new emotion towards the two ladies: admiration.

Tilly was true to her word, or as true as was humanly possible. The woman, helped here and there by an assistant, flitted around her shop like a hummingbird to flowers, grabbing skirts, boots, stockings, corsets, bodices, and even a coat or two.

"Winter is coming, you know," she said.

Tilly never seemed to stop talking all while she went about her work. She and Mina caught up some more, and Camilla joined in as well. Meanwhile, Lenore was measured, dressed, undressed, trotted about, and examined before starting all over again. Feelings that Lenore had kept stuffed down deep inside of her began to creep up during this process. She had gone through this countless times with her mother, and those past memories were pushing against Lenore's heart, demanding to be heard. She forced herself to smile and swallow her sorrow and instead focused on critiquing Tilly's work. It was really very good quality, and Lenore genuinely did smile as she realized that her mother would have approved. Lenore was also pleasantly surprised to find that her opinion mattered in the final decision for every outfit, though how much it mattered seemed to depend on how much her opinion differed from Tilly's. Mina interjected gently when necessary, but Lenore could tell Mina trusted Tilly's expertise, so she tried not to object too much. Finally, after nearly two hours, both Tilly and Mina were satisfied. Mina asked for Tilly to bill her, and Tilly promised to have at least some of the clothes delivered by that evening. Many of the pieces would need to be altered at least somewhat. The appropriate farewells were exchanged, and the three ladies left the shop.

"That was productive," Mina said happily. "Camilla, I think it's time we opened up the practice for today. We'll need some lunch brought in if you could handle that, please. Lenore, are you ready to learn the fine art of healing?"

"Ah, I suppose," Lenore replied uncertainly.

With that, they set off again.

Ready she was not. The beginning of the workday wasn't too bad. A patient suffering from stomach pains was actually waiting at the door for the practice to open. Lenore wondered why someone would wait specifically for Mina, the anomalous female doctor, rather than simply going to a different practice. There were many throughout the city. Later on, she learned that Mina had built up a rather loyal following, which was mostly comprised of women and the elderly. It seemed a woman's touch resonated with these two groups more strongly than whatever the other doctors in town offered. Apparently Mina also offered a "good faith" payment system, which most physicians didn't bother with. For those patients that couldn't pay their bill up front, Mina allowed them to make small payments every month, but with a low interest rate attached to it. Camilla was usually the one to handle the money and other administrative duties, but Lenore began to pick up on those things pretty quickly. It was the patient care aspect that she had trouble with.

Lenore had never had much contact with ailing people. Of course her parents had been sick at times, as had she, and she had known others around her who had fallen ill at one time or another as well. She had never dealt with the issues that Mina's patients brought to her now, however. There was everything from broken bones to phantom pains to pregnancies and other womanly issues to just plain sickness, and every single person seemed to want to tell Lenore their life story up until the time of their ailment. She was surprised to realize that she just wasn't that sympathetic. Lenore felt a bit like, valid as each patient's woes were, they were all being a bit whiney and overly needy. Talking about it—at length—wouldn't help fix them, so what was the point? She held her tongue, however, and nodded appropriately as each person poured their heart out to her. Camilla on the other hand, who knew many of these folks by name, reacted perfectly to every tale, taking hands, offering words of encouragement, and just generally being an angel. It made Lenore want to retch, so she eventually wandered back to see about helping Mina.

That was when Lenore really did almost retch. Lenore had never seen the amount of blood and other bodily fluids in all her life as she did on that day. The sound of a woman vomiting from food poisoning made her queasy, and the sight of a man's bone sticking out through the flesh of his leg from a compound fracture sent Lenore running for the back room. It was a long time before she felt strong enough to come back. The only thing that allowed her to do so was the fact that *this* was her only option. If she couldn't assist Mina, she'd be back out on the street, and Lenore was already getting very used to the idea of not simply trying to survive night by night. Lenore trudged through the rest of the day, splitting her time between the front office and assisting at Mina's side. She made it by sheer force of will, but only just. There continued to be people that made her want to pull her hair out, and there was more than one occasion wherein Lenore feared she would be sick all over a patient. The last patient of the day left after evening had fallen, but the three still had to clean and sterilize everything, which took another hour at least.

Lenore was quiet as they walked to the green-walled Limestone quarter—the Old World denizens thought they were *so funny* with their names—where the attic was so that she could whistle for Bitsy, who was overjoyed at seeing his mistress. Lenore did her best not to look at the family gathering in the front garden to greet the father as he arrived home from work, the family that had bought her parent's house and sold off half the furnishings.

In cases where a house was left abandoned for one reason or another, the house and everything inside became property of the state, which it then tried to sell off as quickly as possible. Buyers could pay a little extra to have the items inside removed and sold for them, but the truly savvy would do it themselves and make a little money on the side. Lenore had sobbed so hard, desperately trying to keep quiet as she'd heard strangers walking through her home and making offers on pieces of the life her parents had built. She knew it wasn't fair to resent the new family, but she couldn't help it. She'd lost so many things to them, and they'd never know it. She quickly told Mina that she didn't need to get anything else from her old home. Everything that was precious to her was carried on her person at all times… just in case. Even with her faithful companion returned to her, her demeanor did not change all the way back to the Allen manor or through dinner that evening. So heavy was the weight she felt pressing down on her that she was not even able to convincingly pretend that everything was fine, though she lamely insisted that she was just tired whenever someone asked what was wrong. Finally, later on that night and in the privacy of her room, Lenore broke down.

It was terrible. She *hated* apprenticing at Mina's practice! It wasn't something that was going to just "get better" either. She really and truly despised the work. It didn't suit her personality, she wasn't comfortable with it, and she just didn't have any interest in it. She admired both Mina and Camilla for their strength and compassion, but that simply was not her. And there was no way out. She was safe and clean and fed now, but she would be miserable every day going forward. She couldn't tell the Allens or Camilla of course, so she just lay in her bed and sobbed, Bitsy snuggling up to her neck to comfort his mistress.

<u>*Ninth Year of the New Age, Ninth Day of the Stone*</u>
*Official report submitted by Fifth Sawyer:*

*Last night around eleven o'clock, I was attacked by a drunkard outside of The Kicking Mule. He was accompanied by what I believe to be a thief. The drunkard rushed me with a dagger as I was questioning him and the thief. I was stabbed in the abdomen. The suspects' descriptions follow this report. I ordered the thief to bring me to a doctor, lest she feel my wrath and the wrath of the entire Enforcer order. I believe this cowed the girl into obedience. The thief helped me to a doctor where I am told I was successfully treated. I lost consciousness just after arriving. I am told I was brought to Doctor Philomena Allen. Why the thief chose to bring me to a doctor so far away from the site of the attack, I do not know. She, unfortunately, ran off as soon as I was in the doctor's care, despite orders not to do so.*

*Suspect 1: Male. Average height. Paunchy build... will probably not be able to escape if pursued. Greyish-brown stubble on his face and short-cropped hair to match. Eye color could not be determined in last night's lighting conditions.*

*Suspect 2: Female. Young, perhaps fourteen years of age. Slight build. Shorter than average, though that may be due to poor posture. Long dark hair. Eye color could not be determined in last night's lighting conditions.*

# 4
# ARCHEOTECHNOLOGICS

The next morning began earlier than the previous. Lenore was awoken by the sound of people moving around the house and the smell of breakfast cooking, so she dragged herself out of bed and began what would become her daily ablutions. She was not looking forward to a new day, but she appeared downstairs an hour later in one of the new outfits that had been delivered from Tilly's the night before. Lenore sat down and thanked Esther when she brought in breakfast. Today it was a steaming bowl of oatmeal with bits of dried fruits in it. Sugar, honey, milk, and butter were waiting nearby to be added as one pleased to breakfast.

"Good morning, Lenore!" Neal said exuberantly.

Much as she liked Neal, his sunny personality was not improving Lenore's mood just now.

"Good morning," Lenore replied, attempting to cover her foul mood with a smile.

"How are you this morning?" Neal asked.

"I'm well," Lenore lied, this time doing a better job of smiling. She was trying to remind herself just how good she had it now, and it was working… a little.

"Wonderful! Ready for another day at the practice with Mina and Camilla then?"

That was when it stopped working. Lenore suddenly remembered every miserable detail from yesterday, the feeling of desperation as she fought to keep her breakfast down, the burning impatience with the woman who just *wouldn't*. Stop. Talking! About her bunions and corns. Lenore urged herself to say yes, to nod her head, something, but her body did not respond. After a few awkward, heavy moments, Mina jumped in.

"Oh, for goodness' sake, Neal! Enough of this mollycoddling. You hated it, didn't you, Lenore?"

"No!" the girl insisted, seeing her new life slipping away as quickly as it had come. "I just… it's new to me. I'm sure I'll get used to it. Please, I'll keep trying. I—"

Mina raised a hand, and Lenore stuttered into silence.

"Lenore, it was fairly clear yesterday how you felt, and Camilla heard you crying last night."

Lenore shot her housemate a withering glare, and Camilla had the grace to look embarrassed.

"It's fine," Mina continued. "It's not the field for everyone, but you need to find employment somewhere, which is tricky considering your past situation."

*That's putting it delicately,* Lenore thought.

"That being the case, what do you think would be an option?" Mina continued.

Lenore's mind raced. She was being given another chance! She couldn't foul this up. What could she do? *What could she do?!*

"I… I could help Esther around the house," she said. "I'll cook and clean and do whatever else needs doing."

"Have you ever cooked or cleaned before?" Mina asked flatly.

"I can do it," Lenore insisted.

She was *not* about to admit that her parents had had a housekeeper and cook for as long as she could remember. Mina was a shrewd woman, however, and saw right through Lenore's evasion.

"Let us look at it another way," she said. "What did you do before you were a thief?"

Lenore's cheeks burned, and she instinctively looked towards the door. Mina and Neal already knew what she had been. Even Camilla had to know now, even if she hadn't known at first, but Lenore couldn't be sure about Esther. Saying it out loud seemed like a bad idea all around. No Enforcers appeared through the doorway, so Lenore looked back and thought hard.

"My mother…" something caught in Lenore's throat, and she breathed in sharp and hard to hold it back before continuing. When she did, her voice was steady and cold. "My mother was a seamstress, though I never took after her much. Sewing just never interested me. My father was an engineer. He was head of a team that developed new types of machines, weapons really, for the government. I helped him at home in his workshop. Women don't really do machine work, so I couldn't ever become an apprentice. My parents were working on finding me a rich husband so that I wouldn't have to worry about employment."

Lenore looked up from the lacework on the tablecloth to see Neal smiling and Mina looking… wry?… pleased?… it was hard to tell.

"That is good information to have. I do hope you haven't had your debut yet. Had your parents introduced you to any suitors? Knowing that will help us to know which circles we need to avoid when we go out."

Lenore's brow furrowed in confusion. She could see the wheels in Mina's head turning. The woman was already planning what galas they could and could not attend? Together? Shouldn't she be thinking of the best way to tell Lenore she'd better start looking for a new place to live just in case this new employment venture didn't pan out?

"Let's discuss that later, my dove," Neal said, putting a hand on his wife's arm. "For now, I think we both know what Lenore can do."

"What?" Lenore asked. "I'll do it. Just tell me what it is."

Mina smiled and kissed her husband, nodding at whatever idea he had had.

"Lenore, I am an engineer as well. I work with machines, but I don't invent them as your father did. I'm more of an archeologist... of sorts. I study machines and other technologies from the Old World for the museum in order to try and figure out how they used to work. For quite a while now, I have been told that I need to take on an apprentice."

Lenore's heart soared. Really? She didn't have to go back to Mina's practice? Anything had to be better than that, but she couldn't believe she could actually do something that she knew she enjoyed.

"Now, be aware that it's not guaranteed. You'll have to prove yourself to the Head Curator."

Lenore blanched, and her heart dropped like a stone. Really? And just how was she supposed to do that? She had only tinkered with her father's machines, discussed schematics with him, some of which had never come to fruition, and now she was supposed to prove herself to someone who had probably collected eight degrees just for the fun of it.

"How?" she managed to say.

"I don't know what he'll ask, but Abraham is a very good man. He'll interview you to see if you show any potential, which I'm sure you have."

Neal smiled, but Lenore was not comforted by it. She'd go,

she'd try, and she'd likely fail. She didn't have any other options just now, though, so she nodded.

"Splendid! I'll set up the appointment today," he said far too cheerfully for Lenore's taste.

Breakfast continued from there. The little family chatted away while Lenore was quiet again. She was glad she'd be left alone today; she really wanted some time to think. Lenore was beyond grateful for everything the Allen family had and was doing for her, but the fact remained she was an outsider. It was only natural that she should feel a bit awkward, which she did. In her heart of hearts, Lenore keenly wished that she might have found a place where she could find a spot to fit in, but it was still far too soon to give voice to that wish. For now, she simply had to figure out a way to carry her own weight. Mina, Camilla, and Neal all eventually left, but asked Lenore several times if she would be alright and assured her that she could ask Esther for anything she needed. Lenore thanked them, and they went their separate ways. It was then that she decided to go for a walk around the house.

Lenore had familiarized herself with some of the rooms by now, of course, and she had seen even more that first night she had met the Allens. The manor was fairly large, though, and so there was more to be discovered. The bedrooms all seemed to be clustered near one another. Next to her own room was Camilla's, with whom Lenore was debating whether or not to be cross, and just down the hall was Neal and Mina's room. Lenore had enough decorum not to go in, but the door was open, and so she did peek in just to see what it looked like. The room was larger than Lenore's, of course, and a sitting area made up most of Lenore's view. Just that indicated how much larger the master suite was than her own room. Lenore moved on and eventually found a small library, within which were two desks, some couches and chairs, a few end tables, and several impressive shelves of books. Lenore decided against exploring this room for now, as she was fairly certain she'd want to spend a good deal of time there, so she made a mental note and moved on.

The rest of the house was pretty typical. The décor was up to date and showed affluence without being ostentatious. There were a few decorative items here and there that were unusual and behind which Lenore could not guess the idea. For instance, a few rooms had hollow glass spheres in them. There was nothing special about them beyond their plainness, so Lenore shrugged and moved on. She suspected several of the items were souvenirs that Neal had collected throughout his career. Everything was clean and tidy, and Lenore could hear Esther singing to herself elsewhere. All in all, it was pretty idyllic, which didn't do much to improve Lenore's mood. She wandered down to the kitchens only to find Bitsy there with a small bowl of fruit in front of him.

Bitsy hadn't been there when Lenore awoke that morning, but that didn't concern her. He always did what he wanted, and she had suspected that he was simply exploring his new home. Now it seemed he had even managed to con some food out of the Allens' sweet housekeeper. It seemed he was adjusting just fine. Lenore smiled and petted her little friend's back. He turned to her and chirped, but didn't leave his food.

"Smart boy," Lenore said. "You enjoy, but come find me later. I'd like a buddy."

Bitsy looked at his mistress for a moment and then turned back to his food. Lenore let him be, wondering at how much his little mind actually understood. Her parents had purchased him a few years ago from a traveling circus. From the very beginning, the ringcat showed great intelligence. He had been trained to do several tricks before coming to live with Lenore and her parents, and it had been Lenore's mother who had taught him—using food as a motivator—how to snatch things from people. The goal had actually been to make Bitsy her little gopher, grabbing bobbins and tape and spools of thread and whatever else was needed during a sewing project. His deft, little paws worked almost as well as hands, but he missed the mark and never grabbed the right thing. How he knew what to take when he and Lenore worked at night was a mystery.

Carrying on, Lenore headed down to the cellar where she'd first met Mina and Neal. She found a lantern at the door and used a match from the box beside it to light the wick. The cellar was, unsurprisingly, stocked with root vegetables, onion and garlic braids, and sacks of dry goods. What was surprising was the little table in the corner. This table held the oil lamp that had been lit the night she'd almost been caught. Also on the table and pinned to the wall were sketches, diagrams, doodles, maps, notes, and blueprints. Most of them showed different types of machines or perhaps ideas for new inventions, but Lenore had trouble telling what purpose any of the machines could have. Looking at one of the more complicated sets of schematics, she thought what she was looking at might be some kind of engine, but what it could power wasn't explained in the documentation. Looking at everything there reminded Lenore about what Neal had said she would have to do to become his apprentice. The thought made Lenore's stomach knot itself up, and she felt herself begin to shake.

*Stop it!* she told herself firmly. *It won't do any good getting all worked up. Go figure something out if you're so worried.*

Lenore knew that this was pretty good advice, so she headed back up the stairs and into the main house. From there, she went back to the library and began searching through the books for something that could help her. It looked like Mina and Neal had simply organized their books by author, so medical tomes were mixed in with history books. There were

53

other genres to be found there as well, and Lenore tried to pair the books she found with an owner. The romances were probably Camilla's, as Lenore couldn't imagine the levelheaded Mina giving into anything so fanciful, while the books of Old World legends likely belonged to Neal. Legends had a root in history somewhere, so it fit that the Old World engineer would have those. It was hard to tell who the art books and mystery novels belonged to, but the *Rules of Etiquette and Encyclopedia of Gentlewomanly Arts* undoubtedly served both Mina and Camilla. Lenore remembered Mina mentioning bringing her to social events, so she suspected it would behoove her to have a flip through that volume in particular. For now, however, Lenore had to focus on not getting tossed out onto the street, so she plucked a history primer from the shelf and began to thumb through it, pausing on anything that discussed technology from the Old World.

Some of what Lenore read was familiar from her school days. The Old World had been full of magic and danger and uncertainty. Unbelievable creatures roamed the land and were a constant threat as towns and villages struggled to survive. Magic had been the only thing that had saved humanity from extinction. Magi, people born with the ability to do magic, worked tirelessly to create devices to protect the people from the creatures that ruled the wilds. Lenore had heard of such things as barrier sustainments and aquadirectors, which had apparently been basic, run-of-the-mill machines for everyday use. Then there were stories of vehicles that could take people underwater or into the air with naught but magic to power them. She and her father had often debated whether or not these things might have actually existed. They had both always suspected there were inventors who had dreamed of specialized boats or tried to create rudimentary zeppelins, but had probably not succeeded to any great extent. As Lenore read, she made mental notes of anything that mentioned inventors, machines, or other technological advancements. Esther interrupted her research at one point to let her know that lunch was ready. Lenore was tempted to tell her that she'd eat later, but simply couldn't resist the housekeeper's inviting warmth. It helped that Bitsy was there with Esther looking just as happy as could be.

Lunch was a simple spread of potatoes, fresh vegetables, and some cold cuts with bread and cheese. Lenore invited Esther to sit with her, and the two chatted idly, mostly about Bitsy and the food. Lenore was still feeling fairly apprehensive, but the cold stone of fear had mostly melted by the time lunch was over. She was preparing as best she could, she was fed, and, if nothing else, if this didn't work out, perhaps she could assist Esther around the house after all.

By the time the Allens were all back, Lenore felt that she was as prepared as she could be, though that wasn't saying much. Without any idea of what she would be asked, she had sort of broadly educated herself, covering as much information as possible.

"Bright and early tomorrow morning!" Neal said upon seeing her in the library. "Scholar Bates is very excited about meeting you."

Lenore paled somewhat at hearing this. Not that she didn't trust Neal—though she didn't completely—but she couldn't quite believe that Neal hadn't talked her up a bit.

"What did you tell him exactly?" Lenore asked.

"Only that you had shown some proclivity for machines and that I thought you had potential as a possible apprentice."

Lenore was still skeptical, but what was done was done. Now it was time to look forward.

"What should I do? How can I be prepared?"

"Lenore," Neal said gently, "even if I knew what Scholar Bates was going to ask you, I wouldn't be at liberty to share it.

Trust in yourself. If you're meant to get this position, you will."

Lenore's insides burned with frustration. She didn't know if Neal was deliberately disregarding the gravity of the situation or if he actually wasn't aware of it. She struggled with herself as to whether or not she should ask the question that had been hanging in her mind since that morning. It was only because Neal had been so sensitive to her feelings so far that she felt she could take the risk.

"Neal, what if I don't get the apprenticeship? What will I do? I'm not so naïve as to think that you and Mina will simply let me leech off of you forever."

Neal didn't answer for a moment, his face inscrutable. "Let's not worry about that just now. I'll leave you to study."

Lenore sighed. That wasn't a good sign.

"Neal," she said before he was gone. He turned, and she said, "Can you please ask Esther to bring my dinner up here?"

"Of course," he replied.

*The gall of that cretin was almost impressive. Surely he had to know he was taking his own life into his hands coming here. Now that the scum was gone, he looked down to the slip of paper he had been given. What an odd turn of events. This could be a trap, though. The Enforcers had every reason to want someone like him off the streets and under lock and key in the Halls of Justice. Something was urging him to follow the lead, though. It was the pulsing in his back. Perhaps this really was as promising as it sounded. Best to bring some extra weapons... just in case. The rat had said he'd be back in a few days to discuss the matter further. Either way, he was looking forward to it.*

Dana Fraedrich

Lenore could scarcely believe she was sitting in the office of the Head Curator for the Springhaven Museum of History and Nature... having tea and biscuits. She had felt eerily calm the night before when she had gone to bed with visions of Old World technology dancing in her head. Now, however, she was so nervous she could barely lift her teacup to drink without shaking. She had already burned her lips on her tea and had almost walked out of the manor with only one glovelet on.

She had wanted to dress in a way that was professional but not too feminine. Lenore had decided that if she looked too feminine, she would appear unsuitable or even incapable of doing the job. Therefore, she had plaited her hair neatly so that it was out of her face, donned glovelets instead of gloves to free up her fingers, and worn a simple but elegant dark blue skirt—none of this bustle nonsense—and white blouse with a silk necktie. She had always heard that dressing well was a surefire way to improve one's self-confidence. That was rubbish. Camilla had helped her get ready that morning, and she looked immaculate. Despite this, if Lenore were any more nervous she would collapse into ridiculous sobs. She was barely holding it together as it was, but at least she was doing that.

It was a small mercy that Neal was here as well, but he wasn't saying much that was helpful. Scholar Abraham Bates was a mountain of a man, which didn't exactly put Lenore at ease. Neal and Lenore had taken a hansom cab to the museum that morning and he had led her straight to the Head Curator's office. Scholar Bates' assistant appeared with the tea service while Neal was making the introductions and, since then, the men had really only discussed how their respective evenings had been.

"Well, Lenore," Scholar Bates said, finally turning his

attention to her properly, "you must have done something to really impress Engineer Allen. I've been badgering him for ages to take on an apprentice."

Lenore swallowed hard and suppressed the urge to turn and glare at Neal. That dolt! He must have exaggerated her qualifications—she used that term loosely—and now Scholar Bates had some kind of ridiculously high expectation of her.

Lenore could do nothing more than smile prettily and say, "Oh, I don't know about that. I think he just saw how badly I need this apprenticeship and pitied me."

Scholar Bates guffawed and turned to Neal again.

"She's humble, Neal. I like that." Looking back at Lenore, he continued, "So what is it that interests you about the Old World?"

Lenore took a deep breath and thought for a second before saying, "It's fascinating to me to think about what was. I believe if we can learn about what the Old World citizens developed, it can help us develop our own technologies. Perhaps we can even replicate some of their inventions."

And so it went. Scholar Bates asked Lenore questions and she answered them as best she could. She was as honest as she could practically be. There were obviously things that she either could not or would not mention, but she had no idea whether or not a mostly honest answer would be good enough. There were some questions that were easy, like what it was about machining that interested her. Then there were questions that were not so easy, like what experience she had with machines. Lenore had to be creative with that answer. Remembering Mina and Camilla's lie from the previous day, she explained that her father was an engineer "back home" and that she had always looked over schematics and discussed them with him, but she hadn't ever been allowed to actually work on his machines. She already had her answer ready when Scholar Bates followed up that question by asking what brought her to Springhaven.

"There are better prospects for me here," Lenore replied easily.

She was beginning to love that answer. It was vague enough that it didn't give anything away but also allowed her audience to make their own conclusions about whether she meant men or work. It wasn't far from the truth either. After all, her parents' ambitions for her had been to marry rich. Looking back from this last-ditch effort to find employment, Lenore now realized what a phenomenally stupid idea it had been and she cursed herself for not pursuing *something*, just in case.

The three continued their conversation, Neal saying very little and betraying nothing those few times Lenore looked to him for guidance, and finished their tea. Finally, Scholar Bates stood and made a pronouncement.

"I think it's time for Lenore to see where it all happens."

"Of course," Lenore said, standing up as well.

Scholar Bates led Lenore out of his office and down various corridors of the staff-only area of the museum, Neal following close behind. Lenore very much wanted to whisper to him to find out how she was doing, but knew she'd never get away with it. It wasn't very long before they arrived at a set of d o u b l e   d o o r s   w i t h   a   s i g n   t h a t   r e a d, *ARCHEOTECHNOLOGICS*.

"Home sweet home," Neal said fondly. "Lenore, this is my department."

"Brilliant!" Lenore said happily.

She assumed this to be a good sign and optimistically f o l l o w e d   N e a l   a n d   S c h o l a r   B a t e s   i n s i d e.   T h e Archeotechnologics department was an entirely different world from Scholar Bates' office. The office had been large enough to be impressive but small enough to be cozy. The dark leather chairs and polished wood had spoken to the station of its well-educated and respected occupant. The Archeotechnologics department space was huge and open. Several desks were placed along the side walls, behind which were aisles of shelving four levels high. All kinds of curious objects were neatly arranged on the shelves with little paper labels beneath each one. Beyond that, Lenore could see a variety of very large objects that she couldn't identify. Lenore was suddenly very keen to start exploring.

"Why don't you look around and see if you can identify what some of these things might have done?" Scholar Bates suggested.

Lenore nodded and stepped forward. Well, she had gotten her wish, but the outcome carried more weight than she had originally thought. She looked all around her as she walked and began to browse the shelves. Picking up a round, brass object that was slightly bigger than a man's fist, she examined it for a moment.

"I think this was meant to be a joint for something larger," she said somewhat hesitantly. "See the tracks here and here? Something fit into each socket and could move back and forth. I don't know what it went with on a larger scale, though."

Neal and Scholar Bates both nodded and made noises of acknowledgement, but nothing more. Lenore moved on.

"This is an arm for something. The claw could grasp objects."

"These are treads for some kind of conveyor or maybe a vehicle."

"Levers for activating something, obviously…"

Neal and Scholar Bates still weren't saying anything. Lenore swallowed hard. She had been right in her last statement; she was picking the obvious things. Anyone with any kind of rudimentary knowledge of machines could have deduced the purposes of those items. She was blowing this!

What could she do, though? Everything on the shelves were single pieces from a larger whole. That pipe could have gone to anything. Those gears served countless purposes. She had to figure out how to show she was better than this, more... imaginative. Lenore walked on very slowly, gazing at each item she passed and trying to think beyond the obvious. Everything here was so mundane, though.

She reached the end of the aisle with her heart beating fast. If all the other aisles were like this, she was going nowhere... except back out onto the street. Standing there, she could feel the two men behind her, their eyes burning into her back. She was resisting the urge to turn around and admit her weakness and ask for help. What else could she do? If she went through everything and failed to say anything impressive and then told them why she was having so much trouble, how would that look? She might not even get that far. She already felt like they might just be humoring her at this point. If she asked for help now, however, they'd surely think she was either lazy or slow. She turned her gaze upward as if for some kind of divine intervention.

"What is that?" she said automatically.

Above her, hanging from the rafters, was... a zeppelin? Maybe. It had a deflated balloon attached to its top, but it had curved, fixed wings as well, which was very odd. It was small, though, and shaped oddly. Modern zeppelins had large, boxy bodies. This one was bulbous on the front end and tapered near the back. The compartment had enough space for maybe two people, but probably only one plus supplies.

"It looks like... is it... a dirigible?" she said half to herself and half to Neal and Scholar Bates. Turning to them, she spoke properly. "Is that what it is?"

"That's probably the closest description," Neal said. "It's one of the only artifacts we've found that was almost completely intact."

"Where did you find it?" Lenore said. "Why is it in here and not on display?"

"It was discovered in the Bladed Mountains to the North," Neal said. "Sadly, we don't know enough about it to display it properly. It doesn't speak well about the museum when the plaque reads, *'Zeppelin-like object. Function and origin unknown'*."

Scholar Bates chuckled at that, and Lenore smiled. She looked back up and spoke again.

"Couldn't we at least take it down so that it can be looked at properly from time to time?"

"That may be a possibility. Why don't you take a look at some of our more incomplete pieces for now, though?" Neal suggested, gesturing behind Lenore.

She turned and saw more clearly now those very large objects she had seen before. She had been so wound up about the interview that she had completely forgotten about them. Now that the shelves were no longer obscuring them, Lenore could see that they were huge machines. Her heart leapt. They were *real*! The undersea vehicles and flying machines she and her father had theorized about all those times were sitting before her. Granted, they were half deconstructed or broken or severely damaged, but she knew these were those fabled machines. She strode forward towards one, clearly an undersea vehicle, and began to examine it closely, being very careful not to touch.

"It has treads," Lenore said more to herself than anyone else. "It could actually travel on the bottom of the sea floor." Losing some of her decorum, Lenore dashed around to the back of the machine. "It has a propeller as well. Buoyancy tanks…" She got down on her hands and knees and tried to look underneath the machine. Not seeing what she wanted to, she called to Neal, "Have you discovered whether or not there are any ballast apparatus? It looks a little too round to be stable."

"Inside the wheels," she heard him say.

"That's brilliant!" she called back. "Very clever…"

That was when she realized she was on her hands and knees, trying to crawl underneath an ancient machine in front of the Head Curator. She shimmied out as fast as she could and was mortified to see how filthy she had gotten in such a short amount of time. Her cheeks burned as she tried to recover.

"I'm so sorry. The subaquatic is in good shape, though."

Lenore mentally cringed. Subaquatic? How stupid could she be? What an idiotic name. Neal had probably already dubbed it something far more academic. Scholar Bates' face was the one that was inscrutable now. Lenore's heart was pounding out of her chest, and Neal was busy looking at his pocket watch.

"My apologies, but I have meetings to attend, so I'm afraid I'll have to leave you two," Scholar Bates said. "Miss Lenore, it was very nice to meet you. Engineer Allen, we'll speak later."

With that, he turned and left. Lenore looked to Neal desperately, who wasn't helping by keeping his face pleasant but closed.

"I'll show you out and call a cab," was all he said.

# 5

# THE FURNITURE RIDDLE

Lenore felt sick and was on the verge of tears. When she arrived back at the Allen manor, she changed out of her dirty clothes and into a clean set. Guilt grew in her heart as she saw another delivery from Tilly's sitting on her bed.

*Such a waste,* she thought to herself.

She politely declined Esther's offer of lunch, but accepted the mint tea she brought. Lenore couldn't focus on anything. Her mind kept drifting back and replaying her appalling performance at the museum. Neal, kind Neal who had been so warm from day one, was probably furious with her. She had humiliated him. Heavens, she was worse than useless. She was damaging. Maybe she should just leave now, save the Allens the pain and awkwardness of having to tell her to go. No, she'd tell them she was leaving. Of all the things she'd done wrong, she at least wanted to do this right. She'd take responsibility and spare them from having to do it. She just had to wait until they got home.

It was agonizing. Lenore sat by a window in the parlor, hiding behind the curtains and watching the drive. It took forever, and, as badly as Lenore wanted to get up and walk around to help time pass, she forced herself to stay put. She'd do it fast, dive into it before she could stop herself. At least Bitsy was there with her. He'd appeared with her tea and never left. Bitsy may not be a faithful dog, always by her side, but he was there when she needed him most, and she was thankful for him. The sun began to dip down behind the chimney pots and roofs, and Mina and Camilla could be seen coming up to the door. Lenore flew to meet them. She slid into the reception hall just as Mina and Camilla were walking in.

"I need to speak with you," Lenore blurted out. "Please, come have a seat in the parlor."

"Lenore, what is it?" Mina asked. "Is everything alright?"

"You needn't worry," Lenore said sternly, forcing herself to be strong. "Just have a seat."

Mina nodded and she, along with Camilla, headed into the parlor. Lenore had actually just meant to speak to Mina, but she supposed it didn't matter if Camilla was there too. Once the ladies were seated, Lenore launched into her announcement.

"I'm leaving—"

"What?!" Mina and Camilla exclaimed together.

Lenore held up her hands and continued quickly before the women could stop her.

"It's fine! I can't expect you all to support me and I won't be a parasite. I'll be out before dinner."

"Lenore, what are you saying? What's happened? Neal, *what* is going on? What happened today at the museum?"

Lenore turned to see Neal standing there and looking as if he were trying to figure out the best way to escape whatever chaos he had walked into. He must have come in while Lenore was talking. Her heart sank as soon as she saw him.

"It went horribly," Lenore told Mina. "That's why I have to leave."

"What are you saying?" Neal asked. "Scholar Bates loves

you. He was so impressed he wants you to start immediately."

"H-he what?" Lenore stuttered.

"He's concerned about your reputation, of course, being a female in a male-dominated field, but we all know how to deal with that, which I reminded him of, so—"

"Oh, my heavens, thank you!" Lenore squealed.

She suppressed an urge to hug him. The last thing she needed to do was make an inappropriate move towards Mina's husband after she had secured a dream position in his department. What happened next, however, was almost as embarrassing. She burst into tears. All of the anxiety that she had held inside for the last two days suddenly burst forth in a great wave of weeping relief. At this, Neal looked terrified and completely lost as to what to do. Thankfully, Mina jumped in to rescue him.

"Lenore, my darling, that's wonderful!" Mina said, wrapping her arms around the sobbing girl.

Camilla joined her and added, "Let's have Esther make some dinner and something to celebrate. Come on, we'll take it in the dining room."

Lenore was able to slow her waterfall of tears to a lazy creek and walked with the women back towards the dining room. Neal followed hesitantly behind. As if by magic, Esther had everything ready right on time. A small pre-dinner tea service was laid out almost immediately, followed up by a dinner of roast lamb with roasted vegetables. Finally, a fruit torte came out made with apples and pears and spices.

"Really, you don't have to do all this," Lenore said at one point, finally having been able to staunch the flow of her tears. "I'm just glad to have gotten the position."

"Nonsense," Neal said. "It's a very exciting event. In this house, we believe in celebrating successes. Scholar Bates doesn't let just anyone work at his museum, you know."

"That brings to mind a question," Lenore said. "They're going to need me to show my papers. What do I do about that?"

Neal and Mina looked at one another blankly.

"Blazes, I hadn't thought of that," Mina said.

"What is your surname anyway?" Neal asked. "It wouldn't happen to be Smith or Johnson, would it?"

"Sadly, no," Lenore replied. "It's Crowley."

"We could call on Gadget," Camilla said.

"Yes, I think we should," Mina said. "We'll visit her tomorrow. Neal, I'm sure Scholar Bates will understand that she can't start on such short notice."

"I don't think that will be a problem," Neal said.

"Who's Gadget?" Lenore asked.

"Our furniture dealer," Neal said with a smile.

Gadget was not what Lenore expected at all. The first surprise was the eye patch over her left eye, followed closely by her mechanical hand. Lenore did her very best not to stare, which only resulted in her looking awkwardly in every direction but Gadget's.

"Lenore, dear, I'd like to introduce a very dear friend," Mina said, "Miss Annabelle Wilson, master carpentry artisan and purveyor of fine furniture. Better known as Gadget."

"It's very nice to meet you," Lenore replied nervously, keeping her eyes down as she curtseyed.

"And you, Miss Lenore," Gadget said with a voice as raw as sandpaper. "Don't bother acting like you don't notice. I won't be offended."

Lenore looked to the mechanical hand and immediately began to deconstruct it in her brain. The real arm ended halfway down the forearm, and the shell of the structure was hammered bronze bound with leather straps, while the smaller, more intricate pieces were steel. Realism had not been the goal when designing the hand. It was mostly metal skeleton from the wrist down with thin fingers. The hand and fingers were jointed and hinged, but showed no evidence of being able to move on their own.

"Can you control it?" Lenore asked.

"Wouldn't that be nice?" Gadget replied. "I can shape it, which works well enough. Perhaps Neal will be able to develop one that moves on its own one day."

She then used her good hand to deftly shape the metal hand and fingers into a scoop and picked up a vicious looking tool from the counter.

"Neal made that?" Lenore didn't even try to hide how impressed she was.

"Dreamed, designed, and constructed."

"What happened to your real hand?"

Gadget chuckled mirthlessly and said, "This is my *reward* for turning over a new leaf. The Enforcers can't stand the thought that someone would jest about turning themselves in. That's the whole reason they instituted the purging, you know. They hate jokers."

Lenore stood there dumbfounded. Gadget was, quite literally, a living legend. It was incredibly rare that someone should actually turn themselves over to the Enforcers, much less live to tell about it. It was a widely believed idea that those that did turn themselves in were masochistically suicidal. Lenore couldn't imagine what had been so bad in Gadget's life that she had felt the need to take that step.

"I think that's enough of that," Mina said. "Do you mind showing us your new pieces?"

"Of course," Gadget said.

She led Mina and Lenore to a section of the shop with a

hand-painted sign that read, *New styles for the modern home!* The pieces here were different from those found throughout the rest of the store. Traditional pieces with curly-cued accents and medium stains made up most of the inventory, but here in this small section were more unconventional designs. Some pieces had squarish patterns and clean lines and were stained so dark they were almost black, while others had incredibly intricate patterns of birds and blossoms and trees carved into them. These looked as if they had simply been oiled to allow the wood's natural tones to show through. These were clearly Gadget's experiments, her pieces that she had made for art's sake, from imagination and inspiration, rather than to simply make a profit on.

"What is it you're looking for today?" Gadget asked Mina as they browsed.

"Something brand new," Mina replied. "Something that speaks freedom and new life. I'll need an entire set."

Lenore looked sideways at Mina. There was something going on. This flouncy, dreamy talk wasn't like her. Even so, Lenore was smart enough to let it go. She simply listened.

"It can be done," Gadget said. "How about this? I haven't thought up a name for it yet. What would you call this set?"

Gadget had stopped at the set of beautifully carved, lightly oiled furniture set with all the tree and flower and bird carvings.

Mina looked as if she were thinking for a moment and then said, "Crowley."

"Crowley? Sounds like lowly. No, no, that won't do. Why not Blackbird? It's a country name, fits the natural accents."

"Oh, darling, it's your work. If you think that's best, I trust you. I'll take the lot."

"Of course. I'll have everything delivered tomorrow."

Lenore smiled. She wasn't sure what had just happened or how, but she was impressed.

True to her word, Gadget's entire "Blackbird" furniture suite was delivered the next day. Gadget came and oversaw the delivery personally, giving orders the whole way. Part of the transaction included Gadget taking the old furniture from Lenore's room to sell in her secondhand shop at a much-discounted price.

"Who's watching your store?" Lenore asked, standing with Gadget as they watched the deliverymen assemble the bed.

"My daughter," Gadget replied. "Oh, don't look at me like that. She's smart as a whip, sweet as sugar, and twice as tough as her mother."

"In that case, she sounds more than capable," Lenore said.

The look Lenore had given Gadget was one of disbelief. Despite the carpenter's wounds, she had a youth about her, and Lenore couldn't imagine Gadget having a child any older than sixteen or so. That seemed far too young to Lenore to be left alone with such a big responsibility.

"Absolutely. I thank the heavens every day that she's as obedient as she is. Otherwise, one of us wouldn't have survived."

Gadget chuckled to herself at that, and Lenore smiled. It took several hours, but Lenore's room was finally completely refurnished. Each piece was gorgeous, and Lenore thought the set actually made the room look brighter. After Gadget and her movers were gone, Lenore began to inspect everything.

The detail was magnificent. Every feature was so lifelike. She cringed to think how much the set had cost and made a mental note to ask Mina about it so that she could start paying her back. The same went for the clothes from Tilly's for that matter. The thought of her ever-increasing debt had been niggling at the back of Lenore's mind for the last few days. Without a job, she had been ignoring it since she had no way to repay it except whatever the Allens asked her to do. Now that she had secured a position, however, Lenore had options. She was definitely going to use whatever money she earned to pay them back.

Despite the high quality of the work, Lenore could find nothing among the pieces that would help her documents issue. She even had Bitsy climb all over and through the pieces to no avail. Thankfully, Lenore didn't need to ask for help. As soon as Neal got home, he asked about the furniture. Lenore explained that everything had gone smoothly and that it was all assembled now.

"But you haven't found the papers yet?" Neal asked. Lenore shook her head worriedly, and he said happily, "Good! This will be fun."

He then headed to Lenore's room, asked if she minded if he went in, and practically ran in and began examining everything.

"What's so exciting, if you don't mind me asking?" Lenore asked, watching him run his hands over the dresser.

"This will probably be our only chance to figure out one of Gadget's puzzles," Neal explained. "Let's hope Mina has an exploding appendix to attend to."

"That's horrible!"

"Baby. Let's hope Mina has some sweet baby to deliver into the world," Neal corrected.

Over the next half hour, Lenore watched Neal comb over every carving, every joint, every inch of the Blackbird set. Finally, he came and sat next to Lenore.

"Alright, Lenore, let's think about this," he said to her. "The furniture has a nature motif. It's probably safe to assume that has something to do with the answer."

"Couldn't we just ask Gadget?" Lenore suggested.

"No! I have to figure this out. There's no victory in asking for the answer."

"If *you* have to figure it out, then why are you asking for my help?" Lenore teased.

"I'm not! I just need whatever information Gadget left for us. What did she say when she left?"

"Not much. She didn't even ask me if everything looked alright."

"She won't have. Gadget knows her craft and part of that is arrangement."

"She did say she was happy that Mina picked out this set. She likes the natural wood tones."

"Hmmm, that is very tricky. With women, you never know if they're just making a harmless comment of if there's a deeper meaning or even a trap to it."

Lenore smiled. She was pretty sure Neal was too engrossed in the riddle of the Blackbird set to realize that she was included in that generalization. Neal sat there staring at the room, talking to himself, while Lenore thought as well. Without any idea of what it was they were supposed to find, however, it didn't do her much good. At one point, Esther appeared and asked if they wanted some tea.

Lenore declined, but Neal stood up and declared, "YES!"

"It'll be ready in just a bit, Master Neal," Esther said and left.

"Excellent, Esther. You're brilliant," Neal called after her.

Lenore then watched as Neal headed over to the bed, then to the side table, and finally over to the dresser. He began to carefully pull some of the drawers open until the stops caught and left them ajar. Lenore felt a little self-conscious, as some of the drawers held her undergarments, but Neal didn't seem to notice. He finally stopped pulling drawers and began to feel around the dresser again. Lenore noticed that all the drawers that were pulled were part of those that made up a large tree—*ah, tea sounds like tree,* she thought—that was carved into the face of the dresser. Neal stopped suddenly, and Lenore saw him lift the top of the dresser up.

"That's not supposed to happen," Lenore said, standing up to get a closer look.

The top panel of the dresser was hinged very cleverly so that it was impossible to see from the outside that there even was a hinge. The drawers must have been the key to unlocking it. Beneath the panel was simply another piece of wood, but laid out neatly across it were papers. These were Lenore's new identification papers: birth record, citizen papers, school records, everything. Lenore lifted a sheet and read it aloud.

"Lenore Blackbird, born in the Ninety-Second Year of the Dawn Age, Second Day of the Star to Erik and Jennifer Blackbird."

She felt Neal put a comforting hand on her shoulder.

"What's the truth of the matter?"

"I was born on the Fifteenth Day of the Earth, same year, to Edgar and Twila Crowley."

"Where are your real papers?"

"I burned them… after my parents were arrested."

"Ah, I see. Probably for the best."

Lenore was struck with a deep sense of loss, though she couldn't exactly say why. Everything before her was looking brighter than it had in a very, very long time, yet she felt as if she were leaving something behind that she could never replace.

"Oh, you discovered the secret. Mina's going to be so jealous."

Lenore and Neal turned to see Camilla standing there looking happy as always.

"Is she on her way back?" Neal asked.

"Yes, very soon. There was a daredevil with a broken arm tonight."

Neal laughed, and Lenore gathered up the rest of her paperwork.

"Will you be ready to work tomorrow?" Neal asked.

"Yes," Lenore said, trying to make herself smile and being mostly successful. "Tomorrow will be my first day."

"Fantastic! Now, let's go have some of Esther's tea."

The three headed downstairs and were met by Mina a little while later. Camilla had been right, she was rather jealous that Neal had gotten to figure out Gadget's furniture riddle. It was the first time Lenore had seen the woman act even somewhat childish. Neal then regaled her with the story of how he had figured it out, which Lenore thought sounded an awful lot more exciting than actually experiencing it had been. Later on when Lenore did ask Mina about the cost of everything, she simply tutted Lenore and waved the question away with a hand.

"It's not something you need to worry yourself over," Mina said to her. "Neal and I are more than happy to help."

Lenore tried to protest further—she still hated the idea of being indebted to the Allens—but Mina was stubborn and rebuffed every objection. Lenore finally dropped the subject, but silently vowed that she would contribute... even if she had to be sneaky about it.

# 6

# HARDLY WORK-APPROPRIATE BEHAVIOR

*inally! There she was, the specter that had evaded him all these long months. The tip he had gotten from that scum proved true. Good thing he had decided against killing him. There was a calmness in him as he looked at Lenore that he hadn't felt in a very long while. But how had she ended up here? He knew nothing about these people she was living with now and would therefore have to proceed carefully. He glanced around again, grumbling inwardly at his hiding place. This area was too exposed. At least now, after all these long and anxious months of searching, he knew where to find her.*

❂

Lenore's stomach refused to stop doing somersaults all the way to the museum, which was located in the very impressive Ivory quarter. Esther had made a special meal for her that morning— her favorite: potato pancakes and eggs and bacon with hot cocoa to celebrate her first day of work. Lenore was thankful that she had been able to enjoy it, but now wondered if it would make a grand reappearance at some point. It wasn't the work she was so anxious about, it was the administrative process of getting hired in. She carried her citizen papers with her in an old satchel of Neal's, which would later be shown to the Museum Administrator so that an employment record could be made. Lenore couldn't help but think the Administrator would take one look at the documents and cry, *Fake!* Neither Neal nor Mina seemed concerned, though. They clearly had a lot of faith in Gadget, though Lenore would always wonder how the woman had ever come up with everything so quickly. She was sure she'd never find out either. Thankfully, Neal never left her side during the entire process. He and Lenore sat in the overstuffed chairs of the Personnel Office while the Museum Administrator, a plump, pleasant woman named Mathilda, looked over Lenore's papers, filled in forms, offered them tea, and chatted idly. It didn't take quite as long as Lenore was expecting. She wasn't sure what she was expecting, but was thankful they got out within half an hour. Then, after Lenore had let out a very relieved sigh, came the fun part.

"So what do I do now?" she asked as Neal led her back to the Arc-Tech department.

Neal had referred to it as Arc-Tech since she had secured the position.

"Everything I need help with," Neal said with a smile. "We'll make discoveries and theorize, in between the department meetings, of course, at which I'll need you to take notes so I can work on sleeping with my eyes open."

"Department meetings?" Lenore said. "What goes on at those?"

"Oh, the usual. New discoveries are praised, expedition plans are announced or updated, failures are tiptoed around. It makes us feel organized. Here we are."

Lenore smiled at seeing the familiar doors before her and followed Neal in after he unlocked them. Work began immediately. Neal explained how archeological engineers— archeotechnologists as some called them—like him must follow due process in order to ensure the legitimacy of their findings. According to him, there were discoveries that had been tragically overshadowed by questions of who and how and where and when. Some had even been disregarded as unverifiable.

"Here, let me show you the notes on the subaquatic," Neal offered.

"Is that what you always called it?" Lenore asked curiously.

"No, I always called it the underwater runner. I kind of picked up subaquatic after you said it the other day. It sounds better, more official, rolls off the tongue more easily. Now, it's here somewhere. I keep the records together to ensure that I don't lose pieces."

While Neal spoke, he was sifting through great stacks of paper on his work desk, which stood against the wall. Lenore noticed that the space exclusively belonging to Neal resembled an overgrown forest floor. Nothing was neat or labeled or sorted. It was all just stacked upon itself in squat towers and broad piles.

"Aha! Here it is," Neal said proudly. "You see, every step, every participant, every detail was documented every time."

"Who are some of these other people?" Lenore asked. "Are there others in our department?"

"There are. You'll meet them today."

"Why aren't they here now?"

"I'm the boss. I have to be here early, and, as my apprentice, so do you."

He smiled, and Lenore knew he was ribbing her, but she didn't care. She had a job and a home and so much more than she could have dreamed a week ago. She smiled back, and Neal began the grand tour, as he called it, of the department.

There wasn't much more to it than what Lenore had already seen. The entire space was basically one large workshop and a lavatory tucked back in the corner. There was also a bookshelf and a few mismatched armchairs off to one side. This was the research corner where Neal and his colleagues would study up on recent discoveries, old theories, and anything else applicable to their field. After the tour, Neal asked what Lenore wanted to start with.

"Um, well, perhaps I should organize things," she suggested, looking back at Neal's cluttered desk.

"What?" Neal said, also looking over at his desk.

Lenore began to panic. Blazes! She'd insulted Neal on her first day. She felt her face flush and opened her mouth like a fish to try and recover. Nothing came out, however, but it didn't matter. Another voice interjected before she would have been able to get very far anyway.

"Brilliant idea!"

The owner of the voice was a well-dressed young man, several years Lenore's senior. Lenore thought he looked a lot like the type she used to steal from. *Quite* a lot, in fact. Her survival instincts kicked in and she kept her face straight and closed just in case he had been one of her victims.

"Everything's already falling into place," the man continued. "This place has needed a woman's touch for a long while. Dempsey, Dempsey Van Pelt. You must be the new apprentice."

He offered his hand. Lenore extended hers carefully, covering it with the guise of being demure, and he kissed it delicately.

*Hardly work-appropriate behavior,* Lenore thought.

"Lenore Blackbird," she said cautiously.

78

"Lovely to meet you," Dempsey said. "Oh, Neal, stop looking like that. Your desk is a wreck. Normal state of affairs, Lenore."

Neal cleared his throat and added, "Yes, Lenore. Dempsey is my post-graduate student."

"You didn't complete an apprenticeship?" Lenore asked.

This was something Lenore's father had often ranted about. University had always been for studying the mental arts: philosophy, history, mathematics, literature, and so on. The practical arts had, until recently, always been apprenticed crafts. The last decade or so, however, had seen students of technologics, mechanics, carpentry, and other hands-on professions through the theory of their chosen professions in school and then into the field. It was a controversial subject, as many believed that one must be physically immersed in the work to really understand it.

Lenore's father had seen too many fresh-faced young men come storming into his workshop, armed to the teeth with knowledge and book sense about how machines worked and were developed and built, but with no practical knowledge of how to actually assemble or design anything. What was worse was that they came with all sorts of idealist theories about how to design and build more efficiently with less cost, red tape, and waste. The issue with that was that the theories often didn't mesh with messy, complicated, contrary reality.

The other side of the argument, however, stated that too many mistakes were made by apprentices, costly ones. These believed that it was better to teach the knowledge of the subject matter first, thus preparing the pupil mentally, and then sending them out to get hands-on experience. Of course, there were others, doctors mostly, that had suggested a healthy balance between the two. After all, physicians had studied both books and cadavers long before ever putting their hands on a living patient. The debate was still in its infancy, however, and would likely continue for a good, long time.

"Ah, no," Dempsey chuckled. "Learn first, then do, as they say."

She smiled a tight-lipped facsimile of primness. Yes, she had to agree with her father on this one.

"Of course. Neal, if it's alright with you, I think I'll begin. I'll keep everything sorted to your liking... as much as possible."

She smiled more widely at him. It was a plea to escape and for forgiveness. Lenore could only hope he understood the deeper meaning.

Neal only smiled weakly back and said, "Very well, but please be careful."

"Of course."

Lenore then headed off towards Neal's desk to begin the delicate and meticulous process of organizing the tornado aftermath that it was. She had to skim the various documents, academic papers, journal entries, and forms in order to know where they would need to go, and Lenore found herself fascinated by what she read.

*Eighth Year of the New Age, Twelfth Day of the Sea*

*The Underwater Runner artifact was brought in today. Arrival time was 1:32 P.M.. Scholar Bates oversaw the transport from start to finish. The description catalogue was taken by myself and Mister Dempsey Van Pelt from 2:14 P.M. until 6:40 P.M..*

*Attached:*

*Description Catalogue—Underwater Runner (unofficial name).*

*Ninth Year of the New Age, Second Day of the Air*

Engineer Cooper Richmond and I began to theorize about the Underwater Runner today. Since we discovered the ballast compartments, we've begun to believe the Underwater Runner could have swum, so to speak, in addition to driving on the ocean floor. If this is true, a rudder would have been required to steer. Engineer Cooper has sketched a deconstruction of the Underwater Runner with the newly discovered ballast compartments and the rudder it may have had. I sent a missive at 12:09 P.M. today to the archeological team at the discovery site to let them know that they may yet find such an item.

P.S.: Happy New Year!


Attached:

Deconstructed sketch by Cooper Richmond—Underwater Runner (unofficial name).

Copy of missive sent to archeological team at discovery site —Underwater Runner (unofficial name).


*Ninth Year of the New Age, Twenty-Third Day of the Sky*

While maintaining the Underwater Runner, I discovered evidence of a hinge at the back of the Runner. The discovery occurred at 8:38 A.M.. Engineer Cooper Richmond and Mister Dempsey Van Pelt were present. The possible hinge is very small. It was hidden amidst all the other damage at the back of the Underwater Runner. Engineer Cooper Richmond and Mister Dempsey Van Pelt both concur that the smooth curve of the hinge and straight cut of its edge makes this a reasonable and acceptable conclusion.

Personal musing: why would the hinge be so small? Surely, a machine of this magnitude would need a rudder of comparable size, which would require similarly sized hinges. Very curious indeed.

<u>*Ninth Year of the New Age, Twenty-Eighth Day of the Fire*</u>

*I let the team go home early today. Engineer Cooper's air cooler failed several times today—again—before petering out completely. Mister Dempsey Van Pelt nearly took off Scholar Lily Grace's head when she questioned one of his theories about the Winged Zeppelin. Nothing of note has or will come while it's so unbearably hot.*

<u>*Ninth Year of the New Age, Tenth Day of the Stone*</u>

*Today, at 7 A.M. sharp, Miss Lenore Blackbird began an interview with Scholar Bates and me. The interview lasted approximately an hour and a half. After speaking with Scholar Bates this afternoon around 3:30 P.M., I learned that he approves of the hire. I will offer the position to Miss Lenore this evening.*

*I will also submit the Request for an Official Name form to the Museum Department Heads at next week's department meeting. Miss Lenore is responsible for the official naming, as it was she that first called it a subaquatic (formerly the Underwater Runner), which I have finalized to Subaquatic Sloop. She called it a "subaquatic" at 8:26 A.M. near the end of the interview.*

*Attached:*
*Request for an Official Name form—Subaquatic Sloop (formerly the Underwater Runner).*

At the bottom of each log entry were timed and dated signatures from each individual mentioned in each entry, as well as a custom stamp. Lenore deduced that this must be what verified the accuracy of the information in each entry. Not a bad system. She was especially shocked and pleased by the last entry, the one she was mentioned in. She was being credited with the naming of an ancient artifact? She had to be dreaming. Lenore smiled, organized all of the papers neatly together, and clipped them with the metal, triangular clips that sat in a small cup on Neal's desk. She then scampered over to Neal, who was going over a machine the size of a large dog with Dempsey. Both men had clipboards and pens in their hands.

"Yes, Lenore?" Neal said, not looking away from the machine.

He was fighting the smile that was trying to spread across his face. He had been carefully watching the girl all morning as she organized his space. Not that he didn't trust the girl, but his desk was his academic sanctuary. It was where he dreamed and thought and mused and deduced. He may have been a little tetchy about it... just a little. He had been very pleased, however, when he saw Lenore losing herself in the details of his and his department's work. After how miserable her experience in Mina's practice had made her, he, not to mention Mina, was very concerned that she would be unhappy here as well. There hadn't seemed to be too much of a chance of that, considering how she had pored over the books in the manor and how well her interview had gone, but it was still a concern nonetheless. The way she was practically skipping now was the final confirmation that this was the right place for her.

"Engineer Allen," she said, trying to sound very official, "I believe I need to sign this, do I not?"

Neal looked at the log entry in Lenore's hand, finally allowed the smile to break through, and replied, "Yes, indeed you should. You'll need a stamp, however, and we don't have one made for you yet."

"Oh, how do I get one?" Lenore asked.

"You'll get one," Dempsey said. "Mathilda has probably already sent off for yours. It will arrive in about a week."

"You can stamp next to any signatures you make after you receive yours," Neal added. "Just be sure to keep track of all the signatures you make. Go claim a clipboard for yourself from the shelf over there, start your list, and then sign."

"I will do so," Lenore said with an enthusiastic nod.

She trotted off again and did as Neal had instructed. Lenore clipped a piece of paper to the back of the clipboard and wrote her name on it in very large letters. She decided she would try and paste something more permanent and official looking to replace the clipped paper later on, but this would suffice until then.

The rest of the day was consumed by organizing Neal's desk. It actually should have taken much less time, but Lenore couldn't stop herself from studying nearly everything she picked up. She tried to be surreptitious about it because she didn't want Neal to think she was flighty and easily distracted. Neal saw it all, however, and only smiled. Lenore was pulled into what she read more deeply than she realized, and would spend stretches of ten and fifteen minutes just flipping through pages and reading. He was pleased about her interest in the work and knew that she was too new to do much else anyway. They both, unbeknownst to the other, decided that this was a good thing because it meant that Lenore would become familiar with the work as she went.

A little while after Dempsey arrived, another member of the department came in. It was Engineer Cooper Richmond, the other person mentioned so often in the official department logs.

He was a shorter, stouter man and very congenial. He greeted Lenore with a firm handshake and a somewhat unorthodox but gregarious welcome.

"So good to meet you, Miss Lenore," Cooper said. "Very good indeed. About blazing time Neal took on an apprentice."

Lenore smiled and replied, "That is the rumor."

"Hah! Indeed! You can call me Copper. Everyone else does."

Lenore could see how the nickname fit. Copper's skin was leathery, probably from prolonged exposure to the heat of a welder and other machinist's tools. Even his hair had a touch of red in it, though his muttonchops looked a little patchy… like they had been burned a few times.

"Just let me know if you need anything at all," Copper added. "These two mean well, but I'm the creative one of the bunch."

"Creative or mad?" Neal called from the small machine he and Dempsey were examining.

"See, he can't deny it. Again, very nice to meet you."

Lunch was a special treat that day, as Neal decided that they should order in to welcome Lenore to the department. All of them wrote their orders down on a slip of paper, which Dempsey ran down to the Administrative department. Lenore was actually familiar with the pasty shop they were ordering from, so she didn't need help with hers, but she was confused as to why Dempsey had volunteered to put in the order. After all, she was essentially the new errand gopher, wasn't she? Copper explained that a member of the admin team would get one of the numerous couriers that were always flitting in and out to pick up and deliver the food. He also explained that Dempsey shamelessly liked visiting all the pretty, young ladies in the Administrative department.

After lunch arrived, the four department members all sat down in the research corner and ate together. They exchanged questions with Lenore about her and her background and she returned the same queries. It was getting easier and easier for her to lie. Using the documents Gadget had created, Mina, Camilla, and Neal had all worked with her to perfect her back story right down to the name of the tiny village she came from to what she had received for her sixteenth birthday. It was a painful process, but a necessary one. Thankfully, rules of propriety kept the questions pretty basic on both sides.

At the end of the day, Lenore went over how she had reorganized Neal's desk for him and showed him all of her documentation.

"So you see, everything pertaining to a single project is clipped together in chronological order. All of those are organized alphabetically by project name. Anything that mentions more than one project, which aren't very many, are waiting to be sorted. I thought it was best to consult you on those to see where they should go."

"Excellent work, Lenore," Neal said. "A very good first day."

# 7
# UNWELCOME VISITORS

L enore was met by another happy surprise when they arrived home that evening. She and Neal had left work early that day. Mina and Camilla came home early too, and Esther was ready with some sweet tea and snacks.

"How was your first day?" Camilla chirped.

"Neal says it was very good," Lenore said, unable to stop smiling.

"You won't believe it," Neal said, "she organized my desk."

"I *don't* believe it!" Mina teased. "Lenore, where have you been all our lives?"

Lenore smiled wider and simply nodded.

"To celebrate such a good first day, Neal, Camilla, and I have bought you a little gift."

"No, Mina, please, no more gifts!" Lenore exclaimed. "You all have already done far more for me than you should have."

"Nonsense," Neal said jovially. "Consider it a tool. You'll need it for work."

That hushed Lenore's objections for a moment, but her insides still squirmed at the thought of taking on a bigger debt.

She watched as Mina pulled a velvet box from her waistcoat pocket and handed it to Neal.

"Would you like to do the honors, Engineer Allen?" Mina said with a smile.

"Thank you, my dear." Turning to Lenore, Neal cleared his throat and said proudly, "Lenore Blackbird, as your mentor, I would like to present you with this gif—erm, tool."

Very carefully, Lenore took the box from Neal and opened it with bated breath. She gasped when she saw what was inside. It was a very fine fob watch with a lightly smoked glass dial that allowed her to see all the gears and inner workings of the watch. The main casing of the watch was bronze with a circular inlay of steel, within which was yet a smaller circular inlay of copper. All of that was covered in elegant, flowing scrollwork embossing. The pieces that made up the clockwork inside were also a mix of metals, and Lenore felt the prick of tears in her eyes.

"This is… this is… this is just so splendid," Lenore said, fighting the urge to weep with joy. "Not that I'm not indescribably grateful, because I am, but why are you doing all of this for me?"

Mina came over and cupped Lenore's face in her hands as she said, "Because, my dear, we are fortunate to have more than we could ever dream. It is only right to help those that life has kicked."

Lenore smiled at that and the thought, but didn't get a chance to respond. The doorchime rang and everyone looked in the direction of the front entrance.

"Are we expecting company?" Mina asked. Camilla and Neal both confirmed that they were not. "Lenore, if you would, make yourself scarce. Just in case, please."

Lenore obeyed and headed out of the parlor and into the dining room. Her survival instincts had kicked in, and her ears were perked, listening for every word. She heard Esther open the door and Mina speaking. There was more speaking and heavy footsteps leading into the parlor. Lenore was then surprised to see Camilla bolt around the corner and grab her hand fiercely.

"Be silent!" she hissed. "Stay here and don't move!"

Lenore was so taken aback by the angelic girl's behavior that she could only nod dumbly. She was shocked to see Camilla's usually soft blue eyes hard and cold. She glared at Lenore for a moment to make sure she wasn't going anywhere.

"Camilla, dear, you have a visitor," Lenore heard Esther say from nearby.

Camilla looked at Lenore for just a moment longer before turning on her heel and stalking off. Lenore leaned back against the wall and listened carefully, keen to know what was going on and ready to run just in case.

"Camilla, my doll," came a man's voice from the parlor. "How are you?"

"I'm well, Father," Lenore could hear Camilla say. Her tone was strained, as if she were barely able to maintain her civility.

*Father?!*

"And how are you, Fourth Hawkins?" came Mina's voice.

Lenore's stomach turned. Fourth was an Enforcer title. A high-ranking Enforcer was here in the house and he was Camilla's father. Lenore could scarcely believe it.

"I'm also well, Mistress Mina," came the man's voice again. "Especially after I heard about what you'd done for my Fifth here. Ladies and Neal, may I introduce Fifth Sawyer?"

"Yes, I recognize him. How are you doing, sir? No problems with your stitches?"

"No, ma'am," came another man's voice. This one was much younger and all-too-familiar to Lenore's ears. "Thank you again for your care."

"Of course, Fifth Sawyer."

"When Sawyer gave his report, he said he was helped to your practice by a suspicious girl," the older man said. "Could you give us a description?"

Lenore's heart began to beat so hard she was sure they could hear it out in the parlor.

"Of course, Fourth Hawkins. Let me think," Mina said. "It was dark, and I immediately focused in on Fifth Sawyer, of course. She was a young girl, though. She looked about fourteen, maybe thirteen. Dark hair, dark eyes. She was pale and rather petite and I would guess poor by her dress."

Lenore felt a sudden warmth bloom in her heart. Once again, Mina was protecting her. Mina's description was vague enough that it could have been anyone. It also described the way Lenore had looked while she was supporting Fifth Sawyer on her shoulders, not how she looked now.

"Does that corroborate with your impression of the suspect?" Fourth Hawkins asked.

"Yes, sir, almost exactly," Fifth Sawyer replied.

"Excellent," Fourth Hawkins replied. "Now, how about some tea?"

From there, Lenore heard Mina ring for Esther to bring a fresh pot of tea. The group discussed tedious subjects like how Mina's practice was doing, how Camilla was coming along in her apprenticeship, and how handsome Mina's new curtain dressings were. It was an hour before the Enforcers left, during which time Lenore never moved. Finally, as soon as the door closed, after Mina had bid the men goodbye, Lenore let out a much-delayed sigh of relief.

"How dare he?!" she heard Camilla snarl.

At this, Lenore left her hiding spot, keen to get an explanation for what she had just learned.

"How dare he come here—unannounced, mind you—and

accuse you?! Never mind that he *still* cannot address you by your proper title. That would be showing you too much respect," Camilla said just as vehemently.

Lenore found her and Mina back in the parlor, Camilla looking furious. With the reminder of what Mina had done, Lenore ran to her and hugged her.

"Thank you!" Lenore exclaimed. "Thank you so much!"

"Of course, darling," Mina said, returning the embrace.

"What was that all about?" Lenore asked, turning to Camilla.

"*That* was my father," Camilla spat. "He came here to interrogate Mina about you, the very person that saved his little pet there."

Lenore blinked and looked at Mina, waiting for the woman to tell Camilla to calm down. She didn't.

"I'm… I'm so sorry," Lenore said, unsure of what else was safe to say.

"I think I need some air," Camilla said and stormed off.

"Is she going to be alright?" Lenore asked quietly.

"Give her time," Mina replied.

What an odd turn to the night. What an odd turn to her life! Lenore never could have guessed that her life would have ended up the way it had over the last year. She wasn't even sure what to think anymore. Should she still be as scared as she had been only a few days ago? Camilla was directly connected to an Enforcer, but it was clear all of them were not just willing to lie, but able to do so very well. She'd probably never completely relax; she'd seen too much. She could already tell that she'd begun to settle in to her situation, however. Come to think of it, Camilla probably had the most to fear of them all. She could never completely separate herself from the Enforcers. For the first time, Lenore saw her housemate as more than just a superficial, fluff-headed girl. Camilla had issues of her own, though Lenore couldn't be sure if the girl's sunny demeanor was a shield or completely genuine.

Camilla was absent from dinner that night, which worried Lenore more than anything. She may not always like Camilla's perpetual cheeriness, but the girl was clearly distressed. She wanted to find Camilla, to make sure she was alright, and to find out more about Fourth Hawkins. She didn't want to appear too eager, though, so she acted as if she were just taking a stroll through the house after dinner was cleared away. Lenore finally found Camilla in the back garden.

Lenore felt ridiculous calling the immense tract of land behind the Allens' stately home a garden, but that's what the rest of the family called it, so she had come to do the same. She preferred the courtyard, which was surrounded on three sides by the manor itself and by a tall stone wall on the fourth. The garden, which was accessible via the courtyard by an old wooden door, was edged by an easily-scalable—an advantage Lenore had discovered during her mad dash through the city— wrought iron fence.

Camilla was sitting on a bench, wrapped in an old blanket. Lenore approached and deliberately made sure she was heard, but said nothing. Camilla turned to look at her housemate and smiled wanly.

"Lenore, I'm very sorry you had to see that earlier," Camilla said. "I was not at my best."

"I'm sure I'll see you in all kinds of states eventually," Lenore replied. "We are living under the same roof after all. Think nothing of it."

Camilla's smile disappeared, and she looked away.

"I just… I just *hate* him so much. He killed my mother, you know."

"He what?"

"Not personally, but he might as well have. My mother was

92

a wonderful woman. How could she not be, being Mina's sister? My father, however, never wanted and never should have had a child. I've been told they were very much in love before my mother got pregnant, but things apparently turned sour after I was born. All I can remember is my father hating my mother, and he never seemed very interested in me on top of that. He eventually turned my mother in for a crime she didn't commit. It was a petty thing—stealing jewelry—but no one believed my mother over a well-respected Enforcer like my father. They made an example of her."

Lenore's heart went out to Camilla. Oh, heavens. Did Camilla think she shouldn't have been born? That things would be better if she hadn't been? And now she had lost her mother to who knew what kind of torment. Lenore wondered if she had seen Camilla's mother. When the Enforcers made an example of someone, it was often public and gruesome, a reminder to all citizens the price for breaking the law. Lenore was thankful she had never seen her parents on display. Perhaps they had been and Lenore, being in hiding, had missed it. She knew she was happier not knowing the answer to that. Despite her willful ignorance, she knew all too well how Camilla felt, what it was like to lose someone dear to those monsters... two someones. Lenore sat down on the bench next to Camilla and wrapped her arms around her, shedding tears with her.

*Ninth Year of the New Age, Thirteenth Day of the Stone*
*Official report submitted by Fourth Hawkins:*

*Fifth Sawyer and I went to the home of Sir Gwenael and Mrs. Philomena Allen tonight to question Mrs. Allen about the attempt on Fifth Sawyer's life the other night. Our questions\**

were answered directly and thoroughly. The Allens showed no signs of deceit. Miss Camilla Hawkins was also present. She was also questioned about the suspect from that night. It is our understanding that the suspect fled before Miss Hawkins entered the room. Sir Allen was reportedly still at work at the time. We will be making inquiries with the Museum of History and Nature to confirm this. We are widening our search to see if we can't find evidence of the girl's movements in other crimes. Sixths Jenkins, Meadors, and Sullivan have been tasked with combing through other reports for any suspect descriptions matching that of the girl who was involved that night. It is unlikely that someone so young, especially a young lady, could operate alone. We suspect she's a small piece in a larger player's game, which means she's likely involved in countless other operations throughout the city.

The search for Fifth Sawyer's attacker is being carried out more aggressively. Fifth Sawyer and I have already begun making calls into The Kicking Mule and other pubs during peak hours to identify the attacker onsite. No luck yet, but a malefactor such as that will eventually crawl back to a favorite hole. People like him are weak to their vices, and I feel confident that we will catch him soon.

*See Fifth Sawyer's accompanying Q&A notes from the interrogation.

Blazes! Enforcers?! Why didn't they just crawl into a pit and die? He had come back once darkness fell to glean more information about the house, its occupants, and Lenore's new situation. All of that went out the window, however, when he realized the vermin were there. And one of them was father to the blond! And the other... oh, he was going to have words with *that one… assuming he made good on his promise to come back.*

*"What have you gotten yourself into, Lenore?"*

*This really could not get any worse. This odd family didn't play by the polite society rules he was used to. Now what? Should he steal Lenore away before she got caught by that ape? He had to admit, he was tempted, but that probably wouldn't encourage her to trust him. He had already decided he needed her to trust him. No, he wouldn't step in until the time was right. He needed more information about the situation first. He'd dig up the family's history first.*

"Do you think we've done well, Mina?" Neal asked that evening, climbing into bed next to his wife.

"What do you mean, dear?" Mina replied.

"With Lenore, do you think we've done well?" Neal explained. "Do you think she'll be happy?"

"Oh, Neal, I like to think so. She seemed very happy this evening."

"I know. I just don't want her to stay out of obligation."

Mina nodded in understanding. She felt the same. After a few minutes of contented silence, she spoke again.

"I imagine if we'd been able to have children, I would like some very much like Camilla and Lenore."

"One to take after you," Neal said wistfully.

"And one like you."

"You think she's like me?"

"She certainly shares your interests."

"What a pleasure it would have been to meet her parents. They must have been brilliant to raise her as they did. Can you imagine living on the streets for over a year?"

"No, I can't. She's certainly something."

Neal nodded as Mina snuggled closer. He eventually felt her fall asleep against him, her breathing becoming more smooth and regular. He did not fall asleep for several hours after that. Thoughts and worries about their new charge kept popping up in his head, and there seemed to be nothing he could do to turn them off.

# 8

# WATCHED

The days began to fall into a regular rhythm, or as regular as possible. Lenore went to work with Neal and learned more about what it was to be an archeotechnologist. There was far more paperwork than she ever could have guessed, but the subject matter remained fascinating. She learned that she could become a scholar on the subject if she went to school or an engineer if she apprenticed. Dempsey was apparently *technically* an engineer already—according to the diploma he had received from university—but the museum wouldn't recognize the title until he had completed three years with them. This was apparently a sore subject, which Copper liked to bring up when Dempsey was being especially himself. He never hid the disdain he felt for the university path.

"Neal and I, we worked for it," Copper told Lenore once. "You can't read some books, write a few articles, and call yourself an engineer. You have to *do* it!"

Lenore tended to agree, especially when Copper taught her to use things like the focused torch or the grit belt. Neal discouraged the use of these tools. He said they were too rough for the delicate work of artifacts.

Copper made a lewd response to that.

Lenore wasn't surprised that Neal leaned towards the more detailed work of his craft after remembering Gadget's mechanical hand. Seeing the wide swath of barnacle residue on the Subaquatic Sloop, though, convinced Lenore that there was a place for the raucous, modern, possibly dangerous machines. She remained a gopher for the most part, but her colleagues were always helpful and even indulgent when she asked questions, which she did... a lot.

Lenore got to better know the family she now shared a home with as well. Neal simply proved again and again to be everything that he had always seemed, though she hadn't expected him to be so... fun-loving. Once in a while, Neal would go out and spend the evening with several of his gentlemen friends and play cards. His favorite haunt was a place called Raven's Tower, which was built into one of the oldest surviving buildings in the city.

The outside of the establishment was a little dilapidated, but the inside was all heavy draperies and dark, polished wood. Lenore only knew this because Mina had been there once, though she didn't like it, and had told Lenore about it. Neal never did. Mina had liked Calandra, the owner, and several of her friends frequented the place, but Mina herself found it to be a bit oppressive. That was probably for the best, Mina told Lenore, as Neal needed a place that was his. Raven's Tower was a good choice for that.

When Neal arrived home from these forays, usually rather late, he smelled of scotch. He never seemed more than a little tipsy, though. Mina would simply roll her eyes at her husband and smile indulgently before taking him to bed with her. Lenore had a feeling that Mina would not be so understanding if Neal let himself go too far or too often. She was very surprised by it, though, because she thought rich people were all straight-laced sticks in the mud. The fact that Neal's occasional indulgences seemed so, well, *normal* was interesting but also somehow comforting.

Mina too had her "girl time", as she referred to it, and Camilla and Lenore were required to join her. This was apparently normal for Camilla, but Lenore objected—loudly— to the mandate. It was the first time Lenore had bucked Mina since she had joined the Allens.

"Mina, I don't know any of your friends or their daughters," Lenore had said. "I'm sure I'll have nothing in common with any of them. It's going to be utterly painful!"

"Lenore, I think you'll be surprised at how well you'll get along with all of them."

"Yes, but none of them are apprenticing in a machine shop."

"Camilla is apprenticing to be a physician."

"And none of them are former criminals."

"Lenore, dear, we've been through this. No one could ever suspect that you are the same little urchin that showed up at my doorstep. That is assuming we play our parts appropriately. It would be suspicious if the young lady we've taken in as our charge never went out with other ladies her age. We're all going to have to move forward as this façade demands, which means *you* are going to have to start accepting the responsibilities that entails."

Mina's words, while true, cut Lenore deeply. It was a reminder that she was a fake the Allens had gotten entangled with, that everything around her was a lie, and Lenore hadn't felt so alone since she had first come to stay with the Allens. Mina apparently saw the effect her words had had on Lenore and apologized.

"Lenore, dear, that's not what I meant. I'm sorry. We are

pleased beyond words to have you. We've adopted you as one of our own, I assure you, so please don't think of yourself as some kind of cuckoo. More than that, never, *ever* think of yourself as a burden. Tell me you believe me."

"I'm trying to…" was all Lenore could muster, not looking at Mina and stroking Bitsy for comfort.

"I know, darling. I know you are. I can't imagine how difficult everything has been for you. We are here for you, though, even through these seemingly unpleasant rituals, and I really do think you might enjoy yourself."

Lenore had nodded and then groaned when Mina mentioned to her they needed to dress to go out with the ladies. She did as she was told, however, and found that she didn't completely hate their time out with Mina's friend and their daughters.

It helped that Lenore had warmed up to Mina considerably since their first meeting. True, the woman was an exacting, shrewd individual with a just-get-it-done kind of determination, but her heart was good and compassionate. She was levelheaded enough to separate facts from feelings—a mean feat for anyone, male or female, indeed!—but seemed to understand the importance of feelings and therefore recognized and attended to them when it was necessary. Lenore respected her more deeply than even she realized.

Lenore chose a cream colored dress for their girl's day out with a rusty orange waistcoat and brown boots and glovelets. The leaves were ablaze now in shades of orange, yellow, purple, and scarlet, and Lenore thought it would be fun to match. She was content with what she had chosen, but Camilla was sent to assist and finish what Lenore had started. Lenore's hair was still growing out, and the girl was not very skillful at hiding the short bits. Camilla, however, seemed to be able to accomplish whatever she set her mind to, and it wasn't long before Lenore had ribbons and even a few feathers woven through her dark tresses in such a way that mimicked the bright beauty of Springhaven's changing leaves.

Camilla also applied cosmetics to Lenore's face for her, which Lenore did not endure with as much grace. Lenore's status before her parents' arrest was never so high that she had been required to wear much in the way of makeup, if any. A little color to her cheeks was pretty much all she was ever asked, and she had even disliked that. Lenore's job only required about the same for propriety. A day out with other high-ranking women, however, demanded much more. Lenore hated the feel of the various creams and powders on her face, but thankfully Mina was sensible enough to know where the line between just enough and too much sat and had taught Camilla well. Camilla, of course, looked perfect no matter what she did.

Lenore was surprised to find that her housemate's constantly cheerful demeanor was genuine. Despite Camilla's painful past, the girl was intentionally happy as often as humanly possible.

"I am alive, healthy, and sane," she had once said to Lenore. "I am warm, fed, and clothed—very well, I might add—and surrounded by love. What do I have to be unhappy about in light of that?"

Lenore admired the girl for her strength of spirit, but couldn't entirely agree. There was bitterness in a small corner of Lenore's heart, but her circumstances had quenched its cold fire for the time being. It was still there, though, and Lenore was aware of it.

The group of women Mina, Camilla, and Lenore spent the day with were all of the same social status as Mina, which did not help Lenore's attitude towards them. They were rich, though not all as snobby as Lenore first suspected they would be. Most of them did not work, but instead acted as spokeswomen for their husbands, many of whom were involved in politics. There was Ophelia Jones, who had brought her daughters, Juliet and Bianca, who were a few years apart. The whole family seemed a bit bossy, and most of the other ladies allowed it for some unknown reason. Then there was Thyme and her twins, Mint and Ginger. Lenore liked them, possibly because Thyme was divorced and unashamed and owned her own business. In fact, she was Thyme of Thyme's Apothecary next door to Mina's practice. Thyme had worked for her status and seemed to be teaching her daughters to do the same. There was also Miss Evangeline Bell, who could have been Camilla's twin, and Mrs. Katerina Holmes and her daughter Beatrice. Katerina was the politician of the family and reminded Lenore a bit of Mina. The biggest difference, however, was that, where Mina had rationality and empathy in equal parts, Katerina's balance was far more on the side of rationality. She wasn't unpleasant really, just matter-of-fact. Beatrice on the other hand seemed to have far more of a sense of humor than her mother, but the same directness, and her humor held the capacity to both heal and harm.

The ladies went out to brunch at a popular but very expensive restaurant in the Ivory quarter. It was the kind of place where there were no menus. Instead, every meal was predetermined based on what was best and available and it was always delicious. The ladies all drank their tea and chatted about the latest fashions and news and even a little gossip. The Joneses seemed most keen to gossip, but Mina objected strongly to it. The funny thing about high society was how much was said without being said.

When Mina said, "Let us not speculate on what may or may not be true of others. Instead, what happy news do we know for certain?" Lenore imagined her actually saying, "Mind your own blazing business, you arrogant cow!" Well, it may not have been as extreme as that, but there was a tension in the air when a subject was danced around like this.

Lenore, thankfully, was only asked questions that propriety allowed, so answering them came almost naturally now. She noticed, however, that some of the girls seemed to think her false history was amusing.

"The city must be so overwhelming for you," Juliet said seriously.

"Not so much," Lenore replied. "It's just a much larger version of home."

"Surely not," Bianca said. "I mean, we don't live next door to cows and chickens after all."

Beatrice laughed, nearly choking on her tea, but pretended to cover it with a sneeze. Katerina shot her a disapproving glare, while Lenore suppressed a smile. Mint, Ginger, and Evangeline all showed a genuine interest in getting to know Lenore better.

"So we hear you apprenticed for Mina," Mint said.

"It was only for a day," Ginger informed her sister.

"Yes, it was... well, it was really difficult," Lenore said honestly. "I simply don't have the stomach or the heart for it."

"Oh, I don't blame you at all," Evangeline said sensibly. "I don't know how Camilla does it. I know I couldn't... oh, I don't even like thinking about all the things she must see in there."

"I know what you mean about the heart," Ginger said. "It's terrible to say, but how long can you really listen to someone about their broken toe? Mint's better about that than I am. She's far more patient."

Lenore smiled. It was good to know she wasn't the only one that had trouble listening to the ailing.

After brunch, the ladies went shopping in the arcade near

the district center. This section of town was even higher class than Tilly's shop.

"Oh, Mrs. Allen, shouldn't we shop for Camilla's debut dress?" Bianca asked. "It's not so very far away, you know."

"Oh, I know, dear," Mina said with a smile. "How well I know. Goodness, whatever will I do? My sweet, baby flower coming out and beginning the search for a husband."

"Mina, dear, have you thought much about Lenore's debut?" Ophelia asked. "She's, what, a few months behind Camilla?"

"I have already begun to think on the event," Mina replied. "I'd like to get through one, however, before beginning to plan another. Even so... Lenore, would you like to try on some dresses today as well?"

"Oh, how fun!" Camilla twittered. "Lenore, I'm so excited! Let's hurry!"

At that, all the other young ladies began to chatter excitedly and followed as Camilla trotted to the dress shop with Lenore in tow.

"Propriety, ladies!" Thyme called after them, but it fell on mostly deaf ears.

Had Lenore not had to focus so much on keeping up the charade—giggling and chirping like a twit—she would have been reeling. A debut for her? What was the point? Did Mina really expect her to get married and carry on the lie forever? Now wasn't really the time to object, though, so Lenore played along.

Thus began several hours' worth of trying on dresses, cooing, oohing, and ahhing. Lenore did her best to transfer all of the attention onto Camilla since her debut was closer, but all of the women seemed too enthralled by the thrill of dress shopping to listen, save for Mina and Katerina. Both these ladies recognized that Camilla's dress was the higher priority, but Mina seemed to want to make sure Lenore didn't feel left out either.

"I promise, I am fine," Lenore assured her with a meaningful smile. "We'll get to me whenever we need to. I'm in no hurry."

Mina smiled back and touched Lenore's nose affectionately. "I understand, dear, but feel free to enjoy yourself anyway. Your time *is* coming."

Lenore nodded and immediately went back to turning the focus onto Camilla… with no more luck than she'd had before. When Evangeline asked her what her ideal dress consisted of, though, Lenore did have a few ideas in mind. Lenore had discussed her debut with her mother a few times before the arrest, though the circumstances were very different. If she was still with her parents, Lenore's debut wouldn't be nearly as grand an affair. From what she remembered, her parents had planned to rent a somewhat large ballroom and invite eligible bachelors from social circles on her father's side. That would ensure attendance by wealthier suitors, to whom Lenore could be married off and live comfortably. Now her potential suitors would consist of politicians, doctors, bankers, and heirs, and Lenore knew her dress would have to be lavish in order to impress.

"I've always liked jewel tones…" Lenore began, looking at herself in the multi-paneled mirror before her. She was currently wearing a beautiful ice blue creation bedecked with crystals meant to resemble snow. It was a dress for a winter debut, which actually suited Camilla very well, as her debut was scheduled for the Ninth Day of the Ice. "My coming out party will be in the au—summer, though, so I suppose I'll have to have a lighter, brighter color."

"Yellow would be lovely," Evangeline suggested.

Lenore tried to hide her distaste for the idea, but mostly

failed.

"Judging by her expression, I'd say Lenore would rather wear a potato sack," Beatrice joked.

"It's just not my cup of tea," Lenore said, trying to save herself. "Camilla, I think this might be your dress."

Camilla then appeared from her own mirrored alcove in a stunning pale gold and ivory number. "Oh my, that is beautiful, but I think I love this one too much."

"It's gorgeous!" Lenore said sincerely. "You look radiant!"

"Sweet Lenore, thank you," Camilla purred. "I think you should wear that. It becomes you."

"No, I think I'll find something a bit more subtle. It's your night, after all."

"I think that will be just fine," Mina said from where she sat in the changing area. She didn't dare come near the ladies at that moment for fear of spilling the red wine she had been served. "If you like it, that is. You do look splendid, though. Also, what about a dusty rose and taupe ensemble for your night? I know pink isn't your favorite color, but perhaps that will be more to your tastes."

"Oh, that does sound lovely," Evangeline agreed, "and it would go so well with your skin tone."

"What about a springy green? You'll have several choices with that, and it will bring out your eyes," Beatrice suggested.

And on the discussion went. Camilla had basically already settled on her dress, and Lenore was content—pleased, really— to brainstorm about possible dresses for her future debut. When Mina had finished with her wine, she got up and helped Camilla with accessories and fitting her dress. The example at the shop was a size too big, so it had to be pinned in numerous places to make sure it would fit correctly. Mina also seemed very concerned with certain details of the dress, mostly the bodice. For that reason, she instructed the seamstresses to add a bit of lace fringe to the sweetheart neckline. This was a detail Camilla rather liked because she was then easily able to convince Mina to agree to some matching engageants. It was also decided that Lenore would keep the ice blue snow dress, but Mina requested for the fullness of the skirt to be taken out.

"We want you to be able to dance in it after all," Mina said with a smile.

She allowed the bateau neckline to remain, however. After dress-up was over, the ladies retired to a chocolate house for their last stop before going their own separate ways. Lenore thought about asking about her debut that evening, but decided against it. She'd see how Camilla's went and then ask whatever questions she still had.

*What an odd place for Lenore to have fallen. Watching her was like watching a nightingale among hens. The nightingale was beautiful and sweet but wild, while the hens were just silly, domesticated, overfed squawkers. He could see everything, the act Lenore kept up, the falseness in her smiles, the calculation of her words. More than anything, though, he saw the carefully concealed guardedness that anyone who's ever lived on the streets never loses. He was sure none of those ridiculous women saw it. Lenore was an excellent little actress, and he knew what to look for. Unfortunately, despite an entire day of watching, he hadn't learned anything that would help him get close to her, much less get her alone. He'd have to keep watching, keep waiting...*

# 9
# CRIMINALS AND MONSTERS ALL

Lenore felt peaceful going to bed a little early that night. It had been a long, estrogen-filled day, but it had been pleasant enough and, despite all the lying, Lenore actually felt like she was settling in comfortably. It was a good feeling.

When Lenore opened the door into her bedroom that evening, however, she stopped short. There, standing by the window, was a tall, gaunt figure with solid black eyes and elongated canines. Lenore screamed and ran pell-mell back down the hall. She was grabbed from behind and felt a searing pain shoot through her neck, down her back, and into her heart. Lenore screamed again and clawed at the head next to her own. It didn't even faze her attacker.

"Kieran! Stop!" came Neal's shout through the pain.

Lenore felt the iron grip loosen and she fell to the floor. The pain was unbelievable and wasn't stopping. Lenore barely caught herself on the wood floor beneath her, but another wave of pain sent her screaming again. Firm but gentle hands were suddenly there helping her.

"Good heavens, Kieran! What's wrong with you?" Lenore could hear Mina snarling. "No, don't touch her! You've done enough damage. Lenore, darling, calm down and breathe. The pain will pass, but you have to let it."

Lenore couldn't calm down, she couldn't think, she couldn't do anything but feel the pain ripping through her. She was going to die. How could she not? Mina was saying something else, time was passing, but all Lenore could do was brace herself against the pain. Somewhere in the background of her senses came a sensation of being pricked, but it was a fleeting shadow compared to her current agony. Then, unbelievably, it began to fade. Lenore's mind grew fuzzy, her limbs felt heavy, and the pain, while still there, dulled to an ache. She felt herself move, she saw the hallway pass by until they returned to her bedroom. A still-sober part of her mind screamed not to return to that room; the creature could get her there. It did no good, however. It was easier to give in to the stupor that had begun to overtake her. She was laid in bed and seemingly left alone.

After Lenore was sedated and in bed, Mina went to find Neal and Kieran. She was furious! How dare he attack her charge?! She correctly guessed that they were in the library. Kieran was sitting in an armchair with a hand over his face. Neal was sitting in the chair next to his friend.

"Well?" Mina said. "What do you have to say for yourself?"

"Exactly what you would expect me to say," Kieran replied flatly. "I am very sorry for attacking the young lady, but I didn't recognize her and deduced that you two must no longer live here. I couldn't risk someone knowing about me. It was a mistake."

"A mistake that could have killed her!" Mina cried. "If you're going to insist on showing up unannounced, why don't you sneak in through our window? That way you would know whether or not we had moved, though why we'd leave a family estate escapes me."

"Humans do all manner of things that defy explanation," Kieran said wryly. "And what if I came in through the window while you and your husband were involved in something... private?"

"Of course, why shouldn't you make lewd jokes? I— Gwenael Allen, I *know* you are not laughing!"

Neal weakly tried to cover his laughter with a cough. Unsurprisingly, it didn't convince Mina. Straightening up, Neal spoke seriously.

"My love, I recognize the gravity of the situation, but let us be glad that everything turned out alright and move on. Lenore will recover. We both know that. We have yet to ask our old friend the reason for his visit."

"Old friend, my eye," Mina growled, glaring at what she envisioned as Neal's blind spot for Kieran.

She was furious with both of them now. Neal wasn't concerned enough for Lenore. True, her injuries were minor now that she had been subdued, but that wasn't the point. Neal, however, was in fact incredibly concerned and angry over what had just happened with Lenore, but he didn't need to say a word to Kieran about it for him to know. Neal would remind Mina of this later when they discussed it, which he knew they would. Mina had that I'm-thinking-about-killing-you look on at the moment. She eventually let it drop for the time being and allowed herself to seethe silently. After all, her history with the Vampyre went back almost as far as Neal's did.

"It is good to see you, old boy," Neal said, turning back to Kieran. "How have you been?"

Kieran shrugged and replied, "I have been traveling and not much else, though I have been searching while I travel."

"Have you found anything interesting?" Neal asked.

"Nothing spectacular, if that's what you mean. The outlying

villages and towns between here and the ocean have nothing to offer. I have heard whispers of remains in the deep, northern forests and Bladed Mountains, however, as well as in the south."

"That doesn't surprise me. The Bladed Mountains are where we found the Winged Zeppelin. Have you been well?"

"Well enough. It's easiest to feed in the most remote areas of the continent, but those places are rife with superstition as it is, and I do not like adding fuel to that fire."

"I understand," Neal said, rolling up a shirtsleeve. "Well, drink up. You're among friends now."

"You have my deepest thanks," Kieran said before biting into the crook of Neal's elbow and drinking the blood that spilled out."

Camilla came in a few minutes later, and Mina looked to her expectantly.

"She's doing fine," Camilla reported. "Her pulse and breathing are steady now. She'll wake up groggy, but I'll be there when she does."

"Thank you, dear," Mina said, "but you needn't do that. I will wait for her to waken. She'll have many questions, no doubt."

Camilla sat down in a chair and waited, averting her eyes from the feeding Vampyre as she did so. Kieran finally lifted his head, licked the wound clean, and smiled at Camilla, who looked at him as soon as he was done.

"Hello, Camilla," he said warmly. "How are you?"

"Very well, and you?"

"Much better now. Thank you again, Neal."

"Of course," Neal said, letting his arm rest on the arm of the chair.

"Are you a doctor yet?" Kieran asked Camilla.

"Oh no, I still have several years to go, plus school."

"Indeed. I'm sure you'll be there in no time considering your teacher." Kieran looked to Mina beseechingly.

"Flattery will—" Mina began.

"Get me back into your good graces?" Kieran cut in with a wry smile.

"Keep at it and we'll see," Mina said. She was still angry, but she'd already forgiven the Vampyre.

The four continued to chat and catch up like nothing was amiss all while Lenore dreamt in her bed. She dreamt of Old World machines and creatures of light and darkness and color and sound and wind. She dreamt of places that didn't exist or perhaps once did or still did but no one knew about. Her dreams were vivid and so realistic that, at the time, Lenore was sure she must actually be there. As she began to wake, however, the colors and sounds and memory of them all slipped away from her until she was only left with snatches and fragments.

*"AHHHHGGGGGGGGG!" he screamed.*

*The pain was unbearable. It was radiating out angrily from his lower back like a hot stone. He needed to get to Lenore, but he could barely drag himself out of his room for all the pain he was in.*

*"Ugh! If you want me to help her, maybe stop kicking me!" he groaned.*

*What the blazes was he supposed to do?! He couldn't sneak over to the Allen manor like this. In the end, he lay on the hard, cold, stone floor, sweating and swearing as waves of sickening pain steamrolled over him.*

When Lenore opened her eyes she saw that sunlight was

streaming in, but it took several moments for her brain to fully comprehend what that meant. The point she finally fixated on was that sunlight meant banishment to the nightmare from the night before. Speaking of which, where was he?!

"Lenore, dear, I'm here," came Mina's voice through the semi-haze.

Lenore turned her head and saw Mina there in a chair beside the bed.

"You're safe, my darling," Mina continued. "You don't need to be afraid."

"Was there... did something... attack me last night?" Lenore asked in confusion.

She could swear she remembered the whatever-it-was from the night before, but Mina was saying she was safe.

"Yes, you were, but it was a mistake. He didn't realize you were with us."

"He? You mean, you know that... thing?"

Bits and pieces of the previous evening were coming back to Lenore, and the more she remembered, the less she could believe it.

"His name is Kieran, and he is a very good friend. He is also a Vampyre. I shouldn't have to tell you that this information does not leave this house under any circumstances. Is that clear?"

"Wait, I'm sorry. You're friends with a... with a..."

"A Vampyre."

"How can that be? They're extinct."

"Clearly not."

"And he's a friend? Of yours? And Neal's?"

"Yes."

"How? How is that even possible?"

"Kieran was human once, when we were all at university together. Well, I was in medical school with Kieran and Neal was apprenticing. Neal and Kieran were childhood friends, and Kieran was courting me at the time. It's only because of him that I met Neal. Kieran and Neal went out one night, some boys' thing in the woods, and Kieran was attacked and turned. Neal was nearby and ran to help, but it was too late. After the Vampyre did what she had to do to turn Kieran, she fled.

"Kieran couldn't come back to school after that night. Neal instantly knew what had happened even though neither of them could believe it. Kieran left soon after, but returned one night several months later. He scared the life out of me, but after I calmed down and stopped throwing things at him, he told me that he was essentially still the same person. We've learned a great deal about Vampyres and a few other Old World subjects thanks to Kieran since then. It's not at all like what so many of the books describe."

"But you're still friends with him?" Lenore asked, unable to wrap her head around that concept.

"Yes. He is, for all intents and purposes, the same person he was when he and I were courting, save for the fact that he needs blood to sustain him now."

"He attacked me."

"I know, and I am so *very* sorry for that. As I said, it was a mistake. Kieran feels terrible about it. He wants to apologize to you this evening."

"He bit me. Does that mean I'm going to turn?" Lenore asked fearfully.

"No, darling, you won't. There's more to it than just getting bitten, thankfully."

"How do you know?"

"One, because Neal has studied these things and knows the actual process. Two, and more importantly, because we've allowed Kieran to feed on us for as long as he's been a Vampyre and none of us have turned."

"You… you let him feed off you?!"

"We feed all the guests that come into our home. Kieran's diet is just unique."

"Is that safe?"

"As long as he doesn't take too much too often, it is."

"I see," Lenore said finally, but she really didn't see.

She couldn't make her brain believe what she had just heard. It was like hearing a fantasy story. She understood all the words and knew what it meant, but it was all fiction in her mind.

"You need to rest," Mina told her. "I'm going to have Esther bring up some food for you, but you'll want to find Kieran this evening and sort things out with him. He'll be staying with us for quite a while and he's very upset about last night."

Lenore nodded but said nothing. Mina kissed the girl on the head before leaving, and Lenore's brain went to work. She thanked Esther automatically when her tea and brunch were brought up, but ate and drank without tasting anything.

Vampyres were real. There was one in the house with them. The Allens were friends with him. What else was real, still existed out there in the world that humans believed to be extinct? She was expected to speak to the Vampyre—Kieran was it?—in the house… like any other person. It was insane! More insane than harboring a criminal. The Allens were apparently experienced extreme risk takers. In light of that, Lenore was somewhat less shocked at their generosity towards her, but still shocked nonetheless.

The day passed, and Lenore spent it simply lying in bed or, when she got fidgety, pacing around her room. Bitsy was there with her, and Lenore looked to him often for signs of danger. She also spent a good bit of time in front of the window basking in the golden sunlight. It was like a guardian companion that would protect Lenore from harm should the Vampyre decide to reenter her room. Of course, the sun had to set eventually, and Lenore remembered that Mina had set a task before her. Mina's cool confidence about Kieran did wonders for Lenore's nerves about the situation. She got dressed in a simple dress that was suitable for around the house but nowhere else and started out of her room. Lenore wondered briefly if she should have dressed better to introduce herself to the Allens' new houseguest, but, seeing as how he had tried to kill her, she decided she got a pass on that. She couldn't find him after looking through the house. Granted, she wasn't trying that hard. She didn't bother asking after him and she especially wasn't going to try and find him down in the cellar or something, so she made herself comfortable with a book in the library and read. If he was really that upset, he'd find her.

And find her he did. When Kieran entered the library, he moved so quietly, like a cat stalking its prey, Lenore didn't even hear him. She was pretty engrossed in her book, too, which didn't help. She didn't notice him until he was sitting on the chair next to her couch. It was the slight noise the chair made when he sat down that alerted her to his presence, and Lenore jumped straight up and out of her seat when she heard it. When she laid eyes on Kieran, everything inside of her screamed for her to run, save for one part. It was her anger. Lenore was angry that he had attacked her unprovoked, and that kept her rooted where she stood. Lenore stood away from Kieran, the two of them staring at one another for a few moments. Then she spoke.

"So you're the real thing? You drink blood and everything?"

"That is correct," Kieran replied flatly.

"You don't trust me," Lenore stated, made curious by the glare he was giving her.

"Also correct."

Dana Fraedrich

"Why not? What could I possibly do to you?"

"You could go to the Enforcers and report me. One word from you and I'd be dead. Frankly, I'm surprised Mina and Neal aren't more worried."

Lenore laughed mirthlessly and said, "Believe me, the Enforcers are the last people I'd go to." She paused a moment as Kieran looked at her curiously now and shrugged her shoulders. They seemed to be on equal ground here, so she said, "You showed me yours… with your teeth… so I'll show you mine. I was a thief. I was almost caught—twice!—and the Allens saved me both times. I'm pretty sure I'd be in the Halls of Justice by now if it weren't for them. I have no reason, least of all you, to go anywhere near an Enforcer, despite the fact that you have actually come closer to killing me than an Enforcer ever has."

Kieran smiled, showing his fangs, and said, "What strange company the Allens keep. Criminals and monsters all. You'd think they'd be more unpleasant than they are."

Lenore smiled. He had a point.

Kieran spoke again. This time his tone was contrite, almost bashful. "I wanted to tell you that I am deeply, deeply sorry for what I did last night. I… I know what a Vampyre attack feels like. It is not something I ever want to inflict on another human being if I can help it, least of all an innocent such as yourself. Could you forgive me… one day… for this grievous error?"

Heavens, this was madness! A Vampyre in the library with her begging for her forgiveness for doing what Lenore had just assumed came naturally. She somehow wasn't surprised at how quickly her answer came or what her answer was.

"Mina and Neal clearly have as much faith in you as they do in me. I'll forgive you now if you promise me you'll never do it again."

"You have my binding word I shall never harm you again,"

117

Kieran said sincerely.

Lenore felt a slight tingly sensation wash over her when Kieran said that, and she was humbled by the power in his words, so tangible she could practically touch it. She couldn't be sure if humans were really bound by their promises to one another the way the Old World stories said they were, but she could tell without a doubt that when a creature of power like Kieran made an oath, it was binding in every way. That instantly created a trust in her like nothing else could have. She then sat down and showed Kieran her wrist.

"Are you hungry?" she asked. "I heard that the Allens were all… donating. I suppose I should too."

Kieran raised an eyebrow at her.

"After I attacked you? That's either very generous or very foolish."

"I have your word you won't do it again. What do I have to fear now?"

"Intelligent girl. Very well, who am I to turn down a free meal? Your elbow, please. People can't see the marks there."

"Will it hurt?"

"It will only hurt when I break the skin."

Lenore nodded and moved over as Kieran took a spot on the couch next to her. Very carefully, he took her arm in his hands.

"Relax," he said, stroking the veins in her arm with a finger.

He then raised her arm to his mouth and bit down. Lenore winced as his fangs sliced through skin and tissue and opened her veins wide. Then he moved so that his mouth was over the wound completely and drank.

Lenore felt a bit like she should feel stupid, but she didn't. Irrationality stated she should be afraid on principle, that she should be running and avoiding Kieran at all costs, and she felt that argument vying for her attention in the back of her mind. Somehow, however, rational reasoning had seized control of her brain and was keeping her cold and logical. The facts of the matter that had been thrust upon her throughout the day were swirling slowly around her head, cooling her fears and giving her clarity. Was this some side effect of the attack? Was it due to something from Kieran's bite, or was this Lenore's survival mode talking? She couldn't be certain, but she wasn't convinced it was such a bad thing.

*Everything looked fine from here, but that was no guarantee. He had eventually been able to drag himself up from the floor, but the painful, lingering throbbing in his back prevented him from any stealth work at the moment. As dawn began to approach, however, he eventually decided he had to tough it out and check on Lenore. He just needed to see that she was safe.*

*This was the closest he had ever been to his charge. It was also one of the worst places he could have picked. The house provided almost no cover, which would be fine if it were dark. As it was, the indigo sky was lightening with hues of pink and orange. The bit of roof on which he was currently perched, however, was also right outside Lenore's window. He had told himself he'd just take a quick peek to make sure she was okay and then leave, but he hadn't moved in over a minute. The calmness that came over him as he looked at her was like opium. She was sleeping, and nothing looked amiss. What had happened that night? He'd felt like he was on fire. He should go. He didn't. What if he stole into her room? No! He was being an idiot! Get out! It's not safe here! He pushed himself away from the window, forcing himself to tear his gaze from the sleeping Lenore. Get a hold of yourself, man! he told himself as he hurried away into the safety of the few remaining shadows.*

Things from there continued almost as comfortably as before, though stranger now than they had been. What baffled Lenore the most was probably Esther's reaction to the Vampyre. She had honestly worried that the sweet, old woman's heart would give out when she learned of their new houseguest. Not the case, not at all.

"Oh, Kieran, my dear boy! It's so good to see you!" Esther had gushed, embracing the gaunt creature as she would a five-year-old grandchild. Taking the Vampyre's face in her hands, she said affectionately, "Let me look at you. Tut tut, pale and thin as ever. Such a shame I can't fatten you up myself. You're sure you're well?"

"Very well, Esther," Kieran said with a warm, fanged smile.

"Just so you are. You can at least join us while the rest of us eat, yes?"

"Of course. I wouldn't miss it for the world."

"Esther's known Kieran since he was a child," Mina explained to Lenore. "This is Neal's family estate, so the boys spent countless days together here."

Kieran really was the perfect houseguest. He was given his own space down in the cellars and followed all rules of propriety, assuming one didn't count his dietary habits. Everyone but Esther contributed, which worked very well, seeing as how Kieran didn't need nearly as much blood as a human needed food to remain satisfied. Mina wouldn't allow Esther to participate due to her age, though the housekeeper always insisted she was tougher than she looked. Mina also made sure to keep tabs on everyone's health to make sure no one overdid it. Kieran, too, helped in this respect. He had finished just over half of his medical schooling when he was turned and used his knowledge and innate senses to ensure he didn't take too much from any one person.

For instance, Mina had had an especially trying time one day in the clinic. A young man who had been trampled by a horse had been rushed in. Mina had done everything in her power to save him, but the extent of his injuries had been too severe. He hadn't made it through the evening. Mina had come in late that night with Camilla and, knowing it was her turn to donate, offered her arm.

"No, my friend," Kieran had said softly. "You are in no state to sacrifice tonight. I will be fine for several days more. Rest and restore yourself."

Mina didn't argue. She had simply nodded and sat with Kieran and the rest of the family while she cried.

It was a lucky thing Kieran had come during the cold weather, as his feedings created the need for everyone to wear sleeves long enough to hide the bite marks. The wounds inflicted by his teeth during these times seemed to heal more quickly and didn't pain the victim the way that normal wounds would, however, so there wasn't much of an issue with that. On the other hand, Lenore did have to wear scarves and wide ribbon necklaces around her neck, which was sore and stiff, for several weeks after the attack. Those injuries took longer to heal than anything Lenore had ever experienced, and Kieran explained a Vampyre bite wound takes on the qualities of the intention behind the bite.

"When blood is given and taken consensually, the wounds heal quickly and peacefully. When it's forcibly taken in an attack, the viciousness of the attack is left behind in the wounds like venom. I'm afraid there's nothing I can do to fix that now. I am so sorry."

Lenore saw the regret in Kieran's eyes when he said this,

and she gave his hand a squeeze.

"I understand," she said. "I can stand it until it heals."

"Perhaps there is at least one thing I can do," Kieran said.

With that, he placed his hand, which was far warmer than any human hand, against the wound and just held it there. The heat from his hand soothed the soreness a bit, and Lenore relaxed against him, glad for the relief.

# 10
# SCHOLAR LAZYBONES

Lenore's responsibilities increased at work as she learned more. She was still mainly responsible for keeping Neal's appointments, paperwork, and general work life organized, but, as she attended meetings with him, she began to get to know the other employees at the museum. With time, Neal sent Lenore on more and more errands to their offices to make deliveries and acquire their signatures. Now that Lenore had her stamp, she could sign off on documentation whenever she needed to as well.

Lenore offered ideas and theories to Neal about the artifacts in the museum's possession, but it was quite a while before she started sharing her thoughts with other members of staff. It was one thing to speculate with the man she had learned to trust with her life, but strangers were entirely different.

When trying to explain these feelings to Mina one day, the doctor had succinctly described it as, "You don't want anyone to call your baby ugly."

From that point on, Lenore had called it Ugly Baby Syndrome, which Neal and Copper gleefully adopted as soon as they heard it. When she had downtime, she would examine the

Subaquatic Sloop or the Winged Zeppelin, which had been taken down as Lenore had requested, or artifact fragments and make careful notes of her thoughts on her clipboard. Neal would often find her musings when he looked over her work throughout the week. When Neal first started inquiring with Lenore about these observations, she was shy and reserved. She believed most of her ideas were silly. After all, many of them didn't have any solid basis behind them. They were just what-if ideas that had come to her during her examinations. Neal, kind as ever, assured her that that was how countless theories by even the most renowned experts began.

"What if the Old World had worked with magical creatures at one point? What if all Old World machines were powered by magic? What if the power source was something we can use now and just don't know about? 'What if' is the most powerful question we can ask. What's important is to go through the proper processes if you're going to try and prove your what-ifs."

Not long after that, Neal began to throw Lenore into the fire, so to speak, at which point she began to have intense bouts of Ugly Baby Syndrome.

During a research meeting with Scholar Lily Grace about the Winged Zeppelin, Neal said, "What was it you were thinking about the Winged Zeppelin's flying ability, Lenore?"

Lenore blanched and shot Neal a terrified glance. Scholar Grace looked at the girl expectantly, her own apprentice there with her ready to write down whatever Lenore said. Lenore swallowed hard and did her best to sound official.

"I, ah, I was thinking to myself recently that there's more to it than meets the eye. The balloon obviously means that it could travel like our zeppelins, but the wings... do they not resemble that of a bird? I don't think they could have flapped... I mean, I checked and there aren't any hinges or anything, but there are pieces on the backs of the wings. They're broken up pretty badly, but I think they were for steering… somehow. Erm, but what if the balloon could be collapsed and tucked away? What if the craft had a way to fly like a bird without the lift of the balloon? There are cleats on the top that indicate that something could be tied down, and I, um… I think that's just what they did."

"Interesting," said Scholar Grace. "I like your thinking, but I just don't see how a machine of that size and weight could get and remain airborne without the aid of a gas balloon."

Lenore swallowed hard and looked down. There it was, her idea had been shot down even as it was meeting the rest of the world for the first time. Scholar Grace might as well have said it was an idiotic theory and questioned Neal's choice in hiring Lenore. Lenore felt her face grow hot and wished to disappear.

"Do you?" Neal asked, interceding for Lenore. "Didn't you just write a paper on some of the possible abilities of Old World magi? Wasn't one of those theories to do with wind control based on accounts of the Battle of Bone Port?"

"I don't think that's it," Lenore said defensively.

She didn't like the idea of her theory being appropriated by magus abilities. That seemed too easy. Too many theories, in her opinion, were chalked up to magical phenomenon. Lenore had researched enough Old World technology to know they'd had an excellent grasp of the natural sciences, better than what was understood now. She was annoyed with Neal over his interjection because he knew she felt this way. Why was he even suggesting the idea?!

"There are obviously some pieces of the puzzle missing," she continued, trying to tone down her huffiness, "but I think it has something to do with heat or speed or something. I'm not sure, but if that machine could fly itself, it could travel much faster than any zeppelin. I don't think magic was involved."

The conversation continued, and Lenore explained her reasoning, citing her observations from examinations of the Winged Zeppelin. After she was done, Neal gave Lenore permission to pursue her flight research with Copper's supervision. Only later, when Lenore questioned Neal about his suggestion, did she learn what he had been really up to.

"You don't like the magical intervention crutch any more than I do," she said. "You don't honestly think magi whistled the wind down to fly it?"

"Of course not!" Neal scoffed.

"Then why even bring it up?"

"Because you're so tetchy about it," he replied, giving her a sly smile.

Lenore made a face at Neal because she now realized what he had done and didn't much like it.

"I don't like being manipulated," she said.

"And I don't like good scientists surrendering to criticism."

Lenore was still annoyed, but it didn't last long. Excitement over her new project was already welling up inside her. She soon began to share her thoughts about it with anyone in the house that would listen.

From then on, Lenore began watching and reading about birds more than she ever thought she would. Modern scholars didn't really understand how birds were able to fly except that their hollow bones made them lighter than other creatures and that they flapped their wings. Sadly, more than one unfortunate soul had been injured or killed by trying out a pair of homemade wings. Lenore had no intention of attempting any such thing, but she did work with Copper to develop a model of a bird. The idea was that, if she could make the model fly, she believed she could gain understanding of how birds flew and then how the Winged Zeppelin might have flown without its balloon. Copper reminded her to the point of madness to make sure she documented everything properly, but Lenore knew how important it was, so she did as she was told. She let Copper know how irritating his constant reminders were with a tongue in cheek comment once in a while, which Copper responded to warmly. Lenore was glad for that because she deeply respected the engineer, but she knew she'd end up snapping and saying something she would regret if she didn't get him to back off once in a while. Thankfully, by this point in time, the two had built up a good, strong rapport, so any tension was soon swept away by a candid, mostly professional— Copper was a little unorthodox in his verbiage at times— conversation.

Lenore also began working closely with the Environmental Kinetics department, though everyone called it EnKin for short. The EnKin geniuses, as Lenore called them, because surely you had to be a genius to understand this stuff, studied the natural forces of the world. Lenore liked them immediately, mostly because many of them agreed with her theories. She had studied basic Environmental Kinetics in school, but that didn't come anywhere close to what the EnKin geniuses knew. Much of her preliminary work with them was simply learning how the world worked, which was difficult to say the least. Lenore had trouble wrapping her head around concepts she couldn't see in action, but she developed demonstrations to use as examples of what she was learning. The more patient EnKin geniuses helped her with these, but it was an uphill battle.

Back in the Arc-Tech department, Lenore's relationship with Dempsey was nothing like what she had with Neal and Copper. From day one, the scholar, as Lenore preferred to think of him just for spite, treated her like a housekeeper more than anything.

The sentence he said to her more than any other was, "Get me a cup of tea, would you, love?"

"I'm sorry, but I'm really busy with this project," or some variation thereof was her most common response. What she really wanted to respond with was more along the lines of, "Get it yourself, Scholar Lazybones!"

Of course she never said that. She may have the respect of most of the rest of her colleagues, limited though that may be, but she knew all too well where she sat on the totem pole. Thankfully, Copper came to her defense more than once.

"What's wrong with your legs?" he had asked once. "Are they broken?"

"No, I just thought since, ah… sorry to have interrupted you," Dempsey had responded uncertainly.

There it was. Dempsey felt that, since Lenore was a female, she would what? Jump for joy at the chance to serve him tea? Dance because her dream of being noticed by a handsome, eligible young man had come true? It was laughable enough that Lenore wasn't even angry about it after that. She did have to restrain her chuckle, however. Even after this, Dempsey still seemed to feel the need to impart his "considerable" knowledge to Lenore. Often, while she was working, the man would sidle up to her and start sharing unsolicited anecdotes from his life. These sessions usually spread to the rest of the department, as Dempsey would eventually address anyone within earshot. Lenore quickly realized Dempsey saw her as an avenue to boast about his perceived accomplishments. Even if she didn't fall at his feet, begging for more stories of his exploits, he could at least share his tales with his fellow men, who would no doubt be so very impressed. Lenore had to smother her grins and laughter when he started to spin these yarns, which she was sure were heavily embellished. One such instance, however, tipped the scales of Lenore's opinion of Dempsey from a mildly irritating prat to a loathsome cur that she wished would die.

"University is the best experience one can ever have,"

Dempsey said almost wistfully. "It's the time when you really become who you will be…"

"Wouldn't know," Copper gibed. "I was busy working my apprenticeship."

"Had you become you by that point?" Lenore asked, joining in. She used Copper as a gauge most of the time, never pushing as far as he did.

Dempsey either didn't hear them or pretended not to.

"I think one of my most difficult times of testing was when we visited a government design shop. They designed defenses and support weapons for the Enforcers, really top-notch stuff. It was headed up by this gent Bentley or Crowley or something-ly. He was brilliant! And a nice enough chap, too. I applied for a position under him, you know. During my interview, however, I discovered he had been selling information about the very same technology they were developing. I had to turn him in. He was arrested, but it was the *right* thing to do, and it makes me proud to think on now."

Lenore forced herself to stay still and silent. Words were churning inside her, questions and accusations were marching up her throat, and she clenched her teeth to keep them inside. What if that had been her father? It certainly sounded like it might have been.

"How'd you do that?" Copper asked incredulously. "I can't believe someone'd be so daft as to just share that information."

Lenore silently thanked the heavens for Copper. He'd asked one of the dozens of questions swirling around in her brain. She risked a glance at Dempsey and saw him beaming. Blazes, that clod thought Copper was impressed! What an imbecile! Then again, that was probably a good thing.

"It was as thrilling an adventure as you'd find in any mystery novel," Dempsey replied dramatically, really getting into the story now. "During my interview, the gent's assistant delivered a message. I snuck a peek. It just said, 'Cobalt Docks, 9 P.M.'. Well, that sounded shady to me, so I informed an Enforcer friend of mine, and they took a team to the docks that night. My friend told me all about it later. They didn't find Bentley there, but he was fairly certain he had only just evaded capture, along with a few other lowlifes. I wanted to stay in the loop, so I started courting his assistant, Marie, who told me about his arrest a few weeks later. She was devastated and rightfully interrogated, but eventually found to be an innocent victim in his machinations. She's doing well now from what I hear… didn't last between us…"

Dempsey's voice continued to prattle on, but Lenore couldn't focus on his words. Marie had been her father's assistant. It was him Dempsey had met. She had to leave, to escape. If she didn't, she'd surely tear Dempsey apart with her own two hands. That arrogant, pompous peacock was responsible for her parents' arrest. Her vision had gone white… or was it red… or black? She couldn't tell, she couldn't see, she couldn't think.

"Lenore, goodness, I've just remembered!" came Neal's voice through the blinding rage.

Neal had been back in the shelves. Somewhere in the back of Lenore's mind, she realized he very well could have been listening the whole time. She hoped he had been. Lenore could only dumbly look at him, though, not trusting herself to make any other move.

"Mina wanted Esther to begin preparing the menu for Camilla's party today," Neal continued. "Oh dear, she'll have my head if everything isn't perfect. Hurry home right now and help Esther. Right. *Now.* You go straight home. You hear me?"

The severity of Neal's command was coming through to Lenore's brain, but her anger screamed back. The small spot of bitterness in Lenore's heart was blazing brightly now, freezing and burning Lenore all at once, pushing her to do and say unspeakable things.

"Lenore, *now*, please," Neal said more sternly.

Lenore forced herself to nod, to put one foot in front of the other, away from the treacherous Dempsey. On she plodded, picking up feet that felt like lead. It felt like an eternity before she exited the museum. She hailed a cab, certain she'd never make the journey on foot. She didn't even thank the driver. She just paid him and nodded after stepping out in front of the Allen manor. Once inside, she felt her rage welling up, ready to surge forward. She ran upstairs to release her fury. Lenore slammed her door shut, buried her face in a pillow and screamed. She roared and screeched and shrieked and sobbed into the downy softness, but her rage refused to subside.

"How can you expect me to work with him?!" Lenore demanded. "That self-serving prat ruined our lives!"

Neal had come home as early as he could, which had actually been rather late that evening, and immediately found Lenore. He had heard everything since the word 'Crowley' in Dempsey's story.

Camilla and Esther were the only other people home at the moment. Earlier, Camilla had found Lenore verbally abusing her pillows and had asked what was wrong. After Lenore told her, Camilla's eyes had grown wide with disbelief and empathetic anger.

"That rat! I always knew he was an arrogant cretin, but I had no idea he was a snitch! Oh, Lenore, I'm so sorry. What are you going to do?"

"I don't know, Camilla. I just don't. I don't even know how I'll be able to look at him without ripping his heart out."

Camilla understood, but she couldn't do anything to help. Lenore knew she felt the exact same way whenever she saw her father.

"How do you speak to Fourth Hawkins civilly?" Lenore had asked, knowing Camilla's distaste for anyone to refer to the man as her father.

"It's… so difficult… so very, very difficult. I know what my mother endures now because of him. I can only believe he'll receive judgment one day, hopefully in the form of one individualized punishment for every day of torture my mother endures."

It was the darkest thing Lenore had ever heard Camilla say and yet it comforted her. Just knowing there was someone that felt the same way she did helped. Now, in front of Neal though, she wanted more.

"Lenore, what would you have me do?" Neal asked softly. "I can't punish him for abiding by the law."

"I don't know," Lenore cried, looking away.

She wanted so badly to pummel Dempsey's face, to light his house on fire, something. She couldn't do any of that, though. She was impotent to enact her revenge. For the safety of her new family, she couldn't move against him.

"Please, you know that we have to act as if everything is fine in order to carry on," Neal said reasonably, echoing Lenore's thoughts.

"Maybe if you all cut ties with me I'd be able to take care of it myself."

"Don't be ridiculous!" Neal said far more sternly than Lenore had ever expected to hear from him. "You're a member of this family. We could no more ask Camilla or Mina to leave than we could you."

That quenched Lenore's anger down to a manageable fire, but it still burned within her.

"We will get through this," Neal said more gently this time. "Just as we get through everything… together. I understand if you need to take the next few days off. I can say you're focusing on your research."

"I think I'd like that," Lenore said softly. "Perhaps I'll do some bird watching from somewhere besides the windows."

"Mina, what can I do?" Neal said, his face twisting in anguish as he discussed the matter with her that night. "He as good as signed their death warrant himself."

"Oh, Neal," Mina cooed softly, embracing her husband. "I don't know. I wish I did."

"Poor Lenore," Neal whispered as a few tears eked out of his eyes. "Sweet Lenore. She has to look at the face of the man who killed her parents every day, and I have asked her to. Blazes! Some father figure I'm turning out to be."

"Darling, you're doing what you can to keep us all safe!"

"I know, but she's talking about leaving. I believe, given the chance, she would do serious harm to Dempsey, and I can't say I blame her. Do you think she'll want to resign? She truly enjoys her work, I can tell. What if this kills her passion?"

Mina stroked Neal's arm comfortingly and asked, "Can you relieve him of his post?"

"Not without proper grounds. He has to commit some kind of violation, which then has to be judged by myself and Abraham."

"And there's no way to plant anything on him?"

"I will not inflict the same mistreatment on Dempsey, villain though he is. I don't know of anything innocent enough to get him dismissed but not arrested." Neal paused and then asked, "Are we horrible people for talking about this as a real possibility?"

"I wouldn't hire him knowing this," Mina replied logically. "And I wouldn't want to continue to work with someone with so few scruples."

There was a long silence wherein both of them were thinking hard about what could be done to help Lenore.

"I could assist," came a voice from the shadows of the room.

"Absolutely not, Kieran," Neal said, cutting his eyes towards the Vampyre. "I don't want Dempsey hurt. I just want to spare Lenore the indignity of having to put up with him. Besides, this isn't your fight."

"I care for Lenore as well. What this young man has done is a horrible injustice. In addition, I can tell how deeply you hurt for the girl, my friend."

Mina smiled at Neal and Kieran.

"No, but thank you for being willing," she said softly.

# 11
# "LOVE" NOTES

Lenore really had done all of her bird watching from the windows of the manor. Most of her free time was in the evenings, which made the activity especially difficult, and her days off were usually spent doing errands or other things with Mina and Camilla. She got the most study time in the mornings before work, which wasn't much time at all. Therefore, she bundled up the next day and headed out to the gardens with a large bag of breadcrumbs and a notebook.

It was odd being out here as a visitor in the daytime after she had spent so much time there by night. She had left Bitsy at home, of course; he would always be too recognizable. He had become quite attached to Esther anyway, which suited Lenore just fine. The housekeeper doted on him like she would a child, and Lenore was glad to see them both so happy. Opportunistic Bitsy still snuggled up to Lenore for warmth at night, though, which was nice too. As an additional precaution, she had taken care to apply some extra cosmetics to make her even more unrecognizable from her former self. It was only after that did she feel safe returning to the scene of her crimes.

She had a lovely time in the gardens studying the birds that afternoon. She sketched their delicate forms in her notebook and noted the shape of their wings, the way the front end was thicker than the back end, the curve of the feathers they left behind, and how rapidly they flapped their wings to take off. She meticulously noted the date and times of all of her notes, looking to her fob watch often. She took some time to watch the ducks in the pond as well and noticed the way they had to get going off the surface of the water before taking off. It was all fascinating, and Lenore's mind worked almost too fast for her hands to move.

She was so engrossed with her work that she didn't realize how late it was getting until twilight had settled over the gardens and everything around her was bathed in the dusky shroud of purple and blue and grey. It was later than she had intended to leave by, so Lenore took a few shortcuts she knew of from her old life to save some time. She was surprised when she found that one of the little alleyways she used to use was now blocked off by a wooden fence. Maybe one of the business owners decided he didn't like people taking shortcuts there, or perhaps the Enforcers had put it up since Lenore had used this way to escape them that night. Either way, it wouldn't be difficult to backtrack. Lenore turned only to see her path blocked by someone she hadn't heard approach, a young man that was eyeing her all too intently.

He was tall and lanky, the perfect build for a thief. His hair was longish and very dark and hung messily around his face. His slender fingers were probably perfect for picking pockets, but his dress said he made a far more lucrative career than that. He had dark outlines painted around his eyes, a trick Lenore had seen before, both to aid concealment and intimidate. His posture was relaxed, but Lenore recognized the forced casualness for what it was. It was a ruse and, like a snake, he'd be able to strike fast and accurately any time he wanted to.

Lenore stared off against the man, ready to fight. Nevermind that she didn't actually know how to fight, not really. Men had sensitive parts, though, and she fully intended on attacking those viciously if it came to it.

"You are a prickly one, aren't you?" the man said.

"What do you want?" Lenore snapped, covering her fear thickly with anger and venom.

"And direct as well. I like that. I've been trying to catch up with you for a while."

"I repeat, what do you want? You're wasting my time and blocking my way."

"Too true, too true. You can call me Rook, and I represent certain interested parties."

"Interested in what?"

"In you, darling. Your father was a good friend of ours."

"I don't know what you're talking about. My father is alive and—"

"Save it," Rook said, cutting her off.

He approached slowly, dangerously, and lowered his voice. Lenore didn't retreat. She knew she couldn't show fear to this man, whoever he was, but she stood ready to defend herself.

"We know your father was Edgar Crowley. He, along with your mother, was arrested over a year ago. And you…" Rook chuckled, "you have done very well for yourself. I don't know how you did it, but you really landed well."

"Very well, if you *think* you know who I am—and you *don't*—why is this the first time we've met?"

"Because we didn't know where you were until recently. Edgar spoke little of you, and you disappeared so completely after the arrest. We only recently put the pieces together. Then there was the issue of catching you alone."

"This is ridiculous," Lenore said, shaking her head and

marching past Rook. "I hope you know you sound mad. Best of luck finding whoever it is that you're looking for, though."

She felt confident and strong and was sure she was getting away with it when Rook grabbed her and spun her towards the wall of the building. He pushed her shoulders back against the stone and hissed in her ear.

"Be careful, little bird. I am taking a lot of care to make sure you stay safe. Don't make me have to protect you from yourself."

Lenore was staring hard at Rook, who wasn't an inch from her face. She was calculating as he stared her back at her. She closed her eyes and sighed, feigning surrender. Rook's grip on her shoulders loosened, and she drove her knee straight up, crushing all manner of soft tissue as hard as she could. Rook grunted and crumpled while Lenore ran. He tried to grab her ankle, but she tore away from him and headed back towards the main road. Lenore was shocked to find she was considering finding an Enforcer. The man was dangerous, without a doubt, but he knew dangerous things. Lenore slowed once she reached the well-lit thoroughfare. Would it do any good? If Rook was as street savvy as he appeared, he'd be long gone by now. She wasn't concerned about him getting her here; he'd know better. No, she didn't want to draw the attention of the Enforcers, even for this. Neal and Mina would know what to do. Lenore hailed a hansom cab and got herself home as fast as possible.

The house was quiet when Lenore returned. She smelled food and deduced that the Allens must be having dinner. She needed to change—the scuffle with Rook showed on her clothes—and so crept up the stairs and into her room as quietly as possible, closing the door behind her. Lenore headed straight to the washroom and splashed her face with water to try and calm herself. She jumped straight up when a growl resounded from the doorway.

"Kieran! What are you doing?" she demanded, seeing the Vampyre standing there. He looked for all the world like a predator on the hunt in that moment.

"What happened?" he asked, the growl still rolling in his chest.

Lenore realized Kieran must have smelled the fear on her—she was sure she reeked of it—and thrown all propriety to the wind in order to check on her. Kieran came closer and drew a deep breath over her.

"Who attacked you? I can *smell* him!"

"He called himself Rook," Lenore sighed. "I don't know who he was, but he knew who I was. I mean, he knew who I *really* was."

"You're telling Mina and Neal. Now."

"Idiot!" Rook cursed himself, as he nursed his wounds in a dark corner of the city.

He had run from the alley as soon as he saw Lenore heading for the main road. She was beyond his reach by that time. He had been hasty and acted rashly. Gaining Lenore's trust seemed impossible at this point, and all that time watching and waiting seemed wasted. Maybe he really would have to kidnap her. How was he to do that, though? She would surely be on her guard now.

Mina and Neal paced in the sitting room thinking to themselves, while Camilla sat by Lenore holding her hand. Kieran was leaning against the wall with his arms crossed and looking dangerous.

The sitting room was positioned deeper into the house, a

comfortable distance from the receiving hall and front windows. It was a smaller room, cozier than the parlor, and felt safer when dangerous conversations were being had.

"He said he was trying to keep you safe?" Neal asked.

"Yes," Lenore said, "and that he didn't want to have to protect me from myself."

"What does that mean?" Mina asked. "Neal, he might have kidnapped her! You haven't been doing anything without telling us, have you?"

"No! You all know everything I do. If I'm not at work with Neal, I'm here or out with you. Today was the first day I went out by myself. I made myself easy to get to by taking the alley."

"She's right," Mina said. "I'm sorry, dear, but that's going to be your last excursion out by yourself."

"Won't she be safe by day?" Camilla asked. "Out of alleys, I mean."

"We can't know," Mina replied. "We can't take a chance."

"I understand," Lenore said soberly.

The experience had shaken her up for so many reasons. Mostly because it had brought up terrifying questions, like with whom her father had dealt before he was arrested and whether he had earned his punishment after all. Lenore had never really believed that her father and mother were really guilty of what they had been accused of. She had always suspected it was a case of he-said-she-said. Someone probably saw someone that looked like her father doing something he shouldn't be doing and it had been pinned on him. She hadn't even really believed that her father was guilty when Dempsey had told her that he'd been the one to report them. She didn't give anything he said any credence anyway. Now, however, she'd gotten proof positive that her father had mixed with the wrong crowd. She just didn't know how to feel about it now.

Lenore gladly abided by the new rule, though nothing

really changed from her old routine, so it was an easy thing to do. The Allens and Kieran were all very supportive and sensitive to her predicament and checked in with her often. Lenore was warmed by how much they cared for her, but still felt guilty that they were entangled in all of this with her. It seemed that Rook didn't give up that easily, however. Letters addressed to Lenore started arriving with the daily mail. Kieran had instantly ripped the first one open because he recognized Rook's scent from the night he had cornered Lenore.

"He's sent you a message," Kieran said, bringing the opened letter to Lenore in the library.

"You opened my mail?" was Lenore's first reaction.

"I could smell him," Kieran said. "There's no telling what kind of tricks he'll play. I want to protect you."

That answer surprised Lenore enough to soften her.

"Thank you, Kieran," she said, taking the note. "What does it say?"

"I hope you can forgive me for my behavior the other night," Kieran recited as Lenore read the note. "It's very important that I make things right between us. Please, come back to our meeting place. I'll always be there for you."

"Blazes, it sounds like a letter from a scorned paramour," Lenore scoffed.

"Better that than something incriminating."

"Hm, good point. I'll talk to Mina and Neal about this tonight at dinner."

Mina and Neal were intrigued by the letter, but not worried, as Lenore strongly rejected the idea of fulfilling the request. More letters came in the days that passed. They all sounded as if they were from a repentant lover and, like a repentant lover, slowly became more desperate.

One actually read,

*Every day I spend without you increases my burden. You must come back to me.*

Despite the gravity of the situation, the letters became a private joke for the family. They laughed heartily at the plight of the fictional, love struck pup out there pining for Lenore. All save for Kieran. He was apparently taking his duty to protect Lenore very seriously, which caused a seed of worry to remain with everyone despite their amusement. Thankfully there was something else that everyone could fix their attention on as a distraction: Camilla's debut.

"Fifth Sawyer, read me my agenda," Fourth Hawkins snapped as he paced the room.

Fifth Sawyer opened the book sitting before him and began to read.

"You have a meeting with Third West and Fourths Pendragon, Waters, and James at 9 A.M.. After that, you have an interrogation session with Edgar and Twila Crowley."

"Why?" Fourth Hawkins demanded.

"Potential sources of information for my assault case," Fifth Sawyer replied.

"Ah, yes. Do we really think there's any connection between them and the little chit that night? It seemed a bit of a stretch."

"No, we don't suspect a connection. They may be able to reveal something of their underworld accomplices, though, which may yet yield something helpful. Fifths Lloyd and Darling are also hoping for any information about their missing daughter since Edgar was a civic weapons engineer."

"Very well. Bring the focused torch. Perhaps seeing a tool

of his trade will move Mister Crowley to speak. What's next?"

There was suddenly the echo of a scream from somewhere nearby within the Halls of Justice. Fifth Sawyer waited until the sound died down again, knowing how difficult it was to compete with that sort of noise.

"At 3 P.M. you have a visit with Adelle Hawkins scheduled."

"Ah, yes. My lovely Adelle. Have you ordered tea?"

"Yes, sir."

"Good. She'll be pleased to hear about our visit with Camilla."

"Yes, sir. That's everything on your agenda today. Will you require anything else for any of your appointments?"

Fourth Hawkins grumbled and said, "I find Third West tiresome. Is it an important meeting?"

"It's your monthly team building gathering."

"Blazes, I hate those. Did we have any arrests last night that will get me out of it?"

"No, sir," Fifth Sawyer said, suppressing a smile.

"Shame. Well, we might as well start making our way there."

Another shriek resounded, and Fifth Sawyer began to follow his commanding officer out, grabbing the agenda book, a key ring, and checking his inner pocket for a small, folded piece of paper as he did so.

# 12
# THE DEBUT

amilla's debut was coming up fast and required a great deal of planning, coordination, and resources. Your average mother of a young lady would simply handle everything herself, but most mothers didn't own their own medical practice. Therefore, Mina recruited the help of Esther, who handled everything with grace and diligence. When Lenore asked Mina why she didn't simply hire an event planner, Mina waved the suggestion away like a tiresome fly.

"An event planner doesn't know Camilla, nor would she have the time to dedicate to the planning in a way that would suit me. In my experience, most planners design events based on their own agenda. You know Esther will do a splendid job."

"Too true," Lenore agreed, thinking on all that she had seen Esther do already.

The housekeeper had already gotten the invitations sent out and a menu planned. She had recruited help from members of her own family and friends. At first, Lenore thought this sounded like a recipe for disaster, but changed her mind when she saw Esther deal with the petulant courier who couldn't get some of the invitations delivered.

"I'm sorry, my dear, but that's your job, is it not? To deliver things?" Esther chided him.

"Yes, ma'am, but—"

"But nothing, young man. If you have a problem, think of way to solve it. If you cannot, ask your supervisor for help. Or at the very least, your mother. I've paid you well and I expect thorough completion of the task. Now, will you be asking your mother for help or do I need to do so? It's but a short cab ride away."

"No, ma'am. I can handle it."

"There's a good lad. Don't doubt that I'll find out if any of these failed to make it to their intended recipients as well. You hear me?"

"Yes, ma'am."

"Thank you kindly. Now, off you go. Be safe, Jeremy. Oh, and take a scone to keep up your strength. Give one to your sister as well."

Lenore ended up with an especially demanding job: acting as a sounding board for Camilla. As the big night drew near, Camilla was filled with ideas, fantasies, fears, and doubts about what the event would bring.

"Do you think everyone will come? What if anyone declines? What does that mean?"

"Do you think I'll know as soon as I meet him? I've met many of the gents at various official functions before, but not all of them."

"Which earrings do you like better? I was thinking the hoops for simplicity, you know, but the updo I've chosen accentuates my neck, and I don't want to look like a goose."

"What's a good way to decline a suitor? I already know of a few I'm not really interested in, but I don't want to offend anyone."

"Have I gained weight? Oh blazes, what if I can't fit into

my dress?!"

Lenore asked the heavens why she of all people had gotten stuck with such a task. She already knew the answer, though. Camilla may be close with Mina, but the fact was Lenore was the closest girl her own age. True, Camilla had her friends, but they weren't often alone to discuss these things without mother figures interjecting their own opinions. It was easy enough to understand, so Lenore was there for Camilla despite how maddening it was. Lenore was sure to make a mental note to get Camilla to repay the favor, though.

The ballroom glittered like a diamond that night, the light of hundreds of petrolsene lamps reflecting off crystal glasses, gemstones in ladies' jewelry, silver flatware, and gilded porcelain dishes. Servers circled the room with shining trays full of delicious finger foods and glasses of wine. A large area in the center of the room was reserved for dancing, and that was where Camilla had spent almost the entirety of the evening. Any fears she'd had about eligible young men not being interested were completely unfounded, as nearly every invitation had been answered with a yes. Camilla was so pleased that the presence of her father and Fifth Sawyer in their dress uniforms barely dimmed her excitement. She was actually more bothered by the advances of some of the suitors that she wasn't interested in.

"What do I say?" Camilla hissed to Lenore and Mina from behind her hand. She was refreshing herself with a glass of wine that matched the color of her dress.

"Say thank you and move on," Mina said. "No one expects you to make any choices tonight."

"It'll give you time to make a list of rejections," Lenore

Dana Fraedrich

teased, knowing how much the girl hated to hurt other people's feelings.

"Laugh now," Beatrice said from beside Lenore, her voice low and dramatic. "Your time is coming."

Lenore made an unhappy sound in her throat. She did not enjoy the thought of playing at marriage.

"She's right," Mina said. "Not too long from now, you too will be swarmed by eligible bachelors, all wishing to have your hand."

Lenore rolled her eyes at that, but her annoyance didn't last. This was just a big party for her. She was off the market, so to speak, for now, so she was free to chat, dance, and flaunt her false identity, which she had a grand time doing. The families of the young men that had been invited were there of course, and Lenore had always gotten along with the opposite sex fairly well. Perhaps that was because she had never really been a dainty flower like Camilla. Lenore remembered all of her manners, of course, but couldn't help but indulge in a little shameless flirting with the young men there that were too young for Camilla but old enough for Lenore. While that wasn't a huge gap, over a hundred families had been invited, so there were enough there to make it very entertaining.

Lenore was having such a good time she didn't even object when someone took her hand and swept her out to the dance floor. It wasn't the first time it had happened that night, after all. She turned to whoever had stolen her for the dance and felt her blood run cold. It was Rook! He was dressed as well as any of the other young men there with his hair slicked cleanly back, but it was him without a doubt. Before she could do anything, he spoke sternly through his smile.

"Act normally. There's more than one Enforcer here."

Lenore held her smile in place as she went through the steps with Rook.

147

"I know. It's Fourth Hawkins, the debutante's father. One of his Fifths is here as well. Why are *you* here?"

"I haven't any other choice. You won't answer my letters."

"You really expect me to come and meet you... alone? You must think I'm a complete fool."

"Look, little bird, I'm trying to help you, so why don't you stop dodging me and listen?"

Lenore wouldn't wish an Enforcer's justice on her worst enemy, so she said, "I suppose I haven't any other choice... until the dance is over, that is."

It was a challenge, and she was surprised to see the corner of Rook's mouth twitch upwards in a genuine smile.

"The Enforcers are looking for you. Not you now, but you from before. They suspect the girl from the gardens is the same one that helped that little pup making eyes at your friend over there."

"You mean Fifth Sawyer?"

"Of course. They're furious she got away, though I'm not really surprised. She's a bit of a firecracker."

Lenore felt the heat of a blush in her cheeks, and Rook smiled again. This time the real smile stayed.

"The description is muddled, but it's close enough to make them pursue the lead. It's doubtful that they can really connect the old you to the Allens, but, if they do, you'll all go down."

Lenore's heart began to pound in her chest. No! It couldn't be true, but if Rook knew about her...

"Keep smiling, little bird," Rook said, bringing his head close to hers and resting his nose against her forehead.

She quickly smirked and said, "Why are you telling me this? Why not just leave us to whatever our fate may be?"

"Because I owe your father a debt, and I'd rather risk the Enforcers than an unpaid debt."

She couldn't blame him for that. It was how she had come

to be with the Allens in the first place.

"What do I do?" Lenore asked softly.

The dance was coming to an end, and she was panicking.

"Meet me tomorrow at midnight behind the pasty shop. We can talk there. *Don't* tell anyone you're coming." He came close again and whispered in her ear, "Promise me."

Lenore didn't have a chance to promise, however. The dance ended. Rook bowed and kissed her hand. She curtseyed appropriately and watched him disappear into the crowd. She would go meet him, but would she keep it to herself?

The evening didn't last much longer after that, for which Lenore was thankful. She didn't know how much longer she could keep up the act. She guessed that Rook had come in when he did because the wine had been flowing for a while. The Allens and Camilla had to stay until after the last guest left, but Lenore was able to slip out before that. The carriage was waiting for her, and she gladly climbed in. When she did, however, she found a note there on the seat. Somehow knowing who had left it, she opened it and read it quickly.

*You looked beautiful tonight. Thank you for the dance. Until tomorrow...*

Lenore quickly stuffed the note into her dress and took a deep breath. She hated to think of what might be coming. Something even scarier awaited her at home, however. She wasn't three steps up the stairs before Kieran was there, blocking her way.

"He found you? At Camilla's party!" Kieran growled.

"Yes, he found me," Lenore replied tiredly, leaning against the wall.

"Why would he take such a risk? Camilla's father was there."

"I know. He said he owed my father a debt."

"Ah, it makes sense now," Kieran said relaxing. "He is wise to respect the burden of debt."

"He said the Enforcers are still looking for me, that they might be able to connect us. Kieran, what do I do?"

"You must tell Mina and Neal."

"He told me not to. He said I have to meet him tomorrow, secretly."

"When?"

"At midnight."

Kieran smiled a fanged smile.

"Excellent."

"No! You can't take the risk!"

Rook leaned back against the wall and breathed deeply as he thought back to his dance with Lenore. Being so close to her had calmed the constant anxiety in him in a way nothing else could. He could still remember the way she smelled, the feel of her hand in his. He prayed she would come tomorrow night. He had taken a huge risk in showing up at the debut after all.

The Allens didn't travel in quite the same circles he once had, but there was enough overlap to make Rook nervous. He had seen one of his many cousins, Mason, there in the crowd, and he had wanted to smack that ridiculous smile off Mason's face. Mason had been trying to entertain Lenore with some story, and Rook could tell Lenore was only laughing at it to be polite. She was too busy watching Camilla try to disentangle herself from an overly amorous suitor to really pay attention to Mason's tale, which had made Rook smile. In addition to annoying cousins, there had been enough people from his past life at the debut to make things dangerous for Rook. He would have liked to stay longer, but even the one dance could have spelled his death. It was a good thing he had grown so much since any of them had last seen him.

*Ninth Year of the New Age, Tenth Day of the Ice*
*Official report submitted by Fifth Sawyer:*

*The investigation into the attack three months ago goes well. The survey of guests at Camilla Hawkins' debut has turned up some interesting prospects. Several guests report having seen a petite figure in the gardens at night. Testimonies collected state that she stalks the area at night, though these could just be fanciful stories. The descriptions, however, match that of the girl I tried to apprehend the night of the attack. She is likely a member of the lower class, so inquiries have begun around the Agate quarter. Knowing the reason* why *this person has chosen to be a thief may yield better leads—is she a member of a larger organization? Does she plan to use her ill-gotten gains to move up in society? Is she homeless? This last option does not excuse her actions, but it may lead us to her. I have cross-referenced my other reports with those of other officers. I have found one that recounts an unsuccessful chase by Fifths Campbell and Ellis. I believe their culprit is the same as my suspect.*

*Attached:*
*Copy of report by Fifths Campbell and Ellis from Ninth Year of the New Age, Second Day of the Earth.*

# 13

# NEW YEAR CELEBRATIONS

"I think it's a brilliant plan," Mina said.

"How can you say that?" Lenore cried. "He risks being discovered!"

"I assure you, no one will know I am there," Kieran said.

"He's right, Lenore," Neal agreed. "Kieran has certain… abilities. He'll be fine. It's you we're worried about."

Lenore looked around at the people in the sitting room, her mouth opening and closing like a fish.

"Are you all mad?!" she demanded. "You've all risked too much for me already, and now you might be caught! I'm not about to put any of you in any more danger! I ought to leave tonight and never come back!"

"Lenore, don't be ridiculous," Mina said with a wave of her hand. "There are more people than you know who oppose the Enforcers. We will be fine. If you don't meet Rook, however, and put this to rest, he may bring unwanted attention to us in pursuit of you."

Lenore sank down onto a chair and put her head in her hands. When did her life get so complicated, not to mention dangerous? It was one thing when she was putting herself at risk, it was something completely different when it was an entire family.

"You'll be fine," Mina said, putting her hand on Lenore's shoulder. "And so will Kieran."

Lenore pushed herself back into the shadows as far as she could. Even though she was covered from head to toe in a black cloak, she couldn't help but imagine herself standing out like a lantern in the darkness. She knew Kieran was somewhere nearby, but she didn't know where exactly. They had left the manor at the same time, but Kieran had left through the window and Lenore through the door. Someone suddenly took Lenore by the hand, and she suppressed a cry. Spinning around, she saw Rook there with a smile that made her uncomfortable. He placed a finger on his lips and gestured that she should follow him. Lenore almost objected, but remembered that Kieran was there. She allowed Rook to lead her by the hand away from the pasty shop and into a nearby cellar.

Once inside the cellar, Lenore felt a stab of panic in her chest. Rook had just closed the door, and they were both in complete darkness. She didn't move as she heard Rook walk away from her. A moment later a lantern was lit and mostly shielded, and Rook motioned for her to follow again. She did so, but kept a safe distance. Rook headed towards the wall and placed his hand there. The stone pushed in and a piece of the wall popped out. Lenore was intrigued and took a step towards Rook. He made a grand sweeping motion towards the secret doorway, and Lenore hesitantly walked through it. She couldn't help but stop and take a look at the mechanics of the hidden latch, however.

"Ah ah ah," Rook tutted playfully. "That's my secret."

He then herded her through the doorway and followed, closing the hidden door behind him.

"Welcome to my humble abode," Rook said happily.

Lenore looked around and was reminded of the attic. Rook's home was nothing more than a large room with a pallet for a bed, a small table, and two chairs. Lenore suddenly wondered just how many little rooms, hovels, and hideaways like hers and Rook's were scattered around the city.

Rook took a seat in one of the chairs, which creaked treacherously beneath him. He motioned for her to sit in the other equally untrustworthy chair. Lenore sat, but remained ready to run.

"Relax, little bird," Rook said.

"Why do you keep calling me that?" she asked suddenly.

Rook smiled and replied, "Because that's what you remind me of. When you wore the feathers in your hair that first time you went out with those ridiculous women, that's all I could think of. A little bird surrounded by pecking, squabbling hens."

Lenore was surprised and afraid of how much Rook knew. He really had been watching her a long time, and he was the kind that noticed details. This was a very bad combination for Lenore. She kept her face closed, however, and betrayed nothing.

"Say what you want to say."

"My, you're in a hurry. Can't we get to know each other?"

"No. I want to finish our business and be done with you… forever."

"You do know what you want, don't you?" Rook laughed. "I'm very impressed."

"Is my family in danger? Tell me!" Lenore said, shooting up from her chair.

"Your… family?" Rook said, his voice dangerously soft. He stood up, standing a whole head taller than Lenore, and she suddenly felt physically frightened of him. "How quickly you forget your *real* family."

"Don't talk about them," Lenore hissed, her anger fighting against her fear. "And don't talk about me like you know me. You said you owed my father a debt. Why don't you repay it and quickly?"

"What do you think I'm doing?" Rook growled. "How long were your parents in the Halls of Justice before you started looking for a cushy, shiny palace to move into? How did you convince them to let you stay? Are you giving the old man some honey on the side?"

Lenore slapped Rook hard across the face.

"How dare you! You're nothing but a liar. I hope you do owe my father a debt, because I plan on letting you burn beneath its curse."

Lenore made for the door, but Rook grabbed her by the wrist. She spun around and punched him square in the nose. He released her and swore, holding his nose gingerly. Lenore was reaching for the door when Rook said something that made her stop in her tracks.

"Your parents are alive. I've been communicating with them."

"I don't believe you," she spat, but didn't leave.

"I'm sorry I said what I did. It wasn't right, but you have to hear me out. The Enforcers have been trying to extract information from them about you, about me, about anything they can get, but they haven't cracked. It's getting more difficult for Edgar and Twila to resist, though, and they're afraid they'll soon submit."

"Why would the Enforcers care about me?" Lenore asked skeptically, thinking back to those first days after her parents' arrest.

She had overheard the Enforcers asking her neighbors

about her back then, but she had just assumed they suspected she was involved in whatever crime had been pinned on her parents. There was never really a proper explanation given for her parents' arrest, at least not to Lenore. When the Enforcers had come to the house to drag Edgar and Twila away, they had just said it was for "attacks against the security of the city".

"Because you've disappeared and they want to know what you know about your father's work."

"I don't know anything, and what does this have to do with the Allens?"

"The girl who delivered that Enforcer to Dr. Allen is supposed to look enough like another criminal they're searching for to make them wonder. If they put all three pieces together, it won't just be you heading for the Halls of Justice. I'd say you're in real trouble if it weren't for the records that miraculously appeared to back your girl-from-the-country story. I'd give my right arm to know how you made that happen."

Rook waited to see if Lenore would give up any of that secret, and, while Lenore thought his choice of words was ironic enough to be laughable, she didn't bat an eyelash. Gadget was not a woman she ever wanted to cross.

"Good girl," Rook said with an approving smile. "I don't know if they'll ever connect all the dots, but the possibility is there. Won't you please sit down?"

Lenore did so, her mind fixating on the idea of her parents in the Halls of Justice. She imagined them languishing there, being tortured, desperate. Meanwhile, Rook checked his nose for bleeding. It wasn't, and Lenore made a mental note in the back of her mind to hit harder next time.

"How is it that you can correspond with them?" Lenore asked.

"I have many contacts including a mole within the Enforcers' ranks. I can only get information through once in a while, though."

"When was your last communication?"

"About a month ago. It may already be too late."

"What information could they possibly get from my parents that could help them find me that they couldn't get from a former neighbor?"

"I don't know. The last message just said they were trying to get information about what your father shared with you and about how they can find you."

"It was unseemly for me to learn about machines, so it wasn't discussed… thankfully. Now, what are we supposed to do? Help them escape?"

"No. They want to be killed."

Lenore opened her mouth, but no sound came out. She turned away and fought back against the tears that burned in her eyes.

"Lenore," Rook said, taking her hand. She ripped it away, and he said, "I want to fulfill your parents' wish. The Halls… it's terrible. The prisoners that aren't put to death are kept healthy but are tortured for information. Many of them go mad. Your mother… she's already begun to lose her mind."

"No, that's not good enough," Lenore said determinedly. "They can't stay there. They don't deserve this!"

"We can't," Rook said softly. "They'd be pursued forever, and they want you to have a future. It's the only way."

"You haven't even tried!" Lenore spat. "I don't care about my future! How can I even have one knowing I've left my parents to die?!"

"This isn't your choice, Lenore. It's theirs. They know what they're losing. They love you too much to choose any other option."

Lenore couldn't hold it back anymore. She squeaked and began to sob. She always knew her parents loved her. That was a parent's job, wasn't it? It came as part of the package, but to see it like this… her parents loved her too much to keep on living, to endanger her with their continued existence. Lenore's heart broke for them, and it was several minutes before she was able to pull herself together again. Rook sat by the entire time, not trying to touch her again, but his hand remained close to her. Finally, she was able to speak again, and she pushed away her sorrow with anger.

"How can you know any of this?" she demanded. "Do they… my parents, I mean, know of my activities now?"

"I told you, I have many contacts. And, no, I can't risk telling them. I've just told them you're doing fine."

"If you found out so much about me, how do I know the Enforcers don't know it already?"

"The Enforcers don't have the trust of the people. I do."

"Why did you have to tell me this? Why couldn't you have just left me out of it?"

"I swore to your father I'd protect you, and knowledge is power. Besides, you deserve to know."

"What did my father do for you to incur such a debt?"

"He saved my life, simple as that."

Lenore paused. She was afraid of asking the next question.

"What are you going to do now?"

"I'm going to do as your parents have asked."

That was the answer she had been expecting, and yet it was still like a punch in the gut. Nevertheless, she carried on with her questions.

"And what about me?"

"I'll still be watching, but keep your nose clean. You're fairly closely connected to the Enforcers now."

Lenore nodded and finally met Rook's eyes again. They were dark brown, she saw now, and softer than they had been thus far.

"Thank you… for sharing with me. I… I suppose it's better to know the truth… in a way. You don't need to protect me, though. I release you from my father's bond… or whatever the way to say that is."

Rook smiled and said, "I'm not convinced it works like that. Besides, you're not so difficult to look after."

Lenore scowled at him, but she couldn't hold it. Rook had done her no harm and had given her some kind of morbid peace about her parents. He had also reminded her about the danger she was in, that they were all still in. Lenore stood, and Rook didn't stop her this time.

"One more question," she said. "When we first met, you said you represented certain interested parties. Who else knows about me besides you?"

Rook smiled and said, "I lied. It's just me, and I intend on keeping it that way."

Lenore was relieved at that and wasn't afraid to let it show on her face. Anyone in her position would feel the same. Rook walked her out silently and saw her as far as the street. After that, he disappeared like vapor into the night. Lenore was careful in going home. It didn't matter who she was or how she was dressed—neither of which were good—being out at that time was more than a little suspicious. Kieran was waiting in her bedroom by the window when she came in.

"Did you hear anything?" she asked.

"Everything," Kieran replied.

"And?"

"He seems genuine enough, if not a bit forward." Lenore snorted at that. "It's you I'm worried about, however."

"I think I'm… alright… with everything," she lied. "I suppose I didn't expect much different, about my parents that is."

"Is there anything I can do?" Kieran asked.

Lenore smiled at him and shook her head.

"You've already done so much. Even so, I don't know of anything you could do anyway. I appreciate the thought, though. Thank you."

"Of course, Lenore. Sleep well."

Lenore nodded, but her mind was still spinning. Ideas were beginning to form, but she dared not give them a voice yet.

Rook stared at the ceiling of his little room. She had been here with him. There was a part of him that wondered if he should have forced her to stay. How was he supposed to protect her in... in that world? There was still a chance he had been recognized at Camilla's debut, but his ears and eyes hadn't reported anything yet, so that was a good sign. This was a foreign feeling for Rook; he had no idea what to do next.

Mina and Neal listened carefully as Lenore recounted what had passed between Rook and herself the night before. Kieran offered details that Lenore had otherwise missed or forgotten. They were thoughtful about what they heard, but did not seem very concerned.

"It's madness for him to think he can infiltrate the Halls of Justice. I'm so sorry, Lenore, but I hope you don't invest too much hope into this wild tale. Even so, it's good to know this seems to be the end of our dealings with him," Mina said.

"There is the matter of his oath to Lenore's father," Kieran said.

"Is there any way Lenore's words last night could have released him from the debt?" Neal asked.

"I cannot say," Kieran replied. "Oaths are an ancient power, far stronger and more mysterious than almost anything I know of."

"Hm, in that case, let us *hope* that's the last of it then," Mina said. "We shall carry on as usual, yes?"

Lenore agreed, but there were misgivings in her heart that simply would not disappear. Mina seemed very sure of her opinions on the subject, but Lenore wasn't so optimistic. Could Rook somehow release her parents from their torment? Should they be released? She still wondered about the secret life she now knew her parents had led. Were they bad people? Or were there simply things she didn't know about them? Lenore suspected the latter, hoped for it really, but that didn't help much. The wonderings gnawed at her when she wasn't otherwise occupied, which made her all the more thankful for whatever distractions she could find.

"How is this even humanly possible?" Lenore asked, her mouth gaping open at the ample decorations festooning the Allen manor. It was a wonder the house didn't sag beneath the weight of them all.

The New Year Celebration holiday approached quickly after Camilla's debut. It was a week of feasting, gifts, frivolity, public festivity, parties, and decorations, all leading up to the first day of spring and the new year, the First Day of the Air.

Neal had taken the day off work, promising Lenore a surprise when she got home and leaving her without him at the museum for the first time. It had been odd and annoying at first, as Dempsey had immediately sought to take Lenore under his wing in Neal's absence. Dempsey had begun to be sort of oddly clingy lately, never wanting to be too far from anyone. Unfortunately, this meant he had started hanging around Lenore more. It had to be obvious that she was ignoring him most of the time, but she just couldn't bring herself to care. Much to Lenore's relief that day—and possibly Dempsey's had Lenore been left alone with him and dangerous tools—Copper absconded with her almost immediately, citing his senior position and a desire to "run some experiments". Dempsey had objected, but they were already off. Lenore didn't much care what Copper's mystery experiments were so long as she was as far from Dempsey as possible. What she ended up doing was far more fun and dangerous than she had dared hope.

"A few of the history scholars and alchemists have been working on an... alteration to Old World weapons," Copper explained excitedly as they walked. "They're hoping to be able to use them for New Year Celebration festivities, and I reckon we're close!"

"So you've been working on this too?" Lenore asked. "Also, what weapons could possibly be used for New Year's? Are you going to shoot sweets from a giant slingshot or something?"

Copper's face lit up, and he exclaimed, "I hadn't thought of that! Right, we'll put it on the list, but this is first priority. We're trying to make pyroprismatics."

Lenore gasped in excitement. The secret to pyroprismatics had been lost with so many other Old World technologies, but the accounts of them were almost too spectacular to believe. Incendiary devices that shot into the air and exploded with light and color and sound and then dissipated into nothing. It was almost enough to make Lenore believe that magic really was involved in their creation.

They soon arrived at the Alchemy department, where a few scholars and more alchemists were gathered. What transpired after that was a day full of noise, mess, laughter, and a few near misses. Copper was insistent that Lenore stay safe.

"Neal will have my head if anything happens to you," he said.

This, however, kept Lenore from some of the more exciting steps in the process… like testing that when the black powder —the recipe for which having been cobbled together from a few old tomes and then loosely packed into a paper tube with colored chalk—exploded, it also blew up the pigment that had been packed with it. After the collected scientists and scholars misjudged the blast radius of the first experiment, however, and everyone was hit with orange powder and obtained some not-too-serious burns, Lenore found that she was less keen to be up close to the action. The group didn't make any major breakthroughs that day, which meant no pyroprismatics for New Year Celebration Day. There were many new ideas and theories born from the experiments, however, as to what compounds could be used instead of chalk—Lenore got to see the vivid colors that many substances burned that day—what new recipes could be tested for the black powder, and Copper and a few others planned on building and testing the sweets slingshot soon. Lenore had been enjoying the work so much, she hadn't realized how late it was getting. She hurried home that evening without a thought about her appearance and stopped dead in her tracks when she saw the manor.

Garlands of holly and pine and mistletoe were festooned back and forth across the front of the house, around the roofs and eaves, and along the doorframes and windows. Bows were tacked onto any visible corner and crossbeam. The light of a single candle was glowing in every window. Finally, to top it all off, there was a massive glittering star of silver and gold attached to the tallest point of the house.

It was not the decorations themselves that shocked Lenore. Oh no, Lenore had seen houses all over Springhaven decorated for the upcoming holiday. Those had all been *tastefully* done, however. Neal's strategy had clearly been to lure tasteful into a dark alley, knock it senseless, and steal everything it had to offer in order to whack it all up together onto the house. How Neal had managed to get everything up so high and attached, much less in just one day, was a mystery.

"Lenore! Finally! You're here!" she heard from across the vast lawn.

Lenore looked to see a beaming and somewhat worse for wear looking Neal trotting towards her.

"What do you think?" he asked, gesturing dramatically towards the house.

Despite herself, Lenore began laughing and replied, "I love it! Blazes, it's awful. How fantastic!"

New Year was Lenore's favorite time of year, even more so now than it used to be. The food, the parties, the general feeling of goodwill, all of it had filled her with warmth for as long as she could remember. Last year had been horrible, as she'd had to spend the holiday alone. Not just that, but she'd used the various festivals throughout the week as an opportunity to pickpocket citizens that were just trying to celebrate the happy occasion. Despite the great deal of success she'd had—better than any other time of the year actually—she'd cried herself to sleep every night for a long time after that because she knew she had contributed to ruining someone else's holiday. This year, however, Lenore had resolved to observe New Year better than she ever had. She encouraged Mina and Neal and Camilla to donate to good causes with her. Lenore also spent nearly all of her saved up pocket money—apprentices made next to nothing, and Lenore had to fight her survival instinct, which told her to hoard as much money as possible just in case things went south with the Allens—on gifts. Now, in addition to her second chance, her gratitude for her adopted family, and her opportunity to be generous to others, she was seeing Neal throw all social custom and aesthetic propriety to the wind in his joy over the holiday, and it delighted Lenore.

Neal's smile grew wider, and he said proudly, "It is rather striking, isn't it?" He then looked down at her and seemed to really see her for the first time that evening. "Good heavens, what's happened to you?"

Lenore looked down at her clothes and saw the various patches of color all over her, not to mention the few bandages that had been used to dress her burns.

"Ar—are your eyebrows singed?" Neal added in confusion.

Lenore, still full of excitement from the day and the shock of the house, could think of nothing better to do than to smile innocently at Neal in response.

"Are you hurt?" he asked.

"Not really."

"Good enough. Wait till you see the inside!"

Lenore laughed again, and she knew in that moment that she had found a kindred celebration spirit in Neal. This was good, as Mina was less than understanding about Lenore's state.

"Oh, Lenore, welcom—what the blazes have you done?! Oh, heavens, your hair! And we almost had it even again. Do these colors stain? It's all over. Camilla, show Lenore how to draw in her eyebrows."

Lenore and Neal didn't stop laughing all week. The color did stain, Lenore's eyebrows never looked better so long as Camilla filled them in, and Mina swore all manner of oaths against Copper. The inside of the manor was decorated just like the outside, and Esther's culinary exploits for the week began that night. There were mince pies and figgy puddings and hot punch and roasts of all types and eggs and traditional gelatin salads, about which Lenore and Camilla commiserated together.

"Cold animal bones and skins soup... delicious," Camilla

said, warily eyeing the lurid pink, jiggling shape on the plate before them.

The top of the "salad", which both girls felt was an overly generous use of the word, was some strange mixture of fruit bits and cheese curds. How it had been turned such an unappetizing color was a mystery better left unsolved. Neal and Mina loved the stuff, however, so it was served at their annual New Year party. Thankfully, that was just one item on the packed table. The house was full of friends and coworkers and their various children. Lenore had counted six belonging to Copper, and Dempsey had brought a lady friend, though Lenore couldn't be bothered to remember her name. Dempsey seemed to always be on his way to another relationship, so it probably wouldn't matter in a few weeks. Gifts were exchanged—Neal gave all of his people gifts, and Lenore slyly passed one to Copper from her when Dempsey wasn't looking—and songs about the new year and new hopes were sung.

Later on in the week, on New Year Celebration Night, the whole family went out to the city center where there was food and dancing and music and sweets that rained down from the sky. They bought crackers from some of the vendors and ran into Thyme, Mint, and Ginger at the spiced nuts stall. They counted down as the large clock, which rose two stories above them, tick-tocked its way to midnight. The first hour of spring was met with uproarious cheering and applause. Not long after that, the Allens and their adopted charges went home to sleep off the week's festivities.

"Happy New Year, little bird," Rook murmured later on that night from his hideaway.

Rook had spent the evening with his men, half celebrating

and half supervising operations. As Lenore knew, New Year Celebration week was a big one for criminals, and Rook liked to make sure his people and contacts were safe—for their sake, his, and the rest of his organization's. As usual, at least one clumsy fool had gotten caught. The oath everyone who came into Rook's employ had to take would protect his interests, as would the many layers Rook had built into the organization, so he wasn't too concerned. Other than that, it was a good haul this year.

After the holiday had passed, Lenore's apprenticeship continued, though the bird project was slowing down. She had gathered piles of data. That had been the easy part... well, easier, as it turned out. The truly difficult part was figuring out what to use and what not to when it came time to return to the Arc-Tec department to continue her progress.

Lenore had begun working with members of the Zoology department when she couldn't gain anything further from observation. These were the people who helped Lenore acquire some live specimens—she didn't bother mentioning the few abysmal attempts she had made at catching her own. Pigeons were the easiest, as the city birds were plentiful and easily lured with food. This had begun some of the most exciting days in the process. Lenore enjoyed working closely with the zoologists, and they seemed genuinely pleased for someone else to be interested in discovering the secret of flight.

Not many scientists seemed very interested in understanding how birds flew, except perhaps avian specialists and a few other non-avian specialist zoologists. Lenore suspected this might be due to the fact that people had devised their own way of flying via zeppelin, so why was there a need to understand how birds did it? The zoologists agreed with her thinking, but they also felt past foolhardy—and usually fatal—attempts had also hurt the cause. Now, though, there was a multi-discipline endeavor taking place, which had a better reason to reveal these mysteries than just "because we'd like to know".

Lenore spent a great deal of time in the Zoology department getting up close and personal with the pigeons they caught. She would watch closely as they fluttered in their cages, which allowed her a better view of the elliptical pattern their wings followed as they beat, though that took a great deal of time and attention. She was less enthused about the study of the subject's internal organs, as this reminded her of her time working in Mina's practice. Lenore was once again thankful for the field in which she worked and its distinct lack of blood and viscera.

After a time, some of the EnKin geniuses were called in to assist the zoologists and Lenore understand what might be happening as the birds flapped their wings and gained altitude. Despite all the combined knowledge between Lenore and the Zoology department, they didn't understand why some birds could fly seemingly effortlessly and others, such as chickens, could not and decided there was likely something happening in the environment that they could not see.

Engineer Cayley and his team of EnKin geniuses devised a number of experiments to understand how the air moved around the birds' wings and bodies. Lenore and Copper designed and built a small steam powered wind maker, angles were measured and tested, wing models of various shapes and sizes were constructed and tried, and the pigeons—as well as a few chickens now—were subjected to their own wind tests. Lenore was both intimidated and pleased by addition of so many other people to the project. All the additional knowledge and expertise was what made their goal possible. Lenore knew had it just been her and Copper, the venture would have died long ago. The assistance offered by her colleagues was invaluable. Having so many members on the team, however, now meant that much more pressure, responsibility, and expectations fell on Lenore.

From the beginning, her instinct was to hide behind Copper as each new scientist joined the effort. After all, everyone assumed Copper was the lead scientist on this endeavor. It would have been easy, but Copper was worse than Neal. Neal at least gradually introduced Lenore to the fire. Copper threw her in without warning. As soon as the introductions were made between Lenore and the newcomer, Copper would jerk a thumb towards his protégée and explain that she was in charge.

"Sink or swim, dearie," he told her the first time she complained about his method.

Lenore *couldn't* sink. She refused to! Neal had put his faith in her. Other people knew about the project. If she failed, would she be allowed to keep her position? She suspected public humiliation would be the least of her worries. The idea of failing scared her more than meeting new people and dealing with their understandable lack of confidence in her. Thankfully, these people knew their fields, and Lenore wasn't so foolish as to think she was smarter than them. Most of the time when she was asked what direction she wanted to take on a step, she would ask a few questions to gain a better understanding of the situation and possible repercussions, got her colleague's opinion on what he or she thought would be best and why, and made her decision based on that.

Despite his lack of sympathy for Lenore's social anxiety, Copper was an excellent mentor and helped her pick out the best materials for her bird's skeleton when the time came to start building a prototype. Thin and hollow metal rods worked best to mimic the lightweight skeleton, but the joints had to be solid pieces. Copper was very good about offering advice, but, when it came time to make decisions, he left that up to Lenore. When she gave an answer, he would ask her why she had made that particular choice, which made her consider her reasoning. Lenore couldn't say how much she appreciated this kind of mentoring, and not just because it mirrored her own style… or had she learned it from Copper? It was challenging, which frustrated her when she was tired or feeling a bit lazy, but she knew it was far better than just being told what she should or shouldn't do. This was also the best time for Copper to really give Lenore hands-on experience with the shop tools.

Equipped with smoked glass goggles to protect her eyes and heavy gloves, Lenore's hands shook the first time she tried to use the focused torch herself. It didn't help that Neal and Dempsey were both watching in addition to Copper, all of them wearing goggles similar to hers. Lenore eyed Dempsey for a moment, wondering if she could get away with lighting him on fire.

She may have questions about her parents' character now, but that didn't mean she could forgive Dempsey for his betrayal. The Enforcers were evil and cruel, everyone knew it, and yet he had seen fit to throw her parents to them like cats to rabid dogs. Oh no, she hadn't forgotten, and she didn't intend to. Miraculously, she had gotten through working with him simply by talking to him as little as possible. She knew this wasn't exactly professional, but it kept the peace, which was far better than the alternative.

No, she couldn't get away with lighting him on fire, but the thought had given her a moment of cold pleasure.

"Steady on, Nori," Copper said to her. "All you need is a little gas. You're just gluing it onto the frame."

Lenore carefully turned the dial a smidge and lit the torch.

It flared to life like a tiny dragon, but Lenore resisted the urge to jump. After a few moments, she had gotten used to the ultra-hot flame that shot from the nozzle of the torch and moved forward. She carefully lifted the hollow rod, this one made of steel, in one thickly gloved hand and held the end up to the partially constructed frame of her bird. This was a piece of the ribs, which wouldn't need to move. Later on, she would use a die to cut a thread pattern into many other rods in order to screw them into miniature bolts and hinges. When the end of the rod was in place, she brought the spitting end of the focused torch towards the skeleton and began to allow the flame to just lick at the two pieces. When the joint was red hot and melted in place, Lenore carefully put the torch onto its stand, turned off the gas, and blew onto the finished joint.

"Nice work, dearie. Nice work indeed," Copper said, patting her on the shoulder gently. "She seems to have inherited your talent, Neal."

"I couldn't be prouder if she were my own," Neal said, beaming.

Lenore smiled widely, never taking her eyes off her work, and thanked the heavens silently.

Meanwhile, Kieran remained a constant presence in the house and seemed to be the only one that still sensed Lenore's distress. That wasn't too surprising considering his supernatural nature. Lenore was thankful, however, that he didn't tattle on her to the Allens. As wonderful as they were, they couldn't understand her turmoil. Camilla's mother was wrongly imprisoned and everyone knew it. Lenore's parents… there was no way to know, and she really wasn't keen to talk about it. When Kieran fed from her, he would simply look at her with that knowing, empathetic look, but said nothing. In an odd way, it made Lenore think that maybe he understood better than any of them, though she didn't know how. That was why she was so surprised and upset when she was awoken one night by Kieran slipping out of her window.

"What are you doing?" Lenore whispered, sitting up in bed.

Had she not been so groggy, she might have wondered at how a creature like Kieran could have slipped up and made noise during his departure. It never occurred to her that something could be wrong with him.

"Hunting," Kieran replied, lowering the window again. "I have fed from all of you too much."

"Mina says it's fine. We're all still healthy."

Kieran smiled and replied, "Too much for my own good conscience. I cannot keep asking you all for your blood."

"Don't be silly," Lenore said, pulling the sleeve of her nightgown up. She waved her arm at the Vampyre and teased, "Eat up." Kieran hesitated and she added playfully, "It's delicious and nutritious."

Kieran finally smiled and swept over to the bed. Sitting down on the edge, he gently took her arm and began to stroke the veins.

"What does it taste like to you?" she asked. "Blood, I mean."

"It's more like tasting a scent. Mina is bold like red wine. Neal's blood is sweeter, and Camilla is floral, like springtime."

Lenore rolled her eyes and muttered, "Of course she is."

"Why do you say that? I've seen you two together. You seem to get along just fine."

"We do, and she's lovely. She's great with Mina's patients and will make an excellent doctor one day, I'm sure. It's just that she's so... perfect." Lenore said the last word with a breathy, high-pitched voice she usually reserved for a very particular type of fluff-headed female.

She smiled sardonically, but stopped and turned her eyes to Kieran in surprise when he put his hand on her face. He was stroking her cheekbone with his thumb and looking at her curiously. Lenore felt her heart quicken, but said nothing. The contact was not at all unpleasant, and she was surprised to realize that he smelled like the forest at night. She had heard stories of Vampyres being able to compel their victims, and she wondered if that's what this was. She wasn't afraid. She trusted Kieran, but she didn't know what he was about at that moment.

"Never compare yourself to others," he said, his gaze never leaving her. "You are unique and not meant to be anything but what you are."

Lenore didn't move, waiting for whatever would happen next. Despite his promise to her, he was still a Vampyre and didn't always operate like a human. After another moment, he released her gaze and looked back to the crook of her elbow.

"Your blood is sharp and crisp and cool like rainfall," he said, suddenly casual again.

He then lowered his mouth to her arm and reopened the puncture wounds that were already there. Lenore relaxed again and sat by quietly as Kieran fed.

"Kieran," Lenore began hesitantly. "Sorry, I don't mean to interrupt you while you're eating…" Lenore still wasn't sure what the proper etiquette was while a Vampyre ate, but she spoke during dinner, so that should mean it was sort of okay, right? "It's just that… I've been wondering recently… wanting to ask you for a favor, really. Um, you have special abilities, right? Could you possibly… would you be able to… rescue my parents from the Halls of Justice?"

Kieran lifted his head from her arm slowly and licked the wounds clean.

"I have been wondering when you might ask me that," he

said.

"Really? You have? I mean, does that mean—"

"No," Kieran said simply.

By his tone, Lenore could tell there was no room for discussion, but she had to try!

"Please, Kieran! You know I wouldn't ask unless I was desperate. I would never ask you to take such a risk… I…"

She trailed off as Kieran shook his head slowly.

"I heard what Rook said during your meeting. He was right; you would have no future. Your parents, too, would never be able to rest. Please, Lenore, you must see the gift they are giving to you."

"I don't want it," Lenore whispered, beginning to cry. "I want my parents back."

"I know, little one," Kieran said, wiping away Lenore's tears. "This world we live in has pain, but your parents will find peace in death. There is no other way."

Lenore fought to push her grief down. She didn't want to feel it if there was no way to stop it. She wanted to be angry. She wanted revenge against the people who did this. She thought about asking Kieran for at least that, but even just looking at him told her she didn't really want to ask him. She sincerely didn't know whether or not he would agree, and that frightened her a little for his sake. Kieran was a good man, a feat surely made more difficult by the creature he had become. At least, that was her best guess based on what she had learned about Vampyres. She didn't want to make his struggle any harder than necessary.

"Sorry I asked," she finally said, getting her tears under control. "Here, finish up."

The next morning, the family was met by a note left on the dining room table.

*My dearest friends,*

*I cannot express how much this time with you has meant for me. I am profoundly grateful knowing I will always have a home with you all, but I regret that I cannot stay. It has become too dangerous for me to remain. I must go where I can feed without restriction, lest I put you all at risk of my hunger. I look forward to the day when we will meet again, and, as we always have, we will meet again as soon as I am able. Please, be safe and take care of yourselves until that time. You will all be in my heart.*

*Sincerely,*
*Kieran*

"He's gone?" Lenore asked, unable to believe what she had just heard.

Somehow, she felt as if she could have, should have, stopped him the night before. Or maybe it was her fault he left.

"I'm afraid so," Neal said, laying the letter back down onto the table. "That has always been Kieran's way, ever since…"

Neal's voice left him, and he looked away. Mina took his hand and squeezed it comfortingly. Lenore laid a hand on her mentor's shoulder. She couldn't imagine what it must be like to lose his best friend in such a way. True, Kieran was never completely gone, and she had seen him and Neal together, talking and laughing as any two old friends did. Kieran was still separated from the rest of them, though from Neal, in a way that could never be mended.

"Still," Lenore said softly, "he'll be back… one day. Perhaps this time without all the death-defying excitement."

Neal turned back to her. He was smiling, but his eyes were

still sad. He nodded, but said nothing else.

Without Kieran, the house seemed much quieter than it had before, but their routine remained the same. That is, save for the still-constant wonderings in Lenore's brain. Without the extra distractions, Lenore began to have other questions, which only bred other questions. Not having Kieran around, that constant mysterious source of understanding, also left an aching hole in Lenore's heart that had not been there before she had met him. The wonderings that plagued her began to become more than a little distracting. Unless she was focusing hard on something, her mind would wander dangerously. More than once she had to be brought to attention by one of her housemates, and they began to notice.

When asked about what was wrong, Lenore couldn't quite get past her misgivings about sharing her doubts. This only made her feel guilty. The Allens had been nothing but wonderful, but she knew they just wouldn't understand. What did they know of questioning everything they knew? Lenore had no idea if her parents had been despicable or noble or liars or just trying to survive. How long had they been at it? Had her entire life been a lie? No, the Allens couldn't possibly understand this. They would, of course, pity her if she told them, but she didn't want pity. Pity would only make her feel more alone, but there was someone who could empathize with her: Rook.

What an idiotic idea! Rook was dangerous, absolutely the last person Lenore should be thinking of as a companion in any sense. She knew next to nothing about him, so why on earth did she think he would fill the empty longing for understanding she felt? Perhaps it was because he was a criminal like her. Sure, she wasn't stealing anymore, but she was still a criminal by society's standards. If the Enforcers knew the truth, they'd arrest her in a heartbeat. It was an absolutely, positively, completely mad idea, yet Lenore eventually couldn't stop herself from sneaking out one night to find him. She remembered everything, and so it wasn't long before she found herself in the cellar of his hideout, trying to figure out which brick to push.

Lenore was so involved with the task she failed to hear the approach from behind her, or perhaps her assailant was just that good. She froze as she felt a blade press against her neck. Despite the light pressure, she felt a trickle of blood run down to her collarbone.

"Turn around slowly or I spill your blood here and now," a soft voice snarled into her ear.

Lenore swallowed hard and began to turn ever so slowly. When she was most of the way around, her hood was ripped back from her head. Lenore found herself staring down the blade of a vicious looking curved knife and into Rook's face. A second later, Rook recognized her and lowered the blade.

"Lenore! What the blazes are you doing here?!" Rook hissed. "I could have killed you!"

"Would you have, though?" Lenore asked before she could stop herself.

"I've killed for far less," Rook said flatly.

Lenore's blood ran cold at that, and she debated whether or not to run while Rook opened the secret door and slipped inside. She took too long deciding, as Rook took her hand and pulled her in after him while she was thinking. He shut the door after them quickly and then headed over to the pallet. Flopping down onto it, he rubbed his back, wincing slightly.

"Why on earth are you here?" he asked, clearly annoyed. "Do you have any idea the risk you put us both in?"

"Are we in danger now?" Lenore asked worriedly.

"No more than we were before. You *somehow* avoided the patrols."

"I did evade them just fine well before I met you," Lenore snapped.

"Wonders never cease. Again, why are you here?"

Lenore sat in one of the chairs and looked at Rook pleadingly.

"I need to know more about my parents," she said. "Have you already... are they dead?"

"Not yet. I have a plan. The timing is tricky, though."

"What are you going to do? They won't suffer will they?"

Rook finally lifted his head and looked at Lenore with soft eyes. He reached out and put his hand on hers.

"Of course not, little bird. They'll simply fall asleep."

"Poison?"

"Yes, poison. My mole has everything he needs, but getting alone with their food is proving very difficult."

"Oh..."

Lenore wasn't sure what to say after that. She had believed she'd said goodbye to her parents long ago. Hearing about them had set her back, though. It was the best thing, or so she was trying to convince herself, but even that didn't make it any easier. Unfortunately, that also didn't quell any of her moral dilemmas.

"How well did you know them?" Lenore asked.

"Your mother, not at all. We never met, and your father only mentioned her one time, when I found out about you and made my oath. I knew your father well enough to know I could trust him. I wouldn't have done business with him if I didn't. I believe he held the same policy about me."

"Why was he selling weapons?"

"He didn't sell weapons, just information."

"But *why*?" Lenore asked, agitation seeping into her voice.

"I don't know. Fighting the good fight and all that I suppose. I think the underground resistance against the Enforcers is larger than anyone realizes."

The good fight. Lenore hadn't thought of it that way before. The Enforcers were so cruel and hateful, unabashedly so, but they were the law. Lenore had never really considered herself on their side or anything, just under their rule. She had always thought of those that opposed them, that broke the law, as criminals, plain and simple. Perhaps… perhaps they were the villains in everything, though. The thought made Lenore feel as if the world had pitched itself upside down, yet provided a refreshing new sense of clarity at the same time. Rook seemed to be able to read all the emotions that crossed her face.

"What's this all about, little bird?" he asked gently.

"I just… I just need to know… if my parents… were they any good?"

Rook smiled. It was not a smile of pity or indulgence. Rather, it was a warm smile of understanding and… was that caring? It was hard to tell, or perhaps Lenore didn't want to comprehend it. He squeezed her hand in his.

"They were absolutely good. Great, even. They saved lives. You can be proud of what they did."

The words warmed Lenore's heart and really did help to fill that hole in it. She believed Rook, and found peace in his words. She smiled and looked at him, though tears were welling up in her eyes. With her joy came pain, the pain of knowing that her parents suffered in their sacrifice for doing good. It was a new hurt, one that cut deeper than anything had yet. She hated that she was learning this about her parents just as she was about to lose them completely and permanently. There was relief too, though, in knowing that her parents were the same people, characteristically speaking, that she had always known them to be.

"Look, it's late. You'd best settle in," Rook said wearily. "Morning isn't for a few hours yet. Go ahead and take the bed."

"I'm not staying here," Lenore replied. "I have to get back. I just, I just wanted to know…"

"You should have thought about that before you came traipsing out here like a lost puppy. Besides, having a late-night rendezvous isn't a crime."

Lenore's tone turned stern as she stated, "Look here, you may be a shadow, Rook, but I am not, and I have to think about my reputation. If you're so talented, get me home!"

Rook groaned but stood and led her out.

# 14
# FEAR OF SUCCESS

Lenore had to give Rook credit; he really was very good. He made flitting from doorway to doorway seem easy. There were a few terrifying moments when the two had to press into a corner or behind a building to avoid the eyes of passing Enforcers—Rook would smile at her annoyingly during these moments as he held her close in the darkness—but it was otherwise uneventful. He took Lenore around the back of the manor and helped her over the fence, which actually concerned Lenore more than anything. How did he know how to navigate their property so well?

"Don't come find me again, *ever*," he told her before they parted. He drew a symbol in the dirt—a slanted line with a narrow triangle at the top—and said, "If you need me, draw this here. I will come to you." He then erased the symbol with his foot.

"But how—"

Rook placed a finger on her lips to quiet her and repeated, "I will come find you."

He then kissed her cheek so quickly she wasn't sure it had happened and disappeared over the wall like a cat. Lenore stood there for a moment in shock before shaking herself and hurrying inside. She was sure that someone would hear her, that Mina or Neal would be up, waiting for her expectantly. There was no one, though. The house was silent as Lenore crept back in. She hadn't lost any of her sneaking skills, and employed every one of them as she laboriously made her way back up to her room without making a sound. Despite this success, she still expected to be already known or later discovered somehow, but nothing came. No clue from Neal, no admonishment from Mina, no nothing. Lenore began to relax as the next day or two passed, and she was overjoyed at being able to return to her life as she had known it before.

True, in her private time, she came to accept that her parents were going to die. They might be gone already for all she knew, and she had thought she had said goodbye long ago. When they had been arrested, she knew they were already as good as dead. Now, however, knowing they would receive their final rest, she cried and mourned them. It was during these times that Lenore began to feel lonely again. Even as a strange kind of... happiness?... relief?... began to creep into her sorrow, she had no one to share her feelings with, except for Bitsy, of course. She couldn't be sure what this new feeling was, but she began to feel calmer about the idea of her parents passing from this world, for she knew they would be far better off than they ever could be in the Halls of Justice. Still, she told none of her adoptive family of these things. By this time, they'd be angry, possibly even furious, that she had sought out Rook, and, on top of that, they still wouldn't understand. Well, Camilla would probably understand Lenore's feelings about her parents' death, probably better than Rook even. Camilla might be angry or jealous about it, however, or might ask Lenore to have Rook ask his contact to have her mother killed as well. That would make things very dangerous indeed. No, better that she not tell them anything. She was done with Rook for good this time… really. Everything would just continue as usual now, even if her grief did make her feel alone.

Fifth Sawyer felt the weight of the tiny vial in his pocket as if it were a giant stone. He also imagined that, like a giant stone, everyone could see it. It had been like this for a few weeks now. He had been waiting for an opportunity to poison the Crowleys, but nothing had presented itself yet. Getting onto their meal rotation was step one.

All the Enforcer Fifths rotated positions between patrol duty, paperwork, prisoner care, and interrogation training. This cross training helped their commanding officers figure out where they would fit best when they were promoted… if they ever were. Competition within the Enforcer ranks was vicious, and that's how the powers-that-be liked it. The ruthlessness among the lesser officers hardened them for life in the upper ranks.

This was the third time Fifth Sawyer had been on prisoner care duty, and tomorrow would begin another round of interrogation training. The fewer prisoners Fifth Sawyer had to put through that, the better.

"I hate this," Fifth Jones whispered to Fifth Sawyer as they walked, pushing the cart of food trays down the hall. "Why do we even bother feeding these animals?"

"Because dead prisoners don't divulge useful information," Fifth Sawyer replied flatly.

Fifth Jones just rolled his eyes.

They entered the first room on the row and looked inside through the barred window. The prisoner, Cassandra Black, was sitting on her bunk and looking petulant.

"Cass, it's dinner time," Fifth Sawyer called through the bars sternly. "Stay there on your bunk. If you don't, I'll break your knees."

Cassandra just made a rude gesture back. Fifth Jones grabbed a tray off the cart as Fifth Sawyer stood by to unlock the door. Prisoners were allowed to keep their trays since everything including the utensils was made of a stiff, compressed paper. The Enforcers consolidated visits by using meal times to also check the health of prisoners. Not being medical professionals, the Enforcers only did cursory checks and then reported anything that seemed amiss. Fifth Sawyer unlocked the door and opened it just enough for Fifth Jones to proceed through. Just as Fifth Sawyer was following him, he saw a flash of movement and heard Fifth Jones yell, swearing angrily. The tray went flying as Fifth Sawyer slammed the door shut behind him. Cassandra was on her feet and laughing maniacally at Fifth Jones, who was now covered in grey-brown gruel. She couldn't go any further, however, as the shackles around her ankles pulled against the chains that connected her to the wall. Fifth Sawyer drew his truncheon and struck it viciously across Cassandra's knees. She stopped laughing, screamed, and crumpled to the ground. Fifth Jones, who was still swearing, moved to kick in Cassandra's head.

"Jones, stop!" Fifth Sawyer yelled. Fifth Jones turned on his fellow Enforcer angrily, but Fifth Sawyer cut off any objection he was about to make. "She's down. Killing her destroys evidence. Go get yourself cleaned up and grab a medic. She'll need to get fixed up."

Fifth Jones looked down to the woman who was now howling in pain on the floor and spat on her. He grumbled as he left, and Fifth Sawyer followed him out, locking the door behind him. He watched as Fifth Jones made his way down the corridor and then hurried. Edgar and Twila Crowley were about halfway down the hall. Fifth Sawyer would have to be quick if he was going to make it to their cells before Fifth Jones returned. He yelled at the prisoners as he brought them their food, threatening them, and barely looking over their bodies for any apparent wounds. There were always the ankles to check. Even though the manacles were padded, there was still always the risk of skin being rubbed raw or bloody.

Finally, Fifth Sawyer arrived at the Crowleys' cell. Inmates were sometimes housed together when it served the Enforcers' purposes. The Crowleys, it turned out, were more cooperative when they were kept together. Fifth Sawyer had observed their interrogation sessions carefully. As far as he could tell, they hadn't revealed anything helpful to the Enforcers yet, but Twila's mental stability had begun to deteriorate. She had begun singing songs about her baby girl, and Fifth Sawyer felt that could only lead to bad things.

"Edgar, Twila, time for dinner," he called.

Looking in through the window, he could see Edgar holding his wife as they sat on the floor together. Fifth Sawyer pulled two trays down from the cart and, balancing them carefully on one arm, he unlocked the door. Edgar looked up at him with narrowed eyes, but said nothing. Fifth Sawyer could see Lenore in both of her parents. Her green eyes came from Edgar, while her fair complexion and dark hair came from her mother. Fifth Sawyer closed the door behind him and moved fast.

"I have a message for you from our mutual friend," Fifth Sawyer hissed, pulling the tiny vial from his jacket. "He's spoken with your light. She's fine, she knows, and she loves you."

"My baby girl," Twila suddenly cooed. "She is like a tree."

"Yes, Twila," Edgar soothed. "She is. It's time for us to eat now. Then we'll have a nap. Isn't that right, Sawyer?"

"Correct, sir," Fifth Sawyer replied, emptying the vial into their meals.

He had to be careful. There were but a few teaspoons to share between the two trays, but Rook had assured him it was more than enough. Edgar tried to feed a spoonful to Twila, coaxing her, telling her that Lenore would be waiting for them after they finished their meal. Twila was more interested in recounting a day they had all gone to the gardens to have a picnic, though.

"Yes, my dear, it was lovely. You need your strength now, though. Please, eat."

Edgar knew he had to get his wife to eat first, lest the poison take him before he could be sure she was safe first.

"Sawyer! Where are you?!" came Fifth Jones' voice from down the corridor.

"Hurry!" Fifth Sawyer hissed.

"Twila, please!" Edgar urged.

Fifth Sawyer couldn't wait any longer. He left the Crowleys, tucking the vial back into his pocket, and walked out of their cell.

"There you are," said Fifth Jones, walking towards him. He then called loudly into the cell, "How's our favorite nutcase today?"

"The prisoners are stable," Fifth Sawyer said.

"You are such a bore," Fifth Jones complained.

"I have a job to do, Jones. I mean to do it well."

Fifth Jones just rolled his eyes, and they continued on their route. Fifth Sawyer feared for what might happen to the Crowleys. If they weren't dead by the time he and Fifth Jones made their way back to collect the trays, they likely wouldn't end up that way for a very long time. When they did eventually make it back around the loop to Edgar and Twila's cell, Fifth Sawyer was both pleased and frightened.

"What the blazes?!" Fifth Jones exclaimed, looking in through their window.

"What? What is it?" Fifth Sawyer asked, doing his best to sound alarmed.

"He's dead!"

"What?!"

Fifth Jones threw the door open, and Fifth Sawyer saw Edgar's body lying dead on the floor. Twila, however, was still alive and painting the wall with her gruel. She was painting a scene of three stick figures having a picnic. There was no rise and fall of breath in Edgar, no color in his face, no signs of life whatsoever.

Turning on Fifth Sawyer, Fifth Jones demanded, "What happened?!"

"Blazes if I know!" Fifth Sawyer shouted back. He then looked to Twila and asked, "Could she have killed him?"

Fifth Jones looked to Twila, thinking hard. It wasn't unheard of for prisoners to die at each other's hands. It was just that no one had expected Twila Crowley to off her husband, even after she had begun to go mad.

Fifth Sawyer swallowed hard as he looked at all the gruel smeared on the wall and dripping onto the floor. Extremely deadly gruel. Then every muscle in him tightened as he saw Twila licking the leftovers off of her hands.

The Halls of Justice was a madhouse within fifteen minutes. As soon as news spread that an inmate was dead, the Halls went into lockdown mode. Anyone even remotely involved with the Crowleys or their care was interrogated. Fifth Sawyer donned a mask of professional impassivity. When Twila Crowley collapsed and started having convulsions, theories started to fly between officers. Had Twila killed her husband? Were they both ill? Did they need to quarantine the area and affected officers? What if it was a type of brain fever that had killed Edgar and caused Twila to go mad? The Enforcer medical staff could not find anything wrong with Twila, but her condition worsened as the evening went on.

Fifth Sawyer only discovered what had happened to her a week later when he walked into his third interrogation training session of that day. Twila was sat in a chair in the bare room. Her eyes were sunken, her face gaunt, as her hands were tied to the table. She was crying as she babbled senselessly.

"Took it away… made it dark. Squirrel makes it all go away. Hush… hush… hush. Promised we would see you."

Fifth Sawyer looked to Fourth Hawkins, who was standing by with Fifth Campbell.

"She survived," Fifth Sawyer said flatly.

"So she did," Fourth Hawkins agreed. "The doctors have given her a clean bill of health, but watch yourself for any strange symptoms."

"What do we hope to gain today?" Fifth Sawyer asked.

"Perhaps she'll be able to reveal clues as to what happened to her late husband. I don't hold out much hope, but we must try, hm?"

"Of course."

Even as he agreed, Fifth Sawyer's insides twisted for Twila. The woman was obviously beyond any shreds of reality she had still clung to. He didn't know what kind of poison Rook had given him, but the small bit Twila had ingested had seemed to exacerbate her delirium. Fifth Sawyer knew she would suffer needlessly in his C.O.'s mission to extract information, and he was right.

⚙

It had been over a month since Lenore had visited Rook. Everything was going as well as possible considering the circumstances. On the upside, she was getting along with her adopted family so well now, it sometimes felt as if she had been there forever. She even got into the occasional spat with Camilla over silly things. When it happened, which was pretty rare, it was usually started because Lenore said or did something she knew would get under Camilla's skin. Camilla was fairly predictable and so adamantly sweet and polite, Lenore just couldn't help vexing her once in a while to incite a reaction. In the end, Lenore always apologized and made friends again, sometimes at Mina's behest, but she now completely understood why little sisters tortured their older siblings.

She did begin to check herself, however, when temptation raised its sleek head due to the fact that Camilla had to begin preparing for her entrance exams to medical school. Mina had finally decided her apprentice was ready, and the pressure clearly weighed heavily on Camilla.

"What if I can't get in?" Camilla had once confided to Lenore. "Mina will be so disappointed. You know how people see a female in our profession. Do you think Mina would be able to keep me on as her apprentice?"

Lenore understood this kind of pressure all too well. Just months ago, she had experienced the exact same turmoil as she had worked to secure her position with Neal. Lenore couldn't even bring herself to tease her housemate on this matter. Instead, she placed a comforting hand on Camilla's and spoke honestly.

"You don't have anything to worry about. If you fail, which you won't, Mina will turn it into a learning opportunity and work that much harder to help you."

"Do you really think so?"

To that Lenore just gave Camilla an are-you-kidding-me look, and Camilla smiled.

"I guess you would know," she said remembering Lenore's previous trials and felt instantly better.

They both knew that, while Lenore had been adopted wholeheartedly by the Allens, Camilla was family by blood and therefore had less than nothing to fear when it came to her family's support. Neither said anything about the distinction between the two's family ties. Camilla felt it wasn't necessary, but Lenore didn't like how it felt to be singled out, so she didn't mention it.

Lenore's own work was still steady but slow-going. Lenore continued to sift through her bird data and set up experiments and make notes about every little thing. She felt a great responsibility to do this right and wanted to have everything laid out in black and white before the real scientific work began. She didn't like to admit it, but the pressure was beginning to take its toll on her. Nothing extreme, but Lenore found herself lying awake at night thinking about the information that circled around in her head until sleep decided to stop evading her. Her biggest fear was achieving her goal, discovering the Winged Zeppelin's secret of flight. Most of the museum staff now knew of her ambitious project, and everyone knew what a discovery, or failure, of that magnitude meant. Lenore was a little nobody apprentice from nowhere. Succeeding would mean honors and distinction and recognition and more. She had begun to regret her decision to set out on this path. She didn't want any of that, but she couldn't just quit. Neal, kind Neal who placed so much trust and faith in her, would be so disappointed. What had she been thinking? That was the thing, she hadn't been thinking... of the big picture, that is. She had been thinking only of the Winged Zeppelin and unlocking its secrets. She hadn't thought any further than that and now she was committed, and there was no going back.

Lenore lay in bed one night, thinking about the project when a noise at her window drew her attention. At first she was thrilled, thinking it was Kieran. He had said he'd be back, hadn't he? But something was wrong. There was too much struggling with the lock, too much effort to get in. It couldn't be Kieran, who could inexplicably slip in and out without a sound, lock or no. Lenore didn't know who it could be, but she didn't care. She flew out of bed, grabbed an iron poker from next to the fireplace, and hid behind the changing screen. Bitsy was there with her, tense and ready to strike or run. Probably the latter; Bitsy was no fighter. She heard the *whish* of the well-maintained window opening and shifted slightly, ready to strike. Lenore stood there behind the changing screen, trying to breathe as little as possible, and saw a tall, lanky figure creep into the room. The shadow crept closer, past the screen now, and Lenore made her move. Striking out, she pressed the poker against the figure's throat and gathered her courage before speaking.

"Don't move or I'll spill your blood here and now."

"Really? You can't even think up your own threat," said an all-too-familiar voice.

"Rook! What the blazes are you doing here?" Lenore hissed, lowering the poker.

"Such language, little bird," he tutted.

"Answer me!"

"I need your help."

"I beg your pardon?"

Lenore couldn't believe her ears. Rook, careful streetwise Rook, was actually asking her for a favor. That would put him in debt to her. This had to be serious.

"What do you need?" she asked.

"One of my contacts, my mole actually, wants to meet with

you."

"Your mole? Your *Enforcer* mole? What does he want with me?"

This sounded like a very bad idea to Lenore. She wanted to meet another Enforcer about as much as she wanted to walk over flaming metal shrapnel in bare feet.

"If I could have made him tell me, I would have. He wants to speak with you, though."

"Will you be there?"

"I'll be nearby."

"Rook, I don't think I can."

"Please, Lenore. He won't accept my payment. He wants it from you. We're both dead if he decides he doesn't want to play anymore."

"Payment for killing my parents?"

"…Yes."

Rook could see the situation going downhill quickly. He decided it was time to show his hand. He reached out and took her hands, looking down into her eyes.

"If nothing else, do it for me. I don't have any other options. Please, Lenore, for me."

Lenore felt her heart skip a beat. Rook really was desperate, and who knew what would happen if she denied him. It could be the end of him, of her, of everyone she had come to love. She couldn't take that risk. As much as she hated it, she would step in and play a part in Rook's deadly game.

"What do I need to do?"

"Meet him at the Corner Cafe tomorrow at one for lunch," Rook said, relief flooding his voice. "He'll be at the table with the white daisy." Rook then leaned forward, kissed Lenore's forehead, and then rested there before saying, "Thank you, little bird. Thank you."

Lenore was very uncomfortable with her current situation.

Not the lunch meeting, but Rook leaning against her, brushing his nose against her forehead. The closeness, the darkness, the room, and the feelings all of that stirred within her made her uneasy. She stepped back.

"You have to stop," she said firmly.

"Why?" There was a note of mischief in Rook's voice now that unnerved Lenore even further.

"You just have to. If that's all you had to tell me, leave. I'll be there tomorrow."

"Very well, my lady," Rook said with a bow and a grin.

He then headed for the window. Lenore didn't watch him go, but she spoke once more before he left.

"Rook."

"Hm?"

"I might know what I want as repayment for this favor."

The next day, Lenore told Neal that she wanted to go out for lunch to which he made no objection. She arrived at the restaurant a few minutes late and quickly looked for the table with the white daisy. After passing over the red rose, pink carnation, orange lily, green clovers, and purple iris, she spotted it. The table was set towards the back of the dining room, if it could be called a back.

Part of the cafe's charm was its entirely al fresco setting. Instead of walls, the cafe had heavy canvas blinds that could be pulled down at night and during bad weather. As it was, the rain today convinced patrons to eat out elsewhere, leaving the restaurant mostly empty and the staff bored and inattentive.

Lenore swallowed hard and took a deep breath. This was it. She was about to come face to face with her parents' killer. Mercy killer, yes, but killer nonetheless. The man was turned towards the opposite direction, more than likely looking for her approach. Then he turned back and looked straight at her. It took everything in Lenore to keep moving forward. There at the table was Fifth Sawyer. He wasn't wearing his uniform, which was probably why she hadn't recognized him. His hair, which was usually slicked back neatly, was allowed to hang loosely now. He didn't bat an eyelash when he saw her. Why should he? He was the one that had asked for this meeting. Fifth Sawyer stood as Lenore approached and bowed as was appropriate.

"Miss Blackbird, I'm so delighted you could join me today," he said congenially, and Lenore almost believed his smile was genuine… almost.

"Fifth Sawyer, it's a pleasure," she lied pleasantly.

Inside, a voice had begun to screech furiously. *You liar! You killed my parents. I'll rip your eyes out, you worthless piece of —*

Lenore shut the voice away, reminding herself why it had had to be done. The knowledge brought her relief, but there was still a part of her that raged, knowing it had been him that had snuffed out her parents' lives. The two sat, and Lenore waited. Fifth Sawyer wasted no time.

"I don't know if I ever told you, thank you for your service to me." He was speaking of saving his life. "And I am very sorry for your loss."

Lenore's smile tightened, but she didn't falter.

"Thank you, Fifth Sawyer—"

He held up a hand to stop her and said, "Please, call me Dmitri."

*I hate you, Dmitri.*

"Thank you, Dmitri. I appreciate it. How can I ever repay you for your, erm, *kindness*? I don't suppose my service to you covers it?"

The word tasted foul in her mouth, but she had said it anyway.

Dmitri smiled and said, "I was all too happy to help. I do feel as if I repaid your service, however, by seeking out work with our friend instead of elsewhere. All I would ask in return for the kindness I have shown is that you speak to your lovely cousin for me."

Lenore's mask finally failed. The combination of learning that it was her selflessness... foolishness... whatever... that had sent Dmitri to Rook and that Dmitri's favor was matchmaking overpowered her good sense. She was somehow pleased and proud of herself. The good deed seemed to have set unbelievable things into motion, but why on earth would he ask for something so, well, frivolous?

"My... you mean Camilla?"

"Who else?" Dmitri smiled at her and nudged her boot beneath the table.

Lenore readjusted her countenance and asked, "Whatever do you mean?"

"I must confess I am quite taken with sweet Camilla. My position, however, is intimidating..."

*Loathsome, repugnant, vomit-inducing...*

"...and I believe this is why she has rebuffed my advances. I do report to her father after all."

Lenore giggled foolishly and twittered, "Dmitri, what would you have me say to her?"

Leaning forward, Dmitri smiled at Lenore, but his eyes were sharp and hard. His voice betrayed nothing, however.

"I know how you ladies are. The power you wield with mere words is greater than any other force. I'm not asking for much. I just want her to agree to see me. Just once. I know you can think of something."

Lenore realized her misstep. She had laughed at Dmitri and

belittled his request. If there was one thing she knew about men, it was that they couldn't stand to be disrespected. They were really very fragile creatures. She let the silly chit act fall, but retained the smile. She was sincere now… or she appeared to be.

"I'll speak with her, but you have to be the one to capture her heart."

Dmitri's eyes softened and he replied, "Too true. I shall do my best. Now, shall we have lunch?"

Lenore faltered again.

"Ah, should we?"

"Why not? It's why we came here isn't it?"

"And what we've discussed?"

"All true."

He smiled conspiratorially at her and waved a server over. Lenore sat back and thought. He was right. It was all true and not suspicious at all. The two were acquaintances, and it was nothing more than what any other pair of young people did. The entire meeting was brilliant, really. The two ordered their lunch and discussed Camilla the entire time. Dmitri simply wanted to know about her—her favorite flowers, preferred colors, etc.—and, while his questions seemed innocent enough, Lenore was careful with what she revealed. She didn't trust Dmitri in the least. In fact, his request made her think he might even be dangerous. Just how taken with Camilla was he that he would refuse Rook's payment for a chance to court her? Lenore wasn't about to throw her housemate to a wolf like Dmitri, but she would make good on her promise. He was someone she wanted to pay as soon as possible.

Rook came to Lenore's room again that night. She was

expecting it this time. Somehow Lenore knew he would want to know Dmitri's price… and hers. They discussed the latter first.

"So you've got me over a barrel," Rook said, smirking at her as they sat in front of the fireplace. "What is it you want from me?"

Lenore narrowed her eyes at Rook. He was playing a game, and she knew it. Rook took debts as seriously as she did, and this little act was a ploy to cover up whatever he was really feeling about their current situation. She wondered if Rook would really ever fret about any request she could make of him. Rook had admitted to doing things that made Lenore's blood run cold. Even now, as she thought about her request, she wasn't sure she really wanted to ask him… mostly because she was pretty sure he'd do it. What did putting this into motion make her?

"There's a man…" she began uncertainly.

"Oh, someone I need to watch out for?" he teased.

Lenore involuntarily gagged, and Rook laughed quietly, lest they be heard.

"Dempsey Van Pelt. He's the reason my parents were arrested," she blurted suddenly.

Rook's smile instantly disappeared, and his face grew stormy. Lenore grew nervous looking at him now. His eyes had become deathly cold.

"I don't want him killed," she hurried to add. "I just…" Her voice caught in her throat as her anger welled up again. She hated Dempsey with every fiber of her being. Just thinking of him fanned the flame of bitterness in her heart. "I do *not* want him dead," she repeated, as much to emphasize her point as convince herself. "I want him punished. I want him to live in fear, knowing he's not safe, knowing that people know what he did, people with the power to hurt him."

"I think he needs to be hurt on the front end to make our

point," Rook said, his voice calculating and thoughtful.

Lenore swallowed hard. She couldn't quite bring herself to agree. She wanted that. If she was honest with herself, she wanted Dempsey crippled in some way, but she couldn't actually bring herself to say it. There was a line, and Lenore wasn't ready to cross it.

"Sweet Lenore," Rook said softly, though there was still an unnerving edge to his voice.

He stroked the back of her hand with his fingertips as he spoke, but Lenore pulled away. She didn't want to be sweet just now. She didn't want mercy for Dempsey, but she couldn't bring herself to say any more on the subject just now. As if he could sense her feelings, Rook abruptly changed the subject.

"So what did Dmitri want?"

"He wants me to convince Camilla to see him," Lenore told him despondently.

"And?" Rook asked.

"That's it."

Rook looked perplexed.

"Are you sure?"

"Yes, absolutely. He wants to court Camilla."

Rook finally shrugged and said, "I suppose if you like that —"

"This is serious! She's my friend. What am I going to do?"

"Do what he asked. It seems simple enough."

"Why do you both think this is so easy?"

"Oh, you know how women are. You plant a seed in their minds and they fixate on it."

"You don't know Camilla. She has no love for Enforcers."

"But she does have love for attention, as all ladies do."

Rook leaned close to Lenore, smiling that maddening smirk.

"Stop. You're being annoying," Lenore told him flatly,

pushing him back to where he had been.

Rook snickered, and Lenore rolled her eyes.

"You don't see the problem, do you? He could be mad, giving up his payment from you in return for a favor from me."

"Or he could just be smart enough to know you're his best chance at getting to the forbidden flower."

"You are impossible."

"Think about it. You're the closest thing to a sister she has. You're the best card he has to win this hand."

Lenore said nothing. She was tired of this conversation for so many reasons. Rook leaned into her side, but she still didn't respond.

"Don't worry so much. I know Dmitri well enough to know he's not mad. He's a good man; he won't hurt Camilla."

"You know all your contacts so well?"

"I know them well enough to know how far they can be trusted, and I trust Dmitri as far as the Halls of Justice."

# 15
# MATCHMAKING

Lenore's opportunity came a few days later with a letter. Lenore came down the stairs just as Camilla was bidding the messenger goodbye. She watched as Camilla opened the note in her hand and snorted derisively.

"Not another one," she said, flipping her hair back in a very unladylike manner.

"What is it?" Lenore asked.

"Oh, just another pathetic invitation from Fifth Sawyer. He wants me to dine out with him tomorrow."

Lenore smiled, calculating the tone of her voice to insinuate that to do so would be naughty.

"That's very exciting."

"No, it's tiresome. It's the fourth time he's asked."

Lenore fixed her face to look surprised and followed Camilla into the parlor.

"Really? And you've denied him?"

"Of course I have. He's an *Enforcer*."

Camilla handled the word like she would a parasitic intestinal worm.

"True…" Lenore pretended to think and then added, "but

he is your father's man, plus he's handsome."

"You've clearly lost your senses, Lenore. Why would that make him any more attractive to me?"

"If he weren't handsome…" Lenore teased. Camilla was sweet, but so easily played when she was in a foul mood—a rare occurrence indeed.

"You know what I mean."

"How would your father feel if you courted one of his men? How would it affect Fifth Sawyer's work?"

Camilla sat down on the sofa and thought. Lenore sat at the other end.

"I hadn't thought about it that way before," Camilla said. "I don't know how my father would feel. He might love it. Then again, it might make him furious. We've never spoken about what he intends for me in the way of marriage before. He's always left that to Mina. I'd have to ask her of course."

Lenore swallowed hard. She hadn't thought about that. She had to recover.

"Well, like I said, this could be advantageous. Men are so weak when it comes to a pretty face. Oh, stop it. You're radiant *before* you're ready in the morning, not to mention after. Perhaps we could get information from him… or simply sabotage his illustrious career."

Camilla giggled and placed a hand on Lenore's.

"Lenore, dear, your mind works in such devious ways." She turned serious then and said, "But we must be so careful. Enforcers cannot be trusted, and I have no mind to become a spy. This idea has potential, but risks to match."

"Very true," Lenore said. "Perhaps we should just focus for now on how angry your father would be over the match."

She then smiled again, and Camilla followed.

Mina wasn't in love with the idea. She strictly forbade Camilla from trying to extract information of any kind from Fifth Sawyer, saying it was too dangerous, and also expressed her disapproval at vexing Fourth Hawkins. Fifth Sawyer was clearly earnest in his desire to spend an evening with Camilla, however, and Mina didn't like the idea of the continued attention on her house.

"I think it would be wise, my dear, if you agreed to see him," Mina said, "but under no circumstances should you encourage him or lead him on in any way. You know I don't believe in all of those silly games women play with men anyway, and to play with an Enforcer is just foolish."

"You mean to say you didn't play those games?" Lenore asked, truly curious.

"Oh no," Neal answered for her. "She only went out with me the first time because she was tired of me chasing her. She told me so herself. She also told me she didn't want to see me in the first place because I was silly and frivolous."

Lenore was honestly taken aback and asked, "So how did you win her heart?"

"Determination, my dear girl! The determination of a man madly in love."

"Humor," Mina added, looking at her husband with big, soft eyes. "He made me laugh in a way no one else could."

So it was decided that Camilla would accept Dmitri's invitation to appease him, but would make no move towards him. A letter was sent back and another returned quickly, this one addressed to Mina and Neal asking for a meeting at their home. Mina sent a terse reply, reinforcing that she didn't want Dmitri getting any wrong ideas. A few days later, Dmitri came to the Allen residence and asked Mina and Neal for their permission to take Camilla out.

It was a tenuous conversation at best. Mina and Neal, not

knowing that Dmitri was a mole, were very careful about not offending the young Enforcer, but also very concerned about the idea of Camilla going out with him. Dmitri won them over in the end, however, with—relative—candor and sincerity. It was decided that he would take Camilla out the following night to dinner and a show at the local playhouse.

Lenore only learned all of this after the conversation had taken place, as she was not a part of this meeting. Besides the fact that it would have been considered improper, she had no desire to sit in the same room as Dmitri and pretend not to know him. She wasn't sure she could pull off a deception like that with her adopted family. True, she could have simply feigned hatred for the Enforcer simply because it wouldn't have been feigned, but the point was moot anyway, so it didn't matter.

During the time leading up to the night out, Mina seemed to have lost much of her even rationality and became positively overbearing. She peppered Camilla with advice at every turn about what to say, how to act, what to wear, and anything else she could think of. Mina was clearly concerned about her beloved niece, but even the sweet Camilla's patience was tested under these conditions. It was yet another time where Camilla decided to confide in Lenore, who didn't have the first clue as to what to tell her.

"I understand her concern," Camilla said, as Lenore pitifully tried to help Camilla get ready for her outing.

The reality was that Camilla was more than capable of getting herself ready, but having Lenore there to "help" was a good pretense for excluding Mina, who had wanted to be heavily involved with the pre-dinner preparations. Mina had smiled knowingly when Camilla had said she preferred Lenore's company, but it was clear she was still deeply disappointed. Lenore was pretty much only good for holding extra tresses of Camilla's flaxen hair while she wove the rest of her locks into a complicated style.

"I mean, I'm going out with an *Enforcer* for goodness' sake, but I'm a smart girl. I know what I'm doing."

Lenore simply nodded and made a noise of acknowledgement.

"Do you know he calls Mina by her proper title?" Camilla continued. "I wonder if he actually respects her—goodness knows his supervisor has never been able to do that—or if he's just doing it to butter her up."

"I didn't realize he did that."

"I wonder what he thinks of my chosen career path. You know he has to have thought about us as a married couple already."

"It wouldn't surprise me."

Lenore was trying to remain neutral, but Camilla was making that very difficult with her incessant chatter. She had held up her end of the bargain by getting Camilla to agree to see him, but she didn't want to risk fouling that up by putting Camilla off Dmitri again before their date. Then again, she didn't want to push her housemate into his arms either. What kind of friend would she be then?

Camilla looked spectacular without even trying on any day of the week, but she looked positively ethereal when she was finally ready to leave.

"I thought you weren't trying to give him any wrong ideas," Lenore couldn't help but say as Camilla stood in front of the full-length mirror, inspecting her reflection for any flaws. "He might not be able to resist proposing as soon as he sees you."

"Oh, Lenore, you are too kind," Camilla said humbly, but Lenore was still genuinely concerned.

Her concerns only increased as she descended the steps

with Camilla. Dmitri had already arrived and was waiting in the reception hall for her. His eyes widened when he saw her, descending like an angel from heaven in a flowing peaches and cream colored dress.

"You look beautiful," he said after taking a moment to catch his breath and bowing.

"Thank you," Camilla said demurely, accepting the kiss that Dmitri gently planted on her hand with complete grace.

"And you must be her lovely cousin Lenore," Dmitri said. "I don't believe we had an opportunity to meet properly at Camilla's debut."

He was so convincing and genuine that the hairs on the back of Lenore's neck stood up. A well-practiced liar was all she saw. That, and the source of a deep, inexplicable hatred. Lenore was an excellent liar as well, however, and didn't bat an eyelash as he also bowed to her and kissed her extended hand. She did have to force herself to curtsey as low as his station demanded, but she did so smoothly enough to be convincing. Any hesitation that Mina, Neal, or Camilla saw could be easily attributed to the fact that she was a fugitive in disguise and simply nervous about being so close to an Enforcer.

"It's a pleasure to meet you, Fifth Sawyer," she cooed.

"Dmitri, if you please. We're all friends here."

Lenore felt her body tense. That's right, she hated him because he was a self-righteous prat, and she hated herself for encouraging Camilla as she had. She couldn't respond, but simply smiled wider and nodded demurely. Mina and Neal bid Camilla good night with tender embraces and kisses on her forehead, but nothing more. After Camilla was gone, Mina wiped tears from her eyes and let out a breath that seemed as if it had been held for years.

"My baby girl is heading out with a potential husband," she said wistfully.

"Let's hope not," Lenore blurted before she could stop herself.

Mina laughed in the way people in shock did when some small sign of relief finally comes and said, "Oh dear, we can only hope."

Dinner was a quiet event that night, and Mina was still consumed with worry. Neal was trying to be comforting, but it was only helping so much.

"She's a smart girl," Lenore said after a while. "She takes after you so much, how could she not be? Camilla won't lose her good sense to a silly boy... no offense, Neal."

"None taken, my girl, none taken," Neal replied, looking affectionately at his wife, pleased with Lenore's words.

Mina too looked like she was taking comfort from what Lenore had said, but they all knew nothing would really make her stop worrying completely.

Lenore was anxiously trying to read by dim petrolsene light in the library, but wasn't having much luck. She couldn't help but think she had made a huge mistake. True, she really hadn't had much of a choice when it came to Dmitri's request... well, maybe he had, but what was she going to do? Endanger her newfound family? Let Rook burn beneath his debt to Dmitri? She didn't know how that worked. After all, she didn't know what the initial agreement had been or how it had changed or how oaths and debts worked in the first place, but now she was thinking about all the ways she should maybe discourage Camilla. Lenore had done her job, hadn't she? Despite her comforting words to Mina, Lenore wasn't completely sure Camilla wouldn't be swayed by Dmitri's charms. She couldn't help but think of her housemate as at least a little fluff-headed, despite all the evidence to the contrary. She also didn't trust Rook's judgment of Dmitri. What did he know of or care what was good for Camilla? Yes, she thought that perhaps she would say something to poison Camilla against Dmitri. The chance of her falling for his false kindness and faked sincerity was too great.

"Trouble sleeping?" came a voice out of the silence.

Lenore jumped and tensed her muscles in preparation to run when she saw who it was. Rook was sitting languidly on the couch. She had been so involved with her own thoughts that she hadn't even heard him come in. All that nervous energy that had prepared her to flee then released itself by striking him in the arm.

"Why do you keep sneaking up on me?!" she hissed.

She tried to hit him again, but Rook caught her arm in a grip that was strong enough to stop her but just gentle enough not to hurt her. It had been a reaction. Rook was as streetwise as they came, and those that survived on the streets were not the kind to suffer any kind of abuse from others, vow to protect Lenore or no. The speed with which he had been able to catch her and the carefully restrained strength she felt in his hands unnerved Lenore, and she stared at him for a moment, worried that he might actually hurt her. Rook looked back at her for a few moments, studying her. He seemed to read her thoughts simply by looking at her face, and he gently transferred her arm into his other hand, stroking it gently where he had caught it so swiftly. His caresses seemed to be a kind of apology, but he also didn't seem keen on letting her go now that he had her. Lenore cleared her throat and carefully took her arm back, feeling afraid of Rook again for the first time in a while. Somehow, she knew he was sorry but wouldn't say it.

"You shouldn't be here," she whispered. "Mina's probably still up. I don't think she'll be able to sleep while Camilla's out."

"That's actually why I came," Rook whispered, scooching closer to Lenore on the sofa.

He placed a hand on her arm again and traced his fingers back and forth across her skin. Lenore suspected that he was still trying to apologize, but was also just trying to take advantage of the moment.

"How do you think it's going?" he added.

Lenore thought about lying, knowing how invested Rook might be in the match. Who knew if Dmitri had demanded anything of Rook in addition to his payment from Lenore? She was honestly too concerned about Camilla to maintain a deception, though, so she decided against it.

"I hope he's falling on his face."

"Such venom, little bird," Rook said with what sounded like true sincerity and care. "Why do you wish them such ill?"

"I don't wish *them* ill, I wish *him* ill. Camilla can do so much better. She could have any suitor, preferably one who doesn't arrest people and send them off to torture and madness, one who actually cares for human life and happiness."

Rook's eyes searched Lenore's face in that uncanny way he so often did, as if he could read her thoughts if he just looked hard enough. She flinched when he touched her cheek with a gentle hand. He paused as he would with a wild, injured animal, and then reached out again even more softly.

"Where is this coming from?" he asked, stroking her face. "Dmitri's a good man. He's trying to make our world better at the risk of his own life."

"He's an Enforcer," Lenore whispered. "How good can he really be?"

Rook's gaze made her uncomfortable, as did his touch, so she shrugged him off and looked away. There was so much said in that gaze of his, so much he knew, so much he wanted. For once, Lenore knew what he was thinking. He was wondering how she could hate Dmitri so much when he had spared her parents so much agony. It was a great kindness indeed, but, as much as her head knew this, her heart just wouldn't accept it. Her heart still grieved for them. If it hadn't been for Dmitri's infernal order, her parents never would have been ripped from her. It never would have been necessary to put them out of their misery in the first place. Blazes, she hated them, all of the Enforcers! But Dmitri was the only one she actually knew, and so all of her bitterness and contempt was focused on him and him alone at a pinpoint, focused torch level of intensity.

It was clear that Rook was fighting the urge to reach out for her, to comfort her, but Lenore wouldn't have any of it. She didn't want to be comforted. The cold fire in her heart kept her from breaking down like the sopping milquetoast she never wanted to be. Instead, the two sat there in silence, Lenore refusing to look at Rook and thinking of the best thing to say to Camilla and Rook looking at her as if keeping his eyes on her would somehow prevent her from drifting too far from him.

When Lenore heard the front door open, she was on her feet in a second, Rook right behind her. Unfortunately, she heard the sound of slippered feet *shushing* down the hall at that same moment.

"It's Mina!" Lenore hissed, turning towards Rook. "You have to leave!"

"I suppose I should," Rook whispered with that maddening smirk.

Then, before she knew what was happening, he was leaning down, brushing his lips against her cheek, and whispering in her ear.

"Don't let it consume you, little bird. You are too good and too precious to be eaten up by malice."

And with that he left with as much swiftness and grace as a

spirit through the library windows and out into the night. Something in Lenore's mind was urging her to think on what just happened, but Camilla's return was too pressing, and she turned on her heel and rushed out of the room. She had lost time dealing with Rook. Mina was already downstairs with Camilla. Lenore could hear Mina asking her questions, and it sounded like Camilla was trying to put her off.

"I'm so tired, Mina. Can we please talk in the morning?" Camilla was saying sweetly.

Lenore wasn't quite down the steps when she suddenly, inexplicably, decided that she didn't want to be found staying up for Camilla. With feet as soft as a cat's, she dashed back up the steps and into her room, leaving her door open an inch or two, and flew under her covers. A few minutes later, she heard the sound of two sets of feet approaching, passing by, and then walking away.

Lenore waited, not quite knowing what she was waiting for. Perhaps she would sneak into Camilla's room after Mina was gone and try talking to her then. She wasn't really sure what she was doing, but she just didn't want Mina getting a chance to talk to Camilla before she did. Who knew what Mina would say? She might send Camilla running into Dmitri's arms with her relentless nagging... or something. Fine, she might be blowing things slightly out of proportion, but she was now so consumed with the idea that she had to reverse what she had set into motion. Then it hit her. She was trying to protect Camilla just as any true sister would. Lenore was trying to figure out just how this had happened when her door opened and Camilla's head poked in.

"Lenore, are you still awake?" she whispered.

Lenore nodded silently, and Camilla slipped in, closing the door behind her carefully. She then trotted over and climbed into bed with Lenore. Bitsy, who had been sleeping on the pillow, glared at the two balefully for disturbing him and moved to higher, less squashy ground.

"I'm sorry for disturbing you," Camilla said, "but I want to talk to someone, just not... not Mina. Does that make me a horrible person? You know I love her dearly. She's basically a second mother after all, but... it's not the same as talking to someone my own age. Her perspective is different, and, well, it's not really what I want to hear right now. Am I an awful daughter?"

"Of course not," Lenore said sincerely.

She was ecstatic Camilla had shaken Mina off and come to her. Now was her chance, but, more than that, she cared for her housemate and was genuinely concerned for her feelings. Lenore smiled to herself, thinking back to a time not so long ago that she had trouble being in the same room as Camilla.

"How did it go?" she asked simply, taking Camilla's hand.

Camilla then began a lengthy tale of how Dmitri had been the epitome of gentlemanliness. There were pink azaleas, her favorite flower, on the table, and dinner was delicious, but dessert was a special assortment of candied dates with various accompaniments of cream, fruits, syrup, and more. They then walked in the dying sunlight through the gardens before heading to the playhouse. The show was a whimsical tale of lovers and people who fought against becoming lovers and trickery and separation and, of course, a happy ending for all, save for the dour villain. Dmitri had been so sweet and complimentary and kind all night, and Fourth Hawkins had even objected to their outing. He hadn't forbidden it, however, presumably because there was clearly no better match for Camilla than a member of their order.

Lenore's heart sank with every detail. This was just what she was afraid of, and she had helped it to happen. She had been the one to tell Dmitri what Camilla's favorite things were, that she enjoyed funny, romantic stories, and her penchant for gardens. She felt ill, but kept her face steady. Finally, when Camilla was done, she asked Lenore a terrible question.

"What do you think? Should I agree to see him again? I would very much like to, but I don't want to rush into anything, and I trust you to be objective."

Lenore swallowed hard and thought fast. She couldn't attack Dmitri's character, not after the night he had given Camilla. She had to try and sway Camilla's rational side... assuming it hadn't fled before the surge of endorphins that was clearly flowing through Camilla now.

"It sounds so magical," Lenore said, trying to balance dreaminess and practicality, a tricky mix indeed, "but aren't you a little concerned? I just want you to be careful. After all, he is an Enforcer."

Camilla's eyes narrowed at Lenore, and she pulled her hands away.

"Ugh, you sound like Mina," she said petulantly.

"True or false," Lenore said shrewdly.

"True, but he's not like other Enforcers," Camilla insisted.

"How so?"

"He's... he's sweet. Have you ever met a sweet Enforcer before?"

"I haven't met too many in general. They're not very sociable, you know."

"Trust me, he's far better than most, and I've met a few."

"Will courting him pose a danger to the rest of us?"

Lenore stared Camilla down on this one. She hated to pull out such a trump card, but it needed to be done.

"No! I'm not stupid, Lenore," Camilla hissed. "Mina and Neal are too careful."

"Yes, but are you?"

"Very! I thought you of all people would understand.

Surely you're thinking about the future."

Blazes, this was *not* a conversation she wanted to get into right now!

"I'm very excited for you, Camilla," Lenore said, trying to switch gears and salvage any chance she had of breaking Camilla and Dmitri up. "I'm so pleased you've found someone that makes you so happy. I just want you to be careful… for all of us."

"I can understand why you're afraid, Lenore," Camilla said officiously.

"Yes, Camilla, I'm afraid," Lenore snapped suddenly, "but not just for myself, for Mina and Neal and you, too. You know just how terrible the consequences could be if this relationship went south."

Camilla stared hard at Lenore for a few moments silently, hurt, guilt, fear, anger, and disappointment all distorting her elegant features into little crimps and corners and sharp angles. Without a word, she got up and left Lenore's room. After she was gone, Lenore groaned and leaned forward, burying her face in her duvet. She had failed and, more than that, she was pretty sure she had convinced Camilla that she was her enemy. And to whom would Camilla go for comfort? Her new beau. Mina and Neal would repeat what Lenore had said, so there was no one else for Camilla to turn to. Lenore hadn't been wrong in anything she had said, but being right wasn't helping her any at the moment either.

She felt a familiar hand on her shoulder and instantly knew it was Rook. She wasn't surprised. He sort of seemed to come and go as he pleased. He had to have been there the whole time, and Lenore knew there wasn't much she could do about it, just as she hadn't been able to do anything about her predicament with Camilla. Therefore, she resigned herself to Rook's presence and sat up, looking at him expectantly. Maybe he would finish whatever business he had with her quickly and leave, but she doubted it. Still, a girl could hope.

"That was a valiant effort on your part," he said, placing a finger under her chin playfully.

Lenore just narrowed her eyes at him and let out a huff.

"I told you, Dmitri can be trusted," Rook added.

"I don't believe you," Lenore said, letting her head drop in defeat.

She didn't object when Rook wrapped his arms around her and held her close. Being a thief, Lenore knew Rook understood her mistrust. She could feel it in the way he held onto her. It was a knowing embrace, even if they didn't agree. Rook sat down on the bed with Lenore, but she gently pushed him back off. She may be freer with Rook than her new station deemed appropriate, but she wasn't so foolish as to allow him onto her bed with her. That just invited too much temptation, and Rook was not someone she wanted to tempt. He smiled at her admiringly when she enforced these boundaries, and stood like a gentleman to see if she would join him elsewhere. Lenore slid down to the floor and sat there, pulling a blanket down with her to ward off the chill of the floorboards.

"She's being foolish, even if you do think he's trustworthy," Lenore said finally.

"Maybe," Rook said, sliding over so that he was pressed against her side.

As she spoke, Lenore leaned sideways into him. After a moment's hesitation, she began to open her heart to him only because she knew he would understand in a way no one else could. She confided to Rook how she felt about Dmitri, why she hated him so much, and why she feared for Camilla. Lenore vented all of her fears about what could happen to the entire family if Camilla continued this relationship and how utterly selfish an idea it was. She told him how much she regretted her part in it all, though she felt it was necessary to let Rook know that she didn't regret helping him. Most of all, she shared how this whole thing had resurrected all of her fears of being revealed. After all, Dmitri knew her secret. What was keeping him from turning on them all?

"I know him," Rook assured her softly. "That won't happen."

Lenore said nothing and just pulled the blanket closer around her. She had to admit, confiding in Rook had helped to quell the tumultuous feelings that had been churning inside her for the last several hours and had even dampened the cold, bitter fire in her heart without breaking her. He had sat and listened patiently the entire time.

"I will protect you to the ends of the earth," Rook said, his voice low and serious now. "If anyone betrays you, I will know and will have their life before they can even get near you."

Lenore looked at Rook. She was so tired and defeated and frightened, but she felt better looking at him. There was a determination in him that told her he was telling the truth, and she believed his vow would allow him to do everything he said. For the first time, she saw him as an ally, maybe even a potential friend, but she couldn't be sure about that yet. He was still unpredictable and dangerous and secretive, but she believed he had her best interests in mind. She was just concerned about what exactly he thought was best for her.

Rook leaned forward and let his forehead rest on hers. Lenore took a deep breath and closed her eyes, confident that Rook was not a danger to her in that moment. This idea was reinforced by the fact that, even though she didn't remember falling asleep, she awoke the next morning carefully tucked into her bed. Lenore got up and quickly got ready that morning, feeling anxious about seeing Camilla after their quarrel from the night before, but she somehow also felt like she couldn't just let it lie. Every moment Camilla had to stew was one step closer to Dmitri in Lenore's mind. She trotted down the stairs but slowed when she heard raised voices from the dining room.

It was Camilla and Mina. Lenore could hear most of what was being said, but it seemed unreal because Mina was simply playing Lenore's part from the night before. Her arguments were Mina's arguments, her tone was Mina's tone, and Camilla's words were the same as before. This time, however, Camilla was really and properly upset. Last night she had merely been angry and hurt. This time, Lenore could hear Camilla's sobs through her angry, irrational words. It was so strange. She had only ever seen Camilla in such a state when Fourth Hawkins had come to interrogate Mina about the night Dmitri had been wounded. How on earth could Camilla be so upset over one night? Lenore shivered to think how convincing Dmitri must have been to have made Camilla's heart turn so completely towards him. And it was back, that same burning hatred that so often blazed up when Dmitri was involved.

Yes, Lenore was to blame for enough of it. She had been too forthcoming with information about Camilla, too exact in her answers to Dmitri's questions. Lenore guessed that Camilla's fluff-headedness had gotten the best of her and was convinced that she and Dmitri were fated to be together because he "knew" so much. Blazes, in her twitterpated eyes, Dmitri must seem a perfect match after all of that, and Lenore hated herself for this unintentional betrayal. Still, Dmitri was the real enemy, but nothing seemed capable of convincing Camilla of that.

Mina was pleading with Camilla to calm down, to think rationally, but Lenore knew it was impossible at this juncture. Her housemate was probably riding so high on her wave of emotions that nothing short of seeing Dmitri kill in cold blood would convince her of the truth. Camilla declared that she couldn't believe that everyone was being so unfair and stomped out, presumably to the garden. Lenore then carefully descended the rest of the way down the steps and crept into the dining room. Mina was sitting there at the table with her head in her hand, an untouched tea service set out in the center.

"If it makes you feel any better, I said the same things," Lenore offered. "Camilla wouldn't listen to me either."

Mina sighed and said, "Sadly, it does not, though I appreciate you trying." Lenore began to serve the tea, and Mina asked, "Did she come speak to you last night?"

"She did. It was after you saw her to bed."

Lenore didn't mind telling Mina this. For one thing, it seemed she had already guessed. For another, they were allies in this.

"Yes, I thought so. I suppose there's always been a pseudo mother and daughter line between us. We just didn't come upon it until now, however. I appreciate you trying to speak rationally with her, but matters of the heart are never rational."

Lenore merely nodded in agreement and sipped her tea.

"What are you most afraid of?" Lenore asked after a moment.

"The same thing every mother is afraid of: her child getting hurt."

Lenore nodded again, willing Mina not to ask her what she was most afraid of. Mina didn't, and Lenore had a feeling it was because she already knew. It was an endless list of precious, little things that terrified Lenore to think of. The two sat in companionable, if not uneasy, silence drinking their tea and thinking of Camilla. Neal appeared a short time later, as if he had been waiting for the tide of estrogen and emotions to go out before not-so-bravely striking out into the aftermath.

# 16

# TORTURE

This braggart was a real piece of work. Rook had begun watching Dempsey since Lenore had made her request. An attack on someone as well connected as he needed to be planned and executed carefully.

Dempsey lived alone in a flat in the Rose district of Springhaven. The place was decorated with as many awards, signs of privilege, and books as possible while still being tasteful... mostly. Rook suspected Dempsey had never even cracked most of the books he owned. Then again, he was more than a little biased. Rook sneered at the pictures Dempsey had displayed of himself—another show of wealth. Image-stills, which many people called momentos to be cute, were expensive and required the services of a specially trained technician to both capture the image and then develop it onto paper. The fact that Dempsey's flat was littered with momentos garishly screamed that he had oodles of money he obviously didn't know what to do with.

Dempsey was out late, as he often was. Rook had already learned the git spent most nights out drinking with friends. Thus, Rook was taking advantage of his absence. He was seriously considering a more direct route. It wouldn't be enough just to hurt him, though, as tempting as that idea was. Edgar and Twila hadn't deserved the horrors held within the Halls of Justice, but this Dempsey had reported Edgar anyway. He probably hadn't even given it a second thought. That in itself deserved a good beating.

Since beginning his investigations, Rook had also discovered if it hadn't been for Dempsey, he wouldn't be indebted to Edgar in the first place. Rook didn't know how to feel about that. He had always hated the idea of being beholden to anyone except himself. Then he had sworn his oath to Edgar, and it had changed him. The oath had changed the way he thought, the way he felt, at least when it came to Lenore. What if that night at the Cobalt Docks hadn't gone south? Would Edgar and Twila still be alive and well and free? Would Rook even know about Lenore? If he did, would he have fallen for her the way he had now? The oath bonded her to him in a way that went deeper than a typical relationship. She was his world now because of it. He knew when she was in danger. He was compelled to care for her, to protect her, but was it because of his debt that he loved her? That was the part he wasn't certain about.

Rook looked around the flat again. Much as he wanted to, he didn't think a direct, physical attack on Dempsey was the right move... at least not now. Rook wanted to meddle with Dempsey's head, steal his peace of mind and feeling of security. He would torture Dempsey, slowly, bit by bit. It was a longer play and would take more effort and planning, but the payoff would be worth it.

Rook left his first "gift" for Dempsey that evening. It was a note pinned to the ceiling, which Dempsey would see when he awoke the next morning. Written on the note in large letters were the words,

## *THE VICTIMS REMEMBER YOU*

Rook had thought about writing the message in red ink to imitate blood, but he thought that might be a bit too dramatic. Still, the idea of making Dempsey think a poltergeist of a former victim was haunting him was attractive. This and many more ideas for small acts of mental torture were forming in Rook's brain, and he smiled cruelly as he thought about his new, ongoing project.

Camilla and the rest of the family eventually made up, but her mind had not changed. She was still enamored with Dmitri and wanted to see him again. Mina and Neal agreed, but only because, as much as they hated to admit it, Camilla would more than likely continue the relationship whether they liked it or not. She was an obedient girl, but she was still subject to the hormones that currently raged inside of her. The Allens would rather unhappily agree to the courtship and keep that dialogue open rather than forbid it and give Camilla cause to keep secrets from them. The permission came with one main stipulation, however. Should Dmitri attempt to gather information from Camilla about any member of the family, she was to break it off immediately. Camilla readily agreed, insisting that she understood the gravity of the situation but also that Dmitri would never do such a thing. Lenore, who hated the decision, safeguards or not, had to admit that it was probably the best route available. She silently commended Mina and Neal on their rationality during such an emotionally trying time while simultaneously condemning Camilla for her stupidity and selfishness. Nevertheless, she played the part of the—somewhat

—supportive sister. She did this partially because Mina had asked her to in order to both actually be supportive and to listen for any important information that Camilla might reveal to a peer that she wouldn't to a parent. Lenore also did this because, well, as furious as she was with Camilla, she still cared for the foolish little twit very much and still desired to protect her.

Dmitri and Camilla's courtship was, thankfully, rather slow, as these things went. Despite her twitterpated state, Camilla was still determined to follow in Mina's footsteps and become a doctor. That meant that she still had several years of schooling after her entrance exams, all while still balancing a partial apprenticeship—a difficult task indeed. That brought deep relief to everyone else in the family, as that meant that it would be several years yet before the two started thinking about marriage.

Things were still tenuous at best between Dmitri and Lenore, though mostly because Lenore couldn't bring herself to be more than civil with him. He got on well enough with Mina and Neal, however, but there was always a disapproving undercurrent of tension, though no one actually mentioned it. The only good thing that the Allens—sans Camilla—thought might come from the match was that they might hear important Enforcer-related news from Dmitri. True, none of them would ever go so far as to outright ask for it—that was too big a risk—but there was always the hope that he might mention something, accidentally or otherwise, of note. No such luck, however, especially when a city gathering was called by the Enforcers.

Every able-bodied man, woman, and child was required to attend, though the aristocracy was allowed special seating, so Mina and Neal went off separately to sit with them. Those noble families that sided against the magi during the War of Light were given magisterial roles in Springhaven's parliament.

More seats to which one could be elected were later added. Neal's family was one of those that had a permanent seat, which he had accepted more out of obligation than interest. While Neal's family name was very old and well respected, only one seat had been awarded, unlike some other families who had been given multiple—the Pendragons held six. This meant that Neal's appointment was of less consequence than others, which resulted in only minor perks for him and his family.

The assembly took place in the city center, a large open space where the Copper, Sand, and Limestone districts converged. This space was usually used as an open-air market where any number of vendors could set up a small booth for a fee. On any given day, a vendor here stood to make anything between a killing and a significant loss. Lenore often enjoyed wandering through the market, especially at the turn of the seasons, to see what new and interesting things people had made and were selling. Today, however, a large stage had been erected over the gazing pool in the center of the square. This was to ensure everyone could clearly see and hear everything that happened during the gathering. Each level of society had its own section to stand in, though, despite what some said, no one section was any better than another. It was always an unpleasant affair from every angle. Lenore held Camilla's hand as her "cousin" led her through the crowd to their assigned area since Lenore had never been to one of these since beginning her new life. Once there, they stood patiently, waiting to see what the Enforcers had to say.

Gatherings such as this happened occasionally. There was the annual address made every summer, during which the Enforcers reminded everyone just how safe they were keeping the city, usually accompanied by the severe public beating of a known criminal. Lenore believed the Enforcers chose the height of summer for these events because they could usually rough up some disgruntled audience member for whinging about the heat, further exhibiting the "need" for their order. When an especially dangerous criminal was caught, the initial punishments were usually before the populace as well, so Lenore and Camilla both assumed this was one of those times.

As Lenore looked around the crowd, she wondered how on earth the Enforcers could ever hope to be sure that every citizen attended. She had heard that some Enforcers would walk the streets, idly looking into houses through windows or down alleyways for any stragglers, but she wasn't sure that was true. It was something she had wondered many times before, but now she had a real reason to be afraid. What if they were looking for her? Would they start with the middle-class section of the square? Then, failing that, would they move onto the other sections to continue their search? Lenore tried to tell herself that she was just making things up, that she didn't have any reason to think the Enforcers were looking for her in this crowd… except that she knew there was a search effort on her to some extent. She just didn't know how far that extent went. She also tried to remind herself that, even if they were using this time to search for her, she looked so different now, there was little chance an Enforcer would recognize her as matching the description that was out on her. She was suddenly thankful for the cosmetics she was wearing. True, they weren't going out to dinner or anything, but they were still going out in public and, abhorrent as the event might be, Mina had insisted that the girls dress appropriately for a public outing. Thinking on these things, Lenore's heart calmed slightly, and she was able to relax a bit as they waited.

Lenore and Camilla stood by one another and watched the platform for what would come next. A man walked up and came to stand in front of all the people. He was First Iago, the head of the Enforcers. Dressed in the blue and grey and gold livery of his station, he looked for all the world like a general on a campaign, which he apparently was at that moment.

"Good citizens," he called out to the crowd, "we have long vowed to serve and protect you from those that would hurt you, steal from you, and bring chaos to our fair city. Those evildoers have continued to strike out against us, however, and refuse to capitulate to justice and truth. It has gone on for far too long, and we have been too patient, too merciful. The time has come to remind them what awaits if they do not surrender themselves to the law."

First Iago then turned as a group of his Seconds dragged the first in a line of people up to the platform. There were eight of them in total. One was an older man, hunched under the weight of age, and there were two women with grey streaked hair. The other five were younger, the oldest in her mid-thirties perhaps and the youngest... the youngest looked to be the same age as Lenore or younger. They were all chained together, some crying and whimpering for mercy, others doing their best to stand straight and tall despite the weight of their thick, heavy bonds. Lenore was shocked at the size of the links. Each one had to be the size of a man's fist. She wondered how any of them were able to walk with such a burden. The old man certainly wasn't able to, and one of the younger men could be seen carrying his for him. Sweat rolled down his face as he grunted with the effort. One of the Seconds smacked him across the arms with his truncheon, and he crumpled but didn't fall. When he didn't drop his load, the Second hit him again, this time behind the knees. The man went down, and Lenore and Camilla fought to hold their gasps of horror within as they saw the old man get pulled backward by the weight of the falling chains. The old man landed hard on his back and cried out in pain. Lenore could feel the tremble of urgency within Camilla.

She was a caretaker, a healer. Every doctoring instinct in her was pushing her to help this poor man who had very likely just broken a hip or displaced something. She could feel Lenore's fingertips pressing hard into her arm, holding her back. Camilla swallowed an angry sob for the man and his comrades onstage.

"These are your neighbors," First Iago explained. "They are millers and bakers, tradesmen, mothers, laborers, and artisans. They all had a good life, families and friends, comfortable homes. Yet they all betrayed our trust and our city. Each of them, in their own way, supported the criminal underworld. They were discovered, arrested, and brought to our Halls of Justice to receive their deserved punishment. The criminals that remain free, however, cannot see these punishments and have therefore perhaps forgotten about them. We are here to remind them of what they will reap by sowing their anarchy."

What followed was enough to make Lenore and Camilla hold onto each other for support. Their knees threatened to give out on them as the poor men and women on the platform were tortured and beaten. Some begged, apologizing for their crimes or pleading their innocence. A few bucked the authority of the Enforcers and tried to speak out. These were beaten more brutally and gagged. It was by far the largest display either Lenore or Camilla had ever seen. Never had either seen more than one criminal publicly beaten at a city gathering. Even on the rare occasions someone turned themselves in, there was only one victim. Eight was beyond belief. There were angry murmurs throughout the crowd, gasps and cries of horror. Numerous people were ill. Lenore and Camilla were shocked that the Enforcers were able to keep order, but the horrific scene before them was enough to cow all members of the audience into acceptable behavior. Both girls could only think of their mothers—and Lenore her father—as the victims screamed and cursed and cried out for mercy. It went on for an hour before the Enforcers finally stopped. First Iago stepped before the crowd again and addressed them one last time.

"Remember, my friends, crime cannot be allowed under any circumstances. To do so is to open the door to more, but to fight back, to show it will not be tolerated, is the path to peace. This is but the first example that will be made. More will follow to remind them, to remind us all, of the consequences of lawlessness. We have been lenient for too long, but it stops today!"

The crowd was deadly silent as First Iago left the stage, followed by the Seconds and their prisoners. Only after they were gone did the crowd begin to disperse. There was no murmuring now, no whispers, no nothing. Lenore and Camilla left, holding onto one another and feeling sick.

Fourth Hawkins and Dmitri watched from atop a small stone wall as the crowd dispersed. They were on the lookout for anyone who matched the description of any of their cases' suspects. The likelihood of any of them coming out into broad daylight like this was low, but they had to try in case one of their targets did happen to show up.

"Brunette, two o'clock," Fourth Hawkins said, nodding towards the entrance to the Limestone quarter.

Dmitri followed his commanding officer's gaze and stared at the figure for a few moments.

"Too well fed," he decided quickly. "I could feel her ribs under my hands like the spokes on a wheel."

"What about the little waif there? 9 o' clock."

Dmitri looked again and immediately said, "She's practically a ginger."

"It was dark."

"Check my scores for nighttime observation, sir," Dmitri said respectfully, though there was a note of pride in his voice as well.

"Indeed," Fourth Hawkins replied, knowing his man was correct.

In truth, he didn't like cases like this. They weren't even sure the garden thief and Fifth Sawyer's suspect were the same person. It was like searching for the ghost of a needle in a haystack. These were not the cases that got you promoted. Only if they led to something bigger did they receive notice from up the ranks. Fourth Hawkins had a feeling this case would be a disappointing dead end, but the prospect of it yielding more kept bringing him back to it. Nevertheless, he decided to switch targets for now.

"What about the blond next to the posts there? Could that be our assault perpetrator?"

"Potentially," Dmitri said, studying the man Fourth Hawkins had indicated.

He fit the body type and basic description, so that was a start. The cheeky git was known for standing out in a public place before slithering off to a dark alley to lie in wait for his next victim. Every Enforcer preferred a case like this one. Whether it was out of cruelty or a deep sense of justice, it was easy to want to catch people like this new suspect. It made the Enforcers look good and proved why they were so necessary. The latter, in Fourth Hawkins' mind, was sorely needed after a day like today.

"How can they do this?" Camilla demanded over dinner. "It's… it's barbaric!"

Dinner that night was a simple salad, which seemed wise. Esther's choices always were. No one was really eating anyway, and it would have been a shame for something like a roast to go to waste.

"It cannot last," Mina said soberly. "They only hurt their cause by exhibiting such violence so publicly. There will be a high body count before the end, however."

Lenore was quiet. She knew what Camilla was thinking. She was thinking of her poor mother being subjected to that heinous treatment. Lenore, however, felt happy in a twisted kind of way. Her parents were dead, free of that torment. She felt the urge to retch, though, when she thought about what they had endured before their deaths.

"I wonder what spurred this new zeal," Neal said.

Lenore felt her face prickle with heat and knew. The Enforcers must be furious that two of their prisoners had died. They had to know it wasn't natural, but, judging by Dmitri's capabilities, they didn't have a clue as to how it had happened. Did they know it was an inside job? Perhaps it was because they hadn't yet caught Lenore. She hadn't a clue as to how many criminals evaded capture as she had. What if it was a rarity? Had her good fortune brought this wrath on those poor people today? She felt her face grow hot with guilt. She caught Neal looking at her and tried to give him a... what? Some kind of glance that didn't say *it's all my fault. I'm the reason for this brutality*. She didn't know if she was successful, but the moment was interrupted anyway.

"I am so sorry for what you two must be feeling," Mina said looking to the two young ladies there. "I know... I just can't stand to think of what's happening to Adelle... sweet Adelle..."

Mina's voice broke, and she covered her face with her hands. Neal wrapped his arms around her, and Camilla joined the embrace. Both Mina and Camilla cried openly for the woman they knew was wrongly imprisoned. Neal too even shed tears, though Lenore couldn't be sure if it was for his wife and niece's pain or for his sister-in-law or both. Lenore was sure she was going to be sick. It was because of Rook or Dmitri or her or all three of them that this was happening now. Blazes, why did the Enforcers have to be so bloody cruel? Lenore burned with her hatred towards them. Dinner was pretty much over at that point, and the evening closed sadly with Mina and Camilla both heading to bed early, leaving Neal and Lenore alone. Later that night, while the two drank chamomile tea together, he spoke to Lenore directly for the first time that evening.

"Copper for your thoughts?"

Lenore didn't look up from her cup. She could feel her face flush again. Guilt and gratitude were twisted together inside of her like a thorny, vicious bramble crowned with full, beautiful roses. She felt pressure to share. Could Neal tell she was hiding something? What about that look from earlier in the dining room? She had good relationships with everyone in the house, but, in some ways, she felt the closest to Neal. They shared a common passion, and she knew him better than Camilla and Mina simply because they spent so much time together. He had even learned to read her a bit, but how well? What would happen if she came clean? What if she didn't? More guilt filled her stomach. What if she didn't say anything now but it came out later? Lenore suddenly realized she was afraid of the consequences not just because she might lose her home and security, but because she might lose her friends. Well, she wasn't sure what Mina and Camilla would do, but surely Neal would understand, right?

"I... I think... I have a theory as to why the Enforcers are taking such vengeance on their captives. You remember when I met with Rook and found out that he planned to... to have my parents killed?"

Lenore pushed past the oppressive sickness she felt in her gut and began to reveal what she knew. Neal listened intently, keeping his face neutral. Unbeknownst to Lenore, he had seen her expression at dinner and strongly suspected she knew more than she was telling. He hadn't any idea how much that was, however. When she finished, Neal thought silently for a while about everything he had heard while Lenore waited fearfully. This silence terrified her more than she had expected it would. As she had spoken, the gravity of the situation became more and more apparent. She had snuck out in the middle of the night, put her life at risk, potentially put them all at risk, and she felt sick at the idea of Neal hating her. When he finally spoke, his tone was flat and serious.

"I think it's time we met this Rook. Get him here tomorrow night, and we'll deal with Dmitri after that. In the meantime, make yourself scarce. *I* will deal with Mina and Camilla. You will not speak of this to them unless they bring it up to you first. Is that understood?"

Lenore nodded earnestly.

"And, Lenore…"

Lenore sensed something terrible was coming judging by the lowered, cold tone of Neal's voice.

"…don't you ever hide something like this from us again. Ever!"

Lenore nodded again and whispered, "I'm sorry."

That admonishment from Neal was worse than anything Mina or Camilla could have said.

The air in the sitting room was thick with tension that night. Esther was gone for the evening, and Rook stood leaning against the wall next to the doorway looking suspicious and angry. Lenore knew he wanted to be as near to the exit as possible. He had appeared on the stairway a little while before, which meant he had come in through an upstairs entrance. Lenore knew it had more than likely been hers, but she kept that to herself. Camilla had shot Lenore a quick, burning glance when he appeared like this, and Lenore knew her housemate must have figured out that this was not the first time he had gotten in near all their bedrooms. Lenore had winced beneath Camilla's glare, holding Bitsy close to her for comfort, but she remained silent as she had been told. She had spent most of the day in her room to avoid Mina and Camilla. Earlier that morning, she had heard angry shouting from somewhere in the house, but couldn't make out the words or the speaker. Now they were all gathered together, and Lenore couldn't be sure what would happen to either her or Rook.

*Perhaps if they kick me out, Rook will help me find a new place to live,* came unbidden to Lenore's mind. Oh heavens, she selfishly hoped it wouldn't come to that.

"Now that we're all gathered here," Neal began, "Rook, perhaps you'd like to fill us in on just how mixed up you are in all of this."

"As I understand it, Lenore has told you quite a bit," Rook replied evasively.

"Yes, she has," Neal replied calmly, "but she has spent limited time with you, which does leave some gaping holes in the story."

"And how do I know you all won't take anything I say straight to the Enforcers? I don't fancy being on display as the next torture show."

"Yes, that is what's brought us all here, isn't it?" Mina said. The restraint in her voice was apparent, and Lenore's stomach turned guiltily at hearing it. The fact that Mina was so angry was a very bad sign. "One could say you're to blame for all of this. Just why did you feel the need to do something so reckless and tip them off?"

"I owed Edgar a debt. What did you expect me to do?" Rook snapped.

"Sacrifice yourself for the good of all," Camilla replied waspishly.

"Oh, stop," Rook sneered. "You know as well as I do that every poor soul in the Halls are subjected to that sort of treatment on a regular basis. They've just started bringing what was inside outside."

Camilla glared hard at Rook, but said nothing. He was right; everyone knew it.

"You needn't have involved Lenore," Mina said. "She's already in enough danger as it is. Part of your debt is to protect her after all, is it not?"

"Yes, and I believe knowing is a far better defense than not knowing."

"Yet you asked her to go to Dmitri and help him as well," Camilla said.

"Again, it was to pay a debt. You would have done just the same to save your own skin."

"I think we're getting off point," Neal said, seeing things beginning to get out of hand. "Let us remember that we don't actually know for certain why the Enforcers have begun this crusade. Hopefully, we'll learn more after we speak with Dmitri. Rook, like it or not, we're all in this together now. As you said, it's better to know than not know, so, if you would, please enlighten us as to how you came to be involved in all of this." Rook shot Neal a piercing glare, and Neal held up his hands in a peaceful gesture. "I swear to you, we have far more reason to avoid the Enforcers than go to them with any information about you. Your secrets are safe with us."

"I doubt that," Rook spat. "Camilla's father is a high-ranking Enforcer. You could go to him and make a deal to save yourselves in exchange for Lenore and me."

"We would *never* do that!" Mina snarled, standing up from her chair angrily. "Lenore is part of this family, so you can take your victim act and shove it up your—"

"Mina, please!" Neal interrupted sternly.

Rook smirked, but said nothing.

"Rook, you have my solemn vow Mina, Camilla, nor I will betray you," Neal said gravely. "By my blood and soul, you have my word."

Rook, Lenore, and Camilla looked to Neal in surprise. That was an oath-bond he had uttered. In the Old World, those words would have bound you by your promise, and the consequences were grave if you broke the vow. Mina was the only one who wasn't fazed by the statement. Finally, Rook sighed and spoke resignedly.

"I must be getting soft. I just hope I don't regret this. I met Edgar, Lenore's father, several years ago. I had heard through my network of a government defense engineer that was selling information on the side. He'd apparently been at it for years, along with his wife, Twila, but they kept their circle small. Smart. I approached Edgar… carefully… to inquire whether or not he wanted to do business. Edgar was sharp, though, and vetted me thoroughly before agreeing to my deal. His terms were… severe. He made me swear if he was ever caught I would make every effort to make contact with him and fulfill any request he made.

"I think he always knew that he planned to have himself killed should the worst happen. I know he always wished to spare Twila from it. He once told me that he hated that she was involved, but she refused to let him go it alone. I never thought anything of it, seeing as how the Halls of Justice are impenetrable and the Enforcers are *supposed* to be untouchable. That was my first debt to Edgar.

"The second came during one of our meetings. We were ambushed by Enforcers. I was shot in the leg by one of the very same handheld crossbows that Edgar had designed. We had been discovered. He got me out of there, but made me promise to always protect Lenore no matter what. He even brought me back to their house to patch me up and show me where they lived. That was when I started watching Lenore. I'm fairly certain Edgar knew what was coming, thus the reason for his request, because he and Twila were arrested not long after that. Had I been there when it happened, I would have taken her in then, but by the time I heard about it, she was gone. Where did you stay anyway?"

"The attic of my house," Lenore replied softly.

"Did you really? I never found you there. Very well done." Rook smiled at her. "Perhaps you were better than I give you credit for."

Neal cleared his throat, and Rook turned his attention back to him, but not before winking at Lenore. Lenore blushed hotly. It was one thing for Rook to flirt with her when it was just them, it was another in front of her adopted family.

"I checked into any potential loose ends, anyone who might have known more than I was comfortable with or would now be willing to make deals with the Enforcers. There weren't very many of either. Edgar was a careful man, but not careful enough in the end, I suppose. I've made friends with those I could. Those who would turn on their fellows… let's just say I took care of them. Don't look at me like that. Only the worst of the worst would even think about working with those—"

"Erm, there are ladies present," Neal cut in.

Rook smiled and said with a deferential nod, "My apologies, ladies. As I was saying, only the worst of the worst would even consider working with the Enforcers. I did those curs a favor. I was in a hurry and so made their deaths quick. Had it been anyone else—and believe me, anyone else would have been just as quick to deliver justice—they would have made it long and painful.

"Once that was taken care of, I began to look for Lenore. It took a long time before I even heard a whisper about her. You are nothing if not a very discreet thief. It was that fiasco in the gardens that tipped me off, but I lost her as soon as I'd found her. Over a month later, I heard that some little chit had saved an Enforcer from death. Lucky for you, no one knew who you were or got a very good look at you. Even after that, though, I couldn't pick up her trail. It wasn't until Dmitri came to me that I finally learned where Lenore was.

"Turns out, he heard everything Dr. Allen said in the infirmary. He had already decided, however, that he couldn't turn Lenore in. She had just saved his life after all. He told Fourth Hawkins that he passed out around the time of their arrival. After that, it wasn't long before he knew the truth. Dmitri's contacts go deep, possibly as deep as mine, and he does his homework. With access to Enforcer files on top of all that, he was able to put all the pieces together. He came to me knowing that I was looking for Lenore. Once we made that connection, I convinced Dmitri to get a message to Edgar. Little did I know he was biding his time. You see, he already had eyes for you, Miss Camilla. While I waited on Edgar's return message, I worked to get Lenore alone so that I could speak with her. That too took a long time, but at least I had a target to track this time. I still regret how I handled our first meeting."

"I'm sure you do," Lenore said, remembering how hard she had kneed Rook in the groin.

Rook groaned at the memory and continued. "I received a response from Edgar. As you know, his request was death for himself and Twila, for their sake and Lenore's. I was bound to fulfill his request. After that, Dmitri gave me the information about Camilla's debut so that I could sneak in. I like to hope I'll receive a proper invitation to Lenore's."

There was a long pause wherein Mina just glared at Rook.

Clearing his throat, he continued, "I believe you all know the rest. Lenore came to visit me that night, and our communication continued while Dmitri worked to deliver rest to the Crowleys before calling his debt. The assassinations are what have sent the Enforcers into a frenzy, or so he tells me. And now here we all are in your lovely home."

There was silence all around for several minutes as the information sank in. Finally Mina spoke soberly.

"It seems fate has seen fit to entangle us all together, so let me speak my mind. Camilla, dear, I don't know what you intend to do about Dmitri now, but tread carefully. He seems a good man, but he is also an Enforcer."

"If I may, Miss Camilla," Rook added, "while I don't know Dmitri very well, I know him well enough to say with confidence that he is not the kind to play with a woman's heart. He is sincere in his affections for you."

Camilla glared at Rook, but said nothing.

"Lenore, I believe you will know better than to keep secrets from us in the future," Mina continued. "We would have supported you, and you put yourself and all of us in danger. Rook was right about one thing: it is better to know than not know."

"I don't know about just one—" Rook began.

"Enough!" Mina snapped, cutting him off. "Rook, I don't like you, I don't trust you, and I especially don't like your attitude towards Lenore. I understand that you're bound to protect her, but I won't have you making inappropriate movements towards her."

*Blazes, do we have to discuss this now?* Lenore thought, feeling the blood hot in her cheeks.

"Seeing as how we are all in this together, however, we need to establish how this arrangement will work. I understand that Lenore already has a way to contact you?"

"She does," Rook replied.

"Good. And if you need to contact us?"

"To respect your wishes, how about I enter through the kitchen door?" Rook suggested.

"Perfect. Neal, dear, do you have anything to add?"

"What are our plans going forward?" Neal asked. "Is there anything we need to do to assure our continued safety?"

"Carry on as usual," Rook said, "and do nothing to attract undue attention."

"You should talk," Camilla said.

"We've already covered this, powderpuff," Rook said. "I just did what I had to, as did we all."

"Rook," Neal said warningly, "let us also establish the same rules of respect for *all* members of this household."

Rook met Neal's eyes and held his gaze, but said nothing.

"Very well, then," Neal said. "I think we've all said what we need to say. Rook, truly, thank you for coming and for the information. I trust you can see yourself out."

"Of course, sir," Rook said with a salute of his hands, suddenly jovial again. "Till next time, my good ladies. Do take care."

Lenore didn't watch him slip out. She was looking down, exhausted emotionally, physically, and mentally. After they were satisfied that Rook was gone, Mina turned to Camilla and spoke gently.

"Camilla, dear, what have you *not* said?"

Camilla's pretty, delicate face was still twisted in anger, and she turned her glare onto Lenore again. It looked as if she were trying to decide between several things until she finally threw up her hands in frustration.

"I don't know what to say to you. I really don't. You manipulated me! How could you?!"

"Camilla, I'm *so* sorry," Lenore began emphatically.

"I know you're *sorry*," she spat. "I'm very well aware of it, and I'm sure you're sincere. It changes nothing, however."

"What can I do?" Lenore pleaded.

"Nothing," Camilla replied, looking away. "No one can do anything. It just is."

Mina placed her hand on Camilla's, but said nothing. There was nothing to be said anymore. There was just anger and hurt and danger now, and they were all stuck together with it. Once again, Lenore found herself profoundly wishing she had never come to the Allens. That would at least have spared them all of this.

"That little... ugh! Neal, this is unacceptable!" Mina railed.

"I agree, but it is out of our hands," Neal replied less vehemently than his wife.

Neal and Mina often joked that they took turns being rational. Tonight was apparently Neal's turn, despite the fact that he dearly wanted to find Rook and tell him exactly what he thought. Rook very obviously had feelings for Lenore. Now, whether that was because of the oath or simply because she was a brilliant, talented, wonderful, and lovely young lady—Neal and Mina both thought it was likely a combination—was up for debate.

"I don't think he's going to hold up his end of our arrangement," Mina sneered.

"He might not, and Lenore might not tell us if he doesn't.

She didn't trust us not to react badly when she first went back to see him."

"That's another thing! Why wouldn't she trust us?! What reason have we given her not to trust us?"

"Have some compassion, my dear," Neal soothed. "She's in a unique situation. Her parents just died. She lived completely alone and only by her wits for over a year. Trust is likely hard to come by in her situation." The next words Neal said were even harder than the last to utter. "We just have to believe she'll be a good girl."

Neal had been furious when Lenore had revealed her interactions with Rook. She had risked all of them. He'd been so livid he actually considered making Lenore swear silence should the Enforcers ever catch her. That way, they'd have a safeguard against her foolishness. In the cold light of day, however, he'd seen the folly of that idea. Not only would it drive Lenore further from them, but it also didn't account for literally every person who had met Lenore in her new guise. No, that was the worst idea he could have possibly had. Neal spoke again as much as to convince himself as Mina.

"Remember when Camilla started seeing Dmitri? Do you remember how strongly we rejected the idea?"

"But Rook is a *criminal*!" Mina insisted. "Dmitri is…"

She trailed off, knowing the next words wouldn't help her case.

"A sadistic, torture-loving Enforcer. At least we thought he was, though now that's a bit less clear," Neal said. "My point is we had to trust Camilla then just as we have to trust Lenore now. She's a smart, strong girl."

Mina was loath to agree, but she knew what Neal said was true. Just like with Camilla, they risked pushing Lenore away if they reacted badly in this situation. As they fell asleep that night, though, Neal sighed heavily. Even though he had been sensible, it had exhausted him. He still worried about Lenore, about what Rook's oath to her father meant for their relationship. And there was nothing he could do about the bond that created between them.

# 17
# HOT PEPPERS

mitri was invited over two nights later. Camilla's note had betrayed nothing specific but carried an undertone of impending conflict.

*Dmitri,*

*I wish to speak with you on a matter of great importance to me. Please come to supper tomorrow.*

*Camilla*

When Dmitri arrived, Esther welcomed him in as warmly as she did everyone else, commenting on how handsome he looked and how she had wondered when she would be seeing him again. She'd made his favorite that night, roasted chicken.

Lenore, who was sitting in the parlor reading a book, had to suppress an eye roll. She felt the fact that Dmitri's favorite meal was chicken said volumes about him, heartily denying the idea that it had anything to do with him, his station, or the fact that he had once almost tried to arrest her. Dmitri was led through the parlor—where he bowed courteously to Lenore in greeting, who tipped her head ever so slightly in response—and into the dining room. Lenore got up a moment later and followed. Camilla had said she only wanted Lenore there, though Lenore could never guess why. Mina would be a far better ally in this situation, but Lenore agreed nonetheless. After all, she was beyond relieved when Camilla had made her request. Perhaps this meant she didn't entirely hate her. On top of that, the idea of seeing Camilla ream Dmitri gave Lenore a twisted sort of pleasure. All in all, things were actually looking up. She had asked Camilla about having Rook there, but Camilla hated the idea and rejected it immediately. Lenore knew it was because Camilla probably felt the same way towards the rogue as Lenore did towards the Enforcer. Ironic world they lived in.

Dmitri was standing at the table across from Camilla when Lenore crept in. Camilla was staring daggers at Dmitri, while the Enforcer was actually looking a little scared, but he waited for Camilla to speak.

"We met Rook," Camilla said matter-of-factly.

*That didn't take long,* Lenore thought. She rather liked the way Camilla cut to the chase.

"I know what you did for him," Camilla added.

"Yes," Dmitri said carefully, "we struck a bargain."

"And I was the payment?" Camilla said waspishly.

Lenore did her best not to smile as she saw Dmitri begin to squirm under Camilla's searing glare. It took a few moments for him to collect himself.

"Perhaps we should sit," he offered. "Clearly we have much to discuss."

"Very well," Camilla replied.

The two sat, but Lenore remained in her corner, mentally urging the other two to remain focused on each other. She did want to be there for her housemate, but she didn't want to get involved in their quarrel.

"Camilla," Dmitri began, "yes, I killed Lenore's parents for Rook."

Hearing it out loud rent a gash in Lenore's heart so suddenly that she couldn't stop herself from needing to grasp the sideboard for support. She thought she saw Camilla look her way for just a moment, but it was over too quickly to be sure.

"I knew what would happen," Dmitri continued. "I knew it would infuriate the order. First Iago hates surprises and likes to take out his frustration on the prisoners. Scuttlebutt around the Halls leads me to think they suspect foul play but have no evidence, just paranoia."

"So why on earth did you do it?" Camilla asked, her tone as cold and steady as ever. She really was a lot like Mina in some ways.

"Because Rook was bound by a debt. Because the Crowleys were suffering. Because it was the right thing to do."

Lenore narrowed her eyes at Dmitri, hating him. She dearly wanted to slap that moralizing look off his face. Camilla seemed to be considering his words carefully, however. After a long moment, she spoke soberly.

"We should eat. It would be a shame to waste Esther's cooking."

With that, she stood again and began to serve. Lenore pressed herself back against the wall, full of anger and spite. She wasn't sure whether or not she was supposed to stay now, nor was she sure she wanted to. She waited a few more minutes until it was pretty clear her presence was no longer needed. Camilla wasn't saying anything else, and Lenore sensed she was just waiting for her to leave, so she silently did so. Lenore knew Mina and Neal were dining in the conservatory, a room mostly reserved for Esther and her gardening, so she went there for lack of anywhere better to go.

After she was sure Lenore was gone, Camilla spoke again.

"Do you have any idea how you've affected our life?!" she hissed, not wishing to be overheard.

"Yes, Camilla, I—" Dmitri began before being cut off again.

"No! You don't!" Camilla snapped, pointing at Dmitri with her carving knife.

Dmitri eyed the knife carefully. He could defend himself, but Camilla knew exactly where she could stab him in order to end his life in a moment. She was obviously furious, and he cared about her, so he said nothing and waited for her to continue.

"You steered that ruffian towards Lenore! He admitted—without an ounce of remorse, mind you—to killing people. He's dangerous! And obviously besotted with her. We're lucky he hasn't done something truly terrible to worm his way into her life."

"I had to investigate Lenore to ensure she wasn't a danger to you," Dmitri explained evenly. "When I discovered that Rook was searching for her, or at least someone close enough to her description for me to take a chance, I had to go to him. If I'd been wrong, he would have killed me. I didn't know he would ask me to pass messages back and forth with Edgar or to kill him and Twila. I don't even know why it was so important, but it was a way to make things better. What the Enforcers do, it's awful and so unnecessary, so I agreed. I won't lie, I also saw an opportunity to get close to you and I took it."

"You could have tried a hello."

"I tried, but I don't think you remember."

"Oh? When was that?"

"At your debut. I asked Fourth Hawkins to bring me along for a case. In truth, I wanted to catch your eye. You were getting punch for yourself. I took my chance and walked over. I said hello. You turned, looked at me, and curtseyed. Then you walked away. You were perfectly respectful, but the disdain in your eyes as you looked at me made it evident that I was scum as far as you were concerned. And I don't blame you. My order has ruined your mother's life."

At the mention of her mother, Camilla saw an opportunity that had not yet presented itself in her short courtship with Dmitri. She pressed her advantage.

"And what do you know about my mother?" she said softly but coldly.

"Adelle Hawkins, imprisoned for stealing. Fourth Hawkins protects her, citing the need for delicacy due to a weak constitution. She gets better treatment than any of the other prisoners, but she is still occasionally abused when another officer can make an argument that she might have information about a different crime, usually theft and usually one of Fourth Hawkins' rivals. It's a constant battle, especially because she hasn't uttered a word in years. It was because of Fourth Hawkins' visits with her I first learned of you. He can see her expression change when he speaks of you, so he keeps her apprised of your progress. She's proud of you, Camilla. She's proud of your accomplishments and happy that Mina has raised you so well. I can tell because her eyes are expressive, just as yours are."

Camilla said nothing. She was barely holding her composure in check. This was not the time to break down, so she drew on her training as a doctor, and got back to the facts.

"You treated me as a prize. I'm not. You used Lenore to learn about me, to convince me that you were something special. Tell me why I should trust you. Give me one reason I should continue to see you."

Dmitri swallowed hard. He knew he didn't have much of a leg to stand on, and he didn't want to manipulate Camilla further. One, he hated to have done so in the first place and, two, because that would only make things worse at this point.

"Because we care for one another, Camilla. I know what I did was wrong. I knew it even as I did it. I'm sorry. Truly, I am."

Camilla did not respond. In her rationality, she recognized and appreciated Dmitri's honesty. He wasn't bargaining, bullying, or begging. He was in a position to do any one of the three, though, and that knowledge frightened Camilla. He may yet use what he knew against them. He wasn't wrong, though. Camilla cared for Dmitri deeply. A selfish part of her wanted him to give her a good reason to stay with him, and she was relieved when he said what he did. Given their current circumstances, staying with him seemed the wisest—not to mention the easiest on her heart—option. Camilla was wary of Dmitri turning on her now, but it was better this way now that she was no longer ignorant of the danger. She nodded and continued to carve the chicken.

Both Mina and Neal had no talent or interest in gardening, much less time for it, but Esther had used the conservatory to create an impressive edible garden replete with herbs, vegetables, and even a few strawberry plants in oddly shaped pots. The herbs were scattered artfully in containers of varying sizes all around the room, while the vegetables were in larger containers in a more orderly arrangement. It certainly wasn't a traditional use of such a room, but the Allens were hardly a traditional family.

Lenore sat down at the table without an invitation, not that she needed one. She said nothing of the meeting in the dining room, and no one asked. Instead, they chatted with Esther, who was tending her leafy charges. The old woman occasionally tutted Bitsy, who was eyeing the tomatoes and other vegetables greedily.

"You want something, eat this," Esther finally said after the fifth or sixth time of catching Bitsy before he could help himself to a snack.

Esther was proffering a small, green vegetable that Lenore didn't recognize. It was like a very large green bean, but fatter and shiny. Bitsy took the offering without hesitation and began to eat like he hadn't been fed his whole life. After a few moments, he stopped and began to chitter madly, dropping the vegetable and leaping like his tail was on fire. Esther suddenly began to cackle wickedly.

"That will teach you to steal my berries! I know it was you!"

Bitsy finally alighted to Lenore and began devouring her bread while Mina, Neal, and Lenore looked on in amazement.

"What on earth did you give him?" Mina asked, picking up the dropped bean.

"Oh, you don't want to try that, Mistress Mina," Esther said breathlessly, trying to calm herself and only being somewhat successful. "Those peppers pack a punch."

"Peppers?" Neal asked. "Peppers from the south?"

"Aye, Master Neal. Thyme came by some seeds and gave me a few to try out. I can't say they'll be making it into any of my dishes. Whoo! No, sir. I didn't realize just how hot they were until after I tried a bit for myself the other day. I'm just glad none of you fine people were there to see me. That's no way for a woman my age to act, not to mention speak."

Lenore was smiling now. Somehow, Esther could always cheer her up. Bitsy, however, was scowling at the old woman, looking for all the world like he was plotting revenge. He settled for perching on Lenore's shoulder instead as things returned to normal in the conservatory.

⚙

Rook slipped in through Dempsey's window as he had more times than he could be bothered to count now. He came round a few times a week, usually just to move some items around and reinforce the poltergeist idea. He didn't actually know or care if Dempsey thought he was being haunted. All that mattered was that the prat's sense of security disappeared, and signs had begun to show it was working. Rook had seen Dempsey question people and make reports to the Enforcers, but there was no evidence to prove anything, not even the note Rook had left that first night.

As soon as Dempsey had seen it the next morning, he went straight to the Enforcers. He had been furious that someone had dared enter his flat, his *personal property*, and done this. He'd left the room exactly as he'd found it so as to not contaminate the crime scene. Dempsey was a good scientist and knew the Enforcers were more likely to catch the culprit if the evidence remained undisturbed. There was no evidence to be found, however, when he returned with two Enforcers in tow. They'd opened an investigation but found nothing. After that, Rook never left anything that couldn't be removed from the room, and all traces of his visit were gone again by the time Dempsey returned with Enforcers, every single time. By now, Dempsey had been warned about "false reports", so he'd been left to his own devices. Rook noticed the window locks had been upgraded—nothing he and his good lock picks couldn't handle —and there was a patrol in the hallway. That had to cost Dempsey a pretty penny, not that it would do any good.

Rook felt a cold satisfaction in his chest as he thought of Dempsey convincing himself that he was going mad. It was the least he deserved. Tonight, Rook was going to give Dempsey another good scare. On the large mirror in the washroom, Rook wrote *REVENGE* in blood. Then he just had to wait and clean up when Dempsey left.

Camilla came to Lenore a few days later to hash out her feelings… sort of. The conversation began oddly.

"What do you see in Rook exactly?" Camilla asked.

The girls were sitting in the conservatory enjoying the dying sunlight. Camilla was poring over some medical textbooks of Mina's, while Lenore was sketching some ideas for her bird project. She'd had success in sorting through her data and had made a list of catalysts for flight that she wanted to try. Now she just had to figure out how to enact them without destroying her precious creation. The biggest issue was that of powering the thing. The bird was far too small for any kind of steam engine, so Copper had recommended a power pack.

Power packs were basically small, condensed power plants. They were very new technology, however, and very expensive. Lenore objected to the idea at first due to the cost and because she couldn't wrap her brain around how it worked. There were apparently chemicals in the pack that reacted together to create energy, but even as Copper explained it, Lenore still couldn't *see* how it all worked, and that frustrated her. What finally convinced her was the fact that the museum had a few power packs on hand already that they could use and that the packs could be refueled and reused.

That being the case, Lenore was trying to sketch out the best placement of the pack in the bird. It couldn't be placed somewhere that would unbalance the bird, but it had to be protected. Destroying a museum-issued power pack was the last thing she wanted.

It took Lenore a moment to pull her mind away from her work to focus on the question she had been asked. When she had, Lenore was very tempted to ask the same thing about Dmitri. As fragile as things were at the moment, however, she decided that wouldn't be wise.

"I'm not sure what you mean," Lenore replied. "You must know I don't plan on courting him or anything."

Camilla laughed at that, which both surprised and pleased Lenore. Camilla was not the type to laugh except when she was truly humored. She wasn't dark enough for any other type.

"Oh my goodness, no. I know that. I mean as an ally. What do you see in him?"

Now that was a really interesting question. She knew Camilla didn't trust Rook, so she was likely looking for some kind of assurance that he wasn't a threat to them. Lenore sincerely didn't think he was. He'd probably have nothing to do with the family if it were up to him. As he was bound to her, however, that changed things, and she thought about it for a moment before responding.

"I don't know. Having been a thief, I think we understand one another a bit. And the fact that he's a criminal means he's as likely to go to an Enforcer as I am. Him being bound to protect me helps too, since he can't do anything that would bring harm to me." Lenore also knew Rook's skill set would be an advantage if she ever was in danger, but she decided it was best not to mention that to Camilla.

"Do you believe oaths are really what the old stories say?" Camilla asked.

"I do. I think I've always suspected, but recent events have pretty much solidified that belief for me."

Camilla nodded thoughtfully and said, "Yes, I suppose that's true. Kieran certainly believes it, and if anyone knew for sure it would be a Vampyre. I suppose that means that Rook had no choice then… to kill your parents. I mean have them killed… I suppose."

Lenore nodded silently and swallowed hard. The knowledge of it all caused a dull, deep ache in her heart no matter what happened or how much time passed.

"I'm envious," Camilla said softly. "It just doesn't seem fair."

Camilla thought about her mother in the Halls of Justice as she said this. What Dmitri had told her had provided a small iota of relief in her heart, but it was overshadowed by the horrible weight of knowing her mother was no longer free, hadn't spoken in years for who knew what reason, and that she was subjected to torture when her father wasn't able to protect her. It made Camilla feel sick whenever she thought about it.

"None of it's fair. And, as… *good* as it was," Lenore said, almost choking on the word, "knowing that is still only a basic bandage on a much deeper wound." There was a pause before she added, "Dmitri was the one that poisoned them. Perhaps he could do the same for your mother."

"I have thought of that," Camilla said, her voice catching in her throat. Tears began to fall as she said, "I can't ask him, though. It would be too risky for him, for all of us. Think of it, another prisoner falls dead while on Dmitri's watch. Dmitri is courting me, the victim is my mother, and the Enforcers look to me and this family. They might discover you, which means Mina and Neal would likely be arrested for harboring you. It's just not an option."

Lenore moved over to the sofa where Camilla sat and took her housemate's hand in her own. Camilla laid her head on Lenore's shoulder, and the two shed a few tears together. Camilla had revealed the gist of what Dmitri had shared with the rest of her household, not that there was terribly much to tell. Because of that, Lenore knew Camilla's mother still lived and suffered. Lenore wouldn't talk about these things, though. She would simply sit here and comfort her friend as best she could.

After that, things returned mostly to normal for the two girls, though Lenore's heart was softer towards Camilla now. It had already softened significantly, especially considering where they had begun, but it was yet another step in making them as close to real sisters as possible.

Meanwhile, Rook remained in Lenore's life, despite the fact that she didn't see him for a while after that night with the entire Allen family. He occasionally left notes for her on her nightstand, which she knew flew in the face of Mina's request for him to enter through the kitchen. Well, he was a criminal, so that probably wasn't too surprising. Lenore had a feeling he just wanted to vex Mina as well, but she couldn't be sure of that. Rook's notes said nothing of importance—*I saw a little bird that reminded me of you today*; *I'm glad you're safe, but don't take that road at night again*; *How does Camilla stand that Jones girl? I thought you might trip her, the way she was prattling on*; and so on—which is why Lenore kept their existence a secret from the family. Showing the notes around would be like throwing petrolsene on a fire. They didn't cause any harm, and it wasn't worth the conflict. She also didn't despise Rook the way the rest of the family did. It felt good to have someone in her life who uniquely understood her position and her past. That didn't mean that she wasn't glad he was keeping his distance, however. Rook's presence was a risk.

"Sir, a visitor for you," a thickly muscled man said.

Rook looked up from his work. He looked to the man tied

to a chair there and then back to the muscled thug.

"Marlowe, who is it? I am in the middle of something," Rook said blandly.

"Ermine," Marlowe said simply.

"Was he followed?"

"None of the lookouts have reported anything."

Rook had people stationed all over the city, as well as runners on standby to deliver urgent messages to his base of operations in the Char district. He paid his people well, which garnered loyalty, and he made an excellent profit from running the underground market. He was careful to build in safeguards, such as nicknames for his contacts, and no one person knew too much. The man currently tied to the chair was one of his former employees who had tried to sell information to another crime syndicate in the city. Rook wasn't concerned, as the man was fairly low level. In truth, he wasn't even high up enough to know who Rook was. The man had worked for one of Rook's many other sub-level hirelings, but he still wanted to know what the man had shared.

"Very well. Let him in."

Marlowe nodded and left. While he was gone, Rook struck the man across the face again.

"Do not think this little interruption changes anything," Rook growled. "You can talk now or you can talk later. It's up to you."

The man groaned in pain and then spat on the ground.

"Suit yourself," Rook sighed.

He then pulled a knife from his belt and began to slice away one of the man's fingernails from the nail bed. The man screamed and struggled, but his bonds were too tight. They had already rubbed his wrists and ankles raw.

"Am I interrupting something?" came Dmitri's voice over the screams.

Rook shouted back, not looking away from his work, "You'll have to excuse this. I'm a busy man. What did you need?"

"I have news for you," Dmitri shouted. "It's of a sensitive nature."

"Good or bad?"

"Good."

Rook said nothing for a moment as he finished, peeling the fingernail from the man's finger and then throwing it into a bin. Rook then carefully removed the gloves he was wearing and placed them on a small table full of cruel looking implements.

"Sorry for my manners," he said, shaking hands with Dmitri. "It's good to see you."

"When I have good news, you mean," Dmitri said with a smirk.

"No, I think you might be growing on me," Rook joked. "Come, have a drink."

Rook then guided Dmitri to a table on the other side of the expansive room. There was a bar set up against the rough stone wall here, and their little corner was dimly lit by no more than a few sconces. Rook liked to keep this room dark. He liked the mood it set for both enemies and friends. It also meant he didn't have to work too hard to decorate this vast, dingy space. With what went on in the room most of the time, he didn't see the point. He saved the really good décor—dark wood paneling, porcelain tile floors, hand carved furniture, and a few ornamental pieces—for his office.

Rook asked Dmitri what he'd like to drink, and he laughed when Dmitri asked for scotch.

"You've been hanging out with your lady's father too much," Rook said.

Dmitri looked back to the man in the chair and asked, "Can he still hear us?"

"No. Also, I'm going to kill him later. Traitor, you see."

"Indeed," Dmitri said.

Dmitri understood Rook in a dark way. They both had jobs that demanded difficult and horrific things, but it was for the greater good. Dmitri knew Rook had to keep up a cruel image, but he wasn't convinced Rook didn't get at least a little enjoyment out of the punishments he doled out. He was pleased, however, that Rook was still careful with his words even when he was certain their conversation wouldn't leave the room.

"Sorry about not giving you a heads up on the ambush waiting for you a few weeks back," Rook said. "I was in hot water myself."

"No, no, I understand. I think it was better that way. Keeps me honest, you know?"

"I do. So what's this news you've got for me?"

"You'll be pleased to know we're closing up all accounts on your interest."

"*All* accounts?" Rook asked incredulously. "Every one? Pre and post decline?"

"Every. One."

"But why? That has to sting."

"Bigger fish. Resources don't need to be spent on minnows. Minnows don't bite, they just get eaten by bigger fish."

"Well, well. In that case, have another drink!"

Dmitri laughed. Rook was clearly pleased about this turn of events.

"Do I have you to thank for this?" Rook asked, beaming.

"I played a part, but I cannot claim all responsibility. Only one of them was a possible prizewinner to begin with, but it hasn't produced anything new as far as anyone has seen. Thus, not worth pursuing."

Rook raised his glass to Dmitri, and they toasted. Dmitri

stayed a while longer as the two discussed further details of that conversation and then progress on their other endeavors. Nothing big was in the works now, but every little strike, every little push helped. As Dmitri was leaving, he looked to Rook's prisoner in the chair and then back to Rook.

"You know, if you sprinkle a clotting agent on an open wound like that, they stay alert and live longer," he suggested.

Rook bumped the heel of his hand against his forehead in a dunce gesture.

"Why didn't I ever think of that? That's inspired, man! I'd much rather get it all over with as quickly as possible. Thank you!"

Dmitri smiled a little and nodded. That certainly made it seem like Rook didn't enjoy extracting information any more than Dmitri did. Bully for him. The man in the chair looked at Dmitri with wide, terrified eyes, and Dmitri left.

"You heard the man. What do you say? You can tell me what you told Price, or I can send someone out to find a clotting agent to make this last much, much longer. You've got another nineteen nails after all."

In the end, after far more blood and effort than Rook had expected, he got his information, but it didn't make him happy.

"I told him about Chrys," the man had revealed, gasping through tears and pain. Chrysalis, better known as Chrys, was the woman this one had reported to. "I also told him about your treasure."

"My treasure?" Rook asked. "What treasure are you talking about?"

"Not your money. Something else. I told him there was something else you valued more."

"And where did you hear this?" Rook growled. "Tell me now, or you'll lose the rest of your nose!"

"The girl, Fetch!"

Rook swore. He hated Fetch.

✿

The next time Lenore saw Rook, she wasn't expecting it in the least.

Lenore was alone in the house curled up on a sofa in the library reading a book when the sound of someone clearing their throat startled her. Lenore jumped at the intrusion, but her surprise changed to annoyance as soon as she saw who it was.

"Rook! What are you doing?" she snipped, looking back to her book. She didn't actually care what he was doing.

"Where is everyone?" Rook asked. "I have news."

"They're all out having dinner with Dmitri and his parents. Mina and Neal are vetting them."

"Ah, how exciting for her," Rook said flopping down on the couch with Lenore. "And what about you? Are they going to be vetting anyone for you any time soon?"

Lenore rolled her eyes at the exaggerated leer Rook was giving her.

"I have no plans for them to need to," she replied simply. "Why? You have a candidate in mind?"

"They could vet me," he laughed. "It'd save time."

"And just how would that work?" Lenore asked. "I come visit you in the middle of the night? You build a hideout in our cellar?"

"You could get some of those fantastic papers made up for me. With those, I could at least secure employment. I have considerable skills, you know."

Lenore wanted to quip back, but a deep growl stopped her. A tall, dark, pale figure was suddenly there lifting Rook up by his collar.

"What is *he* doing here?" Kieran roared.

"Put him down—gently! He's a friend!" Lenore commanded. "We trust him... for the most part."

Kieran half-dropped half-threw Rook back onto the couch, who moved protectively in front of Lenore. Oddly enough, the fact that Kieran was very clearly not human and that this fact wouldn't escape Rook was the least of Lenore's concerns. Like Lenore, Rook would never go to the Enforcers about him. Rather, Lenore was worried Kieran might kill Rook outright. She knew how protective the Vampyre was and, last he knew, Rook was a dangerous enemy.

"You know this... person?" Rook asked angrily.

"Blazes, yes," Lenore said. "Relax, both of you. Rook, this is Kieran. Kieran, Rook."

"What business do you have here?!" Kieran demanded.

"I was visiting the lady, if you must know," Rook snapped back.

"It sounded more like you were making a marriage proposal," Kieran growled.

"Is that what that was?!" Lenore asked, suddenly feeling very self-conscious.

"No," Rook sneered. "If I was proposing marriage, believe me, you'd know it. So Kieran is your, what? Guardian? Chaperone?"

"Funny you should ask," Lenore replied. "Kieran is a friend and has vowed to never harm me. Rook, you've vowed to always protect me. I've never felt safer."

Lenore smiled at that, as did Kieran. Rook did not. Lenore decided it was time to change the subject.

"Kieran, it's so good to see you. Please join us. We'll catch up later. Rook, you said you had news."

"I do," Rook replied, settling back onto the couch.

He placed a protective hand onto Lenore's ankle and glared at Kieran. Kieran glared right back, but said nothing.

"So?" Lenore said, wishing to move them out of this tense moment. "What's your news?"

Rook turned to Lenore and smiled that shameless smile of his.

"The Enforcers have given up their search for you," he said.

Lenore sat in shock for several moments before a realization dawned on her.

"Do you mean me, Lenore Crowley, or the other me, criminal-failure-and-sometimes-Enforcer-savior?"

Rook laughed heartily at that and replied, "Both. The search for the girl that saved the Enforcer tapered off a while back. I suppose they figured that anyone willing to save one of their own couldn't be too much of a threat. They've stopped searching for Lenore Crowley now because no new weapons have appeared on the streets."

"That's wonderful!" Lenore exclaimed, wrapping her arms around Rook's neck before she could stop herself.

She was just so ecstatic! She then got up and hugged Kieran, who lifted her off the floor without so much trouble as it would take to lift a kitten. She then hugged Rook again, somehow feeling that it was appropriate seeing as how he was the one who delivered the news. She suddenly felt free, like a bird released from its cage. Not that it really changed anything practically in her life, but knowing the cases on her had been closed was like a breath of fresh air.

"That is splendid news. Mina and Neal will be very glad to hear it," Kieran said.

"You should be the one to tell them," Lenore said to Rook. "Maybe it will improve their opinion of you."

Rook smiled at that and couldn't help but agree.

⚙

Mina and Neal really were elated, thanking Rook for the good news. Camilla was ecstatic for her housemate as well, though her reaction to Rook was less energetic. She was kind enough, however. That, coupled with Kieran's return, made for a very happy house indeed.

"With that out of the way, we can focus on the next item of business," Mina said clasping her hands together.

"What's that?" Lenore asked curiously.

"Your debut, of course," Mina replied. "We should have started preparations already."

Lenore groaned inwardly and slumped outwardly. Brilliant, just when she thought she could relax.

# 18
# THE FUN OF BEING INCONSEQUENTIAL

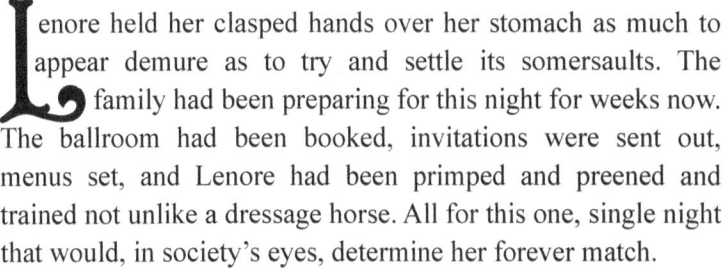

Lenore held her clasped hands over her stomach as much to appear demure as to try and settle its somersaults. The family had been preparing for this night for weeks now. The ballroom had been booked, invitations were sent out, menus set, and Lenore had been primped and preened and trained not unlike a dressage horse. All for this one, single night that would, in society's eyes, determine her forever match.

Meanwhile, in the background of all this production, two more torture shows, as Rook had called them, were held. Camilla's mother was, thankfully, not a victim, but that did little to quell the girl's emotional turmoil. It was during this time that Lenore was half tempted to talk to Dmitri herself about Adelle Hawkins. Surely he could do something to ease Camilla's pain! Lenore shook her head at herself at times like these. Things must be really bad if she was looking to Dmitri for solutions. Camilla was obviously going through something like Lenore had, though. Lenore had been doing her best to comfort Camilla, to let her know she wasn't alone, sharing her own feelings about losing her parents. Camilla was obviously grateful, and Lenore even thought she saw improvement in her housemate at times when she shared these things, but only time would really heal Camilla. And not even that would do the job completely.

She still couldn't understand how Mina and Neal expected her or Camilla to pull this off tonight, especially with everything that was happening. Oh, she knew why—to appear normal—but the *how* seemed to be entirely up to them. Well, Camilla seemed to be doing well. She was chatting away like nothing was wrong. Good old Camilla, proficient at everything, no matter what it was.

The room was full of eligible bachelors, some of whom had been at Camilla's debut because they were either a brother to a man of appropriate age for Camilla but not Lenore—what difference a few years made, Lenore would never know—or because they fell into the small overlap of being of acceptable age for either of the girls. And then, of course, there were the new young men that hadn't been at Camilla's debut at all. Lenore had not added up the numbers earlier, had not wanted to know, actually, and her heart quailed at the knowledge that there were more suitors than she had expected.

Blazes, what was she supposed to do?! Smile and laugh like everything was going to be fine? How would it ever be fine? She was a formerly-wanted criminal, and she'd have to lie about it. Forever. How could she put someone through that? Not even her father had done that to her mother. She felt unsteady, and put a hand on Mina's arm for support.

Mina looked down at her charge and saw not just the pleading look, but the pure, naked terror behind it. Mina was not so ignorant as to not realize the implications of what Lenore had to do, of what they all had to do. It was so much to ask of a young woman, and Mina smiled warmly at Lenore. She placed her free hand over Lenore's and leaned over, as if to share a juicy piece of gossip.

"I know, it's too much to expect you to bear this on your own, and you don't. We are all behind you. All you must do tonight is circle around and be friendly. One step at a time."

Lenore swallowed hard and did her best to put on a smile. It was mostly successful. If anyone asked, it could honestly be blamed on nerves. She saw Mina turn to Camilla, who was standing nearby with Dmitri, and make a small gesture with her head. From the outside, it could appear as if the gesture simply said, "Look at your sweet cousin, dear. Isn't she lovely?" What it really meant was, "Take care of Lenore. She's going to need us."

Camilla nodded with a radiant smile. "Of course, she's beautiful," really meant, "Don't worry. We'll be fine."

Lenore couldn't say how she could translate these movements. Perhaps it was because she knew the true story behind everything, but she was comforted by the reminder that the Allens were all standing with her. Camilla came forward and took Lenore's hands in hers.

"Come, let us go refresh ourselves and see who we bump into."

Camilla was wearing that perfect, exuberant smile, and Lenore easily fell into step with her housemate, smiling more sincerely now at Camilla's support, and agreed happily. If Camilla could be strong tonight, by the stars, Lenore would be, too! The first step of going out and greeting her suitors was the hardest. After all, how does one begin?

*Hello, yes, I'm expected to marry one of you. Tell me why it should be you.*

Hm, honest, yes, but probably not the most socially acceptable approach. Camilla's idea was perfect, though, because there were bound to be at least a few people there, and food was always a good conversation starter. It also allowed Camilla to tag along but in such a way that it was just two thirsty young ladies getting a drink, not Lenore sticking to her older cousin like a scared child. At the refreshment table, Camilla wandered a short distance away to examine the desserts, leaving Lenore with her favorite savories. There she struck up a conversation with a young man named Grayson who was an acquaintance of Mint and Ginger's. He was nice enough, and very complimentary of both Lenore and the party, but he didn't seem much interested in the debutante. She had a sneaky suspicion that one of the twins was more his type, and Lenore relaxed at that thought. Plenty of these young men were probably only here because society deemed it rude for them to decline. None of them were really interested in Lenore, a little nobody from a rural village far away. They all knew she was only here because of who her "cousins" were. Yes! This was all just for show! The thought lifted Lenore's spirits immensely, and her anxiety melted away. It was just another party, and she treated it as such going forward.

Now that she was free of all the nervousness that had plagued her early on, Lenore came out of her shell like a butterfly from a cocoon, which she somewhat resembled at the moment.

Lenore's dress was greenish-blue with pale yellow accents and had a formfitting cuirass bodice and a skirt of countless, gauzy layers, which flowed and floated around her like water and feathers. Her hair was done up with a multitude of gemmed pins and a gold comb, all of which glittered and sparkled whenever she moved, while her jewelry was subtle. Just a simple gold chain and earrings, all of which Camilla and Mina had obsessed over. Lenore wasn't thinking about any of that, however. She was happy just being in the moment.

She talked, she joked, she flirted and danced and ate to her heart's content. She teased the young men who arrogantly tried to tell her what would really happen with her archeotechnology career if they were married and cooed at the ones that made a proper effort at understanding her strange fascination with the subject. There were those that avoided the subject entirely and instead tried to amuse Lenore with their wit, to which she laughed indulgently. She even went so far as to try and pry the shyer or more serious gents from their shells with kind words or a pretty smile. Oh, what fun it was to be inconsequential!

Rook appeared partway into the evening, looking as clean and handsome as he had at Camilla's debut. Lenore was in such a good mood she was barely bothered by his presence. She wasn't sure if any of the guests were Enforcers, but she didn't see any of them in dress uniform, so she guessed not.

Enforcers didn't generally attend debuts and soirees and other "frivolous" events. It wasn't in keeping with their image. Instead, it was publicly understood that young Enforcers didn't need to attend young ladies' debuts to find a suitable match. Rather, it was up to parents to arrange these things. Usually the daughter of an Enforcer or Enforcer supporters were paired up with the eligible young Enforcer and that was that. It had been a special circumstance for Dmitri to attend Camilla's debut, though Lenore wondered if Fourth Hawkins would have eventually tried to match Camilla with an Enforcer recruit of his own choosing. Camilla had once said Fourth Hawkins had always left these kinds of things to Mina, but you could never be sure with Enforcers. Nevertheless, Lenore was, for once, grateful for the fact that society operated in this way. It meant that Rook's presence wasn't a danger to them… for the most part.

"You seem to be having a good time," Rook said, sidling up with a fresh glass of wine for her.

Lenore took it happily, looking at him slyly. Was that a note of jealousy in his voice?

"I am actually," she said, taking a sip.

"That seems... odd, considering the circumstances," Rook said, studying her curiously.

"No, it's really not. You see, I figured it out." Lenore could tell she was being especially free in her conversation with Rook, though she couldn't be sure if it was because of the wine or that they had been through so much together. It didn't matter, though, because she still had the good sense to speak in such a way that their conversation didn't drift beyond them. "These people aren't here for me."

Rook raised an eyebrow at her and looked as if he was thinking about taking the wineglass back. Clearly he thought she was more than a little affected by it.

"Oh, stop. You know as well as I do that it would have been unseemly for any of them to have declined the invitation. They're only here because they have to be and, therefore, they're only here for the *party*, not me."

"You really think that?" Rook said, the note of jealousy now gone from his voice.

"Absolutely. Why would any of these want to marry a little country bumpkin who plays all day in an ancient machine shop?"

Rook smiled at her and said sarcastically, "Of course. Your logic is infallible."

Lenore ignored the comment. His opinion couldn't be trusted; he knew the truth. She turned and saw Mina discreetly glowering at Rook from halfway across the room, and she sobered a little.

"Perhaps you shouldn't stay. Mina might have your head."

"She does look pretty unhappy, doesn't she?" Rook said, a mischievous grin spreading across his face. "We should dance."

"No, you got your dance with me at Camilla's debut," Lenore told him. "I'm sorry."

Lenore could see the hurt and disappointment in Rook's eyes, but he kept his face light. She put a hand on his arm. It was the only gesture she could get away with here, the only contact that couldn't be misinterpreted. She was smiling up at him, but it was a sad smile.

"They're my family," she said, reminding herself to not say his name. "Or as close as I'm ever going to have again. Don't ask me to fight against them. They care for me too much."

Rook smiled back, and some of the hurt was replaced by understanding, though not entirely.

"That's true, they do."

He had seen the depth of the Allens' care for Lenore. For a long time he thought there must be an ulterior motive behind what they did for her, though he could never figure out what it might be. As he had gotten to know the family better, as he had learned their secrets and seen them stand up for Lenore again and again, he came to understand that they loved her. They had adopted her as one of their own, though he still never had figured out why. It made a part of him that he had thought long dead twist with something like envy, though not completely. He was happy for Lenore, glad that she had found such a warm, safe place after the tragedy that had tried to ruin her life, but he wanted it too... with her.

"Very well, I won't stir the pot," he said.

"Thank you," Lenore said sincerely.

Rook bowed for all the world like a perfect gentleman, and Lenore curtseyed in response. He kissed her hand and then he was gone, slipping through the crowd like a spirit and disappearing.

Lenore was unsettled by the meeting and sad that Rook had come all this way, gone through all that effort, and didn't even get a dance. Acting like everything was fine, however, helped her to feel like it actually was a bit—what was that phrase Camilla liked to say? Fake it till you make it?—and it wasn't long before she had fallen back into her rounds of chatting, laughing, dancing, and flirting.

All in all, it was a very good night, and Lenore did her best to remember a little something specific about each suitor, as she knew a stack of blank thank-you cards awaited her the next day.

The sound of the window opening that night was so quiet that it almost wasn't there, but it was not unexpected. Lenore was sitting on the floor in front of the unlit grate, already knowing that Rook would visit her tonight. She couldn't blame him and had mixed feelings about it.

Rook was a nuisance simply because the association with him put her and the Allens in more danger than they were already in. Then again, *she* was a danger to them, as was Kieran, so could she really hold that against Rook? She knew Mina and Camilla didn't like him or trust him. Neal was tighter lipped about the subject, but Lenore suspected he didn't approve. Nevertheless, Rook was bound to Lenore, so there was no helping it. There was also a little part of her that liked seeing him. She couldn't deny that having her own personal defender felt nice, and Rook sincerely cared for and liked her. She felt guilty, though, because she knew it was more than that for him, and she… well, she wasn't sure what it was for her. Deep down, she felt there was something sweet and wonderful underneath that rakish exterior, but she squashed that thought any time it tried to rise to the surface.

Lenore sighed. Why did things have to be so complicated? She didn't move when Rook sat down next to her, nor did she say anything.

"Copper for your thoughts?" he asked, leaning into her side.

Lenore shook off all of her thoughts, not wanting them to show on her face. Rook had the annoying habit of being able to read her expression like a book. She didn't mind sharing one, though.

"I'm sorry you weren't able to enjoy tonight properly," she said, looking at him. "Really and truly, I am."

"I am too, though I was there the whole time."

This didn't surprise Lenore in the least. She didn't know how he did it, but Rook always seemed to be able to spy on her no matter where she was. Perhaps the oath somehow aided him in this way.

"You looked like you had a good time," Rook continued. "So what happens now?"

"Now?" Lenore asked in surprise.

Surely Rook knew the answer to that: nothing, as long as she could help it. She actually laughed when she replied because the idea that Rook would be jealous now was so silly.

"Rook, now I just write my thank-yous and carry on as usual. Remember, they weren't there for me."

"You really think that, don't you?" he said curiously. "You have no idea what a jewel you are."

Lenore laughed again and said, "No, and if I was a jewel, it would be the type that no one really bothers with. Camilla is a diamond and I... I am quartz or pyrite, and everyone knows it."

She was smiling at Rook, back on her cloud of elation at being inconsequential. Rook smiled back.

"You're precious," he insisted, "and I would very much like that dance now."

Lenore shrugged in a very unladylike way. Why not? There was no harm in it. They stood, and Rook slowly, carefully even, placed his hand on her waist and took her hand in his. Lenore rested her hand on his shoulder, and looked into those dark eyes. She noticed something about Rook now that she never had. He was so solid beneath her hands. True, he was thin, but his muscles were hard and wiry underneath his skin, and Lenore suddenly knew that he could defend her, physically fight for her, if necessary. That made her feel safer with him, and she realized that, whatever circumstances surrounded them, however she felt about Rook, she had long felt safe with him and not just because he was bound to protect her.

Rook began to lead her through the steps, pulling her gently but firmly one way, placing just enough pressure in his hands to send her feet gliding back. He was really an excellent dancer now that she thought about it.

"Where did you learn to dance so well?" she asked after a few minutes.

"In another life," he said evasively with that familiar smirk.

Lenore shook her head. She should have known he wouldn't tell her. She then laid her head on his chest and closed her eyes, still dancing through the steps that Rook led her through.

"Why won't you let me in?" she asked.

"It's better if you don't know," he replied. "I mean to keep you safe, remember?"

Lenore felt Rook's grip on her waist tighten at that, and she looked up at him again, honestly thankful for him in that moment because she knew he was being totally honest. The dance finally ended, and Lenore didn't object when Rook rested his head on hers, deeply breathing in the smell of her. Then he spoke.

"You don't have anything to hide from me. I could be the one you choose."

That was when Lenore pulled away and looked at him

beseechingly.

"Rook, don't do this," she said. "I don't have to choose anyone because no one is going to put forth an offer. You don't need to worry about that."

Rook took her face in his hands gently and said, "Little bird, you're being ridiculous. They're going to come calling, and not just a few of them. You are going to have to choose because it will appear suspicious if you don't. Then what will I do? I'll lose you again, and who knows how I'll be able to protect you."

He lowered his face to hers, removing his hands, and rested his forehead against hers.

"I don't know what I'll do then."

Lenore sighed. She didn't believe Rook, but she believed his concern was genuine. His feelings were too, but she didn't know what to say. The wall was just behind her, as their dance had taken them all around the room, and she stepped back and leaned against it, wishing she had words for Rook. He barely let go of her, though, and followed her, also leaning his weight against the wall, as if that was the only thing that could hold them up. Lenore felt safe again, out from the open area of the room, with Rook just in front of her, shielding her from the openness. Like this, she imagined that she could hide behind Rook and be protected from the pressure of the lie that was her life. Rook seemed to like their little space as well, and cozied up to Lenore, breathing in her scent again, nuzzling his nose against her ear. This lit something inside of Lenore, something exciting that she had only barely felt a few rare times in the past, but those times were nothing compared to what she felt now. She reached a hand up and placed it on the back of Rook's neck. Her intention was to have him stop that wonderful nuzzling before she said or did something she would regret. Rook took her gesture as encouragement, however—the way she had run her fingers through his hair at the same time might have been the reason for that—and brought his lips to hers. Lenore turned her face away, fighting against the feelings and desires that were rising inside of her.

"Why do you keep deflecting me, little bird?" Rook asked, his breath warm on her face. "We both know what this is. Why fight it?"

"Rook," Lenore breathed, "this can't happen. It will never work."

"Tell me you don't have feelings for me," he said, stroking her jaw tenderly.

"I… I can't…" Lenore stuttered.

"Of course you can't," Rook said, turning her face towards him again.

She let him because she wanted this too. He pressed his lips against hers then, and Lenore felt her heart sing. She kissed him back, his lips impossibly warm, and relished in the feeling of his strong body against hers. His kiss was eager and grateful, like it fed some kind of need in him. His hands were steady, holding her tightly, clearly wanting to keep her here against him forever. His slender fingers stroked the skin of her face and arms and neck. Lenore loved it, the feeling of being understood and protected and wanted. In that moment, Rook was perfect. There was something in the back of her mind, though, telling her to stop. She wanted to pull away, but she wanted Rook more. She kissed him more passionately, and he responded in kind. She ran her hands over his strong back but stopped when her hand hit the hilt of a knife. It reminded her what was at stake. Lenore hesitated for a moment, hating the idea of stopping this. It was like rising water, however, and Lenore knew that if she didn't get out now, she would be overcome. Finally, with a great surge of effort, she pushed him away and hurried past, breathing deeply as if she had actually been in danger of drowning.

"No! I can't do this, Rook! I can't jeopardize myself and throw everything the Allens have done for me back in their face for a tryst."

"A tryst?" Rook snarled. "You think that's what this is? Oh, Lenore, you have no idea. I would turn myself in to be with you, and all you would have to do was ask. Is that what you want?"

"No, don't be insane!"

"Then what? What do I have to do? I can't buy you anything you don't already have, so what is it going to take?"

"Nothing, Rook," Lenore said, tears welling up in her eyes. "I don't want you to do anything."

Rook sighed and began to head for the window, but Lenore grabbed his hand to stop him.

"Please," she whispered, "don't go."

"You must be joking," Rook said scornfully.

"We can't be together, not like that, but I don't want to lose you. You're important to me. I know it's too much to ask, but no one really understands… except you. I love Mina and Neal and Camilla, but you're different, more like me. I need them and I need you. You're all precious to me in your own ways."

"I understand." Rook sighed and said, "It's not like I can leave you anyway, but I have to go for now. I'll be back."

Lenore felt her heart sink, and it must have shown on her face because Rook placed a gentle hand on her chin and lifted her head to look at him.

"I will *always* come back for you, little bird," he said softly. "You have my word."

He then kissed her forehead and slipped out through the window. After he was gone, Lenore felt very alone. She needn't feel so for very long, however, because Kieran materialized out of the darkness not long after Rook left.

"Have you been there the whole time?" Lenore asked dejectedly. She was feeling so sorry for herself that she barely registered embarrassment.

"No, but I heard everything," he said softly. Kieran's tone was sympathetic, which Lenore was thankful for. "Matters of the heart are never easy. I am sorry for your situation. I know what it feels like to love someone that you cannot be with."

Lenore looked at Kieran carefully. She had never thought about what it must have been like for him when he was turned, having to leave Mina, the woman he loved, and then to see her marry his best friend. She wondered if he still loved her. The two sat down on the floor together and began to talk.

Kieran, it turned out, did still love Mina just as much, just not in the same way as he had. Vampyres, it turned out, didn't feel things the same way as humans did... whatever that meant. Lenore, on the other hand, had no such clarity. She admitted that she wasn't sure what she felt for Rook, save for the fact that she cared for him a great deal. Kieran understood this, but could offer no help.

Rook banged his fists against the wall of his office in frustration. He'd returned to his base of operations to sort out some things, unhappy and unsettled about what had transpired tonight. He'd done everything right, Lenore wanted to be with him, yet he was back here. Rook closed his eyes and envisioned her in her debut dress again. Heavens, she was beautiful. That's all those puffed up ponces tonight saw, though. They didn't see her strength, her determination, her intelligence. Lenore was loyal and true... if only he'd found her before the Allens had. Perhaps then she'd be here with him instead of there with them.

Rook hit the wall again. Blazes! What was he going to do?!

She would have gentleman callers soon. She wanted to be with him. She'd made that very clear tonight... he sighed remembering their kiss. It was like a drug. He had felt calm, like all was right with the world. Was that the oath telling him she *needed* to be with him to be safe? He wasn't sure, and he didn't want to guess for multiple reasons. *Get it together.* He needed to be sharp, smart... *don't muck this up.* He needed a plan for when she started getting invitations. He needed to be the one she chose, and it needed to be her choice and hers alone. An idea began forming in Rook's mind, and it made him sick to his stomach.

Lenore heard nothing from Rook for a long time, and his absence hurt her. To escape the pain, she buried herself in her work. Not so much the work of writing her thank-you notes, which she did as quickly and efficiently as she could because thinking about the debut and what had happened afterwards hurt, but rather her work at the museum. It was a whole week before she thought of that silly event again after she had finished her cards. When she did, she was in the department by herself, as the senior engineers—and Dempsey—were in a meeting.

"Hello?" came a voice, echoing through the great expanse of a department that was Archeotechnologics. "Is anyone here?"

"Back here!" Lenore called, not taking her eyes off the red-hot tip of the soldering iron. A minute or two later, she heard footsteps approaching, and she called, "I'll just be a few minutes."

She paused, listening and ready to shut the iron off if need be. She really didn't want to. This was pretty involved work and she wanted to get to a good stopping point first. She heard the footsteps come closer and then silence. Satisfied, Lenore continued her work. Even though she knew someone was waiting on her, Lenore did not hurry. Her work was too important, and she wasn't about to start rushing and make a mistake. She connected the delicate wires of the motor to the power pack, checked her work, and set the soldering iron down in its stand. After carefully making sure everything was in its place and secure, she turned around in her chair and pushed her magnification goggles up onto her head.

There before her was a young man about her age, and she recognized him, though she couldn't place from where.

"How can I help you?" she asked.

"I'm here to return some books to Engineer Allen. Is he around?" the man asked politely.

"He's not," Lenore replied apologetically, "but I can check them back in for you. You'll just need to fill out the log."

"Fantastic." At that, he flashed a smile that was warm and genuine, which Lenore found she liked immediately.

Lenore smiled back, hopped up from her seat, and began to lead the way over to the bookshelf. As she did, she noticed the young man's signet ring. It showed his family crest, a single rearing lion with the name Lee inscribed below the shield. Then she remembered. The debut! Eamon Lee was one of the invitees. He had been charming and funny, but in a subdued kind of way. He hadn't been one of those that tried to show off. What had she written in his thank-you card? She couldn't quite remember; she had written them all so swiftly. Maybe something about being amusing? Oh, who could remember anything after a hundred-something notes?!

She smiled again and settled on the present, saying, "So, Eamon, I don't remember you telling me you worked here."

"That's because I didn't tell you," Eamon replied with a

smirk.

"Why not?" Lenore asked, honestly curious.

"Oh, you know. It was your debut, so, social niceties being what they are, you would have been required to request another meeting with me here, I would have had to accept, it would have been forced and awkward. It's just better that I didn't."

"Better that you didn't indeed!" Lenore laughed. "Because I had no idea I would have had to request anything of you. The whole thing would have been a disaster. Here, fill out a line for each book, sign, date, and stamp."

Eamon looked curiously at Lenore for just a moment before turning his attention to the task at hand and said, "My, Neal certainly has gotten more organized. I used to just leave the books on his desk with a note."

"That's why he has me," Lenore said not a little proudly.

Eamon didn't respond to that but instead just smiled that warm smile again. Lenore remembered liking Eamon at the debut simply because of all the things he was not. He was unassuming, not pretentious, not overeager. He was just... himself it seemed. Lenore could see herself getting on very well with him.

As if reading her thoughts, Eamon asked, "Have you eaten yet? The museum's new cafe just opened up a few weeks ago."

Lenore was surprised to find herself enthused about the idea. What was wrong with her? She should be avoiding things like this at all costs. After all, she wasn't going to marry him or anyone else as long as she could help it. Then she realized it was twofold. One, she remembered that she was—in her mind —of no romantic interest to any of the young men she had met at her debut and, two, she was lonely.

In that moment, Lenore realized that, as kind as most of the young ladies she knew were, she missed spending time with gents her age. She'd had friends of both genders in her old life, but had cut ties completely with all of them when her parents had been arrested. It was a lucky thing Springhaven was such a large and heavily populated city, lest she run the risk of running into one of them at some point. Granted, she had transformed over the last year or so, but who she intrinsically was had obviously stayed the same, and that person thought gentleman friends simply had different benefits than gentlewoman friends. Mostly, they were funnier and more easygoing due to the expectation on young ladies to be demure and polite.

"That sounds brilliant!" Lenore said.

Eamon finished filling out the log, Lenore replaced the books and, after Lenore had scribbled a quick note for Neal, the two headed off to try out the new cafe.

It was simple but delicious, Lenore decided. The cafe offered basic pastries and sandwiches, one type of salad, two soups, as well as tea and, later on in the day, wine. She and Eamon chatted idly about things as they sat and ate, mostly about work. Eamon was an apprentice in the Anthropological department.

"We study dead people," he joked.

Lenore smiled at that because, when you looked past all the titles and fancy words, that was pretty much all there was to it. She was fascinated by his line of work, though, as she had always been curious about the Old World. She asked questions about what he liked studying best, and was pleased when Eamon showed a return interest in her work. Much of what they studied overlapped, as the technology of people long dead said much about their society. When Eamon asked about Lenore's bird project, she shied away from the subject, sharing only that it was a little daunting.

Eamon nodded and simply said, "I'm sure it will all come out splendidly."

Lenore felt herself breathe an inward sigh of relief. How

refreshing it was to not be pursued or bothered about the things that vexed her. The two finished their lunch and parted ways, Lenore feeling happy but nonplussed by the whole thing. She was pleased, though, when Eamon came round again the next day to see if she wanted to eat with him again... and again the next day after that. Lenore was happy to have a male friend again and began to look forward to their lunches together.

# 19

# "I HAVE NO IDEA WHAT THAT MEANS"

L enore was surprised and a bit anxious when Rook's prediction proved true. Invitations began to trickle in from a number of the young men that had attended her debut. They were nowhere near as numerous as those that Camilla had received, however.

Camilla had answered all of her invitations with perfect grace, turning down those that she was not interested in with the kindest of words and demurely accepting the most casual of the invitations. To those that she might be interested in but offered too much too soon, Camilla had tactfully suggested alternative outing ideas, ones that didn't require much of a commitment. Even then, before Dmitri, Camilla had known that she couldn't even begin to think about marriage and pursue her medical career at the same time. She had to explain this to some of her more insistent suitors, which was a turnoff for a number of them. These, Camilla and Lenore and anyone else listening agreed, were not worth Camilla's time. In the end, she had only gone out with a handful of young men before her courtship with Dmitri began. She had said that they were all lovely, which was what anyone could expect after so many others had been filtered out.

Lenore, on the other hand, was neither perfect nor graceful. When the first invitation arrived, she went straight to Mina.

"What do I do?!" she asked with wide, fearful eyes.

"You decide whether or not you might be interested, of course," Mina replied calmly.

"But I'm *not* interested," Lenore said. "I'm not interested in anyone."

"I wouldn't expect you to be." Mina's voice was still infuriatingly calm.

Lenore huffed in a very unladylike way and was about to protest, but Mina beat her to it.

Placing a hand on Lenore's shoulder, she explained, "How could you be interested? You don't know any of them yet."

Somehow, this frustrated Lenore even more. Mina's words, while true, were completely unhelpful.

"Then what on earth am I supposed to do?" Lenore demanded.

"What do you think your mother would have told you to do?" Mina asked.

The question quite literally knocked Lenore off her feet. She had to sit down in a chair until the sharp pain in her heart subsided. Lenore wondered why Mina would bring up her mother, why bring up something that was so obviously painful? Could it be Mina was worried that Lenore thought she was trying to replace Twila Crowley? Was Mina testing Lenore, fishing for information about Twila since she knew nothing of the woman who would have led Lenore into womanhood if things had not gone the way they had? Lenore didn't think Mina meant to hurt her by asking the question, but still felt strangely sick about it. It didn't matter what Lenore's mother would have told her to do, though, as there was a more pressing issue to deal with.

"Mina, I can hardly remember who was who," she sighed.

"There's an easy solution for that," Mina said gently. "We'll help you."

And so they did. Camilla and Mina and even Neal filled in details for faceless names on the invitations that Lenore received.

"Sebastian Kincaid, he's a fine catch," Camilla said admiringly. "His family owns a shipping business. They do very well, and Sebastian is very down to earth. You remember him. He had those gorgeous hazel eyes and asked if you all had discovered any ancient locomotives. I think he was joking, but don't hold that against him too much. He was trying."

Neal explained that Mason Pendragon was a distant cousin of the very wealthy, very successful, very everything political family there in Springhaven. "He's not someone you want to get tangled up with unless you like endless family melodrama and infighting."

"Gaston Marseille... yes, he's not terrible," Mina said, thinking back. "He's not... well... at least he's very nice to look at."

"Heathcliff, oh no," Camilla said. "He's not very nice at all. Who's next? Seamus Gaskill. Not bad. He was quiet, if you remember, but he smiled when you remarked that you liked his cravat. You said it was a dignified, classic style, and he seemed happy for that."

"No!" Mina, Neal, and Camilla all said at once to Percival Van Pelt, Dempsey's half-brother. Lenore didn't need to be told twice.

In the end, Lenore figured out what her mother would have told her to do about all the attention she was receiving. Twila would have told her to find out whether or not she was interested by spending some time with the suitors that Lenore didn't dislike. Lenore couldn't be sure whether or not this is what Mina would have advised her to do because, when Lenore shared this insight, Mina had just smiled and nodded and said that it sounded like a good plan.

Like Camilla—and with a good bit of help from her—Lenore kindly declined a number of the invites and further pared the remaining down by requesting more casual ideas from the ones that were too serious. When all was said and done, Lenore ended up with plans to go out to lunch with three of the suitors: Sebastian Kincaid, Seamus Gaskill, and Jasper Nichols, third and youngest son in a family of jewelers. Jasper's brother, Jett, had expressed interest in Camilla, and the two girls were somewhat acquainted with their sister, Carnelian. It was decided that the families would be as little involved as possible, as this was simply the getting-to-know-you step of the process.

The evening before Lenore's first date, her stomach was so twisted and unsettled about it she decided to call on the only person that would understand: Rook, her only fellow criminal. She snuck out to the courtyard at dusk and drew his symbol in the dirt, partially hidden beneath a hosta. She worried for a moment that he wouldn't see it, but then instantly knew that he would. Sure enough, as Lenore lay in bed unsuccessfully chasing sleep, she heard the *shush* of the window and rolled over to see Rook creeping in.

"Hi," she whispered, sitting up.

"Hey. You okay?" he asked, the slightest note of worry in his voice.

"Yes, I'm fine."

Lenore climbed out of bed, bringing a throw blanket to wrap around her. She felt a little awkward around Rook now after their last meeting. Blazes, she was needy and selfish. She had spurned him the last time he was here with her, and now she was going to whinge at him about her three eligible bachelors. She was suddenly worried that she was about to shred whatever sort of—or remains of—friendship that they had, which was odd enough in itself for several reasons. Maybe she shouldn't have asked him to come. No, she shouldn't have. It was stupid and risky and selfish. Lenore sighed and sat down on a sofa across the room. She would send him away.

"I'm sorry," she said, trying to hide her feelings behind a light, glib tone. "It was stupid to ask you to come here. You don't need to stay. I don't know what I was thinking."

Rook's eyes narrowed slightly the way they always did when he was examining something or thinking hard. His eyes were on Lenore's face, and she looked away as soon as she saw it. She knew what he was trying to do, and she didn't want him to succeed. Rook walked over to the sofa and sat down across from Lenore, who continued to hide her face from him behind a wall of long, dark tresses. She felt his fingers curl around her chin, and he gently raised her head so that he could face her.

"What's wrong, little bird?" he asked softly.

Lenore pulled away slowly and said, trying to maintain the same tone as before, "It's nothing, I promise. I thought it was a big thing, but it turns out it's not. You're sweet to have come, though."

She smiled at him, but Rook's expression told her that he wasn't the least bit convinced.

"You are a terrible liar."

"No, I'm not," Lenore protested, dropping the act. "You can just somehow always see through me."

She looked away again and didn't bother to stop Rook when he casually tucked a few locks of her hair behind her ear, allowing him to see her face more clearly. He stroked her cheek gently, urging her to look at him again. She placed her hand on his and pulled it down, but didn't let go. He was silent as she worked herself up to telling him what was on her mind, simply watching as she traced the lines of his hand with her fingers. Finally she spoke, and her voice was soft and sad and a little ashamed.

"I'm sorry… for how our last meeting ended. I mean, it's all still true, but I'm still sorry for it."

"I know, little bird, I know. I'm sorry too."

Lenore dared to look at Rook, and was relieved to see him smiling at her. It was a sad smile, but it was a smile nonetheless. Now came the hard part.

"You were right, you know?" she continued.

"Of course I was. About what?"

Lenore smiled at that and shook her head.

"About the men from my debut, they've come calling."

Rook's smile disappeared, and Lenore's heart sank.

"Of course they have," he whispered. "How could they not? How many?"

"At least a dozen, I suppose. I lost count. I'm only seeing three of them, though."

"Who? When?"

She told him the names and provided brief descriptions, followed by her outing schedule. Rook was silent for a while after that.

"Rook," Lenore said, scooting closer to him, "I don't know what to do. I don't really care whether or not I like them or they like me or any of that. I can't risk getting involved with anyone."

"I know," was all he said.

"I've told Mina and Neal this, but they tell me I have to, lest I create suspicion. How am I supposed to do this, though? It's one thing to lie and pretend to coworkers and friends, it's something else to carry the charade on into a marriage."

Rook sighed and asked, "Lenore, what do you want from me?"

Lenore's heart finally sunk down into the pit of her stomach. Even Rook was tired of dealing with her and her drama. As much as she hated it, as much as she tried to fight it, she couldn't stop the first few tears from welling up and spilling from her eyes. She managed to stem their flow a bit after that, but she couldn't stop it completely.

"Nothing," she whispered. "I'm sorry. Like I said, I shouldn't have bothered you."

She pulled the blanket more tightly around her and hunched down into it, letting it be a barrier between her and Rook. He didn't need this silliness complicating his life. She would let him go. He didn't go, though, and it wasn't because of his oath. No, he slid over and pressed himself against her, wrapping his arms around her, and it had nothing to do with his vow to protect her. This was all simply the fact that he cared for her, which made it that much worse. Feeling guiltier than ever, Lenore tried to shake him off.

"Don't. Just leave. You're better off spending as little time with me as possible."

"Don't be ridiculous." Rook's tone was not condescending or patronizing. Rather, he was deeply sincere. "I won't abandon you, no matter what. I wouldn't even if I could."

He placed a gentle hand on her head and pulled it onto his shoulder as he ran his fingers through her hair. Lenore breathed deeply in the feeling of security he gave her, even if she did hate herself for taking advantage of him.

"I don't know what you should do," he said, his lips close to her ear. "You know what your choices are."

These words landed painfully with Lenore and weakened her grip on the flow of tears. Rook was right, she knew her choices: stay with the Allens and continue down this insane path of lies or leave and be a criminal again with Rook. Lenore wondered desperately if there wasn't a third option, but she knew there wasn't… not really.

"What if I hate them all?" she asked. "Or what if knowing what I would have to do to them makes my brain tell me I hate them?"

"Sadly, I find when it comes to survival, your brain does whatever's necessary to make sure you come out ahead."

"I can't abandon you either, even if I do have to get married one day."

"Technically, you can, though it wouldn't do any good."

"You know what I mean!" Lenore insisted.

"I do," Rook said with a chuckle. "You're just too fun to tease." He nuzzled his nose against her and breathed deep. "Thank you. You're precious to me too."

They stayed there for a long time. Lenore couldn't be sure how long because she eventually fell asleep huddled against Rook. She stirred only slightly when the first rays of pink were coming over the horizon and Rook was carefully moving her so that he could get up. She felt him kiss her on the forehead, move a stray lock of hair from her face, and whisper something against her ear before she fell back asleep.

Her lunch out that day was with Jasper Nichols at the Corner Cafe, casual and noncommittal, just the way Lenore liked it… or as close to what she really liked as possible. Camilla and Mina had very firm ideas about how Lenore should dress for the event.

"Just enough makeup to show that you made an effort," Mina said.

"So… what I usually wear to work?" Lenore asked.

"Oh no, dear, more than that, but not so much that you look like you're trying too hard."

"I have no idea what that means," Lenore said flatly.

"And you have to wear something that sends the right message about both you and your intentions," Camilla added.

"I also don't know what that means."

"Here, how about this one?" Camilla said, brandishing a cream colored frock with clover green and lacy accents.

"Oh, yes, Camilla, that's perfect," Mina said. "It says that you're a proper, grown up lady but innocent, and the green will make your eyes pop."

"But what if I'm just a girl who wants to work in a machine shop?" Lenore said. "Where's my dress that says that?"

"Very funny," Mina said, not amused at all.

Lenore was finally ready, though, and arrived at the Corner Cafe just a few minutes after the appointed time. The date went just fine in Lenore's opinion, though she hadn't ever been on one before and so almost wished that she could have somehow done a group thing with another potential couple. Then she could get a second opinion, but that was not how it was done. Jasper was a perfect gentleman and very nice and everything, asking her about her work and hobbies and whatnot. She returned the courtesies, and the two enjoyed their lunch. Jasper reminded Lenore of Neal just a little bit, mostly in the fact that Jasper, like Neal, excelled at working with delicate materials and instruments as a jeweler. The date eventually ended, and Jasper escorted Lenore home, kissing her hand before seeing her inside.

When asked, Lenore let everyone how she felt about the date with a shrug. It was fine and, sure, she supposed she would see him again if she was asked. Even when Rook came again that night—he had, unsurprisingly, spied on Lenore during the outing—and asked, her response was the same.

"He's just… well… I mean, he's fine," she said honestly.

"You're favoring that word 'fine'," Rook said with a smirk. "Clearly, he's lit a fire in you."

Lenore chuckled and tended to agree. She didn't have a better word for it, though, and continued to use it. Jasper apparently had the same opinion of their outing or worse because he did not call on Lenore again. This bothered her far more than she thought it would, but, honestly, she was a little hurt and offended that he hadn't found her more… more… whatever it was that men were supposed to feel about women! Camilla and Mina both simply told her not to fret about it, that it didn't mean anything and that it simply was not meant to be. Rook, on the other hand, said that Jasper was a blind idiot, but was also clearly relieved.

The next two dates went marginally better, Lenore supposed. Sebastian Kincaid was more interesting because he had some knowledge of machines, and this created something for Lenore to speak passionately about. He too was very kind and gentlemanly, but Lenore was slightly put off by the fact that he was a little rough around the edges. He often worked with his company's employees, loading train cars or walking through the warehouses to make sure everything was running smoothly. The occasional rough phrase was not what bothered Lenore, however. It was the fact that many of those employees were either from the same or a similar social class that she had come from. That meant that, if she got involved with Sebastian, there was a higher chance that she would run into someone from her old life or someone connected to it. That was really her only issue with Sebastian. Everyone who heard this point had to give it some credence.

Finally, there was Seamus, who was by far the sweetest of the three. He brought flowers for Lenore and took her on a carriage ride after lunch.

"I know you said you didn't want anything too serious, and I respect that, so please know that I am only doing this because I think a lady deserves to be treated as something special every day."

"Oh, what hogwash!" Rook scoffed later when they talked about it.

Lenore had then turned his statement back on him and accused him of being of the polar opposite opinion. This little tiff ended quickly when Rook offered to prove to Lenore just how special he thought she was.

Seamus was still fairly shy during their time together, but Lenore could see that he was really trying for her sake, and she encouraged him. She did hope that his shyness was only temporary because, honestly, she didn't find a man attractive unless he had a good, strong backbone. Then again, the fact that he was trying so hard spoke to a great strength of character in him. Lenore was especially surprised to learn that Seamus was a horse trainer and breeder by trade—"Ah, hence the carriage ride," Camilla said later—but that did fit with his personality... sort of. His quiet, gentle spirit probably helped him in many cases, but what about when a horse was stubborn? Well, he was rather successful, so he had to be doing something right, and Lenore's opinion of Seamus went up even further.

"He's really very nice," Lenore told Rook that night.

"He sounds like a pushover," Rook said. "Or a complete phony."

"I don't think either of those things is true or that you have the most objective point of view."

"What are you going to do?" Rook asked.

"I suppose just wait and see what happens."

What happened after that was not really what Lenore had expected.

# 20

# EXPERIENCED AT APOLOGIZING

Both Seamus and Sebastian did request another outing with Lenore. The decision about Sebastian was an easy one. No one disagreed when Lenore reiterated her belief that a relationship with him was too risky, so Camilla helped Lenore write another declination. Lenore was still trying to decide on the best way to respond to Seamus and brought it up to Eamon at lunch that day.

Lenore had skipped lunch with him all three days that she had gone out with her potential beaus and had also kept him updated about how each went. Eamon was, as any good friend should be, sincerely interested and asked many of the same questions that everyone else had. Lenore was thankful for how easy it was to talk to him. He was easygoing and said what he thought, all characteristics that she appreciated. That was why his statement to her after she had explained her current situation was so shocking.

"I'd like to take you out… to a proper dinner, I mean," Eamon said, suddenly and seriously. His voice was steady, but Lenore could see the nervousness in his eyes.

She, however, didn't feel nervous. She felt like she had

been struck, a little betrayed maybe. Things were going so well, they were so simple and easy. Why did he have to foul it up with romantic feelings? Lenore tried to respond, but could only gape like a fish and stutter before giving up. She looked away feeling embarrassed. This is *not* what she had asked for. She could feel Eamon shifting restlessly.

"I thought you had to ask my… guardians about that sort of thing," she finally said, landing on rules of etiquette for lack of a better alternative.

"Yes, I generally would, but I wanted to ask you first. Parents have a way of imposing their own ideas on their children in these kinds of situations. I didn't want to put you through that if… if that's not what you wanted."

Lenore's insides twisted at that. Blazes, why did he have to be so kind? His consideration was really inconvenient at the moment.

"If you're not interested, I understand," Eamon said finally, forcing his voice to be brave.

Lenore couldn't look up, but found her voice and said uncertainly, "Please, Eamon, it's not like that… exactly. It's just… I… I don't… I'm not really fit for settling down and all of that. I know it's odd. Every girl's dream is supposed to be the man, the marriage, the family, but… I just don't see that in my future. I'd much rather toil in a machine shop and discover the secrets of the Old World. I only went out with those three because Mina and Neal keep on telling me that I *have to* eventually get married."

She finally ventured to look at him, and her brows furrowed automatically when she saw him smiling at her.

"What?" she demanded before she could stop herself.

Eamon laughed heartily and said, "Oh, Lenore, talk about putting the cart before the horse. I'm not proposing marriage. I just want to take you out and spend some time together. Yes, my intentions are of the romantic variety, but I barely know you and you me. There's no telling if we'd be compatible at this point."

Lenore felt her face grow hot with shame. What else was she supposed to think?! What with her debut and all that it implied just behind her. And that didn't even cover what an outing with a suitor meant to society, especially a *dinner* outing! What Eamon was saying was, while very practical, somewhat unheard of.

"So what? You're just trying out a variety of girls like you would jackets... to see which one fits best?" she said waspishly, covering her own embarrassment with anger. "Or did you see the other boys playing with a toy and it made you decide that you wanted to try it, too?"

"No, don't be silly," Eamon said. "I like *you*, Lenore. I'm just trying to be honest and take some of the pressure off, which you seem to be in sore need of."

Well, he hit that nail on the head, but Lenore was still burning with shame and indignation. She felt so foolish and frustrated and scared and relieved and angry all at once. She didn't know what to say, and was looking more idiotic by the minute.

"Lenore," Eamon said softly, reaching for her hand. She pulled it away, but he didn't retreat as he said, "I'm sorry. I didn't mean to hurt you or whatever it is I've done. Goodness knows I'm just a simple man and will never be able to guess how I've offended you, but I am very sorry for it."

*How can you be sorry for it if you don't know what you did?* Lenore thought angrily.

She couldn't stand feeling so awkward anymore and got up, leaving Eamon by himself at the table.

A bouquet of flowers arrived at the Allens' manor soon after Lenore had that night. There was a note attached to it that simply said,

*Lenore,*
   *Please forgive me.*

                                                                *Sincerely,*
                                                                *Eamon*

"What happened?" Camilla asked. "And who is Eamon? Wait. Is this your lunchtime gent? I wasn't aware he was romantically interested."

Lenore was surprised that Camilla didn't know yet. She assumed Neal had told Mina about today's incident straightaway, who would have in turn told Camilla. Or perhaps that's precisely what had happened and Mina had sent Camilla to gather intelligence. The whole idea of such imagined family intrigues would have made Lenore laugh if they didn't revolve around her. Lenore sighed, resigned to the harmless maneuver, if that's in fact what it was.

"The very same, Eamon Lee," Lenore said, setting the flowers down in the parlor. "He was at my debut and works at the museum. We've been spending some time together—just lunches—and today he asked me out to dinner *after* I told him about Seamus, of course. I got all flustered and made a fool of myself, and he... he... he—"

"He said something stupid, didn't he?" Camilla offered.

"Yes... no... I don't know. I said something unkind back and now I don't know how I can face him again."

"Do you think you'll have to?" Camilla asked.

"What do you mean?"

"In my experience flowers tend to be a last ditch effort for many men. If they don't work, they just give up. Not necessarily because they don't care, mind you, but because they either can't think of anything better, are scared, or they're gambling that they can find someone else just as good or better. The last in your case is a losing bet."

The idea both comforted Lenore and made her sad. She genuinely liked Eamon; he had been a good friend. She wasn't sure the friendship was worth the possible complication, though. Either way, she wasn't planning on crawling back to him. Their conversation had been too humiliating to even think of it. She sighed and allowed Camilla to help her find a vase for the flowers. Mina and Neal had the good grace not to ask about them later on that night, and Lenore was thankful for that.

Despite her best intentions to just let the situation be, Eamon wasn't having any of it. He showed up at their usual time the next day with a picnic basket in hand. Lenore was at Neal's desk doing some organizing when Eamon approached. She saw him there and mentally shrunk behind Neal, saying nothing.

"Apprentice Lee," Neal said formally, nodding slightly.

It was another one of those exchanges where so much was said in what was unsaid. Neal's words and simple gesture were a light warning, just enough to let Eamon know that he knew… and that he took his guardianship of Lenore very seriously.

"Engineer Allen," Eamon replied steadily.

Eamon had the expression of a man standing his ground before a lion rather than a superior colleague. To Eamon, Neal was the equivalent of a father with an emotionally injured daughter, and he was genuinely scared.

Eamon cleared his throat and said, "Lenore, I was wondering if you'd like to join me for lunch today?"

He wiggled the picnic basket slightly and looked sheepish

but hopeful. Lenore looked around. Both Dempsey and Copper were nearby, doing their best to appear involved in their work. Lenore felt the heat rise in her cheeks again. Their little spat had been in a public place the day before. It was very possible gossip had spread their private affairs to every corner of the museum. Lenore narrowed her eyes at Eamon, nodded tersely, and walked out.

The two walked in silence all the way out to the museum gardens, better known as the Botanical department. Eamon chose a secluded, grassy spot with an arbor and set the basket down. He pulled out a blanket and set it down, intending on spreading it out, when Lenore stomped on it, pinning it to the ground with her boot. He looked unfazed by this.

"You cornered me!" she spat. "In my own department! Do you know how hard I have to fight for respect in there?!"

"You only have to fight against Dempsey," Eamon replied blandly.

"He's as bad as three of himself some days! Not to mention whomever he blabs this to. Never mind that the whole museum is probably buzzing about us by now."

"I've already quieted the worst of the gossips."

"Oh, I'm sure you have."

She turned away from him, removing her foot from atop the blanket.

"Lenore," Eamon said, picking the blanket up again and proceeding to spread it out, "what are you so angry about? I told you, I will never guess because I am a male and we're no good at that sort of thing."

"You made me feel stupid!" she snarled. "Like one of those ridiculous, fluff-headed women with no ambition and no brains."

"How did I do that? You yourself told me that you wanted to explore and discover the secrets of the Old World."

"Because you got me worrying even more about marriage! By asking me to dinner with you, you ruined this wonderful, harmless friendship we had with the idea of romantic possibilities."

"So even though I told you I didn't even know if that was an option for us—"

"It was too late by then! The damage was already done. And then you laughed at me. After that, you added insult to injury by acting like I could be tossed aside in the next moment if things didn't work out. I am not disposable, Eamon Lee!"

Eamon sighed and hung his head as he knelt there on the ground.

"My sisters were right. There's no way I can come out unscathed in this." Lenore didn't respond to that, and Eamon stood, approaching her carefully. "I confess, I had good intentions but a rubbish execution. I believe it's a man's curse to never know how his words will affect women. I am truly sorry."

"That's a flimsy excuse," Lenore said, her anger already ebbing away after her explosion.

"Think about all the men you've known in your life and tell me it's not true."

Lenore did so and quickly decided she didn't agree with Eamon. In her mind, the issue wasn't between men and women, it was between human beings as a whole. In her experience, people took even the most simple of statements in different ways. It was maddening to think on but an irrefutable fact of life. Even so, Lenore had to admit that Eamon was making a proper effort to make it up to her. She finally lifted her face to his and saw him looking hopeful again.

"What do you say? Friends again?" he asked.

"Very well," she sighed. "And I suppose I'm sorry for… whatever it is I might have done wrong… if I did."

"What a sincere and convincing apology," Eamon joked.

"I'm still angry!" Lenore said, though not very angrily. "Give me some time."

"Alright, alright, I'm sorry again and likely will be not too long from now for something else."

They sat down on the blanket, and Lenore asked, "So what's for lunch?"

"Only the best to make things up to you." Lenore looked at him wryly, and Eamon said, "What? You think I came armed with only my words? Oh no, Lenore, I am so much more experienced at apologizing than that. Today we have meat pies, fruit salad, honey rolls, and chocolate. Everything I might need to get back into your good graces."

"Meat pie is supposed to entice me back to your side?" Lenore teased, raising her eyebrows at him.

"Don't be coy. I know your weakness for savories."

Lenore smiled. He was too right on that. The two began to eat, chatting about their day—slow—about how Lenore liked the flowers—yellow carnations were not her favorite, she preferred daylilies—and the food. Lenore was very surprised to find that Eamon had prepared everything himself. He argued that it would have meant less if Harriet, their housekeeper, had done it, and Lenore agreed.

"So... at the risk of shooting myself in the foot all over again," Eamon eventually said, "May I try my question again?"

"You *still* want to take me out to dinner?" Lenore asked incredulously. "Didn't you learn your lesson? I'm really not the kind of girl you want to court."

"It sounds so much less romantic when you put it like that," Eamon said in mock disapproval. "And, as for your outlandish claim, I disagree. I think you'd be exciting to court. Who else would verbally flay me in public?"

Lenore groaned and hid her face in her hands. "You're not

making this very easy for me, you know."

"Which part?"

"Any of it."

"Come on, Lenore, give me one chance. No expectations, no pressure, just a night out."

"But *why*?" Lenore asked. "You've never shown any romantic interest before. And why dinner? You know all my other dates have been for lunch."

"One, I have been interested in you since your debut. I thought it was important to become your friend first, however. I know that's not the way it's usually done in our level of society and it's not always plausible, but I think it builds a strong foundation for a romantic relationship. Two, I acted when I did because I realized you were actually beginning to consider Seamus. Now or never, as they say. Three, we have already had numerous lunch dates. I think it's time we had dinner together."

"So what you're saying is, those books were a clever way to get back onto my echoscope?" Lenore teased.

"Yes, it was all a clever and carefully crafted plot. Oh, and I really did need to return them to Neal."

Lenore sighed and said, suddenly adamant, "Fine, one chance, but that's all it is, a night out. We're not courting, our parents… guardians don't need to meet, none of that."

"Deal," Eamon said, holding out his hand.

Lenore shook it firmly and then smiled, suddenly feeling very silly and confident all at once. She laughed, and the two finished their lunch. Lenore asked where they would go, but Eamon refused to tell her. He only said that she'd need to dress for a formal night out. The answer vexed her, and he knew it would, and she knew that he knew it would, and she stuck her tongue out at him.

"My, and to think you just had your debut not too long ago," he said in response.

"We're not at my debut anymore, now are we?" she replied.

"So did you leave his face intact in favor of leaving bruises where they wouldn't show?" Copper asked after Eamon had dropped Lenore off back in Arc-Tech.

"No," she replied easily, "but only because he's not all bad."

"Aye, you could do a lot worse," Copper said with a wink.

Lenore just smiled and rolled her eyes at that and continued her work.

"So who is he?"

Lenore spun around at the voice, shocked at seeing Rook there on her window seat. It was barely dark, and Lenore had only just gotten home. She had been planning on changing out of her work clothes, but that would clearly have to wait. He must have come as soon as he could.

"Blazes, Rook, you scared me half to death," she said in annoyance.

"Who is he?" he repeated.

Lenore sighed. She hated to see him like this, his face dark with jealousy, eyes narrowed mistrustfully, and lounging against the window like a dangerous, seemingly languid cat. Predators were at their most dangerous when they looked the least prepared to strike.

"He is just a *friend*," she insisted firmly. "I have already told him I'm not interested in marriage."

"Did you? And what did he say to that?"

"That he didn't mind, that he doesn't even know if we'd be compatible anyway."

Rook made a thoughtful noise that resembled a growl more than anything. "So why haven't you mentioned him before?"

Lenore stopped, realization dawning on her. Of course, that was why Rook was so upset over Eamon. Or, at least, that had to be part of the reason. She had told him everything about Sebastian and Seamus and Jasper, but had never mentioned Eamon. It must have seemed like she was hiding him from Rook… or something. Did that make Rook think that Eamon was somehow different from those other three? Well, he was, wasn't he? Eamon was her friend first, probably her closest friend besides Camilla and Rook simply because she could talk to him in a way she never could with any of her high-class female friends. And, assuming Rook had seen their entire exchange today, which he probably had, he was sure to have seen how different, how comfortable, she was with him. The other three suitors had simply been that, suitors from her debut, not a good friend with whom she had a well-established rapport. Lenore didn't know whether or not Rook shared the same belief with Eamon about starting romantic relationships as friends, but it wouldn't have surprised her.

"I haven't mentioned him because I never fathomed that it would be anything more than a simple friendship," she said honestly.

Rook said nothing in response. Lenore then slipped her boots off and walked past him to deposit them in front of the armoire, but he reached out and grabbed her wrist before she knew what he was doing. He looked at her intensely with those dark eyes, and Lenore stared right back.

"You can't trust him," he hissed.

"You think I don't know that?" she snarled back, ripping her arm from his grasp. "Yes, let's pretend for a moment that this goes further than a casual outing. I'll never be able to tell him the truth, never be able to explain why I still feel jumpy every time I go out in daylight. I can't trust anyone that might be interested in me."

"You can trust me," he said flatly.

"No, I can't," she said. "Not while you think I'll be better off in the shadows with you. I was an open criminal on the streets, and it'd be the same with you. Here I'm safe, undercover, in disguise. If you really want to protect me, you'd do well to keep that in mind."

Rook scowled at her, and Lenore knew she had pushed him too far. She waited tensely to see what he would do. She couldn't be sure what he *could* do considering his oath. Finally, he turned on his heel and left. Lenore let out a relieved breath and shook herself. Yes, she had been cruel, but she had said what was necessary. It was the hard, cold truth that Rook needed to face. She just hated to be the one to make him face it. Maybe now he'd finally move on.

Dinner with Eamon was a few days later. He'd had to ask his parents and Neal and Mina for permission to take Lenore out, but it was all basically for show. Eamon wouldn't have asked Lenore if he hadn't already figured it would be permitted. The only gamble was Neal and Mina, but that had gone about as smoothly as possible. He had visited the Allens' manor and made the formal request in private... or relative private. Lenore and Camilla were eavesdropping from the dining room. Esther had tutted the girls for such behavior, but it wasn't serious enough for her to actually shoo the two out. Unsurprisingly, Mina gave Eamon a bit of the third degree before agreeing, but it was no more than any protective mother would do. What did surprise Lenore was Neal's hesitation. She almost thought he would refuse at one point, the way he was grilling Eamon about his intentions.

"He's really very fond of you, you know," Camilla had whispered to Lenore. "You're a daughter after his own heart."

Lenore felt a bloom of warmth grow in her chest at this, but said nothing, basking in the feeling of being loved. In the end, however, Neal agreed, and the details were settled. As if they knew they were being spied on, which they may have, Neal, Mina, and Eamon all dropped their voices when discussing where he would take Lenore so that neither she nor Camilla could hear.

When the big night came, Camilla was all too happy to help Lenore get ready. She was dressed in a gown of contrasting green and indigo and gold with peacock feathers in her hair. Lenore was annoyed and surprised to find herself getting nervous as the time for her to leave drew near. Eamon was sending his family coach for her, which would take her to the surprise destination to meet him. Camilla wished her luck, and Lenore smiled prettily at the coach driver while he held the door open for her to climb in. A short ride later, they arrived at a fine restaurant in the Ivory quarter, which immediately made Lenore feel self-conscious. When the driver helped her out of the coach, she looked around to see a number of very rich looking couples milling about, and Lenore swallowed hard. She didn't belong here, yet here she was, looking as fine as any of them. She didn't look to see if any of them were looking at her, as she didn't want to know. Instead, she found herself looking up and around, wondering if she might see Rook's face peeking out of a twilit corner. She almost thought she did. A few locks of dark hair ruffled by the breeze, a glint of dark eyes reflecting the soft petrolsene light, a sense that her protector was here, but nothing more.

"You look lost," came a familiar voice from beside her.

Lenore turned to find Eamon standing there with a smile

tugging at his lips. He gently took her hand and kissed it, lingering for a moment. It was a good thing because Lenore had a bit of trouble finding her voice.

Eamon was attractive, of that she never had any doubt. His well-kept brown hair was always brushed elegantly back. His grey eyes had a mischievous glint in them. He was taller than Lenore and well built, not thin, but not really thick either. There was just enough of him to be a commanding presence without being imposing or overbearing. Dressed to the nines in a waistcoat, the jacket hanging casually over one arm, he was dashing!

"I've never been here before," she said finally. "It's lovely."

"I think you'll enjoy it," Eamon said, placing an arm on the small of her back and leading her towards the door.

Touching. The touching was new for them. Lenore couldn't honestly say she disliked it, but was careful in how she responded. She didn't want Eamon getting any wrong ideas about her intentions.

The two headed into the restaurant, which Lenore was happy to find was nice and dim. Eamon informed the head host that he had a reservation, and the head host breezed them to a private booth in the back of the restaurant and left them there to get cozy, which Lenore had no intention of doing.

"He seemed like he knew you," Lenore said softly.

"My family loves this restaurant," Eamon replied.

"Oh," was all Lenore could say.

She restrained a jump when Eamon placed a hand on hers and said, "Calm down. No one is going to bite you, especially not me."

Eamon was wearing that mischievous look that told Lenore he just wanted to have fun. She smiled, thinking how harmless a bite from Eamon seemed after suffering one of Kieran's.

"Sorry," she whispered. "I'm just not used to… this sort of

environment."

"What? Where people sit down and have a meal together? You have to get out more."

Now Lenore really smiled and pushed Eamon gently.

"You're a cad."

"You wound me," he replied unconvincingly. "Here, let's play a game. I'll ask you a question, we'll take turns answering, and then you ask me a question."

"What kind of question?" Lenore asked curiously.

"If you had to live off one dish for the rest of your life, what would it be?"

"What kind of a question is that?"

"One that makes you think."

He was right. Lenore really did have to think about that. Thus began a lively, albeit unrealistic, dialogue about food, favorite colors, least favorite items of decor, and so on. The courses came and went—this was another establishment that didn't believe in menus—and Lenore had a far better time than she had anticipated, which was saying something considering how much she enjoyed Eamon's company. Eamon rode home with her in the coach and walked her to her door. He didn't try to kiss her or anything like that. Instead, he told her what a wonderful time he had, kissed her hand, and watched her go in. The house was quiet as Lenore walked upstairs, but she somehow knew that someone was up waiting for her. When she entered her room, she found a note sitting on her pillow. She opened it and scanned the contents quickly. All it said was,

*I didn't know you hate cucumber.*

Rook. Lenore sighed and let the note fall from her hand. Of course he had been spying on her during her date. She didn't know what he expected of her, and she couldn't understand why he kept on in his pursuit of her. It was tiresome having to constantly deflect him, especially since she had clearly made her choice. Not to mention how guilty it made her feel. In her heart of hearts she knew that, were the circumstances different, she and Rook would probably already be an item. She truly cared for him, and he excited feelings in her she secretly loved. That's not what fate had dealt them, however, and there was no changing that.

Lenore busied herself with the task of changing out of her evening clothes and washing up, trying to shake thoughts of Rook from her mind. She tried holding onto her happy feelings from the evening, but Rook's note had taken the shine off it.

Rook almost laughed at how easy it had been to infiltrate the Lee family holdings. Gardens, topiaries, and trees all provided perfect cover as he had slipped from shadow to shadow. Nearly every window was obscured by tree branches, which were flush with summer foliage. The window through which Rook had entered the house, Eamon's window, was hidden behind an enormous magnolia tree. Was Eamon Lee asking to be murdered in his sleep? He certainly hadn't safeguarded against nighttime intruders, which Rook saw as an invitation.

Carefully and silently, Rook crept into the room and melted back into the darkness. From this vantage point, he took in the room before him. It was tidy and spoke of wealth and privilege. Old schoolbooks and newer volumes about history lined bookshelves, while various memorabilia were scattered about the room. There was a family portrait above the fireplace on one wall, and various academic awards lined the mantel.

*Always was a little showoff,* Rook thought acidly at seeing the awards.

He then looked towards the bed and saw Eamon. He was sleeping soundly. Rook spotted Eamon's tuxedo lying on a chair nearby where he had discarded it earlier that evening. Rook considered using that to smother Eamon. That idea held a certain amount of poetic irony that Rook approved of. Then again, his knife would be much quicker. Pulling the blade from his belt, Rook approached Eamon as silently as his trailing shadow.

Looking down at Eamon's sleeping form reminded Rook why he had come here, and his anger began to burn at his insides again. There was something off about Eamon, something untrustworthy. He was a danger to Lenore. Rook didn't know why or how, but he knew it was true. Rook's pulse slowed just as it did every time he made ready to kill. The only thing that stayed his hand was the thought of Lenore. Yes, he was protecting her, but she would be crushed. Rook could tell she was already developing feelings for Eamon. He had first seen it that day they had shared a picnic at the museum. What if she found out? Might she suspect? Of course she would suspect. Rook hadn't exactly made his feelings about Eamon a secret. He looked to his oath for direction. It wasn't doing anything at the moment, and Rook growled inwardly. Why did the thing only speak up when it was inconvenient? He considered his options. If he killed Eamon now, he might lose Lenore for good. If he didn't, he could gather information and... what? He wasn't sure. He wasn't sure what he would find, but he had to check. If nothing else, maybe he'd discover something that he could use against Eamon.

Rook made his decision. He retreated, wishing Eamon knew how lucky he had just been. Rook then decided, since he was already out, he'd visit Dempsey's flat and take some of his frustration out there. It had been a little while since he'd terrorized the pompous prat anyway.

# 21
# FETCH

Lenore, like Camilla, wanted to focus on establishing her career before considering marriage, which Eamon already knew and understood. It was simple enough to explain this to the Allens as well, so when Lenore and Eamon's relationship progressed, which no one was surprised at after the two's highly successful first (official) date, it did so at about the same pace as Camilla and Dmitri's. Lenore went out one more time with Seamus, who she still thought very highly of. She was completely open, as she had been the entire time since she had begun this whole rite of passage, with everyone about her current relationship statuses, as Neal called them. That being the case, Lenore had to have a rather awkward, yet rationally factual, conversation with Eamon about seeing Seamus again.

"So you really enjoyed yourself with me the other night?" Eamon asked to confirm after Lenore had given him—rather nervously—her update.

"Yes, absolutely," she said.

"But you want to see Seamus again?"

"Yes."

"Because you think it's fair to give him one more chance to

sweep you off your feet."

"Your words, not mine, but essentially yes."

"So, by that logic, I automatically get another shot too?"

Lenore opened her mouth and stopped, realizing she'd been led into a trap. She scowled at Eamon, who was smiling too much.

"Haven't you technically had far more chances than Seamus?"

"Perhaps, but, you didn't know those were dates. The parameters of the situation were different. If you're going to run an experiment, which you are, you have to have the proper controls in place. The data collected without those controls cannot be counted."

He was appealing to the scientist in her. Drat him!

"Then I suppose it does," she said finally.

Eamon said nothing, but just smiled more.

For their second outing, Seamus took Lenore out to dinner. It was lovely and perfect by every measure, but there was one thing that stood out about Seamus now that was stark in contrast to Eamon. He didn't make her laugh, at least, not like Eamon did. He was kind and sweet, to be sure, but that one thing, Lenore found, was important too. Just as important? She wasn't sure, but it was the thing that had done it for Mina, and it was apparently the thing that did it for Lenore too. Her declination to Seamus came without any help from Camilla because Lenore could honestly write this one from her heart. She didn't write it, however, until after she had had her second date with Eamon. She had told him it had to be a lunch date to make it fair. Two lunch dates and two dinner dates made a well-balanced experiment. Eamon couldn't ignore the logic behind this and agreed. Lenore also kept the fact that she pretty much already knew she would choose Eamon from him until afterwards… for scientific reasons of course.

Her official lunch date with Eamon was much more low key. He bought sandwiches to go for them from the museum cafe and then took her to the museum library. Lenore was very confused already. Once there, he set everything out on a table where a stack of books was already waiting for them.

"These are the best volumes I could find on the Old World," Eamon explained. "Show me what you're really interested in."

Lenore knew it was silly, but she was thrilled at the idea. She was like an addict when it came to discussing the Old World, jumping on every opportunity she could. They talked for so long about machines, magic, people, and creatures. This last one was tricky for Lenore because she honestly couldn't remember what she had learned from books and what she had learned from Kieran anymore, so she avoided the subject of Vampyres altogether. The only damper on the event was that the museum librarian kept on drifting by to make sure they didn't drop meat and cheese onto her precious books.

"You know what the best part of that was?" Eamon asked, as he walked her back to Arc-Tech. "Besides spending it with you, of course."

"What?" Lenore asked happily.

"It counted as work."

Rook crouched on the almost nonexistent ledge and listened. He could hear his target talking with someone else. He recognized the someone else, but couldn't be bothered with him at the moment. He needed to get this done, and fast, but he wasn't confident in his chances. Blazes, he hated this.

Rook waited for over half an hour before he heard the other person depart. Finally! After he was sure that one was gone, he made his move. Rook leapt up and, squirrel-like, was on the roof in two upward strides.

"Fetch!" he greeted congenially, as he would any other fellow professional despite his feelings for her.

The woman sitting there didn't bother to look at him. She simply continued to organize the coins in front of her.

They were currently on the roof of Raven's Tower. Rook disliked it here because Calandra was a good contact, and he didn't like risking her good opinion of him. Fetch was sitting at one of the outdoor tables and dividing up coins according to some system of her own. She resembled a queen as she sat there. Her ample figure dressed in the very best spoke of wealth, confidence exuding from her like a gust of wind, as she reigned over the city from atop this mighty peak.

Rook growled inwardly. Fetch was annoying because she answered to no one. She was as close to a free agent as one could get in Springhaven, indeed a queen in her own right. Actually, she was, in fact, the only true free agent that Rook knew of. She had no network of her own. Rather, she had dirt on seemingly everyone in the city and traded information for what she wanted. And no one knew a thing about her. She wasn't greedy, though. Clever. That was the big secret to survival. She let others come to her and named her own price. How she got her information was a secret Rook and every other criminal in the city would dearly love to know. Even worse, she had safeguards set up, and how those worked was a mystery as well.

Once, a crime lord known as Spades got it into his head that he would capture Fetch and torture her into telling him her secrets. One day into the torture session, the whole of the criminal underworld knew exactly who worked for Spades, as well as the location of one of his hideaways. Idiot.

Rook was sure Fetch didn't work alone, but he couldn't

prove it. All he had was his gut feeling, which was the only reason he didn't just kill her. She was shrewd, smart, skilled, self-reliant, and sly… in short, a thorn in Rook's side.

"Hello," Rook tried again, coming to face Fetch.

She still didn't look at him.

"I want to make a deal," he said.

Now Fetch's eyes lifted to him, and he could see her calculating as she took him in. Rook had assumed his usual business persona: inscrutable expression, black lines around his eyes, well dressed, and a relaxed yet confident posture. He said nothing as Fetch assessed him. If he offended her and she decided she didn't want to play, there was nothing he could do about it. How Rook hated not having the upper hand. It wasn't something he was accustomed to in the least.

"I'm listening," Fetch finally said after a few solid minutes of thought.

"What is silence worth to you?" Rook asked.

Fetch's eyebrows raised in surprise. The request was absurd, as it went against Fetch's entire operation.

"What a question, Rookie," she purred. "I know you don't think I'd consider partnering up. You're smarter than that. What's got you in such a tizzy?"

Rook said nothing. He wouldn't have anyway, but his oath was gagging him, gluing his tongue to the roof of his mouth and holding his lips shut. Fetch was studying him again, but Rook couldn't read her.

"I don't know what it is," she explained. "I just know you've got something."

Rook believed her. Fetch never lied, or so experience and rumor said.

"We both know you'd have to offer me something I can't get myself. I'm not sure such a thing exists, Rookie."

"Me," Rook said simply.

"You're really not my type." Fetch chuckled at her own joke.

"No one is willing to work with you, to get near you. You're too much of a risk," Rook continued. He wasn't even going to pretend to be amused. Flattery didn't work on Fetch, so there wasn't any point.

"And that's just the way I like it."

"No, it's just not an option for you, so you've worked with the options you do have. Quite well, I must admit."

This still wasn't flattery. As much as she infuriated him, Rook couldn't help but respect Fetch. She had made her own way and become quite possibly the most powerful person in Springhaven.

He added, "I do think you'd consider partnering up because you know the advantages. I'm a powerful ally. You are brilliant, Fetch, so I know you will consider this offer."

Fetch smiled at Rook.

"You make an interesting case. Why?"

"We both know I can't play games with you, and you've already shared the only secret I care about. I want your cooperation, and I'm willing to take on the risk to get it."

Fetch looked thoughtful. She didn't ask what that secret was, either because she already knew it, didn't care, or had decided Rook wouldn't tell her if she did.

"I would obviously need to know your terms," she said after a moment.

"Of course," Rook agreed. "You operate however you please. You owe me nothing except silence about my affairs and anything connected to them. If it affects me in any way, I am the only one who hears about it. As your partner, I will feed you information to assist in your endeavors. If we are agreed, we swear this properly. Do you know what that means?"

"It means we pinkie swear," Fetch mocked.

"No," Rook said sternly. "It means you would be bound by the forces of the universe to keep your word. You would have no choice but to uphold your end of the bargain. I could withhold this information from you and trick you into it, but I'm not doing that because I want you on my team."

Fetch looked unimpressed. Rook held his ground and his breath. Everything he was doing here was a huge risk. Rook was angry with himself for even putting himself in this position. He did not make asinine moves like this. This was how people got themselves killed. He had never hated himself more than he did in this moment.

Fetch laced her fingers together and rested her folded hands before her on the table. Rook recognized the ruthless glint in her eye, and his stomach dropped.

"I thought better of you, Rookie," she said, her voice low and cold. "You're letting superstition get the better of you. Now, as much as I appreciate how forthright you've been with me this evening—believe me, that's far more respect than I'm usually shown—I'm not going to agree to that. As you said, I'm brilliant, and that's just an idiotic thing for anyone to do. You either trust me or you don't. I will agree to your deal, sans the swearing of bonds."

*Bloody blazes, Rook! You've really done it now!*

The only saving grace was that Rook's oath was not acting up. That didn't necessarily mean anything, though. The thing wasn't a fortune teller. If Fetch decided to betray him later, he'd know about it, but he might not be able to do anything about it. He had also endangered the precarious semi-peace that existed between him and the other crime lords in the city. Fortunately, none of them would have any better luck than he had.

With no other recourse, Rook nodded and said, "Very well."

Fetch smiled and reached out her hand to shake on it. Rook

followed suit, feeling as if he'd just signed his own death warrant.

Lenore didn't hear from Rook again after she and Eamon began courting properly. She may have been more concerned about that, but she really didn't have time. Besides all of her relationship excitement, Lenore's bird project was complete and her demonstration was coming up.

The last few weeks at work had been consumed with testing the metal bird. The only time Lenore wasn't working on it was when she was organizing Neal's desk, a constant but necessary task, and when she was in meetings. Lenore had never realized how busy a person could be! Being an adult certainly wasn't what she had envisioned as a child. She had imagined work as a school with grown-ups. You attended to your various obligations in an organized and scheduled manner, while someone with more authority and smarter than you provided you with a list of what you would need and instructions for what to do. She laughed mockingly at her childhood self as she remembered these ideas. Honestly, these days it seemed like she needed a double of herself to get everything done.

The bird had officially been named Baby Blackbird in museum documentation after Lenore's false last name, but was affectionately called BB for short. Lenore had outfitted her— they had all come to refer to it as a her—with wing coverings of leather and a body shell of paste and paper. The leather wings had caused a few people to remark that she should perhaps be called Baby Bat, which also fit. Lenore had hastily attached a pitiful looking beak to the bird's empty face after that, though Copper couldn't help but ask what sort of terrible accident had caused BB's beak to be so crooked.

BB's first tests mainly consisted of Lenore having her flap her wings up and down at different speeds and angles. BB couldn't be steered, as all of her movements were either powered by the power pack on her back—that would come into play once BB was actually in the air—or by the tiny, modified rods and cranks that were connected from her wheels to her wings. The wheels created rotating motion in the rods and cranks, which created reciprocating motion in the wings. Lenore had been especially proud of her innovation here, but being able to achieve different angles without making a mess of BB had been tricky. She had always done well with creative solutions and in maths, but she was asking the technology to do something it had not really been designed for. In the end, she and Copper had drilled and threaded various holes into which pins for the rods and cranks could be screwed, depending on the angle they needed. Every test was documented in painstaking detail. By the time the demonstration came, Lenore quite literally had a book on the process.

BB's next tests were more frightening because they involved her staying in the air for more than ten seconds. Lenore had learned from their previous research and tests that some wing angles caused BB to rise quickly into the air, but it was not sustainable, as it created too much lift—a phrase coined by Engineer Cayley from the EnKin department—and put too much strain on the cable. Other angles did not create enough lift or did not create it fast enough, so this step required a whole new series of trial and error runs. Copper was always on hand to spot BB… as well as anyone else Lenore could con out onto the test field, Dempsey included. Her fear of destroying her precious prototype overshadowed nearly everything, including her hatred for Dempsey. Not that she trusted the little cretin's hands on BB for more than a moment, but it couldn't be helped. Horses were brought in to pull BB by a thin cable at increasingly fast speeds. Funnily enough, the horses were provided by Seamus Gaskill, who apparently had no hard feelings over Lenore's rejection because she had done it with such honesty and kindness. Lenore breathed a sigh of relief at this because she needed steady, well-trained horses that would run smoothly while being chased down by a large, metal bird. Oh, and someone to ride them because Lenore was afraid to.

"Why would anyone ever willingly strap a thousand pounds of live, wild animal between their legs, I ask you?" Lenore had said to her department plus Eamon one day when she revealed that Seamus, not she, would be riding the chosen horse during the demonstration.

Copper burst out laughing uncontrollably at this question, but refused to expound upon why. Something about "mixed company" was all Lenore could make out between the guffawing.

Seamus did an outstanding job, however, and Lenore squealed like a little girl, jumping up into the air, when Bolt, a Desert Blaze stallion, carried BB so fast that the metal bird lifted up into the air and began to glide and soar like a real bird. A few moments later, Lenore saw BB's wings begin to flap, and the mechanized bird gained yet more altitude. The chemicals within the power pack required time to activate, and a stopper in the pack had been pulled just before the flight began. Previous tests had provided data to calculate an acceptable window of time, and they'd discovered that, with the help of the horses, wing flapping was not required to create the initially required lift. Alternative designs that negated the need for horses had been proposed, but the power packs simply couldn't produce the amount of energy needed to flap BB's wings fast enough, but the science behind the theory was good. Copper and Lenore yelled and leapt and punched the air for a long time after that as Seamus brought Bolt back around, BB having already been safely caught. To avoid damaging or completely destroying BB, he had to basically reverse the first half of the experiment by gradually slowing down Bolt and allowing BB to gently glide back down to earth where members of the Arc-Tec team were waiting to catch her.

Lenore really and truly believed that she might be ill right there on the platform. The entire museum staff, plus her family, plus the museum board members, plus Seamus and Bolt were watching her. They were all seated in rows upon rows of tiered seats that faced a simple raised platform. It was from this platform all of the appropriate people would address the gathered audience. Behind the platform was the great expanse of flat ground that served as the test field.

She hadn't slept at all the night before and had barely eaten breakfast. Mina had eventually cajoled her into choking down a piece of toast. Camilla had orchestrated Lenore's dressing that morning, as Lenore was barely together enough to tie her bootlaces. Camilla was fastidious about Lenore's appearance that day, putting her in a pressed white blouse, fitted dress trousers with a high-low overskirt—"Practicality and femininity. You are *both* a brilliant pioneer and a proud woman."—fingerless glovelets, and knee-high boots. Her hair was plaited down her back, and, as an especially dynamic accent, Camilla presented Lenore with a set of raven feather earrings and fascinator. Lenore looked immaculate, but felt as unsteady as a newborn foal. Even Dempsey had tried to help, offering her a little white tablet to "help calm her nerves" that morning. Lenore certainly did want a way to calm down, but, not knowing what the pill actually was, she decided against it. It would be better to be on edge—almost falling off the edge was more like it—than to forget there was anything to be on edge about.

"You're going to do brilliantly," Neal had told her before the demonstration had begun. He look fit to burst with pride, which only made Lenore feel sicker.

Scholar Bates had been the one to initially address the crowd, speaking into an amplification cone so that all those many, *many* people could hear him clearly. Lenore knew he was talking about how the museum was always striving to discover new things, unravel mysteries and secrets, and how proud they were to have Lenore and her incredible mind, but her brain kept telling her about all the countless things that could go wrong.

What if the tests were wrong? What if her data and records were lost or destroyed? What if Bolt got spooked stamped all over BB before they even started? What if BB suddenly burst into flames? What if it just didn't work?!

Next, Neal climbed up onto the platform and spoke a bit about the Arc-Tech department, the history of the Winged Zeppelin, which was also on display today, and Lenore's tireless efforts "to bring us this incredible feat of scientific and historical discovery".

Finally, it was Lenore's turn. She actually wished she was wearing a skirt because it would have hidden her shaking legs. Thank the stars she had been allowed to bring speaking notes onstage with her. Otherwise, she would have forgotten everything and really thrown up. At uttering her first syllable, Lenore jumped and gulped. Her voice was so loud! She hadn't expected it to be so loud, especially since she felt like she had only spoken just above a whisper. She swallowed and tried again.

"Ladies and gentlemen, thank you all for being here today.

I am very proud to be standing here before you. This discovery could not have been accomplished without the help of so many people…"

And on and on went Lenore's speech. She took a moment to thank by name every person who had contributed to her project and then began to outline its evolution. Afterwards, she announced that she and her team would explain the science of how birds fly, how that related to the Winged Zeppelin, and then demonstrate those principles by making Baby Blackbird fly as the Winged Zeppelin would have.

Copper then carried Baby Blackbird onto the platform and carefully set her onto a tripod for display. Lenore's heart was in her throat the entire time, praying that Copper didn't trip or drop BB or something equally horrible. None of that happened, however, and in the back of Lenore's mind she was convinced he would have carried one of his own children with no less grace and gentleness than he did BB. Despite this, Lenore's anxiety only increased because now was the part where the entire audience would see her either make history or fall on her face. Lenore began to feel lightheaded, and spots danced before her eyes. Oh no, she was going to faint! Blazes! Then there was the feel of a broad hand on her shoulder, supporting her, keeping her upright.

"Breathe, Nori," came Copper's rough voice softly.

She obeyed and realized she had been holding her breath since Copper had placed his foot onto the first step. Her vision came back after a few moments, just as the crowd had begun to murmur amongst themselves. She looked at Copper and smiled weakly.

"Thanks," she whispered back.

Copper was standing between her and the audience, which meant that he was hiding the way he was holding her up behind his body. She turned towards the audience again and beckoned with her hand offstage. With that, more members of her team ascended the stairs with a few other items: a hooded southern sea eagle—the largest and grandest specimen they could get for today—a caged chicken, and one of the giant wing models.

"I'd like to ask Engineer Cayley, head of the Environmental Kinetics department, to join me now," Lenore said into the amplification cone.

They waited a minute... and then another, this one increasingly more uncomfortable than the last, until someone's voice rang out from below.

"He's gone off sick."

"Oh, bugger me," Lenore thought.

A chorus of laughter rang out from the audience, and Lenore slapped her hands over her mouth. She had thought that out loud and into the amplification cone.

"So sorry, ladies and gentlemen," she babbled into the cone. "I sincerely hope there are no children here."

She was mortified. All kinds of horrible thoughts began to run through her head. Then, a small voice in her head suddenly shouted *STOP*! It waited as Lenore's thoughts cleared and then pushed forward.

"Would another member of the Environmental Kinetics department care to come up here and explain?"

A few moments later, another member of the EnKin department, Scholar Anderson, came trotting onto the stage and took Engineer Cayley's place. Lenore then collaborated with him to explain the forces of lift, weight, drag, and thrust. Using the oversized wings to illustrate, they explained the way the pressure being exerted underneath and over the wing changed when air flowed over it. The importance of the curve and angle of the wing was emphasized. Copper was good enough to put the model wings on and demonstrate the movement of a bird taking off and in flight, which the audience very obviously enjoyed, laughing and clapping politely at Copper's demonstration.

"Before we move on, are there any questions?" Lenore asked at the end of the segment.

There were a few, including one from Scholar Bates. Lenore was intimidated, but she answered the questions as best she could and called on her colleagues when she felt she could not do so adequately. Next was the demonstration of the birds. The chicken, a fat, grey hen called Fryer Cluck who wasn't too pleased to be there, clucked angrily and flapped and tried to peck at the zoologist handling her.

"She looks delicious, doesn't she?" Copper joked.

The audience laughed again. Lenore and her team then went on to explain why Fryer Cluck was not able to fly like her cousin, Arthur the southern sea eagle. They noted the round, heavy body, and proportionally smaller wings, but also noted what the two had in common, such as the hollow-boned skeleton, strong back and wing muscles, and large lungs. These things, they explained, were the reason she was able to fly very short distances. Fryer Cluck was gently but unceremoniously displayed at different angles for this bit, and Lenore smiled to herself as she imagined what horrible things the chicken was thinking about them all in that moment.

"Please give Fryer Cluck a big hand, everyone. And let's bring out Arthur to show us how it's really done," Lenore said.

Lenore moved aside so that Scholar Irwin, an avian specialist in the Zoology department, could tell the audience about Arthur. Meanwhile, Lenore watched as one of the zoology apprentices removed Arthur's hood. A moment later, Arthur leapt from his handler's hand and flew straight towards Fryer Cluck, who was resisting being returned to her cage. The next thing Lenore knew, Fryer Cluck was on the floor of the stage beneath Arthur's now-bloodied talons and no longer moving. This time Copper swore, and Lenore's mouth dropped at what she heard. The zoology apprentice and one of his fellows were fighting with Arthur to try and get him to release poor Fryer Cluck.

"Did you note the vigorous flapping as Arthur took off?" Scholar Irwin said to the crowd calmly, as if nothing had happened. She continued, gesturing with her hands to better illustrate her points, "Even now, he is attempting to use his wings to deter us from separating him from his meal."

Arthur was soon under control again, and Lenore had Fryer Cluck's body removed from the stage. She was panicking underneath; this was a fiasco! Scholar Irwin was wrapping up her piece about Arthur, and, besides the initial gasp and following murmur at seeing Fryer Cluck fall under the eagle's attack, the audience was sitting and listening politely. Wait, what?! Why weren't they all objecting and jeering and demanding an end to this circus? She couldn't do anything about it at the moment, though, as Arthur's flight demonstration was beginning, which meant she needed to check and make sure Seamus was ready with Bolt.

As Arthur—now surprisingly well behaved—went through his various trained routines and what her team had discovered about bird flight was reviewed, Lenore crept offstage. Lenore's stomach did a flip when she saw Seamus and his horse behind the platform.

The horse Seamus had with him was *not* Bolt. She couldn't even tell if it was another Desert Blaze, but it looked nervous. The crowd's exuberant reactions must have spooked it. Lenore could see Seamus whispering to the creature.

"Where's Bolt?" she whispered, doing her best to keep her face pleasant.

"He threw a shoe. I'm so sorry. This is Sunburst, one of Bolt's colts."

"Can he do it?"

"Absolutely."

But Seamus didn't sound as confident as his words, and Lenore's nausea began to come back. There was nothing else for it, though. The show had to go on, and Copper was reiterating the similarities between Arthur's wings and those on the zeppelin. That was the final cue before the big show. She nodded with as much certainty as she could and trotted back to the stairs, willing herself to be calm.

"Thank you so much for that impressive display, Arthur. Now, ladies and gentleman, if I may direct you to your program, there will be a slight change. It seems our testing horse, Bolt, threw a shoe—bless him—so his colt, Sunburst, will be assisting with our demonstration today," Lenore said into the amplification cone. She skipped the customary, "Let's all give him a hand" part.

She didn't need Sunburst getting any more spooked, but the crowd knew the routine despite Lenore's intentional edit. They clapped loudly, evidently excited for what was coming, and Lenore saw Sunburst's eyes roll fearfully. Lenore took another deep breath and took an especially long time to pick up BB, examine her, and get her set up in order to give Seamus time to calm Sunburst. Finally, she handed the extension cable, BB's lifeline, to Seamus to secure and headed back up to the podium.

"Remember about the shape of the wings on both Baby Blackbird and the Winged Zeppelin," she told the crowd.

That was Seamus' cue to begin riding. Lenore turned and watched as he and Sunburst began at one end of the long expanse of land and quickly picked up speed. It was immediately clear that Sunburst did not have his sire's talent for running. He was fast, to be sure, like all horses of his breed, but not fast enough. Lenore thought she might cry now, which may or may not be worse than vomiting. It was hard to say. This was going to fail miserably. She could see Seamus urging the horse on, but he wasn't going any faster.

Lenore was thinking about the best way to admit defeat. She'd blame it on the stupid horse, of course, but that was little consolation. Then how to face... well... anyone ever again. Oh, *there* was her urge to throw up. It had pulled ahead of crying again. Then she heard a frightened whinny from Sunburst.

Lenore looked to see the horse looking behind him. He had seen the oversized metal bird coming after him, and he was *scared*. Sunburst ran wildly, as fast as he could, but it was still coming! A whole new fear settled onto Lenore. Sunburst was going to kill himself and Seamus. Then a spark of hope ignited. BB was *rising up into the air*! It didn't take long for her to pick up speed and rise higher and faster.

"There's lift at work for us," she heard herself saying into the amplification cone. "And our Winged Zeppelin, powered by something far more advanced than a horse and a cable, did the same thing hundreds of years ago!"

The crowd suddenly went mad. Lenore wasn't sure if they had just doubted her at first or if they had been holding back until now. They weren't holding back anymore. It certainly was not the level of decorum one would expect from a large group of scholars and engineers, but what Lenore and her team had just done was unprecedented. A rush of pride and self-consciousness ran through Lenore, and she felt heat rise in her face. She curtseyed the way Camilla had shown her—it was different when you weren't wearing a proper skirt—and motioned for Copper to bow as well. Two major multidisciplinary discoveries in one day? It was unheard of! It was monumental! It was... terrifying Sunburst to the point of madness. Lenore watched in horror as Seamus leapt off the crazed animal. He rolled to safety and was on his feet again in a few moments, but Sunburst was gone, off to who knew where with Lenore's prize creation. *This* was why she hated horses.

# 22

# BB DOWN

I t was almost pandemonium at the demonstration grounds. Most of the crowd was still cheering, though a large enough contingency had seen what had happened with Sunburst and Seamus and were running down to help, though no one seemed clear on how to do so. Someone was going to get hurt.

"Hold it, everyone!" came Copper's gruff command booming through the amplification cone.

The crowd stopped dead and listened.

"That's better," Copper said. "Now, you lads in front, break into two teams and go search for Sunburst and Baby Blackbird. I'd suggest *not* going on foot. If you can find Baby Blackbird, assuming she's not shattered to pieces…"

Lenore's heart dropped like a stone to the bottom of her stomach at that.

"…be very careful with her. That's official museum property. Also, will Doctor Philomena Allen and Miss Camilla Hawkins please come to the stage? I think Mister Gaskill needs attending to. The rest of you, let's hear it again for Lenore Blackbird!"

The audience members that had not been given a task

erupted again, and that was officially the end of the demonstration. Lenore had just made it to the bottom of the steps before the throng of her adoring fans arrived. It was not soon enough to hide the glimpse Lenore got of none other than Rook smiling from beneath the seats. Her view of him was then blocked by Neal, who nearly crushed her in such a colossal hug it pushed the air from her lungs. She was back on track in a second, hugging Neal back and laughing. She had done it! She had actually done it! Then Eamon was there, spinning her around as she was wrapped up in his arms.

"I told you it would turn out splendidly," he whispered into her ear.

Scholar Bates congratulated Lenore with a spirited pat on the back, which knocked Lenore forward a step or two, and there were so, *so* many others that followed.

Scholar Lily Grace, who had been there when the idea had first been brought up, said to her, "I knew you could do it, honey. You made us women proud today."

It wasn't long before Lenore was thanking people she didn't even know. Mina and Camilla arrived a little later after checking Seamus. The young man had escaped with only cuts, bruises, and a sprained ankle. He was limping along, his arm around Camilla's shoulders for support. He was the only one who looked unhappy.

"Lenore, I am *so* sorry. I'll replace everything, I promise. Heavens, I'm so sorry. I…"

Lenore stopped him with a raised hand.

"Let's not worry about it now. Perhaps they'll find it."

Her tone was hopeful, but her heart was not. BB was probably completely destroyed now. She'd have to attend to both the situation and her feelings about it later, though.

⚙

It had basically been declared an unofficial holiday at the museum. Only the tour guides and most necessary attendants were working, and these were rotated often to give everyone a chance to participate in the festivities. The jovial mood spread quickly to the museum patrons too, as news of the day's epic events spread. A big party with tea and cakes and fruit and all kinds of other goodies—no one would ever know how Mathilda had pulled it all together so quickly—was thrown in the largest conference room. Despite all the hullaballoo, Lenore was sure to find Copper and give him a big hug and a kiss on the cheek.

"Thank you," she said happily. "I couldn't have done it without you."

"'Twas nothing, my girl. 'Twas nothing."

It was most certainly something, though, and Lenore made sure to let everyone know just how big a hand Copper and everyone else had had in the process. After all, she knew there would be articles in the paper, journals, and so much more about the discoveries, and heaven knew she wasn't about to have to be in them by herself! She did eventually remember to ask why no one seemed too bothered by how badly some parts of the presentation had gone, though.

"This one ran more smoothly than most," Neal replied. "We've seen people light themselves on fire."

"Blow up museum property," Copper added.

"Endanger the crowd," Dempsey put in. "The death of one chicken is really quite minor."

"Makes a good story, though," Lenore said, suddenly feeling immense relief.

Now that she knew that, she allowed herself to laugh about it. All in all, it had been, hands down, both the best and the most exhausting day of Lenore's life.

Kieran was waiting expectantly when Lenore arrived home that evening.

"Welcome home, Lenore. Congratulations," he said warmly as he hugged her. Lenore squeezed Kieran tightly in return, knowing she couldn't hurt him and still high on exhilaration from the day's successes. As she did, he then whispered in her ear, "You've had a visitor in your room."

The excitement and joy of the day instantly faded into the background. Not counting her glimpse of him that day, she hadn't seen Rook since she had begun courting Eamon, and she had spurned him so callously that night, too. Now that so much time had passed, she wondered if she had been too harsh.

"Oh! My little Nori!" came Esther's voice, shattering Lenore's pondering. "Look at you child, such a celebrity. And for your brains and talent, not like those silly women that are only known for their looks. I told Master Neal and Mistress Mina the day I met you, 'That Lenore, she's a sharp one, she is. She's going to surprise us all.' I said it. Didn't I tell you I did, Kieran?"

"That you did, Esther," Kieran agreed. "And I seem to remember you mentioning once that she was, what was it? Delicate as a flower and tough as nails too."

"I did indeed!" Esther crowed.

"I don't know about all that," Lenore replied bashfully. "Honestly, I was nearly ill today."

Her anxiety over Rook was gone as swiftly as it had appeared. Esther had that effect on her.

"But you weren't. You rose above it like a Phenix of old! My darling, beautiful, smart girl."

Esther embraced Lenore with a strength that belied her age and stature, and Lenore suddenly felt like a little girl again, the happiest little girl with her family, odd or not.

Despite the fact that they were all full—the food had just

kept coming all day—the entire family couldn't help but break open the Allens' finest bottle of wine to toast the occasion. At first, Lenore had objected, doubly so when she learned the bottle was almost a hundred years old.

"Nonsense!" Neal said. He was still giddy with pride. "It's not doing us any good just sitting down there and collecting dust, and what better day than today to celebrate?"

"Hear, hear, my dear!" Mina agreed heartily.

"Hear, hear!" everyone else chimed in.

And that was the end of that argument. Esther even contributed some of her blood to Kieran's glass so that he could participate. Mina protested, but it was already done. Esther had not bothered to ask, so there really wasn't any point in arguing about it.

"Mmm, Esther, you add a lovely sweet and spicy kick to this wine," Kieran remarked. "It's almost like the spicy chocolate they drink in the south."

"Must have to do with those hot peppers I've been growing," Esther replied, and everyone laughed, remembering the story about Bitsy's run-in with them.

The ringcat, who had been given a bowl of fruit on the table, somehow seemed to glower at everyone for this.

It was late when Lenore finally made it up to her room. When she entered, she immediately saw what Kieran had been talking about. Rook most certainly had been here and had left a gift. It was BB, or what was left of her anyway.

She had certainly fared better than Copper had predicted, but she was still in sad shape. One of her legs was completely gone, as was her beak and half of the tail. Some of her framework was badly bent, and most of the wheels were either damaged or gone. The wings seemed unscathed, however, which somehow made Lenore feel better about the whole thing. There was a note sitting underneath BB's now-damaged body. Lenore picked it up and read it.

*My little bird,*

*I am so proud of you. Tomorrow, I will make you proud of me.*

*Rook*

Lenore wondered what on earth that could mean. She knew she should be more worried about it, but her buzzing brain just couldn't focus. She carefully stepped around BB, flopped into bed, and fell instantly to sleep.

Rook opened the window to Lenore's room and stopped, savoring the moment. Lenore was asleep in her bed. She looked happy. She was safe. He wanted to remember her just like this.

The necessary arrangements had been made. His business would continue to function under his man Marlowe. He had been promised Fetch's silence, and she seemed to be holding up her end of the bargain. Rook still didn't like the arrangement, but that was his own fault. Nothing to be done about it now. He had checked in with all of his direct reports. They were all well positioned and well provided for. Only Dmitri knew what he was about to do and the Enforcer had his instructions. Now... now was Rook's time. He needed to be close to his charge. He needed to draw strength for what was coming.

He slipped through the room like a breeze and knelt before the bed. He had to be careful. He couldn't risk waking Lenore, even though his fear—yes, Rook was so afraid just then—

pushed him closer to her. He whispered to her, his voice more breath than sound, as she slept. He encouraged her, told her how proud he was of her, chuckled softly as he remembered her swearing in front of the whole crowd. He apologized for frightening her those times and told her she needed to be strong. Rook gently ran his fingertips over Lenore's face, her hands. The thought of leaving her crushed his heart. He risked a soft kiss before he left and then forced himself back out the window, nearly gasping at the pain in his chest.

Lenore dreamed of someone with her, someone speaking softly to her, stroking her hair, resting their forehead against hers. It was not just a moment in her dream, it was the entire thing, but she wouldn't be able to remember who it was or what they had said the next day.

Lenore awoke late the next day. She wondered if she should be alarmed, but no one had come to wake her up, so she supposed it was okay. What actually did concern Lenore was that, when she awoke, she found flowers—daylilies—lying on her bedside table. It had to be Rook. The note, the dream, he had been here, but why was he acting this way? What was he up to?

Lenore dressed quickly and headed downstairs. Esther told her that everyone was already gone, but that they had let Lenore be to do whatever she wanted that day. Lenore was taken aback. What did she want to do? The only thing she knew she wanted she couldn't have until that evening. She would summon Rook with his symbol and try to make things right with him. Until then, she could at least get BB back to the museum.

✿

Lenore was still the talk of the town that day. Every person she passed at the museum stopped to talk to her, to congratulate her, or to shake her hand. Everyone was thrilled to see that BB was in such good shape considering the circumstances, and did she know that they found Sunburst? It was true! The search party found him in some nearby woods. Poor thing was so worn out. Lenore personally didn't care about the traitorous beast, but was glad for Seamus' sake. Scholar Bates was in the Arc-Tech department when Lenore arrived and was only too glad to see her, especially with BB in hand.

"Look at her!" Scholar Bates beamed. "Oh, she's not so bad, is she?"

No one seemed to care how BB had gotten back to Lenore, and she liked it better that way.

"No, she should be pretty easy to repair," Lenore replied.

"Repair? Nonsense!" Scholar Bates said. "Those are battle scars. It'll make for an even better exhibit."

"Exhibit?"

"Of course. We've already begun the design. That was a big step you took yesterday, you know. Baby Blackbird will be featured along with the whole story and image-stills and everything."

"I, ah," Lenore began.

"Do you mind if I take her?" Scholar Bates asked politely. "I know she's your baby, but I promise she'll be safe in my office until the exhibit is opened."

"But... I was going to fix her," was all Lenore could say.

"I know, my dear, I know, but she's lived a good life. The poor girl needs to retire."

Lenore looked into Scholar Bates' wise, kind face. He wasn't teasing her. On the contrary, he knew just how hard it was to give up a project to the rest of the world. Yes, it was for the best. Lenore wasn't sure what purpose BB would serve now anyway, even if she did repair her. Lenore nodded and carefully handed BB over to Scholar Bates.

"Thank you, dear, and remember, you're welcome to visit anytime. We'll have tea and chat."

Lenore smiled and thanked Scholar Bates. After he left, Copper sidled up next to Lenore.

"He'll be walking on cloud nine for a while now. Pretty incredible feat for a man of his size." Lenore smirked at that, and Copper added, "You should probably go home. There isn't any work getting done in this department. Dempsey's handling the worst of the press. He does so love the attention, but he's been given his lines to say and knows to stick to them. Kind of a perfect solution, if you ask me."

"You're sure I can't do something?" Lenore asked.

"No, ma'am. Soon as they find out you're here, they'll be on you like rabid weasels."

Lenore heeded Copper's advice, but it did her no good. The Enforcers had called an unscheduled city meeting while Lenore was making her way home. Lenore was one of the first ones to her section and was thankful when Camilla found her. Now it was just a matter of time before they found out what new horrors the Enforcers had devised. Once again, Lenore couldn't help but wonder if this was somehow about her. She scolded and told herself that not everything was about her, but it was so close on the heels of her rise to fame that she couldn't drive the thought away completely. Eventually, the square was full on all sides, and the whatever-it-was began.

First Iago climbed the stage looking especially happy—

never a good sign—and waited for the last of the murmurs to die down. Camilla squeezed Lenore's hand. Both of them were terrified of whatever was coming, though Lenore knew Camilla was most afraid of seeing her mother. First Iago looked over the crowd smugly.

"Good people, I bring happy news! A member of the underworld has begun a new life today. He's turned himself over to justice and, if he survives the purging, will be a free man, his slate wiped clean as freshly driven snow."

A chained figure then trudged up the stairs, followed closely by two Seconds. The figure's hands were manacled, but he stood straight and confident. Lenore felt her stomach drop. It was Rook! He really had turned himself in, and she knew why.

"Keep it together," Camilla whispered in her ear.

It was only then that Lenore realized she was only still standing by Camilla's support.

"Give them your name, criminal," First Iago commanded.

Rook took a few steps forward, his gaze fixed on the horizon. He knew the Enforcers would be watching him to see if he made a connection with anyone in the audience, and then they would drag that person into their so-called Halls of Justice. Rook could find Lenore in any crowd of any size from any distance now. His oath and strengthened connection with her now somehow gave him the ability to do things like that, like the way it was forcing him to look forward now as if he were a horse in a tight bridle. One wrong move and it would be over for Lenore… and her adoptive family, too. Not that Rook was about to endanger her like that anyway. He would never.

"Varick Pendragon," he said loudly.

A murmur went through the crowd then. The Pendragons were a huge family, wildly successful and rich and influential. The fact that one was an admitted criminal was a huge scandal. Lenore couldn't care less about that. He was Rook to her. He would always be Rook to her. He was *her* Rook, and he was going to die.

"So you see, my people," Iago crowed, "*no one* is above the law. Only you can choose to obey it, but no one can escape Lady Justice's mighty clutches in the end. Begin the purging!"

It took every ounce of Lenore's self-control not to cry out. It took Camilla's suddenly-iron grip to hold her back when the first lash of the whip sent Rook to his knees. And it was something else entirely that held Lenore together as she watched Rook being tortured, heard his screams, and saw his blood run for the next hour.

"Why the blazes would Rook throw his life away?" Mina asked, pacing anxiously around the room.

Lenore barely knew how they had made it home. After Rook had been taken away, Camilla had managed to get Lenore home without incident. Just in case, she planned on telling anyone who asked that they were just faint from seeing such a violent display. Anyone who knew Camilla would know what a lie that was, but they weren't the only people who were walking away disturbed, so they blended in well. She would have called for a cab, but all the drivers were still making their way from the square. Lenore had collapsed into a pile of sobs as soon as the front door was shut behind them. Camilla did nothing but wrap her arms around her housemate and hold the sobbing girl. Mina and Neal had arrived home not long after that to find the crumpled heap of the two there at the foot of the staircase. Lenore hadn't stopped crying since.

"He did it for me," Lenore replied, tears running down her face.

"Did you know about this?" Mina demanded.

"He said he was willing to do it, but I told him I never wanted that."

"Blazes, this is horrible," Mina said turning away. "Could it have something to do with his oath?"

"It doesn't matter," Lenore said. "He belongs to them now. There's no telling if he'll survive. I should have asked Gadget for help when he asked."

"He asked for Gadget by name?"

"No, he just wanted false papers like mine. Had I helped him…"

"Lenore, you couldn't have given up her secret. It's not your fault."

"But, Mina, he's… he's… and I could have…" and Lenore's words disintegrated into sobs again.

"Oh dearest, I know, but you couldn't have done anything."

"Do you think he'll be given clemency because he's a Pendragon?" Camilla asked.

"There's no way to know," Mina replied. "Do you think he'll tell them about us? I mean, I know he doesn't want to, but there's no telling what kind of brutality they'll subject him to. I don't know who could resist that."

"He has to protect Lenore."

"That's no guarantee for the rest of us."

Just then, Neal came in with a tray of tea. Esther was at home attending to her family, as she often was after these sorts of events.

"Here now, poppet," Neal said kindly. "Have a cup, it'll make you feel better."

"Can I… can I take it into the other room, please?" Lenore asked. "I just… I just want to be alone for a bit."

"Of course," Neal said before Mina could object. "Just be careful; it's hot."

Lenore nodded and unsteadily took her teacup into the

sitting room. She thought she could hear Mina and Neal arguing as she left, but found that she didn't care. Lenore folded up into a corner of one of the sofas there and just held her teacup in both hands, leeching warmth from it, as all of hers seemed to have run out of her with Rook's running blood. She ended up drinking the tea and putting the cup down eventually, but couldn't remember doing it. Lenore had no idea how long she had sat there and only came out of it when she heard the sound of someone entering the room. Then it was like she'd never changed, like she'd never met the Allens, and she was on her feet and ready to bolt in a second. Old habits died hard, she supposed.

"Eamon?" she asked in confusion, like she was waking up from a dream.

Eamon was clearly shocked at the state she was in. Lenore could only assume the Allens had told him that she was upset, but nothing could have prepared him for the shattered mess that stood before him.

"Lenore, what's wrong?" Eamon asked worriedly.

He stepped forward and put his hands on her shoulders. Lenore twisted her face in determination, fighting against the tears that were trying to surge forward again, knowing she couldn't tell Eamon the truth, knowing he'd had a part in Rook's destruction, as had she. She turned, pushing Eamon away, but she wasn't alone for long. There was but a moment's pause before Eamon closed the gap Lenore had made between them and wrapped his arms around her tightly, enveloping her in a fierce embrace. That was all it took to break the fragile walls of her resolve and free the deluge of tears again. Lenore, wrapped securely in Eamon's arms, began to weep with deep, anguished sobs that racked her body even worse than before.

Eamon did not ask anything else of her. He simply stood there, holding Lenore up, letting her cry into his shoulder, holding her tightly. Later Lenore would realize that, even though she couldn't share the reason for her sorrow with Eamon and had pushed him away, he had pursued her and been there for her. No words could have ever done for her what Eamon's emotional support had. In that fierce embrace, he had shown her what words could never say.

Fetch looked out into the night. She was up on the roof of Raven's Tower again. It was not as late as it had been the night she and Rook had made their bargain, which meant there were other patrons around her at the moment. They all chatted and laughed and grumbled to one another as Fetch sat alone, drinking her gin-gin thoughtfully. It was Rook that Fetch was thinking of now, reminiscing on that late night meeting they'd had not too long ago.

He had turned himself in. Why the blazes would he do that? Fetch had to wonder if it was because of whatever had driven him to see her in the first place. There was something strange about that man. She couldn't read him at times. Something shielded him from her. It wasn't consistent, though, which was the most curious part. She never spent much time thinking about it, though, as there were plenty of other marks in the city. She could never cross paths with Rook again and be just as well off as she was now... or better. That's how it was looking now, though, that she never would cross paths with him again. Fetch wasn't concerned for herself. Even if Rook revealed that they were partners, the Enforcers couldn't touch her. Still, she hated what they would do to him, what they were probably doing to him right now. Any decent human being, criminal or otherwise, would. Shame. He was one of the better ones.

Eamon didn't leave the Allen manor until very late, far later than was proper. He dearly hoped none of his family heard him come in. He really didn't want to answer any questions about his evening, mostly because he didn't have any answers to give.

Why was Lenore so upset? Eamon couldn't help but think it had something to do with Varick's purging that day. What else could it be? She was so happy about the success of the bird project. She didn't tell him what was wrong all night, and he didn't ask again for fear of making her even more upset. He had pressed the rest of the family, but to no avail. Each one firmly stonewalled him. If it was Varick, though, why? Lenore had seen other prisoners tortured. They all had. Eamon knew she couldn't know him the way he had. Lenore hadn't grown up in Springhaven.

Thinking about Varick brought back memories that Eamon hadn't thought about in years. When the little pest had disappeared, Eamon and his family had been respectfully and appropriately distraught for the Pendragon family, but it was eventually forgotten with time. Eamon had never wondered if he would ever see Varick again, though now he did.

# 23
# NIGHTMARES

ook braced himself and closed his eyes as his face rushed towards the hard, stone floor. He felt his nose break and begin to gush.

"What do you say, mate? Do you want to come clean? Tell us who you're working with."

"No one," Rook croaked painfully.

Despite all the pain that currently racked his body, Rook felt no push whatsoever to give up any of his people, Dmitri, Fetch, Lenore, or any of the Allens. It was as if the oath that bound Rook was a creature there with him, independent of him. It saw how dire the situation was and grew strong and fierce. Rook was willing to die well before he ever betrayed any of his contacts, especially Lenore.

"That is an unfortunate choice of words."

Rook screamed then as hooks were dug in behind his shoulders and he was hoisted up by his own flesh. An Enforcer physician stood by to monitor Rook's condition, as was common practice with the more intensive interrogation sessions.

"Who are you protecting?" came the voice again.

Dmitri crossed into Rook's view. He was the Enforcer assigned to Rook's interrogation today. Rook spat on him.

"Wrong answer," Dmitri said, his usual cold work persona in place.

He then punched Rook in the gut, sending him swinging back, gravity tearing at the flesh that was looped over the hooks.

Lenore was home for the next few days until she could collect herself enough to appear in public again. With her celebritydom so fresh and her emotional turmoil so deep, Mina didn't want to take any chances. The story went that Lenore had a severe stomach virus and wasn't fit to see anyone. Eamon was the only one outside of the family who knew the truth as far as Lenore knew, and he had adamantly sworn not to tell a soul. Lenore wanted so badly to move on, to be normal again, but she knew what was happening. She was mourning Rook's death. True, she didn't actually know if he was dead, but he was as good as, and there was no point in hoping otherwise. Eamon, mercifully, didn't demand to know the real reason for her severe distress. She later learned that he had inquired with the other members of the family, but her secret had been safe with them. Try as she might, she couldn't force herself to move past this more quickly, and it didn't help that she couldn't sleep.

The night of the purging, Lenore had woken up thrashing and tangled in her covers. Kieran was the one who had woken her up, and she was terrified when she opened her eyes to his face. She had been dreaming of seeing Rook tortured and screamed for him in her dream. The Enforcers had arrested and dragged her onto the platform with Rook and tortured her beside him. Kieran listened patiently, as he always did, and stayed up with her for the rest of the night. He had simply sat there with her, a steadfast companion, until he had to retire to the cellar just before dawn.

When Lenore told Mina about her sleeplessness, Mina offered her a sleeping draught, but Lenore refused. She didn't want to be stuck in a nightmare from which she couldn't wake. Mina understood and didn't force the issue. After two more nights of the same, however, Kieran offered an alternative solution.

"I can make sure you sleep and do not dream," he said. "But you cannot tell Mina or Neal. They would not approve."

Lenore wasn't as surprised at this as she thought she might be. After all, Kieran had been there all those times that Rook had come to visit Lenore in the night. He probably knew every word that had been said, yet never told Mina or Neal. Lenore suspected he might have if Lenore had done something that would have put herself or the family in danger, so she supposed she had done some things right. She was admittedly nervous about what was about to happen, though. What could Kieran do that Mina and Neal wouldn't approve of? For goodness' sake, they let him feed off of them.

"Look at me," Kieran said.

Lenore did so and was frozen in place. Kieran's dark eyes were endless, and they held her perfectly in place.

*Now, close your eyes,* she heard in her mind.

Lenore did so and felt Kieran place a gentle hand on her face. Then there was some kind of sound. It was like singing but completely otherworldly, and it was only in her head. The music, if it could be called music, enveloped her, wrapping around her, slithering over her arms and legs, across her body and through her mind. She felt as if she were floating now, and she remained there, floating with the music, swimming through it, letting its current take her wherever it would.

Lenore awoke sometime the next day. It was the slow, luxurious type of waking up that only someone with no cares and everything to look forward to got. She lay in bed for a while, thinking about nothing, as the world and all that was in it and all that had happened slowly ebbed back into her consciousness. Later, Lenore would learn from Kieran that he had hypnotized her in a way that only Vampyres could. It was an ability they often used to subdue their prey, though Lenore got the feeling Kieran was using the term "prey" loosely. Kieran explained that Mina and Neal would never approve of him using such a mind-trick on any member of the family, but not just on principle. It was also because there was a slight side effect.

Lenore found herself thinking about the music and the euphoric feelings it had induced, and she found herself wanting that again. All at once, she understood the morphine addicts that sometimes came to Mina with phantom pains or made up stories or whatever it took to get another hit. Mina had said it was a double-edged sword because the medicine really did do good things and helped people, but it could also be destructive when misused.

Lenore also understood what a dirty, underhanded trick this was for Vampyres to use. With this ability, there was no need for them to hunt. Their prey would surely come back again and again for an opportunity to go back to the musical dream world, assuming they weren't killed during one of these trips. Being aware of these things helped Lenore to resist the temptation whenever it arose—it was strongest at night—but it still lingered for many days after that night. Thankfully, however, there was one good side effect as well. The nightmares did not return, and Lenore's nights were blissfully dreamless for some time after the experience.

Lenore was finally deemed well enough to go back to work

the next week, though a new ache had settled into her heart and refused to leave. It was perfect timing apparently, too, because now that the initial hysteria had died down over Lenore and her team's discoveries the frantic, clawing tabloid reporters had left to go seek fresh news, making way for the writers of scientific journals and other far more serious publications. She was surprised to learn that Neal, not Dempsey, had ended up dealing with the bulk of the press while Lenore was out. All the ravenous reporters hoping for a quick, flashy headline to help them sell more papers hadn't been interested in the official remarks that Dempsey had to share. Instead, they wanted to know things like,

"Do Copper and Lenore plan on starting on a new project soon?"

"Who is Lenore seeing, if anyone? She just had her debut, didn't she? Surely that means she'll be getting married soon."

"How is it that a country girl like Lenore was about to achieve such an incredible feat of science?"

"Where does Lenore live? We'd like a face-to-face interview."

"Tell us about Lenore. Who's the girl behind the bird?"

"Tell me, did Lenore ever think during this process, 'I'm changing the world. I'm going to be famous. Everyone will know my name'?"

Dempsey, either too daft to know better or too bored or proud to stick to his script, had begun to indulge the reporters. And he had begun to bring his own name into it, more with each new interview. Dempsey also allowed himself to be fooled by their devious trick questions. Thankfully, Neal had gotten involved before too much damage could be done.

"Sixteen years I've known Neal, and never in all that time have I seen him so angry," Copper confided to Lenore. "I thought he was going to either rip off the lad's head or fire him.

He might have if he'd done worse. As it is, Dempsey's sentence might be lengthened. Something about not being able to follow instructions."

The "sentence" that Copper was referring to was the three years that Dempsey had to complete with the museum in order to earn the title of Engineer. As far as Lenore understood it, he was close to halfway there. She knew it had to burn that pompous prat up to have to wait even longer for his title, and that gave her a sick sort of satisfaction.

"Lucky thing Miss Camilla's beau… what's his name, Despereaux?"

"Dmitri," Lenore offered.

"Right, him. Lucky thing he was there when a few of them decided to show up at your house. One look at him in his uniform and off they ran."

"I didn't know he had been over," Lenore confessed, and found that she was thankful for it.

If the reporters decided to write about the Allens' affiliation with an Enforcer, it would only make them look less suspicious. It was hard to say whether or not that would happen. No one dared write, much less say in public, anything negative about the Enforcers. Knowing some of those reporter types, however, they'd probably spin it just the way they needed to.

Lenore and Copper met with a group of journalists that arrived that day in Scholar Bates' office. Neal was there too, though he wasn't required to say much, and BB too, of course. She was sitting on a stand that allowed her to remain upright even with her missing leg, and the writers made sure to take lots of image-stills of her and her creators. Lenore had been coached on what to say, which was easy enough. She was sure to listen to every word of any question she was asked, however, just in case someone tried to slip her a trick question. Thankfully, there were only a few of those, and the reporters seemed mainly interested in the process of the experiment and what impact the results would have on future projects. Lenore breathed a sigh of relief. Finally, something she felt more than prepared to discuss.

Lenore cited and credited the other scientists and scholars who assisted with BB, but her true passion and excitement showed as she discussed the Winged Zeppelin and what the project had taught them about it. Seeing as it was the original inspiration for the whole endeavor, she felt rather beholden to it, more so than she did to BB, she discovered. After that, Lenore felt better about losing her mechanical bird to a museum display.

Well, Lenore thought today was going so well... until Dmitri showed up that evening. The fact that his presence had scared off any nosy reporters didn't change the fact that he was an Enforcer, and Enforcers were scum. Lenore had retreated to the sitting room when she heard him come in through the front door. This was not something she wanted to deal with at the moment. Sadly, he and Camilla came and found her. Camilla took a seat, which meant that they planned on staying. Fortunately, there were other places for her to hide in the house. Unfortunately, she had to get through the irritatingly necessary pleasantries first.

"Lenore," Dmitri said sternly, bowing slightly.

"Dmitri," Lenore replied, curtseying back automatically.

Her form really wasn't correct, especially considering Dmitri's station. She had barely dipped, but the combination of her distress over Rook and her dislike for Dmitri made her cease to care. Lenore turned to leave, but Dmitri annoyingly spoke again, stopping her.

"I need to speak with you about Eamon Lee."

Indignation flared inside Lenore. It was bad enough that his thrice-cursed order had their hands on Rook, and now Dmitri had the gall to bring up one of her closest friends? More than that, her… whatever it was that they were in this long courtship. Lenore barely stopped herself from telling Dmitri where she wished he would go and instead just stared at him coldly, waiting.

"He's not all he appears to be," Dmitri continued.

Lenore chanced a glance at Camilla to see if this blather was worth her time. How her housemate tolerated, much less cared for, the sanctimonious, overbearing Fifth, she would never know. Camilla nodded calmly, and Lenore looked back to Dmitri.

"You're going to have to be more specific," she said flatly.

"He's not just a wealthy aristocrat," Dmitri explained steadily. "He has connections in the underworld."

"Again, specifics, please," Lenore said.

Now she was concerned, but wasn't sure if she could believe Dmitri. Enforcers saw crime everywhere, after all. She covered all of that up with annoyance, however.

"I don't know much more than that. Rook asked me to investigate him before he… before he turned himself in."

It was the first time Lenore had actually seen something like compassion in Dmitri. It would have sent her for a loop had she not been so blinded by rage and fear in that moment. Both came exploding forth at once.

"You *knew*?" Lenore screeched. "You knew he was going to turn himself in, and you didn't stop him? You useless wretch! Rook's going to die now because of you! That's assuming he hasn't already! And now you're investigating Eamon? How much danger is he in? If you found out about him, how long before the other devils do? I should have let you die in that street!"

"Lenore, that's enough!"

Lenore looked and saw Camilla standing now. She could tell her housemate was restraining herself from saying more. Lenore sneered at her. Of course Camilla would take her precious Enforcer's side. She turned back to Dmitri, her resolve undiminished but a good deal of her rage gone.

"Answer me," she said simply.

"As much as you'd like to think so, I'm no fool, Lenore. No one can find out the things that I do because I have access to both sides and I am very, *very* careful."

"You are a fool; you joined the Enforcers," Lenore spat.

"I joined the Enforcers so that I could fight against them."

"Then why did you approach me that night?" Lenore demanded. "You were going to arrest me."

"I have to be convincing, don't I?"

"How convenient. You still haven't answered my questions."

"As I said, I am very careful. Eamon is in no danger, I assure you, just as Rook was never in any danger. That is, until he turned himself in."

"So why didn't you stop him? Or was that one of the times you chose to be convincing?"

"You don't think I tried? He knew the cost, though I can't imagine why he thought it would be worth it."

"Dmitri!" Camilla snapped.

Lenore allowed herself to be ever so slightly impressed. Camilla seemed to be keeping at least a little objectivity.

Dmitri actually softened as he said, "Apologies, my dear. My apologies to you as well, Lenore."

Lenore just rolled her eyes. Why did he bother? They hated each other, plain and simple. There was no need for these pretty pretenses.

"I really did try," Dmitri said, more sincerely this time. "No one deserves that kind of treatment."

*Except the Enforcers who inflict it,* Lenore thought acidly.

Lenore sighed and turned away, sitting down onto a chaise.

"You're sure Eamon's safe?" she asked, suddenly weary.

"Yes," Dmitri replied.

"Do you think Eamon's a criminal? I mean, do you think he's *actually* doing something wrong?"

"Not from what I've gathered, though that's not much. He's very well cloaked. Money tends to help with that."

Lenore nodded and thought back to something she'd heard before. Both Mina and Rook had said in the past that the resistance against the Enforcers was large, possibly larger than anyone knew. The Allens certainly hosted their own small rebellions with Lenore and Kieran, Rook was a criminal, Dmitri was a mole, and even Lenore's parents had been a part of it. Now it seemed Eamon too may very well be a member of this at-risk collective. Lenore sighed, not knowing what to make of it. Thinking about all of it at once was terrifying to say the least.

"I suppose I should say thank you for telling me," she said to Dmitri, who had joined Camilla back on the loveseat. "So thank you."

"I just want you to be careful," Dmitri said.

Lenore shot him a glance. His words seemed kind enough, but his tone told her that his concern was for Camilla and not Lenore.

"Of course," she said bitterly, looking away.

The walls of the Halls of Justice were cream. The floors of the corridors were white marble streaked with black and grey. It was a magnificent structure. It had been built during the War of Light and was supposed to be magic-proof. There was no way to tell that now, but most people believed it. The grandeur of these paths belied the cold stone and metal that hid behind every cell, within every interrogation room. Rook was staring down at the floor, his eyes listlessly following the patterns of the marble as he was half dragged back to his cell.

It had been another successful day, which meant every bone and muscle cried out in pain. He imagined the pain was even in his blood, running through him and refreshing the places where it had begun to dull.

"Come now, Twila," a voice cooed.

Rook, ever wary and alert, looked in the direction of the voice. He didn't recognize the woman herself, but he recognized her features. There was no mistaking the family resemblance. The fair skin, the long dark tresses—though this woman's hair was long and matted—she favored Lenore very much. Rook kept his face closed, but his mind was suddenly scrambling. Twila?! Twila Crowley was alive?! Dmitri had failed! But the oath... Rook's first oath had only required him to make contact with Edgar, which he had. He had also made every effort to fulfill his request, so what did this mean for Rook now? He felt no urging, nothing. He had, as far as he could tell, fulfilled that promise and was now therefore free of it. Even as he thought this and was pleased somewhere in his mind, his heart hurt for Lenore. Twila was nothing more than a huddled mass on the floor. She was babbling incoherently and tracing her fingers along the wall as she wept. The pair of Enforcers with her—Smoke and Tanner, Rook knew—seemed to be handling her with kid gloves.

"Come now, Twila," one entreated her again, firm but gentle. "We're going to try a new treatment regimen for you today, see if we can't piece that broken mind of yours back together."

Rook looked down again. Blast it! He didn't know anything about medicine, but if there was a way to make Twila sane again, that could spell doom for Lenore. His oath was quiet now, but what he had heard was repeating loudly in his head. The sound of Twila's weeping was the only other sound he could hear over his own thoughts.

Rook lay awake on his meager bed of straw that night. Prisoners had different living conditions depending on the severity of their crimes, their state of health, and favoritism by the Enforcers. Rook was no one's favorite, as he spent every interrogation session in silence. He was healthy enough considering his substantial injuries, and his crimes… well, they had wanted to get someone like him for a long time. Rook had to confess his crimes when he turned himself in, but he betrayed no one, not a single person. He was thinking about Twila, about Dmitri, about Lenore, about everything. Mostly he was weighing the pros and cons of an assassination attempt. Death was the greatest mercy Twila could receive at this point. Even if he could get close enough to her, he'd never be free again. He was supposed to be rehabilitating here. If he committed murder, he'd be written off as unredeemable. No, he couldn't risk it. He had a life to get back to. He'd be sure to make sure Dmitri did, though. No one deserved this, and the original job wasn't yet complete. No one failed a job for Rook without consequences, especially after he had already paid.

Lenore had no idea what to do with the information she had been given about Eamon. Part of her, a big part of her, didn't want to believe it. Dmitri was an Enforcer and simply couldn't be trusted. That was that, but Rook... Lenore did trust Rook, very much so, despite anything she might have said to him. Even so, Rook was not objective, not when it came to her and especially not when it came to her and Eamon. Had Rook really asked Dmitri to investigate Eamon? It was perfectly plausible, likely even, but what on earth could Eamon be involved in? She knew him so well, had met his family, and worked with him. She couldn't imagine that he would ever be involved in something even remotely shady. Then again, he probably thought the same thing about her, and that certainly wasn't the truth.

She was scheduled to have lunch with him the next day. When he came by to fetch her at their usual time, Lenore's heart fluttered a little at seeing him. She hadn't actually seen him since that night she had broken down on him, but she knew he had been by the house a few times to make sure everything was okay. Lenore had spent nearly all of her time in her room that week, so it wasn't too surprising that he hadn't come up to see her. She hadn't exactly been inviting, and it wasn't appropriate for a young man to enter a young lady's bedroom, despite Rook and Lenore's all too common practice. One look at that caring, earnest face told her that, no matter what Dmitri said, he was still her same Eamon, and she promptly pushed the whole thing aside.

# 24
## VERISAP

he months passed, thankfully, without any more tragic incidents. Lenore's fame burned steadily on for a while, and it was clear that many people were taking what she had done as a sign that she was some kind of prodigy. She was asked in multiple interviews for her opinion on other archeological mysteries and even occasionally non-archeological ones. To these questions, she answered as honestly as she could, and usually began with, "From what I know, it might be…" simply because her knowledge was worse than spotty compared to that of an expert's. If she didn't know about the subject matter or wasn't familiar with what was being referenced, she said that too. She continued to focus on the Winged Zeppelin as much as she could and steered the press towards Engineer Cayley and his team for the bird side of things as much as possible. She neither wanted too much attention nor to undermine any of her colleagues' efforts and hoped with uncertainty that she was successful. Neal was more than pleased with these answers, though, which encouraged Lenore. He commented more than once on how much he disliked scholars and engineers who thought they had to know everything about everything and therefore came off looking like a prat when they tried to speak to something they didn't understand.

Things got a little chaotic again when the papers caught wind that Lenore and Eamon were courting. It was apparently a darling match, and the "vultures", as Copper called them, clamored for image-stills and interviews with the happy couple. Eamon tried to politely turn down their requests for information, and, when that didn't work, Lenore surprised everyone when she doused their fire with this official statement:

"It's very nice that you all are so interested in our relational well-being, which I'm sure you are, but that's our business. Please, desist with this line of interest."

There was an occasional flare of interest after that when a few of the reporters tried to insinuate that Lenore was trying to hide something, but it died quickly as they were stonewalled at every turn by everyone they tried to interview about the couple. Every potential interviewee said the same thing. She's made her request. You should be a professional and respect that.

Her relationship with Eamon remained steady, and soon felt very much like their friendship had, comfortable and safe and dependable. It really couldn't progress very far due to the fact that Lenore had years before she would be ready for marriage, which she still hated to think about, but it wasn't quite as unbearable now. She supposed that, if she had to marry someone, Eamon would be a pretty splendid choice. She didn't ask because she didn't want to broach the subject—ever—with him, but she often wondered if he was okay with the fact that it would be several years before he could propose to her and therefore their courtship had to remain very casual. Eamon could have any young lady he wanted, that was certain, and yet he was stuck waiting for her. If he minded, it never showed, and the two were seemingly happy and content.

Thankfully, Lenore's work at the museum didn't change. She was still lowest-totem-pole-spot-holder, apprentice to Neal. She was happy to avoid big projects for a while and simply get the Arc-Tech department into better shape. She improved some processes, organized some areas, and assisted with the other engineers'—and Dempsey's—experiments. As for Dempsey's sentence, it was extended, but only by six months. He was furious about it for several weeks, and Lenore wondered if he might quit, especially since much of his anger was directed at Neal.

It was no secret that Neal was the one that had recommended extending Dempsey's sentence. It was documented in numerous official museum records, but it was not the controversy that Dempsey tried to make it into. Lenore once asked Neal why he didn't punish Dempsey even more for making such a fuss of the recommendation.

"You have to pick your battles, Lenore. The fact that Dempsey is throwing a tantrum doesn't worry me. The people whose opinions I respect will not be marred by it. He'll get over it or he'll leave."

He did end up staying, however, and he did seem to get over it. Whether or not he was humbled by the experience was debatable, and the Arc-Tech department returned to normal.

The Allens received more happy news at the height of summer. Camilla passed the medical school entrance exams and was officially enrolled in the fall semester. The Allens threw a party for her and invited all of Camilla's friends. It was quiet and tense for about an hour as Fourth Hawkins made an appearance, but the rest of the event was perfect. Dmitri came in his street clothes, as he called them, and Lenore had to begrudgingly admit that he was very supportive of Camilla. She even told him so... after her third glass of wine, and he had actually genuinely smiled at her. Mina was uncharacteristically emotional over the whole thing, overjoyed that her little baby was going off to school to be a doctor!

Camilla's hours at Mina's clinic were cut by half or more, and Mina had to hire someone to fill the gap. Being interviewed by Mina was probably one of the worst experiences Lenore could imagine. It took quite a while, and everyone was worried that they might not find anyone before Camilla's first semester began. It didn't help that it was such a radical thing for Mina to be a doctor. Many would-be candidates didn't even bother to inquire for fear of being looked down upon by the medical community. The whole situation had Mina more flustered than Lenore had ever seen her. Mina was so strong and independent, but the possibility that her clinic would suffer clearly affected her. Thankfully, they did land upon a fantastic replacement in the end: Eamon's younger sister Emily.

Eamon had three sisters, Eloise, who was older than him, Emily and Elizabeth. Why they all had names that began with E, Lenore didn't know. It always baffled her when families did things like that. Emily took after her brother in that she said what she thought and had a good sense of humor. The fact that she had disagreed with Mina about something during her interview was what convinced Mina that Emily was the right choice.

Kieran stayed for a little while longer, but eventually left again. Neal didn't take it nearly as hard this time, though Lenore didn't know why exactly. She had a feeling, however, that it had something to do with the way the two had locked themselves inside the library for hours at a time during Kieran's last few weeks there, poring over maps and books. They left these out when they left to attend to other business, and Lenore had snuck in at every opportunity to see what they were looking at.

The maps were mostly of the continent they inhabited, Invarnis, and the surrounding islands. Unfortunately, the little buttons and doo-dads they used to mark whatever it was they were marking told Lenore nothing, though the majority converged in the south. The books that were left out all pertained to the Old World in some way or another, which was no surprise.

The family bid Kieran a heartfelt goodbye the night he left, and he promised he would return as soon as he could.

"When are you going to tell me what you and Kieran work on together?" Lenore had asked Neal as they headed to work together the next morning.

"When you're older," Neal said with a smile.

Despite all the joy those months brought, in all the excitement and chaos and changes, a keen pain in Lenore's heart persisted. There were many days where it was a single, discordant note in the background of her life and other days where it was distracting enough to interfere with her work. Lenore couldn't prove it, and she often thought she might be mad for thinking it, but she believed she might actually be experiencing some kind of echo of Rook's pain. She just couldn't believe such a feeling could be produced by emotions, especially since she felt his absence in a different and distinct way.

There were nights where she would wake up and have forgotten that he was gone and swear that he was coming into her room to visit. Then she would remember, and the grief in her heart would pulse painfully until she fell back asleep. Lenore dreamed of Rook occasionally too. They were mostly replays of things that had happened in the past. Her and Rook dancing in her room, her going to visit him at his hideaway in secret that one night, him surprising her at Camilla's debut, and more. And then there were the dreams where she was an invisible observer in the Halls of Justice, watching as Rook was tortured in so many cruel and inhuman ways. Lenore would scream and shriek for the Enforcers to stop, but she couldn't move, and no one could hear her. Lenore would wake up with her screams caught in her throat after these dreams, her heart beating wildly. Thankfully, these horrors were rare, but still always left Lenore shaken for the entire next day.

How could Rook's oath not be linking them somehow if she was experiencing all of these things? But what if he was already dead? Oh yes, a part of Lenore, a large part, believed that he had died not long after he had turned himself in. How could he not have? They had whipped and beaten and tortured him so badly that day in the city square. No one could survive that kind of treatment for long. If he was dead, though, did that mean these dreams, this pain, would never end?

Rook observed the room around him, on guard for whatever was about to come. Today was different. He had not been to this room before. Things were not nearly... violent enough.

The room was plain with nothing but a chair in the center, to which Rook was currently tied. No chains, no whips, no implements of torture lined the walls. There was no smell of blood here, no memory of pain and torment soaked into the walls. What the blazes had happened here? There was... nothing.

The Fifths who had brought Rook here were standing guard by the door. Rook sneered when Fourth Hawkins entered. He looked smug, and Rook suppressed the urge to spit on him. Rook was trying to be better about that sort of thing. He was, after all, supposed to be healing... or whatever rot the Enforcers were pushing. The purging was supposed to be just that, cleansing via torture. It was such rubbish, but Rook needed to get back out, so he was trying to play nice. It was so very, very difficult in the presence of these pigs, however.

"Good afternoon, Master Varick," Fourth Hawkins said cordially. "I trust you're feeling well today?"

Now Rook was really on his guard. He was usually referred to as scum, leech, offal, or any number of other insulting terms. He said nothing in response, not trusting himself or Fourth Hawkins in that moment.

"I have some exciting news for you," Fourth Hawkins continued, not missing a beat. "Your release papers are nearly complete. Just a few more items and you will be free to go. Fifth Ellis here will complete your purging checklist, while Jones will administer your Verisap."

Rook's eyes grew wide despite all his years on the streets. Made from, and named for, the sap of a rare tree that grew along the Bladed Mountain range, Verisap was extremely hard to come by and incredibly effective. Even with all his connections, Rook had never been able to secure the stuff, nor had anyone he knew of. What if it worked? What if the oath wasn't strong enough? From what he understood, Verisap changed the body itself. If the oath lived within Rook, would it break down?

He screamed defiantly as Fifth Jones forced his mouth open and poured the sweet concoction down his throat. Rook's mouth was then held closed as he tried to make himself retch. He was unsuccessful and, after several minutes, felt the change begin to come over him.

Rook's mind grew foggy, making it difficult to string two thoughts together, before it turned fluid, allowing him to see great swaths of memory at once. Rook felt light, like he could float, and a quiet peace came over him. His tongue was the only thing that rebelled. It grew heavy and swollen and stuck to the roof of his mouth. Somewhere far away, Rook heard Fourth Hawkins asking a question. Rook smiled stupidly and opened his mouth to answer.

Fourth Hawkins looked over his report. He had just finished writing it, though reading it didn't make things any better. He had attributed the failure of the Verisap to an adverse reaction, but that wouldn't make any difference to his superiors. They wanted big results, not hints and garbled possibilities. That was all that mattered to them. Fourth Hawkins sighed. This was supposed to be good for his career, getting a major crime lord to out his fellow criminals. Instead, he was liable to get demoted. Besides the obvious humiliation, demotion would also mean he would no longer be able to protect Adelle… in as much as he was able to protect her now with her stuck inside these walls. There was a spot of hope, but it was so small Fourth Hawkins had trouble believing it would yield anything. Still, he had focused on it in the report as a major achievement, despite the fact it could also mean ruin for him. He sighed again. The best laid plans and all that…

"Fifth Sawyer," he said gruffly, covering his disappointment and worry.

"Yes, sir?" Dmitri said.

"Please send a letter to Lady Pendragon with a token of my thanks for the Verisap. Make it something worthy of her ladyship's assistance."

"Of course, sir. Anything else?"

"Prepare the release of Varick Pendragon. The paperwork should all be in order."

"Consider it done, sir."

"Good. Dismissed."

After Dmitri was gone, Fourth Hawkins pulled a sheet of parchment from a drawer. On it were written the words *fetch*, *mole*, *char*, and *deal*. These were the only words he had been able to discern from Varick when he had been under the influence of the Verisap. Fourth Hawkins had no idea what any of these words meant, and had only included mention of the word *mole* into his report. Hopefully, that would give his superiors reason to entrust him with a task force or something to search for a mole within their ranks. It was the only way Fourth Hawkins could think of to try and save his career, though it could backfire badly. There was the possibility that they would see even the mere suggestion of a mole as an insult to the entire order and punish him.

Rook was led by a pair of Fifths, manacled by his hands and feet, to the great front gates of the Halls of Justice. The enormous gates were solid quartz and glittered in the moonlight. He watched silently as the gates were opened—the mechanism for this seemed to be inside of one, or perhaps both, of the towers on either side of the gates. They were opened just enough to allow Rook through. One of the Fifths unlocked his restraints, and Rook was then violently shoved forward and through the gates by the other. Rook stumbled and fell to the ground, as his most recent injuries had not been healed as those before had. The Fifths said nothing to him as the gates closed behind, and Rook was soon left alone and free again.

In his mind, Rook was elated. He had made it! He had survived… pretty worse for wear, but that was minor. Now he had to decide what to do. He had given this question a lot of thought and never landed on an answer. It was possible the Enforcers would keep tabs on him as he left to see where he went. Now that he was known, they just had to not lose sight of him in order to observe his activities. Rook suspected they were smart enough to have thought of that, which was unfortunate for him, so he had to lose his tail first.

Rook was not fit the way he used to be. He had lost strength in his muscles, dexterity from injuries, and currently he was slowed by a limp in his left leg. With all these issues, he wasn't certain how he was going to get away from whoever might be following him, but he would figure that out on the way. He began to hobble away, thinking about his escape as well as what to do once that was done. He couldn't go see Lenore, as much as it pained him. No, it wasn't safe yet. He had to go make peace with his fellow crimes lords, convince them he hadn't ratted them out. He needed to reestablish his network, see about his business, get himself ensconced in the underworld again. These would all take time and no small measure of skill. There was only one person he trusted—a very generous use of that word in this situation, he thought—right now: Fetch. He needed information, which she had, and a safe place—one that wasn't his, just in case—to lay low. He just hoped she was feeling charitable.

"What the blazes are you doing here?" Fetch demanded.

She was not at all feeling charitable at the moment and had been very put out at finding Rook—or was it Varick now?—in her study… helping himself to a drink, no less!

"I wasn't followed," Rook replied sternly.

He soaked the end of a bit of cloth in his brandy and then pressed it to a wound that had reopened on his way here.

"That's not my concern," Fetch said irritably. "That's a three hundred gold disinfectant you're using there."

"Bill me," Rook snipped.

Losing his tail had not been easy, not even after Rook had spotted him. It had worsened some, and put strain on all, of his injuries. This did not put Rook in a terribly patient mood, even with Fetch.

"Get out," Fetch said.

"Or what? You'll reveal some juicy tidbit about me? You have nothing, not anymore. The slime saw to that."

Fetch glared at Rook. For once, he had her. The one bit of dirt she'd had on him, the thing that had brought him to her in the first place, was already out. The Enforcers had revealed the rest, or at least what there was to reveal. There were no names mentioned in the reading of Rook's crimes, but who worked for whom was paltry in their world anyway. Just about everyone worked for someone.

"Do we still have a deal?" Rook asked, getting straight to the point. "Are we still partners?"

"That all depends," Fetch said coldly.

"I didn't tell them anything," Rook said curtly.

He wasn't sure that was precisely true. He couldn't remember anything of his time under the influence of the Verisap, which terrified him down to his core, but not remembering was the same thing as not lying in Rook's book. Fetch said nothing for a long time as she studied him.

"I can't go back out, not until I'm ready," Rook added, hoping that logic would persuade her. "They all know what I look like. They'll try to keep an eye on me, which puts all of us in danger."

Fetch's eyes bored a hole in Rook's face. She detested him.

"I need help, Fetch," Rook said angrily, hating himself for having to be vulnerable like this. There was a pause before he said, "Please."

Rook's stomach dropped as he saw Fetch raise her

eyebrow. It was her one tell, and it never preceded anything good.

"Sister, dear, did I hear… oh, good gracious. I didn't realize we had company. This is a first!"

Rook scrutinized the newcomer quickly and efficiently. It was a man, but a very broken one. His right leg was completely missing, and the arm on that same side might as well have been. It was a gnarled and shriveled mess, looking more like a tortured tree branch than a human limb, right down to the greyish craggy skin that covered it. His face, too, had issues. Over one very wrong eyeball—why was it that size and was it covered in a film or was that just the color of it?—was a strange piece, something like an overly complicated jeweler's loupe, made of brass. His leg and his arm also had their own prosthetics attached. The one on his leg was some kind of advanced peg leg with a working joint at both the knee and hip. Rook could see there was some kind of gear and pulley system at work, but he couldn't work out much more than that. The arm, now that was something else. Strapped around his mangled arm were what looked like a variety of tools, though how they could ever be useful was unclear. Both Lenore and Neal could have a field day studying this man and his… enhancements. Despite all of his physical shortcomings, he was dressed just as finely as Fetch.

"Yes, you did, Lowell, and now is not the time," Fetch said flatly.

"Felicia, my dear, you must grant me this indulgence. We never have guests, after all."

"You know why we don't!" she snapped.

"Too true, too true, but let's make an exception this once, shall we? After all, this is the infamous Rook, is it not? Or shall I call you Varick?"

"Rook," he replied with a quick smile.

Rook sensed that this man could be of use to him and immediately started to make sure to observe the niceties.

"So good to hear! I always liked that name," the man gushed. "And, as you may have heard, I am Lowell, sweet Felicia's twin brother, though she doesn't like me to use that name."

"Lowell! Can I please have a word in the other room?" Fetch growled.

"No, my dear, you may not. I know what you are going to say. You are going to say I am ruining this little ruse we have going. You seem to forget, though, oh sister mine, that we are equals in this arrangement, and I want Rook on our team… *properly*. You knew this."

Rook looked between the two siblings. He was trying to decide if perhaps Lowell was really the one in control here. He couldn't be sure; he didn't see any fear in Fetch. There was… something off in this situation. Either way, he needed to be especially careful in dealing with both of them now, lest he ruin this opportunity."

"We cannot trust anyone, much less him!" Fetch insisted. "I told you that!"

"If I may—" Rook began.

"Shut up!" Fetch snarled at him.

Rook shut his mouth and tried to suppress a smile.

"And, as I told you, I believe we can," Lowell replied adamantly. "He approached you to strike a bargain. The man has something to lose."

The smile was easier to suppress now. Rook didn't like being reminded of the disadvantage he was at.

"You and I will discuss this later," Fetch said.

"Indeed, we're being rude," Lowell agreed. "Rook, my good man, it is an honor to meet you. You are quite the legend after all, even before you turned yourself in."

Rook smiled and nodded graciously. He held back any verbal response, as he was far from convinced Lowell's foppish act was genuine.

"I understand you need something from us, yes?"

"Information, to start."

"Of course," Lowell said. "And a place to stay, I understand. You're welcome here."

"This is a mistake, Lowell," Fetch said.

"Felicia, the man said he didn't tell them anything. If Rook is to be our partner—and he is already yours, after all—we need to show a little trust. If he betrays us, I'm sure he knows what will happen."

Lowell's congenial expression didn't change, though that didn't bother Rook. He was actually glad to finally see Lowell act like something besides an idiotic gentleman at a garden party. And the threat, Rook heard those all the time. He issued them just as often! No, no, that was all fine. What bothered Rook was how Lowell knew what he had said about the Enforcers and needing a place to stay.

"What do you mean you *lost him*?" Fourth Hawkins demanded, his face turning red with rage.

Fourth Hawkins was in his office entertaining one of his commanding officers, Third Jamison, when the scout came in with his report. Fourth Hawkins didn't even know the lad's name, but could see by his uniform that he was only a Sixth, though he could have guessed he was new by the way he simply came in and began to blurt out the information.

"My apologies, sir, but Varick Pendragon has disappeared," the lad replied nervously.

"Why did they send *you* on this assignment?!" Fourth

Hawkins demanded. "Have you even finished basic training?"

The Sixth shifted uncomfortably and did not respond.

"A superior officer just asked you a question, *boy*!" Third Jamison blustered angrily, his bushy mustache convulsing with every word.

"My C.O. thought I would be a good candidate for the job," the Sixth replied, clearly unhappy.

"Why?" Fourth Sawyer and Third Jamison demanded together.

"Because I am one of Varick's cousins, sirs," he explained, barely hiding his disdain for the decision. "Sixth Leopold Pendragon, at your service."

Third Jamison rolled his eyes and moaned, "Good gracious, how many of you are there? You can't swing a dead cat without hitting a Pendragon in this city."

Sixth Pendragon did not respond.

"Just explain how Varick evaded you," Fourth Hawkins said, rubbing the bridge of his nose between thumb and forefinger.

"I wish I could, sir," Sixth Pendragon said. "I was tailing him, following along the road, and had him in my sights for the better part of two hours. He tried running for a while but couldn't maintain speed. We were in the Cobalt district when he turned a corner and disappeared. I retraced my steps, followed every side street there, and looked all night. I'm afraid he vanished."

"And why, pray tell, does your being related to the target make you a worthy candidate for this job?" Fourth Hawkins asked snidely.

"My C.O. believed I would be better equipped to follow since we are family. I believe he thought I would recognize Varick more easily and therefore keep him in my sights better than another officer would. In truth, sirs, Varick is several years older than me, and I only met him on a few occasions when we were very young."

Fourth Hawkins motioned for the Sixth to stop. He had heard enough. Fools, all of them! This was a disaster.

"Thank you, Sixth," he said wearily. "Make sure I'm sent a copy of your report. You may go."

Sixth Pendragon bowed and left. This couldn't have happened at a worse time. Fourth Hawkins had just been making his request to form a task force to find out what Varick Pendragon's confused Verisap-induced gibberings had meant. As a last-ditch effort, he took Third Jamison's glass, refilled it, and handed it back. If anything was going to convince the Third, it was more of his beloved whiskey.

"Well, that's a giant, blazing mess," he sighed.

"Indeed," Third Jamison agreed before taking a long sip of his drink.

Fourth Hawkins allowed for a long silence to pass, hoping for the alcohol to do its thing and quickly. Finally, he spoke again, deadly serious.

"I think this gives me all the more reason to make this request now…"

Fourth Hawkins then summarized what he had discovered during the interrogation and explained what he thought needed to happen now. Third Jamison said nothing all the while, and Fourth Hawkins hoped that glassy look in his eyes was from the liquor and not boredom.

"That's quite a request," Third Jamison said slowly at the end of the proposal. "I'll have to go over it with my people, but I feel confident, given the circumstances, we can enact at least the first step of your plan."

# 25
# ALL HAIL THE KING

During his stay with Fetch and Lowell, Rook found himself both immensely amused and incredibly annoyed. Lowell apparently had no qualms sharing about his and Fetch's life there in their manor. How they had acquired such a fine home in the Rose quarter was a mystery, though Rook made a mental note to look into it later. Much to Rook's chagrin, what Lowell shared was predominantly banal anecdotes about how he spent his time when Fetch was away—his hobbies included doffing his mechanical appendages and dressing as a beggar in order to hobble through the Cobalt and Agate districts and pick up gossip, cooking, gardening, and reading plays (adventure comedies were his favorite)—and stories of Fetch and him growing up in Duskwood, the city-state to the north that was home to the Bladed Mountains. This was not the type of intel Rook wanted, as it was nothing he could use, but the way Fetch seemed to develop a headache anytime she overheard one of these tellings was worth it.

As much as he enjoyed seeing Fetch vexed, Rook found his patience tested by Lowell. The man was perpetually enthusiastic and curious about Rook's adventures as a big fish in the seedy underbelly of Springhaven. Rook had less than no interest in sharing anything about himself, but Lowell would stamp his feet and pout like a child if Rook stonewalled him, which seemed to illicit a strange reaction from Fetch. She seemed both pleased and angry, and Rook couldn't even begin to guess why. Rook, though perplexed by a grown man throwing a tantrum, wanted to stay on Lowell's good side. After all, it was only because of him that Rook was able to stay there, so he humored his host, often interweaving the events of his life with false names and fabricated events.

There seemed a sort of unspoken agreement between Rook and Fetch now. They kept one another's secrets safe in exchange for support. Fetch gathered information for Rook as to who was doing what, what had changed during his incarceration, and what people were planning. Truthfully, Rook was in awe of Fetch, though he'd never admit it to her. Somehow, she was able to uncover secrets Rook knew their owners would never freely tell. The information she shared was invaluable, as Rook needed to be ahead of as many people as possible to regain his position and influence. It was only during their strategy sessions that Rook and Fetch were not openly despising one another, though that didn't mean they didn't still annoy each other. Fetch demanded to know what Rook had planned, which he refused to do at first.

"If you want my help, you need to tell me what you're thinking," she said. "We are, after all, trying to trust one another, yes?"

Rook growled at that. She wasn't wrong; Lowell had been pushing them to work together since day one. Rook, however, was not a sharer, and the idea of letting someone in, especially someone as insufferable as she, went against his every instinct. He turned his thoughts, which had wandered to Lenore, back to what Fetch had just been telling him. The underground market was having trouble keeping suppliers. She didn't know why, though. Rook knew it could be bad management—Marlowe could be cheating his vendors—or competition from someone else. Rook had spent years building that business. He would not see it crumble. He had to go see Marlowe sooner rather than later.

"Are you sure you're fit enough to sneak all the way to the Char quarter without being seen?" Fetch asked.

Rook turned and narrowed his eyes at her. This was not the first time she had strangely landed upon precisely what he had been thinking. She stared evenly back at him and said nothing.

"I'm going to have to be. I need to get this fixed right away."

"If you get caught…" she said with a warning in her voice.

Rook smiled wryly at her and replied, "I know nothing."

"Good boy," she said, smiling back.

"Rook's going back to work?" Lowell asked, hobbling in with a tea tray from the kitchen. It was a marvel the way he never spilled with his strange, uneven gait and the way the tray was balanced on his bad arm. "Can I come?"

"No," Rook and Fetch said together.

Lowell's face fell, and Rook quickly spoke again.

"Not this trip. I think I'm going to need your skills afterward, however. How's that sound?"

During the few short weeks he had been there, Rook had focused on healing and regaining his strength. Lowell, it turned out, had no small measure of talent with wood and metal and the arsenal of tools there on his arm. He was thrilled at the opportunity to build a few training pieces for Rook to use in his rehabilitation, and they seemed to be working well.

Lowell brightened again at the suggestion, but Fetch turned on Rook.

"For what?" she demanded.

"A little renovation project I have in mind."

Rook watched Fetch for her reaction and focused his mind on the changes he wanted to make to his office. Fetch said nothing, gave no indication of understanding, and simply glowered at Rook. He imagined he saw the tiniest flicker of comprehension on her face, a barely discernable softening of the eyebrows, but he couldn't be certain. Turning back to Lowell, he spoke optimistically.

"This is assuming your sister permits it, of course."

Lowell turned to Fetch excitedly, but she held up a hand to quiet him.

"We will see," she said firmly, though the corner of her mouth was turning up into an indulgent smile.

Rook took this moment to study the twins. He still didn't understand these two or the relationship between them, but he had spent enough time with them both to know there was something… strange about them.

Rook stopped outside of his office door and took a deep breath. It felt good to be back here, despite what he had already seen. There were no guards at the door to the office. Marlowe was either getting sloppy or cocky. Rook also hadn't seen as many lookouts as he thought there should be. This was a safeguard against both Enforcers and rivals, though their absence had helped him to sneak in. Rook had taken a peek down at the sales floor… not as many customers as there should be. None of these things boded well for the health of the business. He opened the door and stepped through.

Rook quickly assessed the situation. It was just Marlowe and one other man—Garrick, Rook thought he remembered the man being called—there. He smiled and spread his arms wide.

"Gentlemen!" he said congenially.

"Hey-ey!" Marlowe boomed happily.

He stood up from the desk and walked towards Rook to embrace him, and Rook gladly clapped the behemoth of a man on the back.

"How are you still alive, eh?" Marlowe asked.

"I have things to do!" Rook crowed proudly, avoiding the question.

Marlowe laughed and offered Rook a chair.

"Sit, have a drink, tell me how bad it was," he said.

"The stories I could share, old friend," Rook replied, "but I'm afraid I'm here to discuss less diverting subjects."

The jovial mood instantly dissipated like fog in the sunlight. Marlowe turned to the other man and motioned towards the door.

"Garrick, give us a minute," he commanded.

Garrick wordlessly did as he was told. After he was gone, Marlowe faced Rook, who had not taken the offered seat, again. Marlowe circled the desk again and sat down heavily in the large, leather, wingback chair.

"I never mentioned you or anyone else," Rook said sincerely.

"I know that," Marlowe said, waving the words away like annoying gnats. "I knew those dogs wouldn't break you. Kill you maybe, but never break you."

"Your faith in me is heartwarming," Rook joked.

Marlowe did not reply, nor did he meet Rook's gaze.

"What's happening, Marlowe?" Rook asked. "Why is the market dying?"

"It takes money to make money," Marlowe said evasively.

"I know how to make money," Rook said. "I've been doing it for a long time." There was a long pause, and Rook asked softly, "You skimming off the top, mate? Losing at the card tables? What's. Happening?"

"It's my business to run!" Marlowe snapped, banging his meaty fist on the desk. "Let me run it!"

"It's not yours anymore," Rook whispered, an edge to his voice now.

"You left!" Marlowe bellowed.

"And now I'm back," Rook replied evenly. "We had an agreement. I expect you to honor that."

"No! I can fix this, and I will. Now get out!"

"Marlowe, everything here is mine. You are my employee. Hand over the keys."

Rook held out his hand expectantly, his eyes locked on his former second-in-command. A shadow passed over Marlowe's face as he gazed at that outstretched hand.

"Don't do it…" Rook warned.

Too late. Marlowe pulled a knife from his desk and drove it down towards Rook's hand. Rook dodged, barely pulling back in time. A split second later and the blade would have pierced his palm and pinned him to the desk. His reflexes were still not back to where they had been. In the same motion, Rook used his other hand to pull a small throwing blade from his belt. He let it fly, and it buried itself in Marlowe's shoulder. Rook was on top of the desk now as Marlowe hurled himself at Rook like an enraged bull. Marlowe's massive fist knocked Rook onto his back from midair. Marlowe reached for Rook's neck, and Rook pulled another hidden blade from his boot. He sunk it deep into Marlowe's neck just as the big man's hands closed around Rook's throat.

"I'm sorry, mate," Rook croaked, looking Marlowe straight in the eyes.

Marlowe's face was a war mask of pain and shock and anger and shame. He died quickly like that, falling on top of Rook, blood gushing from the wound.

"Marlowe, sir, I—" came a voice from the doorway.

Rook looked back and saw Garrick standing there in shock. Pushing Marlowe's massive body off of him, Rook scowled at the man.

"Get this out of here," he growled, gesturing vaguely at Marlowe's body. "And, in case you're unaware of how I like things done, weight the body down with stones and dump it in the sewage outlet. Get it done within the next hour and do not allow yourself to be seen. And get me the financials for the last three months!"

Garrick turned, presumably to call for help to accomplish these tasks, but Rook stopped him.

"And Garrick... one whiff of dissention on your or anyone else's part, and you will swiftly follow poor Marlowe here. Am I understood?"

"Aye, sir," Garrick replied.

"Oh, Fetch," Rook purred, opening the door to her private apartments.

"In here, Rookie!" she called back from somewhere within.

Rook followed the sound of her voice and made his way past gilded furniture and finely embroidered window dressings. The wallpaper alone in this room was worth more than most Springhavian families made in a year. It was ornate and boldly colored, depicting scenes from the Duskwood, the forest for which that city-state was named. Rook guessed it reminded Fetch of home. Seeing this garish display of wealth made him pleased about what he had brought back from his office. He passed through another doorway and spotted the top of Fetch's head on the other side of a changing screen. He paused, having no wish to see her in her knickers.

"Calm yourself," she laughed. "I'm decent enough."

He rolled his eyes and kept a scathing comment to himself. He stopped when he caught sight of Fetch's reflection in one of the several mirrors that faced her and the changing screen. In the reflection, he could see Fetch rubbing lotion or oil or some such concoction onto her leg. It was that leg that held his attention. It was badly scarred and missing chunks of flesh, as if sections had simply been sheared off. A moment later, Fetch threw her voluminous skirts back over the leg and appeared from behind the screen.

"Why are you here?" she demanded, suddenly spitting out her words like venom.

"I come bearing gifts," Rook replied innocently.

Fetch glared hatefully at him for a long while. Meanwhile, Rook maintained his innocent gaze. Finally, Fetch spoke again.

"What could you possibly have to offer?" she growled.

Rook bowed deeply and presented a velvet box to Fetch.

"A token of my gratitude for all you have done," he said sincerely.

He opened the box to reveal a magnificent necklace of diamonds and sapphires with matching earrings. Fetch approached him and took the box carefully. She examined the gems closely. As she did so, she spoke with a softer tone than before.

"I take it you had a successful day?"

Rook thought back to killing Marlowe, the man he had trusted with so much. Marlowe had been his bodyguard for years and the closest thing to a friend Rook had for a long time. "Successful" was not how he would choose to describe today. He felt Fetch's eyes on him and was careful to keep his expression neutral.

"You love your position of power so dearly," she said... was that pity?

Rook said nothing in response to that. Instead, he turned the attention back to his gift.

"I could not have done it without you," he said.

"I know," Fetch replied, and she allowed herself a little smile at this.

Rook smiled too, but it was a sad smile. He bowed again and left. He didn't have time to waste now. He needed to begin repairing what had been broken and preparing for what would come next.

Dmitri stood at attention and looked at Fourth Hawkins seriously.

"You understand what this means, don't you?" Fourth Hawkins asked gravely.

"Yes, sir, I do," Dmitri replied.

Next to him Fifths Ellis and Jones also agreed. The three Fifths had been called into Fourth Hawkins' office near the end of their shifts on short notice. They had already been instructed to say as little about the summons as possible.

"This mole issue will bring everything you *think* you know about your fellow Enforcers into question. More than that, it will test you in ways you never expected. No one is above suspicion."

"Not even us, sir?" Fifth Jones asked.

"Not even us," Fourth Hawkins replied simply.

Fourth Hawkins had brought Fifths Ellis and Jones onto his task force because they had been witness to Varick's Verisap confession. Fifth Sawyer, on the other hand, had a vested interest in helping Fourth Hawkins, which the Fourth was not above exploiting. It was Dmitri who would keep watch over the other two as Fourth Hawkins held his leash.

"Begin with everyone's files," Fourth Hawkins then said. "I want to know about any holes, inconsistencies, or outright failures. We'll conduct interviews when we have a list. And do not in any way allow this to affect your regular duties. You are to perform as well as ever. Any questions?"

There were none, and the Fifths were then dismissed.

"I might start with your file, Sawyer," Fifth Jones sneered after they were out of earshot.

Dmitri gave him an even look and replied, "Do whatever you feel you have to, Jones. The important thing is that we accomplish our mission."

Fifth Jones gave him a cruel smile in response and walked off. Dmitri swore silently, cursed Rook, and began to think back over his records for the past year.

Rook slowly thumbed through the ledger before him. His eyes glided over the numbers for the last few weeks, his brain doing comparisons and calculations. It was a slow process, but things were beginning to improve. He'd had to apply every skill and ounce of charm to get certain vendors back. Some were happy to return when they learned that Rook was back in control. Others, however, were now working with rival crime lords, which made things very difficult for both those sellers and Rook. He looked to his liquor cabinet and made a mental note to restock, as business had severely depleted it.

The effort required for this endeavor rivaled that which it took to get Rook's forces organized again. Marlowe had apparently not seen the need for such a large network of thugs and lookouts and informants—*Fool!* Rook cursed—and so had released many of them from his employ. Rook was still working to get most of them back. If a seller of black market wares wasn't keen to switch sides, a hired scout was especially resistant. Merchants rarely favored a single buyer; they usually could not afford to have too much loyalty. The other crime lords, however, took the fealty of their men and women very seriously. Death was on the line for many so-called turncoats.

Because of this, Rook was still working with what he thought of as a skeleton crew. That was likely why he had no more than a few minutes of warning when an unwelcome visitor came calling.

The man opened the door and walked into Rook's office without a knock, without a word, and without an invitation. He was shorter and heavier than Rook with scars to show how he had fought for his position. He smiled pleasantly enough, but there was a murderous glint in his eye.

Rook was sitting at his desk calmly with his feet up and a glass of whiskey in his hand.

"Duke!" he said congenially. "So nice of you to drop by! Can I offer you something to wet your whistle?"

Duke said nothing, but instead took Rook's glass from him and took a long, slow sip.

"Ah, not your best stuff," Duke said, looking at the liquid. "What is this? Killian's 91st Dawn Age?"

"87th, actually," Rook replied. "Not their best year, I admit, but I sometimes like a little bitter in my drink. Reminds me why the good stuff is so good."

"I can relate," Duke said. He then finished off the drink in one swig and placed the glass back onto the desk. "You're the bitter in my drink, Rook."

"I'm crushed," Rook replied playfully. "I thought you liked me."

"I may have done at one point. Well, 'liked' is a strong word. I may have respected you at one point, but after that little stunt you pulled, you scared the piss out of the entire underworld. You're done for, Rook. Pack up and leave while you still can."

"Aw, Duke, are you… are you actually concerned for me?" Rook cooed. He then turned serious and said, "Let me assure you, the Enforcers know no more about you now than they did before. Same goes for everyone else. You know as well as I do they would have kicked down your door by now if I had given them even the smallest scrap of information."

Duke said nothing in response for a long time. Like Fetch, he lived much of his life in the daylight, allowing his wealth to cover his tracks and indiscretions and… lifestyle choices.

"Even if that is true, the balance of power has changed," Duke finally replied. "You're out of the game."

"Are you just saying that because you've poached so much of my business? Word is, you're working on a polished up copy of what I've got set up here."

Rook waited a moment. This was one of the tidbits Fetch had gleaned for him. The project was still in its infancy, but, according to Fetch, Duke wanted what Rook had and was moving to fill the vacuum that had been left. When he saw a muscle in Duke's face twitch, he went in for the kill.

"It's a bad plan, mate. You can't sustain an operation of this size anywhere with halfway decent folk around. You were going to, what? Run it out of your home under a guise of legitimate business dealings? Open a proper shop in the Sand district and have a secret back room? It's too risky. Dressing anything up as more than it is never ends well. In the end, people will always see through the façade."

"Gents," Duke said.

A moment later, two men entered. One of them used to work for Rook. Rook grimaced as he took in their matching, bespoke uniforms, complete with Duke's signature colors, scarlet and plum, for the trim.

"You've dressed up your thugs nicely. Just as I said, people will always see through your façade," Rook sneered.

"I'll give you one more chance, Rook. Agree to leave, and things won't have to get messy."

"I'd rather things just go back to the way they were," Rook said with a crooked smile.

Before Duke could make good on his promise, Rook pushed a lever underneath his desk. Crossbow bolts came flying out of the shadowed corners, but they only impaired the three men there. None hit lethal spots. Rook would have to have Lowell make some adjustments. Limbs flew through the air, kicking, punching, striking anything they could. Cartilage crunched and a bone snapped. Blood spattered. The empty whiskey glass was embedded in Duke's head. Rook felt a blade slice through his side. He was taking blows from all sides. The poisoned whiskey seemed to be slowing Duke down, but not as quickly as Rook would like. One man down, the one who used to work for Rook. That daft fellow always did leave his flank open. Duke stumbled back. Rook focused on his other bodyguard. He was quick like Rook and handy with those knives. Oh, but he wasn't much of a match for a large accounting ledger to the face. Poetically, a few well-placed stabbings with the fountain pen he had been using incapacitated the man permanently, leaving wounds bleeding both red and black. Rook turned on Duke. The man was still alive, but would not be for long.

Rook looked over his work. The butcher paper he had used was a good choice for containing any blood that still leaked out. Just under a dozen large, neatly wrapped parcels sat ready to be couriered to Rook's fellow crime lords. For a touch of drama, he had collected blood from all three men and, once thinned a bit, used it as ink to write each recipient a handwritten note. Each note outlined what Rook knew about that individual and what would happen should any of them get any ideas about challenging his return.

Next, he gave the couriers a chilling lecture about loyalty and following instructions, which in this case referred to theirs: take the package directly to the destination, deliver it directly to the intended recipient, and leave. Do nothing else. You are being paid well and do not want to end up like your bundles there. The men and women conveyed their understanding and began to make their way out.

Fetch was there when Rook returned to her manor that morning.

"All hail the king," she said with a raised eyebrow.

"I hope to be leaving soon," he replied, ignoring her comment. "I truly appreciate everything you have done for me."

Fetch smiled and nodded her head.

Rook gave her a tired bow and then began to make his way out. On his way, he stopped and spoke again.

"Oh, and is Lowell around? I was hoping to speak with him... after a bath, I think."

# 26

# ASSASSINS

Lenore, Eamon, and Neal wound their way through the crowd, Lenore leading the way. As she was both the smallest and a lady, she had an easier time getting the crowd to part for her. Now, if only she could keep herself from trotting so quickly.

A massive technologics fair had come to Springhaven, and Lenore was like a little girl at New Year. Eamon and Neal were not far behind. Copper and Dempsey were supposedly somewhere here as well, but they had come separately, and it would be impossible to find anyone among the throng.

"Eamon, look!" she gushed. "The mechanical animals! How do you suppose they're powered? Let's see if we can get a closer look."

"I say, Eamon, what do you think of this?" Neal asked, examining some very small fob-watch-like contraptions. "It's apparently meant to sit on your wrist. They've done away with the casing, though. What's to protect the clockwork from damage?"

"What I wouldn't give to have that in my garden," Eamon said, staring at a large water moving system. "How much would it cos—Oh, my stars, no! Walk away, Lenore. Walk away quickly before I'm poor."

The fair was open to all fields of new technology. Exhibitors were looking for backers for their projects or customers or trying to build a following or all of the above. Lenore was thankful she saw many other female patrons, but she quickly discovered she was often seen as a pretty, fluff-headed ninny. Depressingly, this was not completely unfair, as it was the way many of her gender chose to act... because being a twittering ditz was somehow attractive. Lenore was determined not to be disheartened, however. She was energized by the sight of so many pushing boundaries and looking to new possibilities. Neal was looking at the technologics fair as a work event, so he and Lenore had dressed for the occasion. She felt a bit as if this too worked against her. After all, why would such a fine lady know anything about these complicated pieces? Her fervor, however, caused her to be dismissive of these attitudes and a bit impatient.

"Now, this is what we call a firebox, my dear," the man said indulgently. "This is loaded with coal or woo—"

"And the water in the tanks is heated to produce steam, which creates pressure, which is then released once the pressure reaches a substantial enough level to push the valve open," Lenore interrupted. "Yes, sir, I am aware. What I am asking is where is the regulator. If I'm busy with the work of cleaning myself, I don't want to have to simultaneously keep an eye on the pressure gauge."

Lenore was currently looking at a "mechanized sauna", as the banner read. She was vaguely familiar with saunas, as they were popular in the cold northern reaches of Invarnis. Those were simple apparatuses, however. A vessel of water and fragrant plant matter was heated to boiling within a small, wooden edifice. The resulting steam and subsequent wipe down cleansed and perfumed one's body, and rocks at the bottom of the vessel retained heat, decreasing the amount of fuel needed to keep the water hot. Lenore thought it was an ingenious solution, especially given how hard life could be in that region. She had always wished to try it and wondered if this mechanized version might allow her to do that. It too produced steam and allowed a person to bathe with much less water than a bath required. It did, however, lack the perfuming feature and seemed to have a few issues. She was becoming more disappointed by the minute.

"If the user follows the instructions, a pressure gauge should not be necessary," the man said, obviously trying to hide some emotion, though Lenore couldn't be certain if it was annoyance or surprise.

Lenore thought hard about his response. He made a good point, but would most people follow instructions? Lenore knew how dangerous an overloaded steam engine could be. That was, after all, essentially what this was. It was rudimentary, to be sure, but the basic concept was the same. There was the potential for this product to literally blow up in someone's face. She decided this was one of those instances where a perfectly good concept was made unnecessarily complicated. Yes, it was new and shiny and modern, but some things did not require modernization, and that was saying something coming from someone who adored new gadgets.

Lenore politely thanked the man and wandered on. A fair number of the goods here were home appliances, and Lenore noticed many of the women in attendance were avidly watching those demonstrations. Steam dishwashers and laundry machines were some of the most popular exhibits of this type, and Lenore suspected these items would face the same issues as the mechanized sauna. She would scrutinize those pieces later, however. She saw miniature home distilleries—"They better have used copper," Neal sniffed, eyeing the various setups with a censorious glare—and repeater hunting bows and diggers for both construction and... graves? Was there really a call for that? Some of the concepts were far-fetched and would never be practical, such as the multi-foot powered people carrier. Others were so simplistic yet incredible, Lenore couldn't help but wonder why these were not already in everyday use. The best example of this was the simple hose irrigation module. A rubber tube, colored green to blend in with garden plants, was hooked up to a water source. A special grommet tool was included so that holes could be made at strategic points in the tube, allowing water to be released where plants needed it. It was coated in a shiny resin that made it weather resistant and could be left alone to do its work. Lenore suspected many a gardener would love such a timesaving device and took a card and pamphlet for Esther's benefit. Finally, there were creations that had no practical purpose but were amazing nonetheless. One of the main stages showcased one of these.

*Come hear the Ether Echo!*
*Instrument of the spirits,*
*Voice of the beyond,*
*Played by Mrs. Theodora Rosencrantz*

The little group walked away at reading the sign. Sensationalized claims such as these were commonplace, but they left a bad taste in Lenore, Eamon, and Neal's mouth. Given their proclivity towards science, none of them liked claims without backing, and they really disliked those that preyed on human emotion. At hearing the demonstration begin, however, they turned back and then stayed to watch. The sound produced by the Ether Echo was eerie and certainly otherworldly, an undulating tone of both low and high notes. It transitioned up and down the scale with almost labored effort, as if it was passing through thick liquid to do so. Indifference soon changed to curiosity, and they found themselves asking questions of Mrs. Rosencrantz after the performance. It turned out her husband had invented the thing by accident, and neither knew how it produced its ghostly music. It was both fascinating and frustrating, but Neal got their concert schedule and said they would be buying tickets to the next show.

Eventually, after completing a circuit through the entire fair, Neal, Eamon, and Lenore split up to revisit their favorite booths. Lenore had seen a curious array of odds and ends for sale in one corner, but hadn't had a chance to really investigate the offerings. The merchant was the son of an inventor of minor notoriety—Lenore believed she remembered her father corresponding with him a few times, but couldn't be sure—who was trying to help clear out his father's workshop at his mother's behest. The son, who simply introduced himself as Victor, had little interest in his father's work and therefore could only offer vague descriptions of what his wares did. Lenore was disappointed, as she would have liked to know the full history of each item, but there was nothing to be done about it, so she commenced her explorations with only her wits to guide her.

Some of the pieces were large, unwieldy things that were obviously for more than Lenore was interested in. There was a large, heavy glass globe that was bisected down the middle and hinged at the edges. It had a handle, but for what it was meant to be used was a mystery. Perhaps another washing machine, transparent so that you could see the garments within? But why? A broken centrifuge? Lenore decided to move on. There was a myriad of small items as well, and Lenore scanned the grabber claws, unfolding supply case, modular toolkit, collapsible bicycle, and more. They were all fairly practical and interesting, but nothing Lenore really wanted to spend her pocket money on. She turned to look over the display again and noticed something iridescent in the very back corner. She started towards it but was distracted by the sound of a heavy, regular clomping. She turned her head and then tried very hard not to stare.

Coming towards the booth was a man with numerous deformities, all wrapped in a very fine package of exquisitely tailored clothing. The man was missing a leg, but he had replaced it with a false one of pulleys and rods and metal gears. His jacket and one-legged slacks, which Lenore's mother would have whistled at, were twill woven wool, perfect for the cooling weather. His arm, on the same side as his missing leg, was wrapped in a bandage, and he wore a mask over part of his face. The mask, Lenore suspected, was no feature of fashion. It was his mechanical leg she was having trouble keeping her eyes off of. She wondered if he was an exhibit unto himself that she had simply missed. His lost appendage had been replaced by quite a marvel.

The man tipped his hat to Victor and began to browse the wares there. Lenore was hovering nearby, trying to pretend to examine her own section of merchandise while keeping one sharp eye on the false leg. She debated just coming right out and asking him about it. No! That would be so rude! But she was at a technologics fair. Wasn't that understandable here? She was still debating with herself when a cheery voice spoke to her.

"Excuse me, miss."

Lenore looked up and realized the man had been speaking to her.

"Do you mind terribly handing me one of those claws?"

She looked to the man and then to the table where he was pointing with his bandaged arm. Picking up one of the grabbers, she spoke as politely as she could, hoping to muster some goodwill.

"This one, sir?"

"Splendid," he replied.

He took it from her and tested it.

"Your leg is beautiful," she blurted.

Immediately, she blushed and started to apologize. Before she could even finish her first word, however, the man replied brightly.

"Why, thank you!"

Lenore was lost for words then. Now what was she to do? She looked at Victor, as if doing so might reveal some secret to how one proceeds in a situation like this. Victor looked embarrassed for her, and she looked away quickly.

"You know," the man continued, "I thought about using bronze instead for the frame. It does look so much nicer."

"But steel is so much stronger," Lenore replied automatically.

The man smiled at her, but Lenore wasn't sure if she should smile back. She felt she had already overstepped her bounds with this man twice in the last thirty seconds, so instead she waited awkwardly for whatever would come next.

"You know your materials," the man said. "I thought I recognized a kindred spirit in you."

Lenore allowed herself to smile now, demure and contrite.

"I apologize for being so bold," she said. "I shouldn't have called attention to…"

"To what?" the man finished for her playfully. "To my leg, which you would have to be blind not to see? Think nothing of it, my dear. The poor chap needs bucking up now and again, so I rather appreciate the praise." He then leaned in and said conspiratorially, "I made it myself, you know."

"Did you really?" Lenore asked carefully. She still felt as if she was being far too brazen.

"Indeed! Let me tell you, every chap here with even an ounce of talent has been eyeing it. I'd best watch out, lest they steal it out from under me."

Lenore allowed herself to laugh at that and then ventured a question about its construction. The two introduced themselves and chatted for several minutes before the man stated he needed to get on with his business and purchased the grabber claw from Victor.

"It was lovely meeting you, Miss Lenore," the man said with an awkward little bow. "Always so nice to meet a like-minded individual. I do hope we cross paths again one day."

"As do I, Mister Lowell."

With that, Lowell tipped his hat again and hobbled away. Lenore was smiling when she turned back to the item that had caught her eye. For a moment, she thought the item was part of the astralscope tucked back there, perhaps a lever of some sort. Upon closer inspection, however, she found that it was a separate piece entirely, though she had no idea what it was beyond that. The iridescence she had seen was a stone set into the pommel of the... whatever it was. It had a handle, a hilt really, that much was clear, but the thin, metal shaft, tapering slightly at one end, made the thing look unfinished. Had it once been meant to be pounded into a dagger? Was that how they were made? Lenore would have to look into that. The metal was dark and looked like iron, but it was lighter than iron would allow it to be. The item fascinated Lenore, and she asked Victor if he knew anything about it.

"Sorry, that's as foreign to me as the rest of these," he replied with a shrug.

"How much for it?" Lenore asked.

Victor looked it over, focusing mostly on the pommel. Lenore was fairly certain he was trying to decide if the stone was perhaps an opal or other precious gem. She honestly wasn't sure either, but the way the light played over the surface, purple and brilliant white and light yellow streaks down the length, she doubted it. Probably some type of pretty quartz or something. Victor then looked to the corner where she had found it. He must have eventually decided that something stored so haphazardly likely wasn't worth much, as Lenore paid less than a gold for it. It was a frivolous purchase, but the item was so interesting and the stone so lovely, she was pleased with her decision anyway. She checked her pocket watch and saw that it was nearly time to meet back up with Neal and Eamon. She shoved her new curiosity into her bag and hurried back to their meeting spot.

Rook waited and watched the street in silence. Even his breath was noiseless as it slipped in and out of him. The petrolsene light washed the green walls of the Limestone quarter with a pale yellow, which made the walls look sick like a half-healed bruise. Rook had been tailing Dmitri most of the night. The Fifth was on patrol duty tonight, and Rook had picked a spot he knew they wouldn't be seen or interrupted. He absently rubbed his lower back as he waited. It was a little sore today, probably from the new rehabilitation regimen he had recently begun. He was still not back where he wanted to be physically, but he had been getting better week by week.

It was to Rook's advantage Enforcer patrols often split up to cover more ground, as there just weren't enough men to cover a sufficient patrol area together. Finally, he saw his target walking by himself slowly down the road. Rook waited patiently and, as soon as Dmitri was close enough, Rook shot out of his hiding spot, grabbed Dmitri, and yanked him back into the alley. Rook's hand covered Dmitri's mouth, preventing him from calling for help. Dmitri fought hard, and Rook swore. He hated fighting Enforcers. They were well trained and disciplined, but Rook was faster and more experienced. He landed a few strategic blows to Dmitri's midsection and soon had the Enforcer doubled over.

"Don't say a word, Dmitri," Rook hissed.

"Rook! What the blazes—" Dmitri whispered angrily.

Rook cut him off with two more strikes.

"I said not a word, scum!" Rook snarled.

Dmitri scowled at Rook, but remained silent. He knew Rook wouldn't take this kind of risk without an explanation.

"You lied to me," Rook began, his voice low and dangerous. "I paid you for a service."

"What... what are you..."

Another hit, this one in the ribs, shut Dmitri up again.

"Don't play stupid with me. We had a bargain. You kill Edgar *and* Twila Crowley, I pay your fee. I held up my end, and now you have your sweet flower. You, however, *failed*! Twila is still alive. I saw her. She's a pathetic wretch now, a plaything for your sadistic comrades. What happened?!"

"Something went wrong," Dmitri explained. "Edgar tried to get Twila to eat, but she wouldn't. I don't know what happened. I had to leave to keep up the ruse. When I came back, Edgar was dead. Twila, I think she got a little of the poison into her, but it wasn't enough. It made her worse."

"And what are you going to do to fix this blunder of yours?"

Rook didn't need to draw a weapon for Dmitri to know his life was being threatened.

"I can't do anything now. They'd know I was involved."

"I suggest you figure something out. Make good on your half of our arrangement, or I will reverse my part in it."

Dmitri didn't know exactly how Rook could do that, but he knew it would involve Camilla. Rook could tell he had touched a nerve, which had been his intention. Dmitri would do whatever it took to protect Camilla, but he now also knew what was at stake if he failed again.

As the two stared one another down, Rook, against every instinct and learned skill, twitched in response to a spasm in his back. This was no response to physical exertion. It was a warning. His oath was demanding to be noticed. Something was wrong. Lenore…

Rook released Dmitri roughly and retreated, his figure dissolving into the shadows.

Lenore trotted down the road, trying to remember to watch the street signs for her turning. Preoccupation was an issue, though. She kept looking around her absently instead while her thoughts whirled around her like Fae, pulling at her and keeping her from her task. She rather liked the city at night. It was beautiful, all lit up but quietly settling in for a nice deep sleep. The silence and dark helped Lenore think.

Lenore had met Neal and Eamon back at their pre-arranged meeting spot only to find they had hit it off with several of the exhibitors and made plans to have drinks together.

"That sounds marvelous!" Lenore said excitedly. "Where are we going?"

At that, Eamon gave her a sheepish look, and Neal looked sympathetic.

"Erm, I'm afraid it… it's just that," Eamon fumbled.

"I'm afraid you wouldn't be welcome," Neal said softly, rescuing Eamon. "I'm very sorry, Lenore."

"I wouldn't be welcome?" Lenore asked, not quite

understanding. Then it dawned on her. "Wait, are you saying... I'm not invited because I'm a woman?"

Both men nodded silently. Lenore gaped and made a noise of angry incredulity. Several different counterpoints went through her head. She felt foolish about the one she finally landed on, but it was the best defense she could muster.

"Do they know who I am, what I've done? Did you tell them?"

Good heavens, she sounded pretentious!

"We did," Eamon said, taking her hands in his. "We explained that you were here too and would love to discuss their work."

Lenore pulled her hands back. She didn't need to hear how the inventors had reacted, and she didn't want to be comforted just then. She was incensed.

Lenore had never really faced this kind of prejudice before. Of course there was Dempsey, but in Lenore's eyes he was just an idiot and everyone knew it. He was no more than a nuisance, like a persistent fly you can't kill for legal reasons, an outlier. The museum was a lovely, idyllic place that encouraged forward thinking regardless of class and gender. Even the resistance she had faced there at the fair wasn't much of an obstacle since Lenore had the advantage of being a paying customer. She had heard plenty of horror stories from Mina and Camilla, of course, but this was new for her. Resentment rose in Lenore like a hissing serpent, and she found herself suddenly angry with Neal and Eamon, too.

"And you two are going anyway?" she demanded.

"It's a good opportunity," Neal said, almost impassively.

His bland tone only increased Lenore's temper. Nevermind that there was something else in his voice, something a small part of Lenore's mind knew she should consider. She shoved that small voice down and looked for something else to say.

There was too much, too many things she wanted to accuse them of, too many things she wanted to insist about herself, about the wrong way of the world. Eamon beat her to the next step in the conversation.

"I'm sorry, Lenore. Give it time. You—"

"Stop," Lenore snapped. "Go. Enjoy your boys' time."

"Lenore," Eamon said plaintively.

"I'm going home. Have a good evening."

She then turned on her heel and walked towards the fair's exit.

Now that she was alone, Lenore replayed everything in her mind over and over again. What a lovely day it had been, only to have a bucket of cold water poured over it. No, not a bucket of cold water. What it actually felt like created a repulsive mental image for Lenore, and she tried to clear her head of it. She couldn't decide if she was upset over her own behavior. She had every right to be angry, but had she dealt with it well? Probably not, and that made her feel worse. She was going to face these hurdles in the future. If she wanted to get anywhere, she was going to have to react with more grace. Wait, no! Why should she?! Because she was a woman? Because being such demanded certain behavior from her? She was furious all over again. What if a man had reacted the way she had? Oh dear, that was a bad example. Now she was embarrassed.

Lenore looked up to check the upcoming street sign and found that she didn't know this one. In fact, she didn't know what area she was in at all. Oh, bother! She must have gone too far. Why hadn't she just taken a hansom cab? Because she had been angry and didn't want to see anyone just yet, that's why. She did do some awfully daft things when she was cross. She looked ahead and saw a man walking down the road towards her. She could stop him and ask. Then again, she could just retrace her steps. Turning around, she looked back up the road.

Another man was walking towards her from that direction. Lenore suddenly felt nervous about her situation, her anger instantly dissipating to make way for fear. She crossed to the other side of the street and began to walk back the way she had come. She did her best to appear casual, but also tried to look purposeful. She didn't know exactly what that looked like, but she wasn't much fussed about looking foolish at the moment. One street up, someone turned a corner ahead of her, but she couldn't make out who it might be. It could be an Enforcer, which she would actually welcome just now. She risked a glance back and saw both men from before walking on the other side of the road in her direction. When she looked back, she saw the figure ahead was not an Enforcer. Lenore sensed a trap, and her old survival instincts came out.

She scanned her surroundings. No escapes. If she ran, she'd be caught by any one of the three.

"Excuse me!" she suddenly called out to the figure ahead of her. "You wouldn't happen to know the time, would you?"

She was shouting, her voice ringing through the still night like a discordant bell. The men following behind her slowed but didn't stop. The figure ahead was now close enough to be seen properly. It was a woman, though that didn't make Lenore feel any better at the moment. The woman's hair was cropped short —an appalling choice in their society; the woman might as well be walking the streets wearing animal carcasses—and she wore a greatcoat that hid her figure. Lenore couldn't help but wonder if she dressed like a man to earn the respect of her peers in whatever line of work she was in or if there might be a more nefarious purpose behind it.

Turning to the men behind her, she repeated the request, praying an Enforcer would hear her. One of the two men crossed the street to Lenore's side, while the other remained on the other side, effectively surrounding her. Lenore narrowed her eyes at all of them, doing her best to feign annoyance. The truth was her heart was beating out of her chest. It was clear these three had trouble in mind for Lenore.

"You don't want to do this," she said as steadily as she could, still loud, though less steady than she would like.

"What's that, dearie?" one of the men asked. He was challenging her.

"Whatever it is you've got in mind," Lenore replied. "Now look, I have money, and I'm perfectly happy to part with it. No one needs to get hurt here."

The three laughed at that, and Lenore swallowed hard.

"Don't worry about that, sweet thing," the woman purred. "We'll make sure to take your money, too."

Lenore did not miss the "too" and so then did the only thing she could, even though she knew it was doomed to fail. She weighed the options and ran for the gap between the man across the street and the woman. There was an intersection ahead, which increased her chances of alerting someone. She shouted at the top of her lungs as she went, knowing she was wasting precious oxygen she needed for running, but she was trying to hedge her bets. If she could get around the other corner, she might have a chance. Also, if any of the three had crossbows, she didn't want to be running in a straight line.

The woman reached her first, but Lenore bit her hand as it tried to muffle her screams. The woman's other hand, though, only tightened around her arm, and Lenore kicked out at the man who was there now too. He caught her foot and held on, unbalancing Lenore. The woman's bitten hand was back and successful in silencing Lenore this time. The man with Lenore's foot drew a knife, but the woman snarled at him.

"Not here! We need to make it look like an accident!"

"So just snap the little twig's neck," the third man whispered gruffly.

"Use your head!" the woman said, turning on him. "She lives with a doctor. She'll be able to tell. We're taking her to the spring."

Lenore either simply didn't know how close they were to Springhaven's namesake or was too frightened to work it out. She continued to struggle, refusing to go down without a fight, but three against one were odds she could not manage. She was dragged back to the footpath and around the corner. One of the men complained about wanting to knock Lenore out, but the woman reminded him about the doctor aspect and that they couldn't afford any suspicious injuries. Lenore could tell they were headed for less well-lit paths, and she knew she was done for if she was taken into that darkness. Her captors adjusted their hold on her, and Lenore was only able to get out a short cry before her calls for help were stifled again. Her heart sank further as another figure descended from above, leaping down from the building ahead like an acrobat. This was surely another thug here to kill her.

The newcomer emerged fluidly from the gloom cast by the building. Lenore stopped struggling. She couldn't move. She couldn't breathe. It was Rook, and he looked murderous.

"Get your hands off her," he said, that dangerous whisper darting towards the group like barbs.

Lenore felt the grip on her loosen but not release. She didn't know if her assailants knew who Rook was or if they could simply tell he was not one to be trifled with.

"Now," Rook growled. "I am not asking."

"Rook," the woman said flatly. "Move along. This is no business of yours."

"My business is what I say it is, Bonnie," he said.

"This is our job," Bonnie said, her mouth twitching up in a smile. "If we don't get our mark, we don't get paid... unless you're willing to make us a better offer."

"Stupidity isn't the same thing as ambition," Rook sneered. "Your disloyalty is going to get you killed."

"And who's going to do it? You?" Bonnie scoffed.

"He killed Duke," Lenore heard the man holding her whisper to Bonnie. "He cut him up and—"

The man didn't finish due to the miniature crossbow bolt that suddenly embedded itself in his face. It didn't kill him, but he did release Lenore in order to howl and grab at the bolt. Lenore had barely seen it happen. Rook was moving so quickly, firing off three more shots from the repeater crossbow before producing blades from thin air and hurling them forward as he rushed the group. Lenore spun and struck out at the body closest to her. She was already losing track of where everyone was, but she didn't much care. Her bag was still looped around her wrist, modern convention being such that allowed a fine lady to use her hand without risk of losing her belongings, which was, in Lenore's opinion, still less useful than her usual side pouch. The bag connected first, and Lenore thought she saw a spark, perhaps from the metal clasp hitting the buttons on the target's coat. The figure, the other man she now saw, stumbled, and Lenore saw one of Rook's throwing knives in the man's shoulder. She grabbed for it, pulled it free, and then jabbed it in again wherever she could. It disappeared up to the hilt just above the man's collarbone. He recovered then and grabbed Lenore by the wrist. She cried out as he simultaneously crushed and twisted her wrist. Suddenly, Rook was there, spinning and slicing with a pair of curved daggers.

Rook moved quickly with a carefully controlled rage, driving his anger behind every slash, every thrust. Bonnie rushed at him with her own blades, small but very sharp and easily maneuverable, which had been hiding within the folds of her coat. Rook used one man as a shield and then threw him forward into his comrades. Lenore looked to see the man who had been shot in the face dead on the ground. The second man was trying to regain his footing, and Rook took that opportunity to stab him in the back of the neck, slicing through his spine. Bonnie, too, took advantage of the situation and stabbed Rook in the shoulder. Lenore kicked her, not knowing what she was doing, and Bonnie turned unscathed towards her mark. As she did, Rook swung his second dagger around towards her, the blade slicing easily through half the flesh of Bonnie's neck. The fight was over almost as quickly as it had begun. The blood that ran out from all the injuries, Rook's included, looked almost black in the dim light, creating dark pools around the bodies, some of them still quivering. Rook was left standing with his rage still pulsing under his skin. When he swept over to Lenore, she jumped.

"We have little time. Collect everything," he said coldly.

Lenore tried to obey but found that her legs were beginning to give out on her. It didn't matter. Rook knew his business, and had everything collected and replaced within moments. Lenore felt sick at seeing how easily he slid each item from the body that enveloped it. They heard footsteps resounding off the street in the distance. They were coming fast.

"We have to go," Rook said, grabbing Lenore by the wrist and pulling her.

She stopped herself from crying out, but only just barely. That was the wrist the last man had hurt. Something was wrong with it, but Lenore couldn't worry about that now. Rook seemed to notice and let go, but he still urged her on. They ran from that place, Lenore following Rook blindly through the night. As they ran and hid and ran again, she began to realize the implications of the last... few minutes? How long had it been? Lenore's thoughts ran faster than she did all the way back to Rook's hideaway. Once the secret door was shut, she turned on him, not that she got far. Rook caught Lenore's incoming fists, though this time she didn't care about the pain that shot through her injured wrist. He said nothing, but looked down at her furious face, his own finally softening.

"How long?" she demanded through gritted teeth.

"Little bird, I—"

"No! Don't you 'little bird' me! I thought you were dead, Rook! Do you understand that? I mourned you!"

At that, she turned away from him, finally allowing herself to cry. She cried for him, she cried for her anger from earlier, she cried from her fear. She didn't object when she felt him wrap his arms around her and hold her tight. She recognized that embrace. It was the same one she yearned to give him, if only she wasn't so consumed by turmoil at the moment. He had suffered without her as well, though Lenore knew she couldn't begin to conceive of what the Enforcers had done to him.

"I'm so sorry, Lenore," Rook whispered into her ear. "I'm so, so sorry. This is not how I wanted to return to you."

"Why did you wait?" she replied softly.

Rook stroked Lenore's hair, and she could feel him breathe in the scent of her. His lips brushed against her ear when he replied.

"I had things to take care of. It wasn't safe for you yet."

At that, a memory rushed back to Lenore. She pulled away and turned to face Rook, feeling frightened of him for the first time in a long time.

"They said you… you dismembered someone?"

Rook reached out to touch Lenore's face gently, and she was suddenly aware of the sticky blood on his hands. She looked down. More blood was smeared and spattered across her clothes from where Rook had held her and the fight. Rook pulled his hand back when he felt her tense.

"Lenore, what I do, the world in which I live—"

"I know that world," Lenore interrupted him.

"No, you don't. Please, I'm not trying to frighten you, but you were a lone petty thief, beholden to no one. I thank the stars and heaven for that. Being a member of an illegal collective is a kind of death sentence unto itself, and running it means being the executioner. Lenore, please know I take no pleasure in these things, but it's what I must to do in order to keep others, not to mention you, safe."

Lenore couldn't bring herself to condone what she had heard, but she also couldn't bring herself to judge Rook. She'd always had an inkling of what the crime syndicates in the city were like—ruthless, underhanded, dangerous—which was much of the reason why she had never joined one, but she had no idea just how barbaric they could be. What Rook said made sense. She was sure he had to be brutal in order to successfully run a gang of criminals. Putting all that aside, though, she realized this was the first time he had ever openly shared about his life, and she didn't want to make him regret it.

"How do you… did you know Bonnie?" she asked, turning the conversation to the attack.

"She used to work for me," Rook replied simply.

"Why would they try to kill me?"

"I don't know." When he said this, Rook's voice was quiet and angry with a vein of concern running beneath it.

He reached for Lenore again, and the touch of his fingers against her skin told Lenore what she already knew. Whatever tonight was about, he meant to protect her.

"You should teach me to fight," she said suddenly.

Rook actually looked surprised at that, but his expression soon flattened into a set of grim lines.

"You're right," he agreed, his voice low again.

Lenore knew he must be thinking the same as she, that tonight might not be the end of it. Either way, being able to defend oneself was a good skill to have.

"Before that," Rook said softly, "may I just hold you?" Lenore hesitated, and Rook saw it. He looked earnestly into her face and said, "I would never hurt you. You know that, even if I could."

Lenore did know it, but knowing the damage those hands had wrought made her shudder on the inside. Even still, Rook was… well, now that she thought about everything he had done for her, he was unfathomable. She looked up at him, the memory of losing him coming at her like a wave on the incoming tide. Other memories followed, all of them pushing everything else that had happened today aside. She reached for him, wrapping her arms around that familiar form. She started to cry again as he returned her embrace.

"I missed you so much," she wept into his chest.

Rook reciprocated her sentiments in the way his hands gripped her, like a man hanging onto a cliff's edge. He nuzzled her forehead with his nose and kissed the top of her head.

Rook was thankful for his oath in times like these. He didn't really know how it worked, but it provided him some kind of advance warning system when someone bore Lenore ill intentions. He knew that was the only reason he had been able to reach her in time. Had it not been for that, she would be dead now. He also smiled as he thought about Lenore's cries. Had she not been such a fighter, he wouldn't have heard her and known where to go. She had been brave and clever even in the face of certain death, and he felt a swell of pride at that. He felt Lenore looking at him in that moment, and he looked down at her with a smile. How badly he wanted to kiss her just then.

Lenore could see what Rook wanted in the way he gazed at her. She would be lying if she said the thought hadn't crossed her mind already. She didn't stop him as he lowered his face to hers, cupping her face with his hands. Rook's kiss was strong and passionate. In it, Lenore could feel how deeply he cared for her, how much he had missed her, how sorry he was for leaving her and putting her through that anguish. When Lenore kissed him back, she told him how she never wanted to be without him again. Lenore eventually broke away as she thought of Eamon. She felt guilty. This was wrong, and it wasn't fair to either Eamon or Rook. Rook didn't seem to mind. He seemed happy for the kiss and said nothing.

# 27
# NOT AS BAD AS IT LOOKS

Lenore and Rook had debated about the best time to take Lenore back home. They did so as they roughly patched up Rook's injuries. Both of them knew they should have done so earlier, but there were so many other things happening. Because of the blood on their clothes, it was easily decided that they should return tonight and soon, definitely while it was still dark enough to conceal them. Lenore wouldn't let herself think about how worried Neal and Mina must be. Rook also agreed that Lenore's guardians needed to be told about the attack. They needed all the allies they could get for this. Lenore had to put her foot down about what entrance they would use, though. Rook voted for his usual window, insisting he could get Lenore up there even with her injured wrist, but Lenore didn't want to remind anyone about that way in, so she insisted on the kitchen door. Rook finally acquiesced to her logic, and they made the harrowing journey back to the Allen manor.

If they were caught, there would be no explaining away the blood on their clothes. Rook had only a small basin of water in his hideout, and much of that had gone towards cleaning his wounds. Beyond that, they had washed their hands—Rook helped Lenore, as her wrist had swollen to the size of a cricket ball—and nothing else. They tried to be quiet as they came through the kitchen, but could immediately tell there was no point. Mina and Neal's voices could be heard from the parlor through the butler's pantry and dining room. They both stared in shock when Lenore appeared with Rook in tow. Mina recovered first, her eyes darting between the two, assessing injuries and triaging the situation.

"Rook, sit. I need to examine you. Neal, get some ice for Lenore's wrist."

"You had best not be responsible for this," Neal said when he had returned with the ice, giving Rook a hard stare.

"It's because of him I'm alive," Lenore said heavily.

"What?!" Camilla exclaimed.

She had been upstairs searching Lenore's room for clues as to her disappearance when she had heard Mina start giving orders. Camilla was now checking Lenore for more serious injuries.

Lenore began to tell the story of the attack. When questioned about how Rook knew Lenore was in danger, he had simply referred to the oath as his answer. Lenore had gotten the complete version, which further educated her about the strange phenomenon. As Mina commenced with her examination, she uncovered far more than Lenore was aware of.

"It's like he's been mauled," came Camilla's disapproving voice.

Lenore turned and was quite shocked to see that Mina had Rook's shirt off of him. She noticed his physique first and was impressed. No wonder he was able to swing down from buildings! Then she saw the scars and gasped. Rook's flesh was patterned with stripes and gouges in angry pinks and old tans. Some were from deep slashes, others stab wounds, some lash marks, and others that Lenore couldn't identify the source of.

"We need to do a full examination," Mina stated. "Let's go into the kitchen."

Rook made an unhappy noise at Mina and looked to Lenore.

"Come now," Mina said sensibly, "none of that. We need to make sure they haven't done any permanent damage. Camilla, is Lenore well enough for now? I'd like assistance."

Camilla nodded, and Mina motioned for Rook to stand, which he did, and Lenore was better able to see what Mina was referring to. In addition to the scars, bruises and wounds were peppered across Rook's body, not all of them from tonight. All of his pieces seemed to be intact, save for a large notch in one ear, and a few fingernails were still growing back. Lenore suddenly realized how much pain he must be in.

"There we are," Mina continued. "Into the kitchen with you. We'll probably need to clean some of these fresher ones."

"What did they *do* to you?!" Lenore demanded.

"Nothing I can't handle," Rook said with a smirk, refusing Mina and Camilla's supporting arms.

Lenore was reluctant to let Rook out of her sight, scared she might lose him again. She got up to follow, but Neal put a gentle hand on her arm to stop her.

"No telling what they're going to do in there," he told her. "It wouldn't be appropriate for you."

Lenore wanted to object, to point out that his adopted daughter and wife were both going to see who knew what in there, but she held her tongue. She'd be of no use to Rook and his countless injuries. She looked back at Neal and saw in his eyes a mixture of deep relief and blind terror. She put her good hand on his and smiled.

"I'm okay," she said comfortingly. "I'm safe."

Neal tried to smile back, but his face broke. Lenore was taken aback when Neal began to cry. She reached out to him, unsure of what else to do, and he hugged her tightly. Lenore was suddenly and painfully reminded of when her own father had hugged her like this.

"I was so scared, Lenore," Neal confessed. "I'm even more scared now."

"I know. Me, too," she agreed. She wanted to be strong for him, so she added, "We'll figure this out."

They stood there in the hug for several more moments, Lenore wanting to comfort the man who had become a second father to her. Neal finally released her and was able to smile weakly.

"You're right. We'll figure this out," he said hopefully.

Lenore smiled back, and there was suddenly a knock at the door.

"Who the blazes is that?!" Lenore hissed, suddenly afraid again.

Surely it was an Enforcer. It had to be. Who else would call at this hour?

"Eamon," Neal said simply and headed for the door.

Lenore's fear escalated to panic, though now for a completely different reason. She glanced back in the direction of the kitchen. Rook was in the house. Eamon was coming in. This was a bad situation. She turned back towards the reception hall and heard Neal speaking.

"It's not as bad as it looks," he said.

"What does that mea—Lenore!"

Eamon was by her side in a second. He examined her iced wrist, barely daring to touch it. He took in the blood and bruises and her disheveled hair. He looked back to Neal with a look that screamed, *not as bad as it looks?!* He then turned back to Lenore and seemed to have trouble finding his voice.

"What happened?" he finally wheezed.

Lenore sighed, not wanting to rehash everything but

knowing it was better to get it over with and Eamon out of the house.

"I was attacked," Eamon paled, and Lenore rushed to finish. "I'm fine now! I'm safe. That's what matters."

"How?! Have you called the Enforcers? Where was this?"

Lenore shot a look at Neal, begging for help. Thankfully, Neal caught her glance.

"Eamon, I understand how you feel," he said. "Believe me, I do. It is very late, however, and Lenore needs to wash and get some rest. I think it would be best if you went home for now to rest up as well. We have much to discuss, just not tonight."

Eamon clearly didn't want to leave Lenore's side, but he nodded respectfully as Neal motioned for Eamon to go ahead of him. Lenore walked with Eamon as far as the reception hall but stopped there for fear of being seen through the stained glass windows on either side of the doors. Eamon leaned over Lenore and placed his hands on her arms, and she was surprised to feel a tremble in them. Eamon snuck a glance at Neal, who had respectfully turned away from them.

"Are you sure you're alright?" Eamon whispered worriedly.

"I am," Lenore replied.

She flowed into Eamon's arms as he embraced her and hugged him tightly, suddenly feeling guilty for how much she had frightened everyone. If only she hadn't gone out by herself.

"I don't want to let you go," Eamon whispered to her.

"I know," Lenore said, feeling secure in Eamon's arms. It was a different kind of security from what she felt with Rook, but it was comforting nonetheless.

She was suddenly immensely thankful for all the wonderful, loving people in her life and allowed a few bittersweet tears to eke out of her eyes. Eamon furtively kissed the top of her head and then pulled back, knowing full well Neal was keeping an eye on them. He gently wiped away her tears and smiled at her.

"I'll see you tomorrow," Eamon said.

Turning to Neal, he nodded and then left. After he was gone, Lenore slumped. Exhaustion was taking over quickly, but she still wasn't ready to abandon Rook. She wasn't surprised Eamon was aware of her disappearance. It was likely Neal would have sent a message to him via swift courier once he realized she wasn't home. That was assuming Eamon hadn't come back to the house with Neal in order to make things right with Lenore. Eamon being involved, though, as much as Lenore cared for him, made things so much more complicated.

"Why don't you head upstairs?" Neal suggested, interrupting Lenore's thoughts.

She didn't answer and looked in the direction of the kitchen again.

"He'll be fine," Neal assured her. "You know Mina and Camilla will take care of him."

Lenore wanted to know if they would send him away once they were done with their ministrations, but she didn't want to ask. Instead, she nodded and very slowly headed upstairs. That was more frightening than she expected, and she gripped the banister for safety as she went. She felt as if unknown assassins were waiting for her in every shadow, a multitude of which were cloaking every corner and room at this hour. Lenore lit every lamp in her room, driving the darkness away before peeling off her sweat-soaked, bloodstained clothes. Both undressing and bathing proved difficult with her pained and swollen wrist, but she did both as quickly as she could, feeling vulnerable by herself, and changed into something that would be acceptable to see Rook in. When she headed back out into the hallway, she heard voices from one of the guest rooms and followed them. There she found Rook levering himself into bed, avoiding his bad shoulder. Camilla was holding a tray of poultices and simples and other odds and ends while Mina helped Rook get settled. At seeing Lenore, Mina spoke more sternly than Lenore expected.

"He needs to rest, just as you do. You should let him be."

Lenore silently remained. Mina motioned Camilla towards Lenore and returned to her patient. Camilla set her tray down and picked up one of the poultices as well as a sling. With well-practiced, dexterous fingers, Camilla bound up Lenore's arm, expertly securing the poultice, which smelled a bit funny.

"Come on," Camilla said gently, turning Lenore away from Rook's room. "I'll stay with you tonight. Mina, you can handle the rest, can't you?"

"Of course. Lenore, darling, I hope you sleep well."

"Good night, Lenore," Rook called cheerily after her.

Lenore smiled, certain he was being cheeky to get under Mina's skin, and allowed herself to be led back to her own room. She was so thankful for Camilla that night. Anxiety sidled up to her and settled in as the lamps were put out, like an overly large, unwelcome creature that had crawled into the bed. Camilla's presence was like a security blanket, though. The killers were under orders to make Lenore's death look like an accident. Therefore, Lenore concluded, they wouldn't try anything with witnesses around. Yes, that was logical. Even so, Lenore held Camilla's hand as they snuggled down underneath the covers together. Bitsy was there, too, and none too happy about his usual spot being taken. He was restlessly trying to find a place to settle amongst all the extra arms and legs.

"He's so very loyal to you," Camilla whispered as they lay there, waiting for the ringcat to stop crawling back and forth over them. "I could see him, always attentive, caring nothing for anything we did. You should have seen his ears perk up when we heard Eamon come in."

Lenore sighed and said, "*That* situation is not something

I'm looking forward to."

"It's time he knew," Camilla said sagaciously. "Rook is only going to become more difficult to hide."

"I know," Lenore said, feeling her stomach twist.

The memory of the kiss was still bothering her. Not that she hadn't enjoyed it. She most certainly had, but she was committed to Eamon, and she and Rook were... they were not, not like that anyway. After learning about Rook's recent brutal activities, though, Lenore was more certain than ever that they couldn't have a future together. She and Rook had something together, though, and the idea that she could be unfaithful unsettled her. Small gestures of affection were a nonissue—definitely something with which the upper class mindset would disagree—but Lenore was actually contemplating whether she was capable of having an outright affair. She honestly wasn't sure.

"What's wrong with Rook?" Lenore asked, both curious and wanting a diversion.

"He's one tough chap," Camilla said, admiration coloring her voice. "Don't get me wrong, that wound in his shoulder isn't doing him any favors, but he's incredibly healthy for having been tortured for who knows how long. It's miraculous, really. Even still, you should make sure he stays put tomorrow as much as possible. His body needs to rest in order to recover."

Lenore thanked Camilla for the information, but it didn't make her feel any better. Camilla sensed her melancholy and squeezed Lenore's hand.

"He's here safe. You're here safe. And we're all with you."

Lenore smiled at her housemate through the darkness and squeezed her hand back.

"You're mad if you think you're coming in today," Neal told Lenore the next morning.

Lenore had gotten up and dressed as usual that morning, feeling oddly uncomfortable about the idea of missing work over the attack last night. She wanted so badly for her life to be normal, and she was going to force it to be, pit of dread in her stomach or no. Neal was having none of it.

"Stay home," he gently chided. "Study up on the southern coasts. I will handle Eamon. I imagine he'll want to come round tonight, so *you* need to convince Rook to stay quiet and in his room."

"You're going to let him stay here?" Lenore asked, a little surprised.

"I know better than to go against Doctor Allen's orders." Neal was smirking as he said this. "Not that I can stop him from leaving, of course. That being said, Esther will be here. I expect you to behave."

Neal fixed her with a serious look, and she blushed hotly. Lenore thanked Neal and watched him go. Mina and Camilla were nearly ready to leave too, so Lenore headed up to the library, grabbed a few volumes, and then headed back to Rook's room, opening the door wide for propriety's sake.

"Hi," Lenore said softly, a smile spreading across her face.

There was a part of her that still couldn't believe he was here and alive!

"Hello," Rook replied, a matching smile spreading across his own face.

Lenore looked around uncertainly. This was one of those times she felt out of her depth. The upper class had stricter rules about men and women together than the middle class. Lenore had been raised with middle class standards, but had learned much about the upper class since coming to live with the Allens. Thankfully, Lenore's fictitious back story covered a multitude of faux pas, so most slip-ups could be blamed on that. Neal had told her to behave, and Lenore didn't want to disobey him, especially with everything going on right now, but what was appropriate behavior in this case? How did one keep a male guardian-companion company while he convalesced in bed from a stabbing without crossing lines of propriety?

"Come on, little bird," Rook said, seeing her hesitation and getting up from the bed. "I'm liable to crack up if I don't move around a bit."

Lenore held his hand as they made their way into the library. She insisted Rook take the sofa while she spread her books out on the rug. Having the books in front of her on the floor was easier than trying to balance them and turn pages with only one free hand. She had selected several geographical volumes that covered the southern region of Invarnis. She didn't know why Neal wanted her to study this, but she did as she was told. Esther came by a few times to check Rook's poultices, something Lenore was sure Mina had instructed her to do, and deliver tea. Lenore wasn't sure what was safe to talk about with Esther milling about, but that turned out to be just fine. Rook didn't seem too keen to talk anyway. He was mostly content to lie there while Lenore read, often looking over her shoulder. Lenore was distracted, though, worrying about him, and he had to encourage her to stick to her task.

"I'm not going anywhere, I promise," he told her. "Not until tonight at least."

"Eamon will likely be over later," Lenore told him, and she watched him for a reaction. "You'll need to make yourself scarce."

"You're still with him, then?" he asked unhappily.

"I am," Lenore said simply.

Despite Lenore's misgivings about her own behavior, she wasn't going to stand for Rook to speak ill of Eamon, just as she wouldn't stand for Eamon to speak ill of Rook.

"I don't know if you heard him last night, but he was very concerned for me," Lenore continued. "Do not roll your eyes at me! Eamon is sincere, and heaven knows neither he nor you would have had to endure what you did last night if it weren't for me."

"Stop, Lenore," Rook said severely. "Don't you dare blame yourself for what happened! Abusing and killing is what those people do. If they hadn't been after you, they would have been after some other mark."

"I went out alone, Rook," Lenore argued. "I am at least a little to blame, for mere stupidity if nothing else."

"You should be able to walk down a street at night without fear of assault."

"That would be grand, wouldn't it? But that's not reality. I should have been smarter."

Rook sighed and rolled his head back onto the arm of the sofa.

"It's not your fault," he said, closing his eyes. "If nothing else comes from this conversation, I want you to know that."

Lenore huffed. Rook was just concerned for her and wanted her to be happy and safe. She shuffled back towards him with her books and leaned against his cushion. She reached up with her good hand and stroked his arm soothingly.

"Thank you for caring for me," she said quietly.

He turned to look at her and smiled a little.

"Always," he said, and ran a finger along her chin.

"Will you stay hidden when Eamon calls on me today?"

Rook agreed, and Lenore suspected he had only done so for her sake. After that, they sat in companionable silence, Rook simply stroking and playing with Lenore's good hand when she didn't need it to turn pages. When Mina arrived home that night —Camilla was out with Dmitri—she immediately checked on

Rook. She was pleased with the effect the poultices were having. Neal was not far behind with Eamon trailing, and Rook had to stifle his laughter as Lenore practically shoved him back into his room. Rook stole a kiss on her cheek right before she shut the door, making her scrunch her face at him, though she wasn't terribly serious.

The embrace that Eamon swept Lenore up into when she came downstairs surprised her in its ferocity.

"Neal told me the whole story today," he breathed into her ear. "I can't believe someone would try to kill you."

"The whole story?" Lenore asked, shooting an indignant glance at Neal.

Eamon's behavior was hardly proper, but Lenore expected an exception was being made due to special circumstances. Well, a small exception. When Eamon's embrace went on too long, Neal cleared his throat, and Eamon reluctantly pulled away. He muttered a halfhearted apology to Neal, at whom Lenore continued to stare.

"The whole story?" she repeated to both Neal and Eamon.

"Indeed," Neal replied. "I'll leave you two to speak."

The bottom of Lenore's stomach dropped out. How could Neal do this to her?!

"Shall we speak out in the garden?" Eamon asked.

Lenore tried to think quickly, but she was still reeling, making her brain sluggish. She nodded, but changed her mind and led Eamon out to the courtyard instead. The Allens' estate sat on a handsome parcel of land, though Eamon's family holdings were even larger. While it was unlikely they would be overheard in the garden, Lenore felt safer in the center of the estate with walls and as much land as possible on all sides.

Once outside, Lenore looked up to the windows on the second story. She saw hers, but only now understood how Rook was able to get in and out: pure strength and skill. The window of his room did not face the courtyard, but several others did. If someone inside the house wanted to eavesdrop, they might be able to, so Lenore resolved to speak softly... whenever she got around to it. There was a stone bench there, and she tried to sit as if staying still might still her nerves as well. She was far too keyed up for that to last very long, however, so she resorted to pacing nervously back and forth before the rosebushes, trying to figure out exactly where to start.

"Tell me what Neal told you," she said slowly, still trying to get her brain to work more quickly. She then added gravely, "Quietly."

"Not as much as I would like," Eamon replied, keeping his eyes on Lenore. "He said you were attacked on your way home from the fair, that they meant to kill you. You, specifically. Then he said a family friend came to your rescue."

Lenore was surprised and pleased at hearing this last part. A family friend was far more credit than Lenore thought Neal would ever give Rook. She was also relieved that "the whole story" to Eamon apparently just meant "the framework of last night". Still, though, she was irritated at having been forced into this conversation with Eamon for which she didn't feel at all prepared.

"Whoever this friend is, I'd very much like to shake his hand and buy him a drink," Eamon said, obviously trying to coax a smile from Lenore. It didn't work. "Have you spoken to the authorities yet?" Eamon tried again. "What about Dmitri? What has he said about all this?"

At the mention of Dmitri, something came back to Lenore. After everything she had recently learned about Rook, she suddenly wanted to know the answer to something she had thought long settled.

"He said you were somehow involved in criminal activity," Lenore said so quietly she wasn't sure Eamon heard her.

Eamon went completely white and sank down onto the bench. He started murmuring to himself about not understanding how they had found out, about needing to leave, to get his family out. He most certainly had heard, and Lenore realized her mistake.

Of course Eamon was scared. Petrified was probably more correct. He had no way of knowing that Dmitri was a mole, if Dmitri's claims of how careful he was were to be believed. Lenore knew that feeling all too well. When they had come for her parents, after her initial terror at losing them, Lenore could only think, *what if they come for me, too?* It was part of the reason that Lenore had become a thief, besides the fact that her parents' arrest had been very public and no one would employ her afterwards. At least as a thief she could hide, she had decided. To think that Eamon was facing that horror now pulled Lenore's heart to him.

"Eamon," Lenore said, sitting down next to him on the bench, "He told me two months ago. He's not coming after you."

Shock, relief, and confusion all suddenly began to fight for a place on Eamon's face. He stuttered until he finally landed on a point to make.

"You have to believe me, Lenore. It's not how it sounds. I… assist with a movement that opposes the Enforcers. It's nothing radical like some of the groups out there. We just want a fair system of justice: trials, the opportunity to defend ourselves when accused, an equitable sentence for crimes that are committed. I'm not directly involved. I just provide resources… alright, money, when I can. Please, tell me you believe me."

Lenore searched his face. Blazes, what was wrong with her?! She knew this man, knew his character, and yet couldn't quite bring herself to do it. She couldn't just trust his word as his word. Lenore looked away, and Eamon took her hand.

"Why, Lenore? Why don't you believe me?" he asked desperately.

Because she had been a criminal and there was no honor among thieves? Very likely. Because she had seen too much? Probably.

"Because people are horrible, terrible, petty creatures that care nothing for the suffering of their fellows," she said bitterly, thinking back to the way all her neighbors had just watched as her parents were beaten and hauled away. "They will betray their fellow man to injustice as easily as they would crush a bug beneath their heel. Because they are cowards and cruel, and their words are meaningless. A person's word is no longer the bond it was in the Old World. It's naught but breath and noise to them."

Eamon was looking at Lenore with sad, soft eyes. This was a side of her he had never seen before. She had suffered something he knew nothing of.

"Lenore, I swear to you that every word I've ever told you is true. I swear to you that what I am saying now is true. And I swear to you that I will never speak falsely to you. I swear by my life and my heart, this is my bond. You can trust me."

Lenore looked at Eamon with wide, surprised eyes. She hadn't asked for this. She hadn't done anything to warrant such a gesture. This was a promise that Eamon would have to keep until the end of his days. They had talked about oaths in the past, and Lenore knew he believed in them at least to some extent. Surely she wasn't worth this.

"My name isn't Lenore Blackbird, it's Crowley," she whispered suddenly, "and it's because of me… sort of, that Dmitri knows about you. Not really, but it is."

"You're not making any sense."

Lenore took a deep breath.

*Oh stars, oh stars, oh stars, what was she doing?!*

He had made her an oath. She was safe.

"Oaths within oaths…" she said, and then began her tale.

She began with telling him about her parents and their arrest and her subsequent disappearance into the world of shadows and near-starvation. She explained how Rook had been looking for her at the same time and how he had come to know her father and become indebted to him. Her story about when she saved Dmitri's life made Eamon smile knowingly and then smile wider when she explained how the Allens had taken her in and helped her with her new identity. Lenore left out Gadget's name completely and didn't even mention anything that was related to Kieran. She had to swallow a lump in her throat when she explained about Rook's task to have her parents killed, and things got a bit dicey after that when she got to the part about how she and Rook had become allies and then friends. She left nothing out as she described the fight from the previous night, but said nothing of what transpired afterward.

"He is my best friend," she said adamantly. "He's my guardian and has gone to great lengths to protect me. He's always been everything I've ever needed."

She did not mention his nightly visits, but her tone implied that he was very special to her and that he was part of the package for anyone that wanted her in their life. Eamon did not miss this. The two were silent for a while afterward.

"So… were you ever going to tell me?" Lenore asked finally. "About your… other interests?"

"To be honest, no. Plausible deniability and all that," Eamon replied. There was a pause wherein he studied her curiously. "Were you ever going to tell me?"

Lenore laughed sardonically at that and said, "Heavens, no! It was too dangerous. Plausible deniability and all of that."

"I had no idea," he said frankly.

"That's kind of the point," Lenore replied with a wry smile.

"So now what?"

"What do you mean?"

"Now that we've shared our deepest, darkest secrets with each other, what do we do with them?"

"Um, nothing," Lenore replied with a raised eyebrow. "Why would we need to do anything?"

"I don't know. It just feels kind of momentous somehow."

"Let's not celebrate our shared criminality, hm?"

"Fair enough. Though, speaking of criminals, why did Varick turn himself in?"

"His name is Rook," she said more angrily than she had meant to.

"Sorry, Rook," Eamon said, backing off. He could tell he had hit a nerve. "Why did he do it?"

Lenore sighed and said, "I honestly don't fully know."

She had her theories, to be sure, but wasn't keen on sharing them with Eamon. She was trying to avoid the subject of Rook's romantic feelings for her as much as possible. Eamon, however, seemed to have already picked up on it despite her best efforts.

"He was at your debut? There's no way Mina invited him."

"No, he came of his own accord. How did you see him? He wasn't there but a few minutes."

"You were the belle of the ball. Is it all that surprising my eyes were on you?"

Lenore rolled her eyes but smiled. Eamon scooted closer and spoke earnestly as he took her hand in his.

"I don't mind if you have another admirer. I expect it, actually… a lot. I just want to know how hard I'm going to need to fight for you."

"You don't need to at all," Lenore assured him. "I'm not going to court Rook."

"I'll still fight for you anyway, just for good measure."

Lenore nudged Eamon with her shoulder and smiled.

"So when do I get to meet him?" Eamon asked.

"What?!" Lenore cried. "Why would you want to?"

"Why not?"

Lenore forbade Eamon from meeting Rook for the time being. There was too much going on at the moment. It was a paper-thin guise, and Lenore was pretty sure Eamon saw right through it, but he was good enough to agree without pointing that out.

# 28
# BEING PARENTS

amon stayed a little while longer, and Lenore debated with herself whether or not she should inquire about his clandestine activities. She decided against it in the end because she wasn't even sure what she thought of it. She had already decided she couldn't be with Rook because of what he did for a living, but was what Eamon did any different? Granted, he wasn't killing his enemies and cutting up their bodies like a chicken for dinner, but what did the people he financially supported do? Eamon might indirectly have just as much blood on his hands. She felt exposed and vulnerable now. She still wasn't completely at peace with having bared her secrets to Eamon, but he had told her his and made a vow to her. That was a great comfort. Would she ever trust him completely, though? Could she ever trust anyone completely? She even questioned Rook at times. Lenore, weary of all the worry and stress that had plagued her for the last twenty-four hours, leaned her head on Eamon's shoulder and closed her eyes. She trusted him enough for this just now. He seemed happy about that, and the two sat in companionable silence for a while. After Eamon left, the silence came to an abrupt halt.

"What possessed you to tell him?!" Lenore shouted.

She had confronted Neal as soon as Eamon was gone. It was the first proper row they'd had, and Lenore found herself furious and indignant a second night running.

"Lenore, he has a right to know!"

"A right?!" Lenore scoffed. "Neal, this is *my life*! Do you have any idea the position you put me in?! You should have asked *me*!"

"We can trust Eamon."

Lenore released a very unladylike sound of exasperation and pressed her palm to her forehead.

"It wasn't your decision to make," she insisted.

"It is because it concerns my household."

Lenore bit back a harsh retort. *That* would certainly not help this situation.

"Why couldn't you let me make this decision for myself?" she asked instead. "Or at least have discussed your plan with me so that we could agree on something together? Or am I just a simple female and therefore have no say in the decisions that affect my life?"

Lenore knew she was being petty but didn't care. She certainly wasn't backing down now.

"Don't be ridiculous! You know very well—"

"Pardon me," came a voice from the doorway.

Both Lenore and Neal looked to see Rook standing there.

"Please, forgive me for interrupting, but I need to speak with the both of you before I go," he said respectfully.

Neal looked back to Lenore and said, "We'll continue this later."

Lenore ignored him and asked Rook, "You're leaving? Now? Has Mina deemed you well enough?"

His eyes soft on her, Rook replied gently.

"I have to. There are things that need my attention."

Lenore didn't doubt it but also didn't like it. She didn't question him further, though. She didn't really want to know what he needed to get back to. Neal had already gotten himself ensconced in a chair there in the drawing room, where Lenore had cornered him after Eamon left.

The drawing room was not often used except when Neal had some of his fellow gentlemen over. Lenore didn't like it because it was dark and smelled of leather. Now, though, she especially disliked the "boys only club" feel it gave her.

"Doctor Allen should be here as well, please," Rook said.

Lenore appreciated the respectful manner Rook was taking, though it also served to raise her already heightened apprehension levels. Neal agreed and asked Lenore to fetch Mina. Lenore bristled at this, still angry about so many things, but wasted no time in doing so. She was keen to hear what Rook had to say. She did not fail to notice, however, that Neal did not offer Rook a drink, which, to her knowledge, he did with every other guest that joined him in this room. When they were all four gathered together, Lenore realized she felt awkward too. Mina and Neal had to have some inkling of her and Rook's... relationship? If that's what it was. Whatever it was, though, it was hardly appropriate.

"First of all, Engineer and Doctor Allen, thank you for everything," Rook began courteously. "Please also pass my thanks onto Esther. She is a gem."

"We know," Mina said, smiling fondly. "And you're very welcome. You did, after all, save our sweet Lenore's life. It is the least we can do."

Was that a note of possessiveness in Mina's voice as she said that? Lenore could have just imagined it, but the idea that Mina was being protective of her was heartwarming nonetheless.

"That brings me to why I have asked you all here together,"

Rook said gravely. "Not knowing who contracted for Lenore's death puts us at a disadvantage. More may come. From what we know, they wanted her death to look like an accident. Now that she's escaped, that may stop them. Then again, it may not. They might try something wholly different. We simply do not know enough of anything for certain. That being the case, I believe it would be to our advantage to create for me a cover, one that is legitimate. Doing so will allow me to be seen and interact with her in the open."

Rook was speaking like a war strategist, examining tactics and creating plans. Lenore was impressed but suspected this was old hat for him. And she wondered why Neal was looking at Rook like that? He hadn't committed a crime. He'd been absolved, in fact. Not that he needed to know what Rook had been up to since being released. Then Lenore got her answer.

"You know it's not appropriate for you to be so close to Lenore. She is seeing Eamon. That, and there is the question of your class," Neal explained sternly. "Are you planning on returning to one of the Pendragon estates?"

Lenore scowled at him. Rook had barely escaped death and then risked himself for her, and Neal was ready to reject his idea on the grounds of propriety and *class*. The Pendragons were as close to royalty as you could still get in the city, and Lenore had grown up below them all. She felt as if her blood was beginning to boil in her veins.

"No, sir," Rook replied respectfully despite the very obvious slight Neal had just given him. "They won't have me, not after the scandal. Ideally, I would find employment. Though that will prove difficult given my history, I do believe my family name will help."

"I think I can assist with that," Mina said kindly. "I'll have Camilla get things arranged for you tomorrow, if that's alright with you, of course."

"I welcome the help, Doctor Allen," Rook said with a smile.

Lenore wondered what Mina had in mind, but felt confident that it was good whatever it was. After all, Mina didn't do anything by halves, and she was too much an enemy of the Enforcers to betray Rook. Lenore sorely wanted to go with Camilla, but wasn't about to ask. Neal seemed too conflicted with the whole situation, and she didn't want to push him any further.

"We'll need to figure out a story to connect you two, but I'm sure we can contrive something believable," Mina said pensively. "Neal makes a good point, however. The matter of Eamon is a pressing issue."

Lenore felt her cheeks flush hotly and shot an angry look at Neal, who did not respond. This idea of her and Rook's… kinship coming out for all to see was attractive but troublesome. It would raise questions. Lenore and Rook were far closer than was appropriate, especially since she was courting Eamon, and, considering the circumstances, she wasn't sure their bond could be concealed so easily. Their relationship had developed in secret under cover of night. How to either pretend they were not as close as they were or explain it? Rook would never stop being her protector, her everything-that-she-needed, and it seemed unlikely that anyone would understand that, much less accept it.

"He… he has already expressed a desire to meet you," Lenore confessed. There was no use hiding it. She didn't trust Neal not to broach the subject with Eamon behind her back, or vice versa.

"Dmitri did give you my message about him, didn't he?" Rook asked, his eyes suddenly sharp.

"He did," Neal replied, "and we have heeded the warning. I know Eamon quite well, however, and I believe he can be trusted."

Lenore could see Rook tense angrily at that. She was also annoyed, mostly because she was not aware Dmitri had spoken to Neal on the subject. Neal had certainly never mentioned it to her anyway. She thought something unkind and likely unfair at that. Neal had never asked her for her thoughts on the subject. Rook still very clearly didn't think Eamon could be trusted at all. Without thinking, she placed a calming hand on Rook's and spoke pointedly.

"*I* believe we can trust him too, but I'll be careful. I promise."

Rook left soon after their meeting. He snuck out through the back door and promised to see Lenore again soon. In the meantime, he would be investigating the attack.

This was not at all the way Rook had wanted things to go. Reemerging above ground, so to speak, was the last thing he wanted, as it would give the Enforcers plenty of opportunities to tail him again. Given the options, however, if Rook had to publicly defend Lenore at any point, it would be better if they already had an openly established friendship. This was a contingency he was prepared to face. Being connected to her put her at risk as well, though. His enemies could use her against him. He considered what might happen if he were to remain a shadow and carry on as he had. There was less risk on the front end, but if word were to get out of their connection, there would be the question as to why he had kept it a secret. Of course, he could always claim he kept his connections close to the vest, but that would still beg the question as to how he knew her. That was the truly tricky part. Rook could bluff, state that it was his secret to keep, but even he couldn't be sure that someone wouldn't uncover the truth. He had put out feelers for Lenore before. That had the potential to eventually catch up with him. Having a cover story to rely on provided an extra layer of protection. It was a lose-lose situation really, but he'd needed to make a decision and quickly. The more time he wasted, the more risk he took with Lenore's life.

As Rook left that night, his heart was pulled back towards the Allen manor. What he really wanted to do was never leave Lenore's side. That, however, was simply not possible.

Not long after Rook was gone, more arguing broke out in the house. This time it was Mina and Neal. Lenore could hear bits and pieces from the library. She still didn't want to be alone, and anywhere but her room seemed like the best option for that.

"Her safety is in danger, Neal, and you're worried about the perception of her honor?!" Lenore could hear Mina yell through the walls. "Pardon me if I fail to give a damn about what others think while Lenore's life is under threat!"

"It's not just her. Eamon's name is mixed up in this, too. He is a good man. I don't want him made a fool for that… that… cur!"

"Rook may well be the only thing between Lenore and certain death. Eamon is an excellent man, but he cannot protect her the way Rook can, nor do I know that he would. We know Rook has both the ability and the will, and if Eamon must suffer a little for it, so be it! If he is truly worthy of Lenore, he will understand and bear that burden with grace."

"Philomena, it doesn't have to be this way. Rook can stay hidden. He's protected Lenore all this time while remaining invisible. He can continue to do so."

"You know I don't like him or his romantic attachment to Lenore, but I trust him to keep her from harm. He understands these things better than the both of us combined. If this is what he thinks is best, we need to follow his lead. If you're that concerned with Eamon's good name, then you should convince him to break it off with Lenore instead of dragging my name through the mud. I've put my integrity on the line by agreeing to help Rook, and I am not going to break my word because you disagree."

"What's happening?" came a whisper from beside Lenore.

She looked up from her spot on the sofa to see Camilla standing there. She must have just come home from her outing with Dmitri. Lenore sighed.

"They're arguing about me," she said softly, unsuccessfully trying to hold back her tears.

Camilla made a sad noise of acknowledgement and sat down next to Lenore. She relaxed into Camilla as her housemate wrapped her arms around her.

"Dmitri says he expects to hear from Rook any time now," she confided to Lenore. "He's aware of the deaths, but there are no legitimate eyewitnesses. Dmitri is going to start pressing his contacts, carefully, to see what he can uncover."

"Thank you," Lenore said, and she suddenly felt very tired, as if she hadn't slept in years.

Mina and Neal continued to argue, but Lenore didn't hear much more of it. Her mind wandered back and forth over everything.

"How do you deal with it?" she asked Camilla suddenly. "Being looked down on because you're a woman, I mean. I can manage it when I have a voice, but being impotent, unable to speak up for myself, it just… even now they're deciding things for me…" Lenore trailed off with a noise that was something between a huff and a growl.

Camilla shook her head and pointed in the direction of Mina and Neal's voices. "*That* has nothing to do with being a woman. That's being parents. Surely your mother and father argued about you." Lenore opened her mouth to retort, but Camilla wasn't done, "And do you honestly think Mina would *ever* take that attitude with you? You know better."

"Last night, though, at the fair—" Lenore started.

"That was something entirely different. It has nothing to do with this argument." Camilla paused and then said more gently, "I know all too well what you mean, though. When people want to exclude you on the basis of your gender, there's nothing you can do but push forward. Persistence unto results unto respectability. You will get there, but it will take time and no small measure of patience."

Lenore made another unhappy noise at that. She knew Camilla was right and simultaneously loathed that admission. Thoughts about what Camilla had said about Neal and Mina's current disagreement pushed at her too, but Lenore closed her eyes and ignored them. She didn't want to think about her parents or why she had forgotten what it was like to have people dote on and worry about her. It was too painful for right now.

Dmitri rubbed his eyes in the dim petrolsene light, willing them to see better, to find more. He had returned to his quarters in the Enforcer barracks several hours ago and was looking over a number of files. Fifths Jones and Ellis, he knew, also had files just like these in their quarters. Their lists of interviewees were due soon, and, while Dmitri did have a list, he had no direction.

The Enforcer barracks were a number of long, low buildings near the Halls of Justice. In the Old World, these buildings had been servants' quarters for the royal palace. Thus, the rooms were small and neatly lined up one hall and down another. The walls were thin, and there were communal washrooms. When he had been a Sixth, Dmitri had shared a room with another recruit who had not been Enforcer material and was evicted from the order. With his promotion to Fifth, Dmitri had moved up to a set of private quarters, though the only real improvement here was the presence of petrolsene sconces. In his first room, he'd had to burn lanterns at strategic points around the room to get a sad but usable amount of light.

Currently, Dmitri was combing the files for something, *anything*, to put his comrades on a false trail for this mole. So far, he'd come up with nothing, and Fifth Jones had been subtly implying that he was onto something.

"Difficult reading?" came a voice behind his ear.

Dmitri shot out of his seat and turned in one smooth, swift motion. His truncheon was drawn and met a blade that flashed gold in the dim light. He found himself face to face with a grinning Rook.

"I can recommend a good tutor for that," Rook whispered, still grinning.

Dmitri disengaged and replaced his truncheon.

"You've truly gone mad," he sneered, keeping his voice below a whisper. "If anyone finds you here—"

"Of course, of course," Rook replied easily, waving Dmitri's words away. "I'm a filthy thief, you're the big hero, and we've never met."

Dmitri returned to his small secretary desk. He hadn't forgotten about his run-in with Rook from the previous night and was none too pleased to see him now, though he knew precisely why he was here.

"I know less than you do," he said brusquely. "I will see what I can discover, however. You'd know this if you would be patient instead of charging in here."

"I didn't charge. Charging is for brutish bulls like your comrades. I crept in like a spider," Rook purred.

"What an apt comparison," Dmitri murmured, looking back to his files.

"Oh, come now, Dmitri. Surely you're not sore with me?"

Dmitri looked to him and raised an eyebrow.

"Can you really blame me?" Rook whispered innocently. "Think about it. If you buy a suit and are only given trousers, you're going to demand some kind of compensation. This is business. I paid for a service, only half of which was rendered."

Dmitri still did not respond and glowered angrily at Rook.

"Very well, I admit I acted rashly. I did not treat you like the valued partner you are. My eyes have been opened."

"You mean circumstances have changed," Dmitri hissed finally. "You need me again."

"As I said, you are a valued partner, and you have my humblest apologies."

With that, Rook executed a florid bow.

"Does this twaddle actually work on anyone?" Dmitri asked sardonically.

"What do you think?" Rook asked, cocking an eyebrow at him.

"Business," Dmitri said. "Don't forget this."

"Perish the thought!" Rook said. "Now, what are your cronies doing about last night?"

"Likely nothing. Once they determine that the victims were all criminals—I'm assuming that's the case—they'll drop the investigation." At the eye roll Rook gave him, Dmitri added, "Why should they care? The more of your kind that kill each other, the easier their job becomes."

"And you?" Rook asked.

"I will make my inquiries with the upmost care, but results will come slowly. I must be cautious. I am under investigation."

At that, Dmitri threw Rook an accusatory glare. Rook's face changed then. His eyes grew sharp and his jaw set.

"Tell me," he said, his voice barely audible.

Dmitri scowled at Rook, angry at his reaction. How dare Rook shift the blame for this mess on him!

"What's happened, man?!" Rook demanded.

Dmitri's face changed then and, fully baffled, he said, "You actually don't know." Rook fixed him with an impatient, expectant look, and he asked, "What do you remember from your Verisap interrogation?"

"Nothing," Rook admitted, keeping his voice soft despite the dangerous edge behind it.

"Truly? We've never been able to verify with any certainty what victims can recall. You told Fourth Hawkins there was a mole."

"What did I say *exactly*?" Rook asked.

"I have no idea. I don't have access to the final report, and there's no telling what Hawkins recorded as compared to reality."

Rook sighed and rubbed his face in frustration.

"Truly, Dmitri, I am sorry. I never meant to put you in this position."

This was a rare show of sincerity from Rook, and Dmitri shook his head. Up until that point, Dmitri had wondered if Rook had traded the snippet for his freedom. Dmitri had cursed Rook for the supposed betrayal and considered what bargains he could leverage. Now that he knew better, his focus shifted. There was no defense against Verisap; Rook had been helpless.

"Nothing to be done about it now," Dmitri said pragmatically. "Our new goal is to put them off this trail."

Rook nodded and looked to the files spread across Dmitri's secretary desk. A knock resounded at the door, and Dmitri gave Rook a quick glance before rising to answer it.

"The files you requested."

It was Fifth Jones looking superior. Was it because he had

found something? Perhaps in the files he passed on now? Dmitri feared for a moment he and Rook had been overheard, but they had been so quiet. There was no telling. Mind games like this among the Enforcer trainees were common as fleas on a dog. Doubly so for ambitious, spoiled snakes like Fifth Jones.

"Thank you," Dmitri said mechanically. "Did you find anything helpful?"

"Maybe," Fifth Jones replied cryptically.

"Keep searching. We'll suss out this traitor yet."

Dmitri didn't listen to Fifth Jones' snide remark as he closed the door. He looked back into the room, his eyes searching for Rook. He couldn't find him at first and wondered if he'd left already.

"Always a pleasure watching you work," came Rook's whisper a moment later.

Dmitri looked in the direction of the voice and watched with admiration as Rook materialized from the darkness, crawling on the ceiling like a spider, just as he had said earlier.

"How?" Dmitri asked.

"Practice." Rook leapt down, landing on his feet as nimbly as a cat. "Now, about these files, do you want to pin it on someone else? On *him* perhaps?" Rook tossed his head towards the door where Fifth Jones had just been.

Dmitri looked back to his door, thinking about Fifth Jones. He was trouble and represented everything that was deplorable about the Enforcers. Dmitri wondered for a moment, but decided he couldn't sentence someone to such a crime, even a villain like Jones.

"No. I want it to appear as if there is no mole. You just muttered that in some Verisap-induced delirium."

"A tall order. We'd best get started."

The two men then began to sift through the information, Rook providing details where he could, and hoped to build a case for nothing.

# 29
# THE MEETING

ork the next day was odd for Lenore, yet she also found it to be both comforting and frighteningly necessary. Having something to do suppressed the horrific wonderings that plagued her mind. Besides her own problems, she also now wondered what Rook would be doing. Mina had assured them she could arrange something, and Camilla was meant to be working on that today. What could they possibly have in mind? The other ladies she lived with were far more enigmatic than Lenore would have ever initially given them credit for. The morning had been good as she worked to catch up on what she had missed the previous day, her progress hindered by her sling-bound arm. As afternoon approached and then drew on, however, her work slowed and her thoughts sped up. She was paranoid, expending considerable energy to keep herself from jumping at every noise and going to great lengths to remain with one of her coworkers at all times. She was the very picture of helpfulness as she volunteered to assist Copper with whatever it was he was off to do. He could be watching paint peel and taking notes for all Lenore cared, just so long as she wasn't alone and could occupy her mind.

"I'm in need of an assistant," piped up Dempsey.

Lenore groaned internally, though not as much as she usually would. Maybe Dempsey's supercilious droning would drown out the questions in her head.

"What are you working on?" she asked, trying to be cheery instead of cautious.

"I need to dictate a letter to a colleague."

Supercilious droning indeed. The specific breed of anger that was quickly becoming familiar to Lenore began to rise, but she swallowed it and began to follow Dempsey.

"Oy, Nori," Copper called after her. "I need a third hand, but not a fourth. Perfect job for you. Sorry, Dempsey. Duty calls."

Lenore silently thanked the stars and turned on her heel towards Copper. She called back something obligatory over her shoulder to Dempsey and hurried to catch up with the engineer, who was striding out the back door to the loading area, beyond which was the testing field. Lenore wondered if perhaps there would be more black powder work today. She knew Copper had made a few improvements, but no breakthroughs yet. Once outside, Copper perched himself under a tree that edged the field and began to pull items from a leather pouch hung from his belt. Lenore's brow creased in confusion. She knew that pouch did not contain tools, nor was it work related in any way. It was where Copper kept his pipe, tobacco, and striker—a compact item that resembled miniature sheep shears, except the end of one handle was flint and the other steel.

"What are we doing?" she asked.

"Taking a break," Copper replied simply, stuffing his pipe with a bit of tobacco.

Lenore liked the smell of it. It had a hint of cherry wood and vanilla. She was not unhappy about taking a break with

Copper. In fact, she was pleased about it, for Copper had become a good friend and a better mentor, and she enjoyed spending time with him. Plus, he never invited her along on his smoking breaks. That was his time, and everyone in the Arc-Tech department knew it well—Dempsey had once tried to show off to Lenore by approaching Copper outside, to which Copper had suggested he sod off. That he'd said he needed her help in addition to this made for a very strange situation indeed, so she asked about it.

"You obviously need a little time away, agreeing to be Dempsey's secretary and all that rot," Copper said bluntly. "Did you crack your head as well as your arm?"

Lenore felt her heart sink to her stomach. Copper was right. Under normal circumstances, Lenore would have refused, probably politely... maybe, yet she had barely wasted a moment before agreeing today. She even had a perfect excuse with her sprained wrist! Dempsey still made no secret of what he thought a woman's role should be, and Lenore had always resisted this proposed subjugation. Honestly, it had become part of the normal routine of their department. It was no wonder Copper was concerned. And Lenore felt ill because there was nothing she could say that was remotely close to the truth. She sat down next to Copper in the grass, chagrinned.

"I must have done. I'll have to solder it back together inside."

While Lenore was back at work, Camilla visited Gadget to inquire about an assistant she might have found for her. It was the Pendragon lad, who'd had a tough go of it since he'd been released from the Halls of Justice. Employment was difficult to find for ex-convicts, and Mina had taken pity on him as she provided him with first aid for his injuries. Mina was known for accepting patients from all walks of life, thus Varick had sought her out. So went the cover story. When she heard about the exchange, Lenore was certain Gadget knew the truth, as she was creating some false medical records for Rook to support the tale. Lenore was more than pleased by the report. It was simple yet cunning. Rook liked it too, for that very reason.

Rook was awed by the woman, and he didn't even know that she had been the one to forge Lenore's papers. He was dubious about two known former criminals working together, however, and suggested that it would perhaps be a mite suspicious.

"The Enforcers come in often enough to check up on me," Gadget croaked. "If they wanted to pin something on me, they would have done already. Don't fret, sweetie, we'll be fine. You any good with your hands?"

"Good enough," Rook said with a smirk.

And so Rook was employed as a whatever-was-needed to Gadget. Not long after, Lenore "met" Rook while picking up a bibelot Mina had ordered as a gift for Camilla.

This was the most difficult part for Rook. He kept searching himself for any indication from his oath that this was a mistake. It was suspiciously quiet, which Rook wanted to believe meant it wasn't working, but he knew that couldn't be the case. Still, his connection to Lenore was about to come out, and it set his teeth on edge.

Lenore went through her rehearsed steps, as did Rook. He "accidentally" bumped into her as he carried a large box from the back of the store to the front. Lenore graciously forgave him and introduced herself. Rook followed, and they met again a few days later at Mina's clinic. Thus, their story unfolded from there.

Lenore did express concerns about Eamon's sister Emily

talking to Eamon about Rook, but Mina assured her that was a violation of Emily's employment contract. Camilla made other points about this worry.

"He used Dmitri to find out about Eamon," Camilla pointed out. "It's only fair."

"He did that to protect me!" Lenore insisted. "He wanted to make sure I wasn't courting a maniac!"

"You don't think Eamon's concerns and motives are of a similar ilk?"

Lenore had nothing to say to that, and she dropped the subject, but her anxiety about it did not disappear. (Eamon did learn that Rook had been to the clinic. Emily couldn't wait to tell her big brother about meeting Varick Pendragon, the infamous redeemed criminal. He did not seem to be able to glean much information, though, as Emily took her job very seriously.) Rook and Lenore had several more staged meetings, wherein she befriended the former, very earnest delinquent. Rook now had to shake off the Enforcers anytime he returned to his other life—it took them almost no time to identify the vanished ex-convict—but that became easier as his injuries healed. In an effort to bore them, Rook spent some nights in Gadget's attic, but the Enforcers would likely always keep one eye on him—at least they could try—as long as he kept disappearing the way he did. Once everything had come together for the most part, Eamon asked about meeting Rook again. Lenore tried not to let her true feelings show on her face. She had been able to forestall this for several weeks now, which had given her at least some modicum of relief while she waited for another attack or for something to go wrong, but it seemed her time had run out. She was out of excuses, so she agreed, doing her best to hide her overwhelming reluctance.

Lenore made the arrangements with Neal, who seemed almost as apprehensive as she. He was no fool. Putting two men interested in the same woman in a room together wasn't generally a good idea, as he knew from personal experience. Best friends or not, he and Kieran had ended up looking like fools and doing things they later regretted when they were both pursuing Mina. This was before Mina had chosen Kieran, of course. Nevertheless, he allowed both of them to come over for tea later on that week.

Rook was the first to arrive, as Eamon wished to go home and change into something nicer than his work clothes first. He lingered, Lenore thought, a bit long when he kissed her hand in greeting. He didn't need to kiss her hand, but she knew why he had... and why he had done it in full view of Neal. He was trying to make some kind of point, which Lenore thought was frankly stupid and only hurt his case, which annoyed her. Despite how this made her feel, Lenore thought he looked very handsome as he did it. He wore a simple vest over his white linen shirt and had left his hair be so that it hung into his eyes ever so slightly. It was a rakish look that she found she liked very much.

The two sat on the sofa in the parlor talking while they waited for Eamon—Neal sat in an armchair nearby—and Lenore was reminded of how comfortable she was with Rook. She asked him about his new job and what he thought of Gadget, and the two fell into easy conversation, completely forgetting about Neal's presence and everything else.

"She's the one that made your bedroom furniture," Rook said, genuinely impressed. "It's very fitting for a little bird like you."

Lenore smiled and nodded as Rook tucked one of her dark tresses behind her ear as he had so many times before. There was the sound of someone clearing their throat from the doorway, and they turned to see Eamon standing there with Camilla just behind. Lenore hadn't even heard him knock when he arrived and couldn't help but wonder if Camilla had been intentionally silent when she let him in, or if she simply hadn't heard anything for being so focused on Rook. Eamon looked angry, which was something Lenore was not familiar with. She didn't like the dark look on his face as he stared Rook down, not at all.

She and Rook had just been discussing her bedroom furniture, which Eamon had never seen because he wasn't permitted near that end of the house, much less in her room. From their conversation, it was clear that Rook had not only been there, but spent enough time in it to get to know her wardrobe and vanity and bedside table. And Eamon had heard it all, not to mention seen Rook touching her so casually.

Rook, Lenore, and Neal all stood to greet Eamon. He seemed to share some kind of understanding with Neal when the two shook hands and was stiff as he bowed to Lenore. She felt awkward as she curtseyed back. Rook and Eamon did not shake hands. Lenore stood there feeling very self-conscious as the two men faced off against each other.

"So you're the one whose been looking after Lenore all this time?" Eamon asked.

"That's right," Rook said. "It's kind of a permanent job, you understand."

"That's what I hear," Eamon said. "So we're kind of stuck together then?"

"That's assuming you stay in the picture," Rook said waspishly.

"I've actually been meaning to thank you," Eamon said, "for keeping her so safe."

Rook rolled his eyes. Clearly he wasn't impressed with

Eamon's noble words. At seeing this, Eamon's tone changed, and it sounded as if he were trying to talk down a petulant child.

"Look, I'm sorry for the way things have played out," Eamon said sincerely. "Had things been reversed, I'd be pretty upset about not being able to be with Lenore too. I just—"

Eamon couldn't continue his sentence because Rook chose that moment to punch him in the jaw… hard. Eamon actually staggered back a few paces before recovering. He stood up straight and wiped the blood from his lip. He clearly wasn't going to retaliate, but it seemed he wasn't able to speak again and still be civil, so he just stared daggers at Rook. Rook, on the other hand, seemed incensed by Eamon taking the high road and looked ready to throw a few more punches just for spite.

"That's enough!" Neal commanded, stepping between the two men. "Sit down, both of you, and take a few moments to breathe."

Eamon sat down gracefully, while Rook flopped carelessly onto the sofa behind him.

"Camilla dear, icepack, please," Neal said to the girl who was looking appalled at both young men.

She did as she was told, and Lenore sorely wanted to go with her. She didn't, though, and instead took a seat in a chair that was midway between Rook and Eamon. She looked back and forth between them, trying to decide which of the feelings tumbling around inside of her to grasp onto.

"You've met now," Neal said, his voice dripping with disappointment. "Are you happy?"

"I am," Rook said, raising the hand with which he had punched Eamon.

"I'll take that as an effort to protect Lenore," Eamon replied tersely.

"Eamon, you requested this meeting. What exactly did you

446

hope to achieve here today?" Neal asked.

Eamon leaned forward and spoke sincerely, "I apologize for stirring things up, Engineer Allen. That was not my intention. I know Rook is very important to Lenore, so I thought I should meet him. What's important to her is important to me."

"Oh rubbish!" Rook exclaimed. "The only reason you were ever interested in Lenore is because you thought she came from money. Had Edgar and Twila thrown her debut and sent you an invite, you'd have turned your nose up in a heartbeat."

"You're one to talk!" Eamon shot back. "You're a Pendragon!"

"In case you hadn't noticed, I turned my back on that life! Men like you only care about whether or not a woman can offer you the two things you like best!"

"How dare you?! I love Lenore!"

"As do I! But I don't see you making any sacrifices to protect her!"

"SHUT IT!"

Eamon, Rook, and Neal all looked in shock towards Lenore. She was standing now with her hands tightened into fists at her sides like she wanted to hit one of them too. She took a deep breath through her nose and let it out slowly. When she spoke again, her voice was calm but cutting as she bit off each syllable with a carefully controlled anger.

"You are both acting like children. In case any of you have forgotten, I am by no means an idiot, nor am I somehow incapable of making my own decisions. You will not fight over me like a pretty bauble."

"Lenore—" Eamon began to protest.

"I am not yet finished!" Lenore snapped, cutting him off. "You will *not* fight over me like a pretty bauble. I care about both of you deeply and intend on keeping you both in my life. If you do not like that, you may remove yourself from it. I will be disappointed and hurt, but so be it if that is what it comes to. Out of respect for me, I would ask that you both remain polite when in one another's presence. If either of you cannot, or refuse to, comply with my wishes, then *I* will remove you from my life. Have I made myself quite clear?"

Silence then descended onto the room like a heavy wool blanket, making it uncomfortable and tense for everyone. Eamon was the first one to speak.

"Lenore," he ventured carefully, "I think it's fair to consider how this—" at this he gestured back and forth between himself, Lenore, and Rook "—might look if you and Rook appear in public as close as you truly are. Neal agrees with me, don't you, sir?"

If Neal had a response, it remained unheard because Lenore spoke again before he could.

"My issues with Neal are my own. I won't have you two ganging up on me, trying to cow me into submission."

"I can assure you that's not what we're trying to do," Neal said gently.

"Then why are you so resistant to Rook?" Lenore had wanted to use a different word than "resistant", but she was trying to keep this argument as civil as possible.

"Because I don't believe things will end well with him," Neal said, obviously also working to keep his temper in check. He raised a hand to stop Rook's forthcoming objection and explained, "Rook, you will keep Lenore physically safe, yes. I know you are bound by the very universe to keep her from bodily harm. However, beyond that, I believe you will bring nothing but trouble. Lenore has a very bright future ahead of her, whatever she decides to do—travel, study, explore, marry, not marry—and I am of the opinion that you will only drag her down and hurt those around her in the process. My apologies, Lenore, I do not mean to speak about you as if you are not here.

Please understand that I only want you to have the full life for which you have begun to work so hard."

Lenore had no response to that. She was still too angry to appreciate everything that had been said. Instead, she focused on a different matter with which she took exception.

"Stop talking behind my back with Eamon. Eamon, you do the same. You both only serve to drive a wedge between all of us by doing so."

Neal and Eamon exchanged a concerned look about that. Rook's expression was neutral, though Lenore could sense he was hiding his usual smirk underneath that mask of inscrutability.

"Rook, I don't want to see you," Lenore whispered, pulling the blanket more tightly around her and still refusing to look at him.

The evening had ended quickly and without resolution after everything came to a head. Lenore had told both Rook and Eamon that she thought they ought to go, and Neal supported her. Eamon tried to apologize as he went, but Lenore wasn't hearing any of it and sent him away. Rook only wordlessly bowed to her and Neal as he left. Lenore spent the rest of the evening with tea and Mina's semi-silent company in Mina's small study, which was tucked up in the one tower the manor boasted. Lenore rarely came up to this part of the house, as Mina's work made her uncomfortable, what with all the diagrams of body parts and organs and the like. She didn't want dinner, nor did she want to be anywhere she might run into Neal or Rook—that included her bedroom in the case of the latter—so she had picked the highest point of the house. Neal would have to intentionally seek Mina out here, and Lenore knew he didn't often disturb her when she was working. Therefore, this seemed the best option. Lenore had been relegated to the opposite side of the room with her tea, as Mina didn't want to risk any of her work coming to tea-stained harm. The silence was a blissful respite after that evening, the only noise being Mina's short instructions to Bitsy to fetch her this or that.

The entire family had adopted Bitsy as one of their own, and he had gotten quite good at carrying out simple orders so long as he was familiar with the materials. Mina was asking for needles and thread and gauze as she practiced her stitches. Lenore was glad for his activity. Bitsy had begun to grow a little chubby before it was discovered what he could do. She was content to watch him and Mina work together, just so long as she made herself forget that Mina was miming stitching together human flesh. Lenore also appreciated that Mina was letting her invade her private sanctum in order to escape, for it was an obvious escape tactic. It could not last forever, however.

When Mina was finished working that night, Lenore was lovingly ushered out, and Mina gave her hand a quick squeeze before leaving her in the hallway. Of course Mina knew what had happened. She knew everything that happened in her house. Nearly everything anyway. She likely didn't know that Rook was waiting in Lenore's bedroom for her, or she might have personally defenestrated him. Lenore suspected he might appear again sometime later, though she was surprised it was that very same night.

"Please, little bird, I'm so sorry," Rook said sincerely.

He reached out to touch her, but she pulled away.

"I'm not interested in your apologies," she snapped. "Just leave."

"Why are you so upset?" Rook asked, not leaving. "Two young men, one clearly more handsome than the other, just professed their love for you. Most girls would be swooning."

"Maybe I'm just not most girls," Lenore said morosely, turning away.

"You are most certainly not. You are brilliant and kind and strong." There was a long pause before he said, "Lenore, please hear me when I say this is not my debt talking; this is me. I won't say that I don't care what you choose to do with your life. It's just not true, but I will be here for you in whatever way you need me to be. If I can throw my two coppers in, though, I don't want you to shut me out."

Lenore often wondered just how much of an effect Rook's oath to protect her had on him, though she never mentioned these wonderings to him. Kieran had commented in the past on how powerful oaths were, so it stood to reason that two people linked by one as Lenore and Rook were operated differently from normal people. She wondered if it was the reason he felt so strongly for her and why she felt... whatever it was that she felt for him. Perhaps it was what had driven him to turn himself in. She had never asked outright and suspected Rook wouldn't tell her even if she did. There was much he kept close to the vest.

Lenore turned back to Rook and sighed.

"I don't intend on shutting you out, whatever Neal says. I don't believe I'm so empty-headed as to go flitting off after you without regard for anyone else." At that, Lenore felt the sting of tears prick her eyes, and she added plaintively, "Why does he think that? How can he claim to believe in me yet think I'm such a fool?"

"In Neal's defense, I don't believe his thoughts on the matter are a reflection on you. From my experience, that's simply the position all loving and protective fathers take. I don't think he trusts Eamon with you either, deep down, though he'd never admit it."

"It's insulting," Lenore scowled.

"It's not meant to be. Though who can blame him? Look at what he's working with."

Rook then grinned and gestured to himself, still in his dapper dress clothes. Lenore considered his jest seriously for a moment. Was it possible Rook's vow was also part of the reason Neal was concerned? He too knew how powerful they were. Perhaps he was concerned about how close the bond would grow if left unchecked.

"Has anyone ever told you how vexatious you can be?" Lenore grouched, deflecting his comment to hide her true thoughts.

"Only those who love me," he teased. There was a long moment of silence and then more seriously, "Do you truly wish me to leave? I will."

"No, you can stay if you like," she said wearily.

A part of Lenore was stubbornly determined to prove to Neal—and possibly to Rook's ego as well—that she was not so easily swayed. She had to admit this, though: once again, he had proven that he was her anything and everything. He would have left tonight had she asked. Lenore believed he would leave her friendship forever and simply be her guardian if she told him to. Alternatively, he would be a friend or even a lover. She just had to say the word.

"Thank you," she whispered, and reached out her good arm to him.

Rook hugged her gently, and Lenore could feel relief in his embrace. Pressed against him, Lenore listened to the beating of Rook's heart, which, for better or for worse, was forever bound to hers.

Mina sat at her vanity table thoughtfully as she brushed through her long hair. She always plaited it before bed, which generated efficiency come morning. Neal was lying in bed staring at the canopy of rich cloth above him. The bed curtains had been recently changed to a heavier, darker material in readiness for the impending cold weather. As she watched his reflection in the mirror, Mina knew he was not admiring the new material.

"You'll give yourself an ulcer if you keep stewing on it like that," she said gently.

"I don't understand," Neal said heavily. "I need to make her understand."

"I hate to tell you this, my love, but it won't happen if you come at it from that angle."

Neal looked at his wife, and she stood as she began her plaiting.

"From what I have gathered, Lenore feels betrayed by you. You sided with the misogynistic cretins that snubbed her because she happened to be born a female. How dare you enjoy drinks with them?"

Mina's tone was light at the end, but her eyes were sharp and without humor.

"She doesn't need to feel that way," Neal insisted. "It was a good opportunity, one that, with time, could afford her a chance to speak with them and show them her talents."

"You'll get nowhere telling her how she should and should not feel," Mina chided gently.

Neal rubbed the bridge of his nose in frustration.

"Tell me, O Sagacious One, what would your wisdom recommend?" he asked.

"Talk to her about her feelings. Don't dismiss them; acknowledge them. Your opinion matters to her a great deal. She needs to know being a woman makes no difference to you."

"She knows this!"

"Her faith in you has been shaken." Neal looked properly angry now, and Mina said softly, "Don't be offended, darling. As a rule, faith and trust are fragile things. With what Lenore has endured, I can only imagine it's more difficult for her than most."

Neal said nothing and turned over in bed to lie on his side. Mina climbed in next to him and placed a comforting hand on her husband's arm, but she was thinking about Lenore.

# 30
# HONESTLY DISHONEST

Lenore didn't have to work again for three days, so she didn't think she would have to deal with Eamon until then. Once again, she thought wrong. A bouquet of flowers, daylilies this time, arrived with a note at midday the next day.

*Lenore,*

*I hate being at odds with you. Can we please talk? Come to my home tomorrow at 11?*

*Forever yours,*
*Eamon*

Lenore cringed at the idea of seeing Eamon again after last night but knew she had to at least hear him out. She cared for him and knew he was truly sorry and did want to make up with him. Plus, Rook had gotten a chance to say his piece. Eamon should too. It was just… she didn't have the same sort of connection with Eamon that she did with Rook. Conflict with him was more difficult and less certain and therefore made her insides squirm. She really did already have plans, though. She was scheduled to go out with the ladies the next day. Therefore, she sent a note back suggesting the day after that, same time. Lenore reckoned Eamon must have made the messenger wait because she received a response within a few hours. The newly proposed time worked for him.

Her girls' day was, like all the others, positively estrogen-centric in every way, but enjoyable. There were still things that Lenore detested about these outings, like getting dressed up and certain members of the company, but there were things she really enjoyed as well. She had developed friendships with Ginger, Mint, and Beatrice, and Evangeline was sweet but exasperatingly naïve. When the subject of men arose, accompanied by the same complaints Lenore heard at every one of these events, she laughed more appreciatively than she used to. It was times like this where Thyme would chuckle to herself and look rather smug. As always, however, Lenore had to leave some major parts of her life out of the conversation, which caused her more than a little consternation. On this day it was mostly because she very badly wanted to vent about how upset Rook and Eamon's blowup had made her, but she couldn't even go near the subject. Thankfully, there was one person she could talk with about it: Camilla.

That evening, Lenore had gone for a stroll in the courtyard with her housemate and shared her feelings about the events of the night before.

"I just don't understand them. Why resort to that kind of behavior? And so quickly! You saw how it escalated."

"Of course it did," Camilla replied reasonably. "They both went in thinking the other is a danger to you and themselves. They were primed for a fight before they even walked in."

Lenore had not thought about that.

"I don't think either one is, no more than we all are to ourselves anyway," she said. "Though Eamon, I must admit, is at a disadvantage."

"Perhaps. You know how I feel about Rook, but Dmitri actually thinks Eamon is a bigger issue, despite my strong objections to that opinion."

"Really? Dmitri is taking Rook's side?"

"He is. I tend to think it's because they're friends of a sort, but he says it's because Rook is more honest about his dishonesty."

"I don't follow."

"Rook was a criminal, through and through. He didn't pretend to be anything else. Eamon, however, is doing the opposite by pretending that he is a wholly law-abiding citizen."

Lenore hated to admit it, but she liked Dmitri quite a bit more in that moment. No one gave Rook any credit because he was a confessed criminal. True, he and Lenore's relationship was less than proper, but it hardly could have developed out in the open like her and Eamon's. Circumstances just hadn't allowed for it, yet Rook was treated like a scoundrel for pursuing Lenore when it was no different from what Eamon did.

"I may have to start thinking better of Dmitri. Maybe he's not as bad as I thought," Lenore said with a smirk.

"Careful, you might actually find that you like him," Camilla teased back.

The Lee family manor was on the edge of the city with far more land than the Allens had. It was a huge structure with columns at the front porch and wings on either side that curved away from the center of the manse like a river from a waterfall pool. Whoever had built the place was focused first on art and aesthetic and second on practicality.

Eamon was waiting out on the veranda of his home with a

simple tea service when Lenore arrived. The butler left them at Eamon's word, and Lenore found herself feeling very bashful suddenly, though not from embarrassment. She was anxious about what was coming. She had meant what she'd said the other night, but she knew it wouldn't be easy if Eamon offered her some type of ultimatum or had decided to break things off with her.

"Hello," Eamon said, sitting down after she had.

"Hello," she replied softly, forcing herself to look at him. Whatever was about to happen, she was determined to face it with courage. Before she could think better of it, she forced herself to say, "Please just say what you're thinking."

"You're never going to give Rook up, are you?" he replied. Eamon sounded like he was forcing his words out too.

"No, Rook is too important to me. He's an integral part of my life, and not just because he's bonded to me, though there is that too. Nothing will change these things. We've been through too much together. I know you don't like it. In fact, I know it must bring you pain and, heaven forfend, possibly even embarrassment, given the standards of your class. I'm sorry for that, but it can't be any other way. I did tell you that I'm not going to court him, though, and I meant it, so you don't have to worry about that."

Her last statement seemed to give Eamon some relief, but he still looked deeply unhappy. Lenore laid a hand on his and met his eyes.

"I promise," she said earnestly.

Eamon smiled at that, and she smiled at his smile.

"I guess I'm just going to have to get used to him then," Eamon said, sitting back in his seat. "You think he'd agree to see me again so that I can tell him?"

"Not likely," Lenore said disapprovingly. "He'd probably just try to hit you again."

Eamon rubbed the bruise on his chin gently and joked, "True. I wouldn't put it past him." Lenore scowled at him, and he added quickly, "I jest! Apologies. I know you're angry about that. I was hoping to bring some levity to the situation."

She rolled her eyes and said, "Why don't you just start pouring the tea?"

"Good idea. I should know better than to almost miss an opportunity to butter you up with tea."

Lenore smiled at that; he really did know her too well. Lenore stayed for a few hours after that, reconnecting with Eamon after their rather awkward separation. Eamon was still curious about Rook, but he was respectful as he inquired about him. Mostly he wanted to know about Rook's oath, how it worked, how it affected him, and so on. Lenore had to tell him that she honestly didn't know much except that it drove Rook to be very watchful and very distrusting, though those might have come naturally to him anyway. Eamon also learned about the nature of their friendship through this line of conversation —Lenore shared only the most noble bits—and Lenore was pleasantly surprised at his final assessment.

"Well, he sounds very sincere and brave. I'd hope for nothing less in your personal bodyguard."

Lenore smiled widely at that and actually had hope about this whole mad situation for the first time.

Being the beginning of the week, the first order of business was the weekly staff meeting. Neal had some kind of presentation to do that morning, so he had left the house very early, well before Lenore. She was relieved by that, as their interactions had been strained and awkward. Neal had not followed Mina's advice, and Lenore had not pursued the issue. When she arrived to the meeting, she was surprised to find the room almost completely full. People usually trudged into these events because no one wanted to start their workweek by listening to a lot of talking. Lenore took a seat by Copper, who had saved a spot for her, and whispered quickly.

"What's going on?"

"Seems like there's some big announcement. You'd think we would know something about it since Neal's involved."

"You would think," Lenore agreed, hiding her disappointment.

Lenore felt a keen pang of regret that she and Neal were at odds. Granted, even if they weren't, he might not have told her about whatever was going on. He might not have been permitted to—she didn't know how that sort of thing worked on his level of leadership—but even still, the knowledge that the possibility had been dashed due to their differences pained her.

There were a few more minutes of shuffling and getting situated and trying to find a good place by the other latecomers before Scholar Bates finally walked to the front of the room and waited for the buzz to quiet down.

"Good morning, gents and gentlewomen," he said in his usual, congenial fashion. "We have a lot of very exciting information to cover this morning and not a lot of time to do it, so let's try to stay on point, yes?"

"Whatever you say, sir!" came someone's voice from the crowd.

There was a polite roll of laughter for several moments before dying down again. It was a well-known fact that Scholar Bates loved to talk and divert onto entertaining little rabbit trails. He smiled indulgently and smoothly moved on. Scholar Bates covered the updates on old business, let Mathilda go over a few policy, procedure, and personnel changes, and then had each department head briefly discuss any new business. Finally, he called Neal up to speak.

"Good morning, everyone," Neal said. "I know the rumor mill's production has been up this morning, so let's get right to it. We're launching a new expedition!"

There was a short, excited spike in murmurings from the crowd, but Neal got their attention again and continued.

"We have discovered evidence of a buried Old World city down near the southern coast. This is just outside of Bone Port. Miss Cooke is passing around copies of the expedition members and their departments. If your appointment or lack thereof is a problem, please don't be alarmed. This is not a final list… except for my team. Heaven knows I'd lose my head if Lenore wasn't here to help me keep track of it."

There was another round of chuckles because… well… everyone knew it was true. Lenore sat in shock. The lists hadn't made it around to her, but she didn't care. She was going on an Old World expedition! She was actually shaking with joy. It was probably better than jumping up and down and squealing. When the lists finally made their way around to her, she scanned it quickly, and her joy grew even more. Hah! Dempsey wasn't going! She could see him fuming as he sat there and did her best not to stare too gleefully. There had to be at least two people in the department staying, and apprentices didn't count. Swell after swell of elation rolled over her, washing away so many bad feelings for the time being. She did feel bad for Copper, but he didn't look bothered in the least. She turned her head to find Eamon and grin at him but stopped when she saw his face. She looked back down at her list and scanned the Anthropology department team members. Eamon was not on it.

"If you wish to change your designation, please submit a letter outlining your request and justification for it," Neal added.

"Engineer Allen, my letter of appeal," Eamon said stonily, brandishing the letter at him.

It hadn't been an hour since the end of the meeting. Both Lenore and Neal were astonished.

"This is a very fast turnaround, Apprentice Lee," Neal remarked.

"It was very easy to justify my request."

"Well, thank you, Apprentice Lee. I will look over your request and have a decision back to you within a week."

"Thank you, sir. And, if I may, my mentor, Scholar Smith, has written a recommendation for me down at the bottom of my appeal. Scholar Nash will be giving you a separate letter to request *not* to go in order to spend some time with his new baby and has said he will recommend that I go in his place."

"Thank you, Mr. Lee. I will take that into consideration when I make my decision."

Neal began to turn away, but Eamon spoke again, stopping him.

"I mean no disrespect when I say this, sir, and I hope I'm not out of line, but please tell me my relationship with Lenore wasn't the reason I was left off the initial list. I respect your charge very much and would never even dream of doing anything inappropriate, especially on such a prestigious and important expedition."

Eamon didn't look like himself at all. He was flustered and had lost his carefree air.

"The selections were made on experience and skill sets and, yes, Mr. Lee, you are out of line," Neal said calmly. "Now, if you'll excuse me."

With that, Neal walked away. Eamon didn't look Lenore's way as he turned on his heel and left.

Neal had numerous appeals and change requests, all of which Lenore had to help organize and keep straight. Eamon was eventually accepted for the expedition, which he responded to with a very ungentlemanly shout and a few good punches to the air. Rook seemed conflicted by this development, but, in the end, told Lenore it was probably a good thing because Eamon *appeared* to also have her best interests at heart.

"How gracious of you," Lenore said in response to that, her voice dripping with sarcasm.

Mina and Camilla were thrilled for the two as well. It turned out that this was the first expedition Neal had ever headed up, though certainly not the first that he had ever been a part of.

Only Dempsey's response to the news was more inappropriate than Eamon's. Dempsey outright said that Neal had made the wrong decision and that it was preposterous that Lenore should go on an expedition before him. Neal calmly reminded Dempsey of the policy that two permanent members of staff had to remain behind, at which point Dempsey threatened to quit. Neal called his bluff, reminding him that, one, he was welcome to do so at any time and, two, all of his time and energy spent there at the museum would be for naught. Dempsey folded, but was petulant and snappish for a long time after that. It got round that he had whinged to some of the girls in Administration about nepotism and "the museum's little darling", but it was all hearsay, so there was nothing to be done about it. Nothing Neal intended to do about it anyway, by all appearances. Lenore suspected this was a battle he didn't think was worth choosing.

That was not the only rumor that circulated the museum around that time. Eamon's concerns seemed to have some basis. Having cornered Lenore in the back of the shelves, Dempsey nastily shared with her that she was the reason Eamon was left off the original list. He didn't state exactly why, but the unsavory look he was giving her gave Lenore the impression that, at best, she was expected to be inappropriate with Eamon or, at worst, with Neal.

"Just what are you trying to insinuate, Mr. Van Pelt?" she asked directly.

It was the first time she had dealt with Dempsey in such a way, usually preferring something sly so as to avoid dealing with him as much as possible. Though she had kept her tone level, she was aggrieved by such an idea, having smashed Rook's nose for suggesting as much once upon a time. Dempsey looked taken aback for a moment, but collected himself quickly.

"It seems suspicious, doesn't it?" he sneered.

"No, it seems like a perfectly rational initial assessment was made. The Anthropology department has at least twice as many members as ours. Eamon is a junior member of that team. It sounds to me as if you're calling Engineer Allen's judgment into question *again*... or are you questioning his honor?"

Dempsey opened his mouth to reply, but the sound of Copper and Neal coming back into the Arc-Tech workroom made him think better of it.

"I'm just telling you what I heard," he said with a malicious grin. "Perhaps you should heed the warning."

With that, Dempsey swept away.

Lenore did her best to forget about the incident, but Dempsey had nettled her. He was probably lying, had probably fabricated the entire thing himself, but she couldn't shake her doubts. She rallied her nerve and went to speak to Neal about it that evening. The idea that such a rumor could actually spread sped her decision.

Things had been better between them since the announcement, but there was still a feeling of unresolved bitterness in their interactions. And Lenore was about to broach a very uncomfortable subject. She was not looking forward to this. She found Neal in the drawing room that night.

"Come in, Lenore," Neal said congenially when he saw her. "You know you can just walk in."

She always felt as if she could no more simply walk into the drawing room than she could Mina's tower. It was just… too much Neal's space. She gave him a weak smile anyway and approached.

"Is everything alright?" he asked, seeing Lenore's hesitation.

"Yes. I mean, sort of? I need to speak with you, please," Lenore answered uncertainly.

"Is this the kind of conversation that will require some liquid courage?" Neal asked, motioning to his bar.

The bar was a clever contraption that doubled as an orbiter. There was a globe, which for functionality's sake was much larger than was accurate, in the center and the sun and the moon on spindles, which rotated around the earth whilst simultaneously spinning on their own axes by way of a myriad of differently sized gears all working in concert. The globe too spun on its axis, but it had to be turned with Invarnis facing the front in order to be opened. Lenore was fascinated by the object but felt as if it was even more hands-off than the room itself.

She wrinkled her nose and politely declined Neal's offer. Her father had let her try scotch once, and she hadn't liked it in the least. She might have taken gin—Mina had turned her onto it—but it didn't agree with Neal, so he didn't keep it stocked.

"Alright then," Neal said, folding his hands before him. "Let's hear it."

Lenore looked down at her hands and realized she had been wringing them together. She made herself stop.

"I've heard a rumor… about the expedition assignments. It

concerns me because, well, because it concerns you."

"Lenore, whatever it is, I'm sure it's not as bad as all that," Neal said, trying to be reassuring.

"It comes to this," she said, trying to blurt it out before she lost her nerve. "I heard Eamon was not included with the initial assignments because…" she took a breath while Neal waited patiently for her. Oh, how to say this? "Because of some perceived inappropriateness… to do with me."

Neal's brow knitted in confusion.

"I heard Eamon's objection, but it… oh, you mean from someone besides Eamon. Well, whoever thinks you would be… wait, what does that have to do with me? That I would somehow be aware and wouldn't put an immediate stop to it?" Neal looked to Lenore and saw in her expression that he was missing a step. "That makes no sense. Why…" And then his eyes widened. "You cannot mean… no! Are you serious, Lenore?!"

She nodded meekly, feeling her cheeks burn awkwardly. Neal spluttered for several minutes, trying to collect himself. He motioned for her to give him a minute, got up, and then got himself a drink after all. He took a deep draught and then waited. Finally, he sat down again with his drink in hand, but still did not speak for several minutes.

"From whom did you hear this?" he asked sternly.

"Dempsey," she replied. She then emphasized, "Just today."

Neal swore and gesticulated a few times before finally landing on a response.

"Firstly, Lenore, I am so sorry you had to hear that, much less from that…" he shut his mouth at that and made a noise like a muffled growl. "Apologies. Blast it all. The little wretch! I cannot turn him out without proof. What did you say in response? Tell me everything."

Lenore did so and tried not to blush so much. She also

shared her fears that Dempsey might have actually spread the rumors. Neal nodded when she was finished and sipped at his scotch pensively for a few moments.

"Thank you for defending me," he said. "I know things have been… difficult between us of late, and I appreciate you saying what you did."

"I simply stated the facts," she replied, bracing herself against the bad memories that bubbled up now.

"There are many who would not have risen above it," Neal replied stiffly.

Lenore paused and, thinking this might be a colossally bad idea, asked, "You did select me for my skill, yes?"

"Yes, without a doubt," Neal said with a certainty that made Lenore feel better.

She thanked him, but wasn't sure what else to say besides that. Neal supplied new conversation material.

"Would it interest you to know what the gents we shared drinks with a few weeks back discussed?"

"No." Lenore's tone was clipped and angry. "They're not worth my time with attitudes like that."

Neal sighed and leaned forward in his chair.

"Lenore, I hope this doesn't rub you the wrong way, and I mean no offense when I say it, but I think it's an important lesson. Even if someone snubs you for being a woman, you might still benefit from what they have to offer. Helpful knowledge to be gleaned and erroneous perspectives can coexist within the same person. You should endeavor to learn what you can from wherever you can, just as we all should. Again, no disrespect meant, but it was my intention to use the relationship I might build with those gentlemen as a way for you to acquaint yourself with them. It's no different than I would do for any protégé of mine, male or female."

"But they want nothing to do with me on the basis of my

gender. Eamon is my equal and was invited along. Therefore, despite your best efforts, it would do no good with them."

"Not at first, no, but we don't know what would happen given enough time. Perhaps we might even change their minds."

Lenore sensed they had somehow crossed into a scientific sort of debate with theories being batted around like cats with yarn. She didn't want that just now; she wanted to be understood.

"It's not fair on a principle level," she insisted.

"I agree."

"It's not even correct!"

"I know."

"Then why… why try to overrule me?"

"Lenore, I appreciate that you are frustrated about the discrimination you face. I'm sure 'frustrated' is a paltry word to describe it, in fact. I know I haven't the slightest inkling of what that's like. After all, I was born into the right class, the right gender, the right everything. However, when I make a decision you disagree with, please do not assume it is because I am trying to undermine or hinder you. Often, I am trying to make the best decision for our family as a whole. Sometimes, I do make a poor one, and I am sorry for that. Try to consider whether I would do that to Mina or Camilla."

Lenore's distrust shot an arrow of doubt through her mind, and Lenore heard a small voice hiss, *I am not a part of your family. Not really.* She quashed the thought immediately. No! That wasn't fair. The Allens had done nothing to exclude her. They had accepted her as one of them, heart and soul. She nodded.

"I will." Turning back to what had brought her here, she asked, "What about Dempsey?"

Neal's features flattened into hard lines at that. "Not much I can do without evidence. Let me know if you hear it from others. I don't know if Dempsey is fool enough to try and spread this around. It makes him look bad, too, but there are some in our workplace that don't have the wherewithal or the decency to know better."

She still felt dubious, still felt as if Neal had not really validated her feelings, but he had made some logical points, and she could work with that. She would have to, as that appeared to be the best she could hope for. Hearing Neal say the expedition team selections were based on ability did help, and all the work that went along with it was yet another buoy for Lenore. It also meant far, far more work.

Copper got himself an apprentice about that same time, a young man by the name of Ezra. He was hired initially to train and fill in for Lenore while she was away, but it was well known that, like Neal, Copper had put off getting an apprentice, and it was about time.

Ezra was respectful, helpful, and smart, but he was very quiet, which made for a very odd pairing indeed. Ezra had been referred by a friend of Copper's wife, though, so there had been no guarantees on the personality type. Thankfully, while he was quiet, he was not timid. When Copper started to go a little overboard on something, Ezra would calmly and politely point out the potential pitfalls of the thing, which ended up working out fairly well. He was certainly better than Lenore in that respect, as she was often happy to get carried away with Copper, as her eyebrows could attest. Unfortunately, Lenore did find that training Ezra actually increased her workload for a while, as she wouldn't turn anything over until he was properly trained. This led to many a late night for Lenore. Despite the fact that there had been no more attempts on her life—neither Rook nor Dmitri had been able to gather much intelligence on the subject, which led them to agree it was someone with a good deal of money—Lenore was forbidden from walking home alone, which suited her just fine, and was always accompanied by one of her family or close family friends. Even Dmitri was called upon one night, which Camilla found highly amusing.

Copper, it turned out, didn't mind being left behind at all. Travel didn't agree with him, as he put it, and Lenore couldn't help but rib him about this, as she almost couldn't believe that anything could bother the thick-skinned engineer. Copper could take it as well as he could dish it out, so he took no offense and told Lenore to let him know how much she liked it when she chose the wrong leaf to take to nature's WC with her.

Rook, who Lenore began to spend time with outside the confines of her bedroom more and more, had mixed feelings about the news.

"How am I supposed to watch over you from so far away?" he asked her one day as they walked through the museum gardens together.

Out of respect for Eamon—entirely at Lenore's insistence —the two tried to avoid doing anything that might seem questionable as far as propriety went, and Rook hadn't been to the museum gardens in many years. That didn't mean that he didn't still make the occasional nightly visit, but that was usually only when there was something one of them needed to discuss that absolutely couldn't be overheard.

"I don't know," was all Lenore could say in response to his question.

That night was one of those rare occurrences when Rook meant to share his thoughts with only her. They discussed the likelihood of her being safer so far away. It was an unknown variable, as Lenore put it, and she began to think again about learning to fight. Rook had agreed, though her sprained wrist and everything else had gotten in the way at the time. Now, however, it seemed more urgent than ever. She and Rook discussed the idea with Neal and Mina together, and it was unanimously agreed to. The next big question was where to do it. That was when another secret about the Allens came to light.

"Haven't you ever wondered where Kieran sleeps during the day?" Neal asked.

He sounded far too pleased about the question as he led Lenore and Rook down the gloomy stairs into the cellar.

"Not really," Lenore quipped. "As it probably has something to do with a grave, I don't know that I want to know."

"Oh, piffle!" Neal scoffed playfully. "Of course you have. Why? Because it's Old World lore."

Lenore cocked a wry smile at him. Right on both counts. The old stories claimed that Vampyres returned to their graves or melted into the earth or any number of strange and unlikely things during the day. Lenore had accepted them at face value and never thought much more about it. Now that they were discussing it, however, she found that she was keenly interested in knowing the truth of the matter.

Neal led them around and behind the cellar stairs, where all three of them had to crouch. Lenore tried not to jump at the fat spiders that had made a home here, and Rook obligingly swept away any that came too close.

"Watch carefully," Neal instructed.

The walls were stone here, the cellar having been carved right out of the earth and then reinforced when the manor had been built centuries earlier. Neal slid his hand down the clammy stone right next to one of the stair's support beams. Lenore watched raptly as she saw some smaller pebbles turn and roll beneath Neal's fingers. She looked for identifying marks on the tiny rocks but only saw that the underside was a paler shade of grey. She made a mental note of it. Neal then depressed a stone at the base of the wall, followed by one on the side opposite the lock-pebbles, as Lenore would eventually come to call them. The wall sank into itself, and Neal pushed open what was now a very low door. Lenore and Rook crawled in after Neal, Lenore cursing her skirts the entire way, and came through to a large open space with a low ceiling, but tall enough that they could stand up again. It was a proper set of chambers!

Against one wall were a desk and a short bookshelf full of tomes. There were no sconces here, but candles littered the area, making it resemble a temple. The floor was hard packed earth and the walls the same stone as in the cellar. Lenore turned to look at the door they had just come through. There was a beautiful and complicated system of gears and a turn-wheel hatch.

"Did you make this?" Lenore asked, awed as she examined the mechanics of it.

"No, but I did make some upgrades. Some of the pieces were very old and worn, so I replaced them with newer versions. Getting the sizes right was a blighter of a job."

"I take it the unlocking... yes! Here! Ah, the hinges slide into place," Lenore observed. "Ingenious! Then the bottom and the sides... I see, the levers push the wheel."

"And *I* have solved the mystery of where Kieran sleeps," Rook interjected.

Lenore looked up at him and saw him grinning as he jerked a thumb towards the opposite end of the room. She followed with her eyes and saw a coffin in the corner. It was very simple and made of grey, untreated wood. No pillow or blankets, but there was a layer of dirt in the bottom. At least it was set upon some kind of raised platform so that Kieran didn't have to sleep on the ground. Lenore gasped when she saw it.

"Is that really..." she began, unable to believe her eyes.

"Yes, it really is," Neal said sadly.

They quickly turned their attention from the macabre bed to why they had come.

"You will be chaperoned," Neal informed them. "If Camilla or Mina or I think it's getting too rough, you will stop."

"Neal, I don't think someone who wants me dead will consider what may or may not be too rough," Lenore reasoned.

"Also, I might have difficulty with that anyway," Rook added.

Lenore realized that this training might hurt Rook more than it did her, and she questioned the wisdom of the entire idea now. Rook insisted, however, and Neal did not disagree. Lenore acquiesced to their logic, knowing she'd feel much safer with some actual defensive skills under her belt, but she was tense and concerned for Rook.

"Let's get started," Rook said with a determined edge to his voice.

Dmitri sat at the table with his hands folded in his lap, his face a moving portrait of impassivity. He had interviewed several of his fellow Enforcers in this very room. Suspect lists for their investigation had been turned into Fourth Hawkins, and interrogations, under the guise of random performance reviews, had begun. These were nothing like prisoner interrogations, but they still reeked of guilt and judgment. Dmitri hadn't been surprised when he was called in as a suspect. He was even less surprised when Fifth Jones entered as his accuser. Fourth Hawkins was right behind him.

"Hello, Dmitri," Fifth Jones purred.

"The appropriate designation is Fifth Sawyer," Dmitri corrected him flatly.

"That title is for Enforcers," Fifth Jones sneered, shifting his demeanor.

Dmitri recognized the tactic. It was meant to make the target uneasy. They had all learned it in training.

"We both know I wouldn't be here if I wasn't an Enforcer," Dmitri said.

"You are not worthy of the name!" Fifth Jones shouted.

Dmitri's only move was the raising of one eyebrow.

The questioning began soon after that. Fifth Jones accused Dmitri of letting the girl from his stabbing incident get away. Dmitri countered that he had been occupied with not dying at the time.

"She should have been detained!" Fifth Jones insisted.

"I was unconscious," Dmitri said.

Fifth Jones took exception with every case Dmitri had worked. He pointed out every missed opportunity, anything Fifth Jones perceived as a flaw, some substantiated by this or that and others conjured from nothing. It was Dmitri's caution that caught him out. By the numbers, Dmitri's performance was poor in comparison to the average Enforcer, his arrest numbers lower than most.

"I don't waste my time chasing after innocent people. How many man-hours do we waste interrogating people we just end up letting go in the end? I wait and watch and catch the *right* people."

"But you never can be too careful," Fifth Jones said with a nasty smile.

"I agree," Dmitri replied, unimpressed.

"You're looking at a suspension, *at least*," Fifth Jones goaded.

"That will be for others to decide, not you."

"It has been decided," Fourth Hawkins said suddenly.

He had been silent during the interrogation. Dmitri looked

to him, failing to keep the surprise from his voice.

"Sir?"

"Your record is under review," Fourth Hawkins replied. "You're suspended for six weeks while we deliberate."

Dmitri gaped at him, unable to believe what he was hearing.

"Turn in your baton and your uniform with the quartermaster this afternoon."

# 3l

## CAMPS

enore stepped back, dripping and breathing hard.

"You know, this would be easier if I was allowed to wear trousers while we trained," she huffed.

"Will you be wearing trousers on a regular basis in Bone Port?" Rook asked calmly. He hadn't even broken a sweat, but he was rubbing his back, not for the first time that day.

"No," Camilla answered for her, not looking up from her book.

The training was not going as well as Lenore had imagined it would. She had imagined herself making great strides, being able to at least push Rook back a step or two within a few weeks. She hadn't gotten a single strike in, not once. Rook insisted she was improving and that he wasn't a good measuring stick for her, which Neal had chalked up as bravado. Lenore, however, tended to believe it, having seen Rook take down multiple foes at once. Still, she was determined to learn something, so she was diligent, even when she had been knocked onto her back for the sixth time in a day.

Lenore's whole body complained every day they trained. She couldn't imagine her muscles ever being so sore, yet parts of her she didn't even know she had ached. Mina and Camilla helped her to hide the bruises that bloomed on her skin, though autumn was in full swing now with winter on the way, so the chilly weather helped considerably. Neal's expedition wouldn't launch until the New Year, as winter meant storm season for the southern reaches of Invarnis. This gave Lenore just under six months to get ready. Rook had asked her how she planned on explaining her toned physique once the gloves and scarves and boots were gone, but Lenore hadn't thought about that, so she didn't yet have an answer. Right now, she felt like the only change to her physique would be her muscles going mushy from all the hits she took.

As for the trousers, the expedition team had been made aware of how oppressively hot it would be in Bone Port, and Lenore had played with the idea of getting some trousers made for her in some kind of durable material that would breathe. Mina had strong feelings about this. She didn't mind trousers in a few specific cases—Lenore had, after all, worn a dressy pair on BB's demonstration day—but Mina suspected Lenore would begin to eschew skirts entirely, even the practical high-low variety, given the chance in such a hot climate, which wouldn't be proper, and said as much. Therefore, rules had already been laid down for when trousers were appropriate and when they were not.

Rook looked at Lenore and smirked. She grimaced in return. All three of them turned towards the door as it began to open. Dmitri stepped through a moment later and looked around him darkly.

"Dmitri? What's wrong?" Camilla asked, standing up and going to him.

"Mind if I have a go?" he asked, looking at Rook and ignoring Camilla.

Rook motioned for him to come over and take Lenore's

place. Lenore had sparred against Dmitri once, and she had enjoyed it... mostly because it allowed her to work out some of her feelings towards him in a safe place. She was still abysmal compared to him, but not as bad as she was against Rook. She had never seen Rook and Dmitri against one another, though, and was curious about how Rook would do against elite Enforcer training. The two men took their positions and began, Lenore and Camilla watching from along the wall.

The differences in fighting style were immediately apparent. Dmitri's moves were precise and accurate. It was clear the Enforcers used katas to train their recruits, relying on muscle memory as much as strength and skill. There was a rhythm to his movements, like a brutal, rehearsed dance. Each strike was designed to do as much damage as possible with the most efficiency. Even the weapons were standardized. Rook, on the other hand, was opportunistic and fought dirty. He was strategic too, but relied on his own instincts and decision making to choose his hits. Dmitri only used his fists and feet to attack, while Rook used fists, feet, elbows, knees, and anything else he could. At first, it appeared that Dmitri was a more effective fighter, but Rook quickly gained the upper hand by sheer strength and skill. The match was shockingly aggressive, but Rook soon put an end to it when he seemed bored by the effort. Using his foot as a stumbling block behind Dmitri's, Rook used his entire body to knock Dmitri onto his back.

Camilla and Lenore clapped politely as if they had just watched a croquet match. Rook bowed graciously, playing along, and was then nearly knocked onto his face as Dmitri swept his leg around and knocked Rook forward. Rook caught himself at the last moment and sprang back up, rounding on Dmitri. Dmitri was ready, however, and landed a vicious blow to Rook's solar plexus. If the sparring match before had been aggressive, this was a small, concentrated war. Limbs flew, strikes were launched and deflected. Rook might have been simply trying to defend himself at first—it was hard to tell—but that changed quickly. Camilla saw for the first time what Rook was truly capable of, and she cried out for them to stop. She even stepped forward to intervene, but Lenore held her back, frightened for what might happen should she get caught in that fray. This fight didn't last half as long as the one before, Rook finishing it brutally and effectively. Dmitri was on his back again as Rook stepped back and glared at him.

Camilla rushed forward and tried to help Dmitri up. He brushed her away and painfully began to stand up on his own.

"What the blazes is the matter with you?!" Lenore exclaimed.

"I agree!" Camilla said, glaring at Rook. "Dmitri, please, let me have a look at you. You might be properly injured."

"I was talking to Dmitri," Lenore said.

"You cannot be serious," Camilla said incredulously, gesturing at Dmitri. "Look at him. Rook, the beating you just gave him was hardly necessary."

"Dmitri attacked Rook," Lenore reasoned.

"Stop," Dmitri groaned angrily. "It was a lesson. I'm teaching her." With that, he motioned towards Lenore.

"A lesson in bad decision making?" Lenore quipped.

"You need to learn to remain focused," Dmitri replied. "Distraction will get you killed, very possibly by him."

"What the blazes are you on about?" Rook growled.

Instead of answering him, Dmitri turned to Camilla and spoke more softly. "Dearest, I think you should have a chat with Mina and Neal. These two are criminals. They have the potential to get you all killed, or worse."

At that, Camilla drew away from Dmitri.

"You know the situation. We can hardly help it," she said sternly, her features pinched in confusion and anger.

"You're one to talk," Rook retorted.

"You could turn her out," Dmitri said, ignoring Rook.

Lenore could see Camilla was nearly at her breaking point. She was visibly shaking, her long golden tresses quivering with indignation.

"Dmitri, that is simply never going to happen, and I think it's time you left."

Dmitri's face finally changed. He looked surprised and then hurt and angry.

"Camilla, I—"

"I said leave."

Lenore watched as Dmitri seemed to gather himself before stalking out of the room. He threw a hateful glare at Lenore as he went, and she returned the same. After he was gone, she released Rook's hands, which she hadn't realized she had taken, and spoke seriously.

"Do not go after him."

"Agreed," Camilla said. "I will deal with him after we've all had some time. I won't have you catching him in an alley and threatening him."

Rook crouched behind a rosebush and scanned the garden. He spotted Camilla further in. She was walking by herself along the path that wound its way past some Echinacea. He looked around again and didn't see anyone else. He was pleased but still concerned. This was not the best time. Anyone could come into the garden, and he needed this to be a private conversation.

He emerged from his hiding spot and whispered her name, hoping to get her attention without needing to venture closer. She heard him, and her expression changed to complete confusion. She opened her mouth to speak, but Rook motioned for her to be silent and to come closer. She shook her head distrustfully and took a few steps back. Blazes! She didn't trust him not to hurt her. Rook tried to make himself appear as disarming as possible—a difficult task to say the least—and laid the knives that were visible onto the ground. He raised his hands and approached slowly.

"Stop," Camilla said, making no effort to keep her voice down.

Rook obeyed and waited.

"What do you want?"

"I need to speak with you." Rook whispered, hoping she would follow his lead.

She did not. "About what?"

"Dmitri."

"Rook, no offense, but you are the last person from whom I wish to receive relationship advice."

"Then call it practical advice. Don't break things off with him."

"That's surprising coming from you, considering the way he treated Lenore."

"I haven't thrashed him for that at your behest."

"Yes, and I meant what I said. He told me about your encounter that night."

"What did he tell you precisely?"

"He told me about Lenore's mother." It was only with this admission that Camilla finally lowered her voice.

Rook felt the bottom drop out of his stomach. He had hoped Camilla didn't know, though he'd had his suspicions.

"You cannot tell Lenore," he whispered plaintively.

"I hadn't planned on it. Nevermind that I am all too aware of the pain that would cause her, but I hardly need to provide her with another reason to dislike Dmitri."

"Thank you," Rook said sincerely. "As for Dmitri, he

knows too much to be thoughtlessly thrown aside."

"You think I don't know that?" Camilla hissed. "Lenore said as much to me after our first outing together, not that I was willing to listen at the time."

"Do you regret courting him?"

Camilla didn't answer for a moment. Finally, she said softly, "No, but his... behavior. I don't know why he's acting this way."

"I can investigate for you."

"No. Stay out of it, Rook. Whatever this is, I will work it out with him in the traditional way."

"My way might be faster," he said with a smirk.

"I said no."

Rook nodded, though he planned on ignoring Camilla and keeping tabs on Dmitri anyway.

Rook slipped through the crowd at Raven's Tower with drink in hand.

"What are you up to?" came a voice from the corner.

He looked and smiled widely at the owner of the voice.

He approached, drew close, and then said just loud enough to be heard, "Fetch, my dear, how are you?"

Rook set his drink down in front of Fetch.

"Better now, thank you," she replied, taking the glass.

The room was heaving with people, so they actually had to speak up even from so close. Calandra was having one of her game nights, which were very popular, and the complimentary refreshments had already made several rounds. The gaming tables were all set up in the center of the large main room. Players filled every spot, chatting and joking and, most importantly, communicating with their partners through code.

The game was called Camps and required two teams of two per game. Partners would sit opposite each other, and cards were swapped between the four in the middle and the players' hands until everyone was satisfied and the next hand began. In the midst of play, partners were meant to covertly communicate to one another when they had four of a kind in their hands. If a player correctly called *Camp!* to signify that his or her partner had four of a kind, that team won a point. How the signals were communicated was up to the team playing. Thus, there was all manner of strange conversations going on. One team was going back and forth naming various animals, while others seemed to be idly chatting. Some of the communication was nonverbal, and many an amusing facial expression could be seen throughout the room. Alternatively, if a member of a team were to figure out their opponents' tells, that person could declare *Camp closed!* when four of a kind was suspected and steal the win. If an incorrect Camp closed call was made, an extra point was awarded to the opposite team.

There were smaller, two person tables set in a ring around the edge of the room for spectators. In some cases, watching the loud, tense stratagems unfold was just as fun as actually playing. Fetch was happily settled at one of the spectators' tables, and Rook joined her in the other seat, leaning towards her across the small table.

"You really don't accept anything but the best, do you?" she asked after taking a sip of the drink. She was looking admiringly at the golden brown liquid in the glass.

"Never," Rook grinned. "Not in drinks or partners."

"You know I hate flattery," she said, looking sideways at him.

"You know I'm not employing flattery," Rook replied, giving her a look.

Fetch smiled at that. "No, you're not." There was a

companionable pause in their conversation, after which she added, "You look horrendous."

Rook smiled again. Fetch was referring to his disguise. He had begun employing this sort of trick since beginning work for Gadget. It made duping the Enforcers that much easier, though Rook didn't like carrying with him everything a good disguise required. Currently, he was dressed as a seaman with features that suggested he hailed from the south. His skin was painted in swarthy shades, and he had on a false nose, which was somewhat wider than his real one. He had put a plant compound in his hair that made it appear thicker and wilder than it truly was, and he was carrying himself with a completely different air than he usually did. Rook only chuckled appreciatively at Fetch's comment.

"So what are you up to?" she asked.

"Whatever do you mean?" Rook replied innocently.

"You drugged that man's drink. Why?"

"Call it a small personal vendetta."

Fetch looked curiously at Rook, clearly trying to puzzle something out. Lenore had shared with Rook about Dempsey's rumormongering, and Rook took that as a reason to up his game on Dempsey's torments. This time, it would be public. As they waited for the show, as Rook put it, to start, Fetch looked to him.

"Something is troubling you," she said. "What is it?"

Rook didn't reply at first. He may have come to trust Fetch fairly well… as well as he trusted any of his criminal contacts anyway, but Lenore was not a subject he wished to share with anyone not already in the know. He searched himself, imagining the possible outcomes if he did ask Fetch for help. He tried to listen for any signs from his oath, but it was silent. He grimaced. Why was it so ambiguous at times but painfully clear at others? He hadn't gleaned anything from the feelers he'd put out about Bonnie and the other assassins so far. Dmitri had also not learned anything, and he might no longer be of use after that display in the Allens' cellar. He had nothing to go on. He sighed and leaned back over towards Fetch.

"I want to know about a hit," he said.

Rook said nothing about the intended victim of the job, only referencing those that had been contracted to carry it out. He wanted to know who had called for it.

"How am I meant to question dead people?" Fetch asked sardonically. "What about the target?"

Rook hesitated again. Still nothing from his vow.

"It was a girl, works for the museum, young."

"Is that all you're going to give me?"

"She's a friend. I don't like it when people try to kill my friends. Let me know if you hear something, anything that might hint at such a job?"

Rook was slightly pleased that having a public friendship with Lenore finally seemed to be paying dividends.

"Very well," Fetch replied. "I'll let you know."

"While we're on the subject, you'll be pleased to know a shipment of Northern Spiced Wine arrived yesterday. I managed to procure a crate of it and made a new friend while I was at it. I'll personally deliver most of the bottles when it's convenient for you."

"*Most* of the bottles?" Fetch asked.

"Handling fee," Rook grinned. "Oh, all right. I'll bring an extra for all of us to share together."

Fetch smiled back at him. They traded a few other helpful tidbits before the shrieking started. On the other side of the room, Dempsey suddenly leapt up from his gaming table and started pointing at the ancient stone walls. He claimed gargoyles were coming through the stones, sent to steal their souls. The gargoyles positioned outside did not respond to his accusations.

# 32

# POISONED

C amilla stood in the receiving area of the Enforcer barracks. There were a few others milling about.

The receiving room was austere with undecorated plaster walls, a few simple chairs, and a bare wooden floor that was somewhere between shabby and adequate. Camilla knew the Enforcers were not well funded by the city—it was hard for the magistrates to justify more than what was strictly necessary with such mixed feelings about the city's peacekeepers—but she wondered if perhaps the off-putting atmosphere of the receiving room was intentional. After all, Enforcers were supposed to focus on the job above all other things. Family and friends and romantic interests, while not exactly discouraged, were seen as potential distractions.

The clerk at the front desk had taken down Camilla's name, Dmitri's information, and the reason for Camilla's visit. *Apologies* was all Camilla wrote for the last. It was vague enough that it shouldn't arouse suspicion, was true, and also verifiable later... just in case. A runner had been sent with the message to track down either Dmitri or his location.

Camilla had sent Dmitri several requests via courier to meet, but every one had been refused and returned to sender.

Feeling anxious and angry, Camilla had finally decided to go to him. Her hope was, at best, that there had either been some kind of mistake or, at worst, her messages were being intentionally blocked for some reason.

As she waited, she saw a pair of Enforcers emerge from the barracks, laughing together. She recognized one, Fifth Jones, whom she didn't much care for.

Dmitri had complained about the man on numerous occasions. Nothing specific, but he often cited Fifth Jones' cruelty with a scowl. Camilla had her own reasons for disliking the man, though. He was the younger brother of Juliet and Bianca Jones, and having spent much of her life in the company of those two ladies, Camilla had had more than one run-in with the little brat. In particular, she still hadn't forgiven him for releasing a box of spiders over the tea table from the pergola above when she was thirteen. The majority of the spiders had landed on her and Evangeline Bell, resulting in several nasty bites and a panic that had overturned the table and sent all the young ladies in attendance running.

Camilla didn't recognize the other man and quickly did a mental run through the rules of etiquette in her head. Under normal circumstances, manners dictated that she should greet Fifth Jones and, at the very least, ask after the health of his family. These were not exactly normal circumstances, however. She was unaccompanied, and he was with another man with whom she was not acquainted. She was, however, in a public place among polite society. Drat it! She would have to say hello. She put on an acceptable smile and approached.

"Miss Camilla," Fifth Jones said far too congenially when he saw her. "How lovely to see you."

Camilla's stomach turned. Heavens, he was slimy. He practically reeked of insincerity as he put on every possible upper class affectation. What was worse, he seemed genuinely pleased to see her.

"And you," she replied by rote. "How are you? Is your family well?"

"Couldn't be better, my dear. Forgive me. Allow me to introduce my colleague, Fifth Falcon Smoke. Smoke, this is Miss Camilla Hawkins."

"Very pleased to make your acquaintance," Fifth Smoke said congenially with a bow. "Any relation to Fourth Hawkins?"

"My father," Camilla replied quickly. "Falcon, what a handsome and unique name."

Fifth Smoke smiled awkwardly and replied, "My parents are avian specialists with the Zoology department at the museum."

Camilla smiled and asked, "Do you have any siblings?"

"Indeed. Lark and Wren."

Camilla gave an appreciative laugh. "You know, your parents might know my cousin, Lenore Blackbird. She's done some work with that department."

"Yes, I believe they both did a bit. I heard about the final results of that endeavor. Jolly good work your cousin did. I wish I'd been able to see the demonstration."

"It was ever so good."

"So what brings you to our dank little corner of the world, Miss Camilla?" Fifth Jones broke in.

Camilla kept her smile in place as she turned back to him, despite the fact that he had rudely interrupted and changed the subject. He always had been a bully.

"I'm here waiting for Fifth Sawyer."

Fifth Jones laughed unkindly at that and then said insincerely, "Oh, my dear, I am so sorry to be the one to tell you this. Fifth Sawyer is not here. He's been suspended, you see."

Camilla allowed the shock to slip through and show on her

face. She collected herself quickly, however, and said unsteadily, "Oh, dear. It must have been my mistake."

"I very much doubt that," Fifth Jones said snidely. "Fifth Sawyer is—"

"That will do, Jones," Fifth Smoke admonished.

Fifth Jones was clearly unhappy with being silenced, but he smiled anyway, an ugly imitation of the real thing.

"We'd best be going," Fifth Smoke said to Camilla. "Have a lovely day."

He then bowed, followed by Fifth Jones, and Camilla curtseyed in response. She watched them leave with her heart in her throat. A moment later, the runner returned and told her that Fifth Sawyer was not available. He apologized and left.

Camilla wondered what to do now. She was beginning to understand why Dmitri had acted as he did. Besides the fact that the Enforcers were dangerous even to their own kind, Camilla knew Dmitri took his job very seriously. It was important to him, and she believed that he took pride in the good he was able to do in his position. But why? Why had he been suspended? Did this mean danger for them all? And why hadn't he told her? Didn't he trust her? She needed to speak to Dmitri as soon as possible. She could seek him out at his parents' house, but that would be the height of impropriety.

Fine young ladies did *not* pursue men no matter what the reason. Camilla was already being inappropriate by seeking Dmitri out, not to mention she had come to his place of work, so to speak. Going to his house would be considered nearly obscene. Mina and Neal didn't know exactly where Camilla had gone. She had simply left a note saying she was going to meet with Dmitri. They'd both be apoplectic if they knew what she was considering now. Even so, answers were required. Outside, she hailed a hansom and gave the address.

Dmitri did not come from means. The little house in front of which the cab stopped was very nearly derelict. Camilla had only ever been to the Agate quarter once, and that had been the night Mina and Neal had vetted Dmitri's parents. She had never wished to return, yet here she was. She told the driver to wait and furtively paid him extra to do so. There was a beggar missing an arm and a leg sitting on the footpath against the building next door, and Camilla avoided eye contact with him.

The house was skinny and squashed between two other taller buildings. One was a shop of some sort, and the other was a multitude of flats sandwiched on top of one another. These houses were made of brown clay and wood, which was chipped and splintered. The scrap of lawn that could be seen was weedy and overgrown. Every door and window was warped. The bottom window of Dmitri's house was being held open by a spare bit of wood, and a thin stream of smoke was trailing out. Camilla knew the stove smoked anytime it was used and guessed Dmitri's grandmother was cooking.

The house was shared by his paternal grandparents and maternal grandmother as well as his parents and younger brother, Boris. Dmitri's father was disabled due to a work accident many years ago, leaving the rest of the family to make ends meet, and they had not been very well off to begin with. The city had several safety nets in place for situations such as this, but they could only do so much, especially for such a large family. A considerable portion of Dmitri's wages went back to his family to help support them.

Camilla approached the door with the same sense of purpose she did with a nasty wound or tricky procedure. Dmitri had it open and shut behind him before she could even knock.

"What are you doing here?" he demanded, his voice hushed

and angry.

"I need to speak with you," Camilla whispered back. "You didn't tell me you were suspended."

Dmitri's face grew dark at that, and Camilla could see his balled fists shaking.

"It's none of your concern," he hissed.

"Yes, it bloody well is!"

"Your paranoia about—"

"I'm here for *you*, Dmitri! I love you, you infantile fool! I'm concerned for *you*, but you're too wrapped up in your own self-pity or bruised pride or whatever it is you're suffering to see it. Why do you think I'm with you, knowing full well how deeply I hate your order?"

Dmitri narrowed his eyes at her and replied, "Go home, Camilla. Don't try to contact me again."

With that, he left and shut the door in her face. Camilla stood there in stunned silence for several moments. Finally, she gathered herself and returned to the cab.

It had been a few days since Camilla's tête-à-tête with Dmitri. The girl had come home and taken Mina and Neal's rebukes in stride. She admitted the subterfuge and impropriety, but she stood by her decisions. Mina and Neal insisted that she must never repeat the behavior, though Camilla couldn't honestly promise this, which only led to more fighting. Lenore was waiting for her when she finally, very wearily, returned to her room that night. It was only then that Camilla allowed herself to break down and weep. Dmitri had shunned her. Their relationship, by all appearances, was over, and Camilla didn't even know what to do. He had said not to try and contact him again. Things had ended so badly and messily, and Camilla was brokenhearted.

"I really do love him," she had said tearfully as Lenore stroked her hair. "He's such a child. Is he ashamed?"

"I don't know," Lenore said gently, though she wasn't so sure.

What if family friends had been willing to take her in after her parents' arrest? None of them had been. Seemingly everyone in the Limestone quarter knew what had happened. She understood shame that deep and knew she had been fortunate to get a second lease on life, though she didn't understand why Dmitri put so much stock in something so deplorable as his position as an Enforcer.

Tension had eased around the house somewhat with the passage of time, but Mina and Neal were clearly still upset. Camilla was putting on a brave face before them. Lenore had been busy with work and various other engagements and so hadn't had a chance to share this new development with Eamon. She was unloading on him in the privacy of his family coach.

"What an absolute ratbag!" Lenore railed.

"Such vehemence, Lenore!" Eamon said, scandalized by her choice of words.

"You don't think his behavior is disgusting? And so help me, Eamon Lee, if you defend him because he took a cheap shot at Rook, I'll—"

"No, no, that's not why," Eamon said, clearly trying to allay Lenore's outrage. "That was an unwarranted attack and a shameful transgression against the rules of fair play."

Lenore made a skeptical face at him and waited.

"Dmitri is proud of his position. His vocation defines him as a man. Having been turned out is a mark against him for all the world to see. He and those around him see him as a failure as a man because of this."

"What trumped up hogwash!" Lenore spat, disregarding her own questioning thoughts from the other night. "If he does see himself as being defined by his profession, he's made a poor choice of it."

"And you don't see yourself as your work?" Eamon asked, raising an eyebrow at her.

Lenore lowered her voice and said, "As someone who used to not know from where her next meal was coming, I'm happy to do anything where I can pull my own weight. I told Neal and Mina I'd clean their house if that's what it took. It's simply miraculous that I've ended up somewhere I can do something about which I'm passionate. If that changes one day, well, I'll have to cope."

Eamon sat back in his seat and nodded, not really believing her, "Still, I understand where he's coming from. I'd be devastated if the same happened to me."

Lenore made a face at him, but they were nearly to the restaurant, so she dropped the subject. It was the same restaurant at which they'd had their first proper date, and Eamon, unsurprisingly, had booked them their usual private booth in the back. Lenore ordered a sloe gin cocktail to go with their meal: duck breast with winter greens on a bed of parsnip and potato mash. Dinner and drinks arrived as Lenore and Eamon were discussing the latest fashion of faux pauldrons— feathered for ladies and leather or even metal for men—which both of them had tried for their outing that evening. The spray of brown and teal wood duck feathers coming off of Lenore's left shoulder kept tickling Eamon's nose anytime he drew near, making Lenore laugh every time.

"At least those on your hat have the decency to stay away from my face," he grumped playfully.

"I shall have to try wearing it backwards in future. Perhaps I'll start a new trend of my own," she said, sipping her drink.

Lenore then made a mischievous face at Eamon and lifted her fork to begin her meal. She jumped when something… someone… alighted from the ceiling and landed softly next to her. Her plate was suddenly pulled away, and she looked to see Rook standing there, his eyes smoldering furiously.

"Rook?!" Lenore hissed.

He cut her off. "Don't eat it! It's poisoned."

"What's poisoned?" she demanded, trying to keep her voice down.

"Your food. Who did you tell you were coming here?"

"Everyone in Arc-Tech knew," Lenore spluttered.

"And you?" Rook asked, turning to glare at Eamon.

"My parents, Doctor Allen, and Engineer Allen," he said, incensed. "And, if you don't mind, we're trying to enjoy ourselves here."

Rook suddenly grabbed Eamon by the collar and yanked him forward. Bringing his face close, Rook snarled at him.

"Didn't you hear me? Lenore's food is poisoned!"

"That's preposterous!"

"Preposterous, hm?" Rook then grabbed the plate and shoved it towards Eamon's face. "Let's see you eat it then."

"Rook!" Lenore hissed. "Let him go! He's absolutely not eating it!"

Rook obeyed… roughly… and stood up straight again.

"He's absolutely deranged!" Eamon insisted.

"Rook, I won't eat anything else. Just, please, leave! Before you get caught."

He nodded before silently leaping up and climbing back into the ceiling. Lenore put her head in her hands. A moment later, a waitress knocked from outside the booth.

"Is everything alright in there?" she called.

"It's fine," Lenore lied immediately. "I don't feel well. We're leaving."

Eamon paid the bill and tipped the wait staff generously. He then led Lenore outside and looked around.

"Where's my coach?" he said immediately.

"Eamon…" Lenore began.

"Richardson knows to wait. He must have been forced to move for some reason. Wait here."

"No, Eamon, stop," Lenore said, grabbing his arm.

He looked back and saw her holding her hand to her head. She was gripping his arm tightly.

"What's wrong?"

"I don't feel right. I need to get home… to Mina."

She took a step and swayed slightly. Eamon held her arm and kept her steady.

"Come on. Let's get started. We'll hail a cab as soon as we see one."

Lenore nodded, though she wasn't optimistic about her chances of seeing a hansom. Her vision was blurring, and the petrolsene lights were blinding to look at. She held onto Eamon and focused on putting one foot in front of the other. Someone called after them, asking if all was well. Eamon called back some congenial thanks and politely declined assistance. Lenore couldn't tell where they were headed, but Eamon knew the way. The streets were darker now, for which Lenore was thankful. Unfortunately, the shadows around her had begun to twist into shapes. They loomed forward, reaching for her, pulling at her dress, her hair, brushing against her. Lenore tried to swat them away, but her hands passed right through them. She leapt in surprise as something else grabbed her hands.

It was a ruddy colored figure, far too tall. It was like a man but stretched out thin. The eyes were white, and its long, snakelike fingers were curled around her arm.

"Lenore, dear, it's me," she heard Eamon's voice from the figure's mouth. Then, in a different voice, it growled, "You won't make it home alive tonight."

She cried out and pulled away. Too quickly. Her balance fled in that moment. She was falling and hit her backside hard against the pavement. The figure came for her again, and another was approaching from behind. This one was darker than the first with a head aflame in blue and indigo. It was more like a thick mist than an elongated specter and wielded a white quill. Lenore cried out in alarm and pointed. The tall one fell to the ground near her. There was a third figure now, a wind made of flashes of light and gusts. It fought the mist, which dissolved quickly.

The wind blew near, but now a black creature of limbs and leaves made of glass appeared behind the wind. It thrust its boughs at the wind, dispersing the wind back into the atmosphere. The creature then drew close to Lenore and, as it drew nearer, she saw it change from black to maroon. Its glass leaves condensed into a more solid shape, covering the creature in armor of liquid gold. It reached out to Lenore, and she knew it was going to destroy her as it had the wind. Time was slow, fortunately, and she was energy. No, she wasn't. She was a conduit for energy. It was calling to her, and she placed her hand on the hilt of a sword. She lifted the sword from the scabbard by her side and saw it had a blade of jagged white and lilac and blue lightning. Without thinking, she thrust the sword at the creature, so close now she could feel the cold emanate from it. The tip connected, and the creature reared back, screaming and juddering in midair as it arched back on itself. Smoke was coming off of it now. Lenore could see its bones cracking beneath the gold armor, but she didn't move until it fell away from her into the darkness.

All was quiet. Lenore didn't know for how long. The wind returned and pulled the tall specter to its feet. Together, they gently helped Lenore up as well. Wherever they touched her glowed orange and yellow, and they whispered comfort to her, though she couldn't always make out the words. The wind led them through the dark, which still moved like liquid.

Lenore twitched away from the thing that claimed to be Mina. Blazes, the light was horrible here. There was far too much of it. The visions that plagued Lenore had subsided a bit, but her heart was still racing, her head hurt, and her mouth and throat were painfully dry. In addition to the pain, her head was spinning, and though she could hear people talking to her, her brain sometimes garbled what was said.

From what Lenore heard, the entire family was there including Esther, as well as Eamon and Rook. Lenore could tell they were talking about the attack, though the rendition she heard now did not line up with her own memory whatsoever. Mina was questioning Rook about poison and Eamon about the meal.

"She didn't eat... drank a little."

"Slow. Siren berries."

"Tipped me off... he likes plants... to prove... garden."

"Samples? Fluids."

Lenore was eventually placed on something that felt like a cloud, after which she drifted in and out of a strange sort of half sleep. She was tired and wanted water. Someone helped her to drink a little something, which felt nice, before drifting off again.

"What progress have you made in your search?" Mina asked sharply.

Everything she'd done that night had been sharp and

precise and exacting. Seeing Eamon and Rook appear with an obviously very ill Lenore had set off every instinct in her, both as a mother and a doctor. She'd begun firing off orders and questions as quickly as her mind and tongue would allow. Now that Lenore was tucked into bed with a care plan in place, she was able to slow down, but only slightly.

"Little. I have my best people on it, but—"

"I don't want to hear your 'buts'," Mina snapped. "I want to know what you're going to do next."

Rook narrowed his eyes at Mina.

"With all due respect, Doctor Allen, I can only press so hard before my own investigation becomes a danger to Lenore. There are people who would be more than happy to use her to get to me."

"Fine," Mina agreed brusquely. "Eamon, no more nights out. Neal, that goes for lunches as well. Esther is to oversee all her food preparation."

"Do you trust Esther to—" Eamon began.

"Implicitly," Neal cut in. "That woman has been with my family since before I was born. Even still, I believe she's due for a wage increase."

"She identified the most likely source of the poison before I could even begin narrowing it down," Mina added. "Esther is Lenore's best defense against this new method."

There was a heavy pause in the conversation then.

"Neal, could you send Lenore ahead of you to Bone Port?" Mina asked softly. "Perhaps she would be safer there."

Neal shook his head. "I'm afraid we don't have the permits. Besides, she'd be in more danger there without all of us."

"I know," Mina said resignedly. "I just want to get her away from here, remove her from the situation."

"As do I, my dove," Neal replied, placing a hand on her arm. He then looked to Rook and Eamon and asked, "Any other ideas? Eamon, don't you have some… connections?"

Eamon looked surprised and then rubbed his ˈneck uncomfortably.

"I didn't realize you knew about those, though I suppose I shouldn't be surprised. I do, but they're not really that sort."

"What sort are they?" Rook asked.

"They provide… influence," Eamon explained. "Professional persuaders, if you will."

"You bankroll crusaders?" Neal asked, disdain coloring his voice. "Heaven above, I cannot stand those conniving ratbags."

"And now I know where Lenore learned it," Eamon mumbled to himself.

Rook smiled at that.

"Crusaders" was an unpleasant term for someone who made it their profession to sway the vote of the magistrate council. Bribing a magistrate was illegal, but crusaders used other, more cunning methods to ply their trade, and many believed Enforcers often looked the other direction when it benefitted their cause, though no one could prove anything either way. Who was to stop someone from gifting a fine bottle of spirits to a friend just because they value the friendship or to say thank you?

"It's for a good cause," Eamon insisted.

"Neither here nor there," Mina said. "Can you use them?"

"That's not really what they do," Rook said. "And I wouldn't trust them with a thimble."

"Agreed," Neal said. "Rook, is there anything we can do to assist you? Do you need money? Weapons?"

"How about information on that magic stick in Lenore's bag?" Rook said, raising an eyebrow. "What do you know about it?"

All four of them looked to the small console table upon which Lenore's accessories—hat, bag, and gloves—had been set. The hilt of the small baton was still sticking out of the top as it always did. Lenore had taken to carrying it with her, as she thought it could be used as a sort of weapon in an emergency. It certainly wouldn't feel good to be hit with it, she had reasoned. The gem in the pommel was dull and dark grey now, and no one had dared touch it since hearing what had happened. Unbeknownst to Lenore, the man she had struck with it was left lying in the street, a charred and blackened husk of what he once was, his clothes being eaten away by small, residual flames.

"You said it shocked him?" Neal asked carefully.

"Not just shocked," Eamon explained. "It was as if she called the very sky down on him."

"Though nothing specific comes to mind at the moment, I will certainly look into it," Neal said, "The Old World denizens harnessed all kinds of power through their enchantments. There's no telling what this thing might be. For all we know, it could be an incomplete experiment."

"If she can safely use it again, I want her carrying it with her at all times," Mina said.

"With all due respect, Mina, it killed a man," Eamon said.

"Yes, and a bloody good thing it did, too," Mina said, her sharp eyes focusing in on Eamon. "As far as I'm concerned, anyone who dies in the attempt on an innocent's life has it coming."

Rook smiled again, more widely than before, at this.

Camilla and Mina watched over Lenore in shifts. They monitored her heart rate and pupils and kept her hooked up to an intravenous tree, which they called an IVT for short, for fluid therapy. Rook refused to leave that night, though Eamon was the only one who objected with any kind of energy. Eamon eventually went home after sharing a drink with Neal so that he could honestly tell his parents he had done so, thus providing an acceptable reason for being so late. Rook's suggestion that he could just lie was met with contempt. As for Richardson, the Lee family coach driver, Eamon was going to have to find out what had happened to him. He sincerely hoped the man wasn't dead. After he was gone, Rook and Neal were left alone, as Mina had left to check on Lenore again and help Camilla refresh the bulky saline bags, which had an annoying tendency to make a grand mess if the switch was not performed just right. On more than one occasion, Mina and Camilla had sworn they were going to invent a better version.

After an awkward period of silence, Neal gestured for Rook to follow him. The two men made their way up to Neal's drawing room, and Neal opened his bar.

"Would you like something?" he asked tiredly.

"I'd be honored," Rook said, and his voice was sincere. "I'll have whatever you're having."

"What I'm having is pretty strong." Neal looked at Rook and thought for a moment before adding, "Which will probably suit you just fine."

Rook smiled and said jovially, "Be careful, Engineer Allen. That sounded dangerously close to a compliment."

Neal said nothing to that and poured two small drinks. Rook thanked him and took a sip. His eyebrows shot up appreciatively.

"My, that is good. Do you mind sharing where I might procure some for myself?"

"Dawn's Light, 1st year. You can't get it anywhere. This bottle has been in my family for generations."

"That's incredibly magnanimous of you," Rook said slowly. "I notice you didn't pour any of this out for Eamon."

"No, and I'd prefer it if you didn't mention it to him. I don't need there to be any more competition between you than there already is." Neal paused and sighed. "We may not like each other, but the fact is you've saved Lenore's life twice now, possibly more. This is the least I can do."

"You sincerely see yourself as a surrogate father to her, don't you?" Rook asked curiously.

"I can only hope Edgar Crowley would be pleased."

Rook was silent for a little while after that, pensively swirling his glass around in his hand. When he finally spoke again, his voice was soft.

"I think he might have been."

"And you?" Neal asked.

"And me what?"

"Do you sincerely love Lenore?"

"Yes, sir. Everything about Lenore is sincere for me."

Neal made a noise of acknowledgement at that, but it was impossible to tell what the feeling was behind it. They sipped their drinks in relative silence after that.

Dmitri stared at the drab, cracked ceiling and tried to block out the noises that surrounded him... the sound of his elders chatting on the floor below... the baby crying in the flat squashed next door... the sound of the arguing couple in the shop on the other side... Boris playing pretend in the hallway outside. How he hated this place. The people were not the problem. No, he'd seen enough all over the city to know people were all the same no matter what walk of life they came from. He hated the uncertainty, the fear. His family did well enough covering it up, trying to be hopeful and happy with one another, but there was always that thread of apprehension that wound its way through and around them. It drew tight some days, spoiling moods and stealing joy, making everyone feel trapped.

No one had said anything to Dmitri. No one had asked why he had been home more in the last two weeks than he had been in the last two years. No one would ask at the end of the month when he didn't bring home any money. Four weeks. That was all that was left until he received the decision from the order. There would be no trial, no chance to defend himself. There would only be their verdict. Even if he was accepted back, he would be a walking disgrace. Doubtless Jones had already told everyone what had happened; only his version would be heard.

Dmitri turned over and noticed something sitting on the short box that served as a bedside table. It was a piece of paper, small and folded tightly. He picked it up and unfolded it. He immediately recognized the handwriting and almost threw it. The second sheet was what stopped him. The first was short and simply read,

*You're an idiot. Come by. There's a glass and opportunities waiting for you.*

Dmitri growled. He didn't need Rook's charity. He didn't want it anyway, especially not when he was considering trading information for his position. Dmitri crumpled the first sheet. He was lying to himself. He'd never do that. The only reason he had joined the Enforcers was to try and make a positive difference, to try and stem the tide of cruelty. If he turned on Rook, he'd be no better than that weasel Jones. Not to mention the threat that now posed to the Allens... to Camilla via Lenore now that she and Rook had a public relationship. Dmitri swore, thinking of Lenore. The little cuckoo had caused him nothing but grief. He brushed that thought aside as he began to read the second page of the note. It was from Camilla.

She acknowledged—not apologized for—contacting him after he'd told her not to. She expressed condolences for what had happened to him and listed his good qualities. She wished him the best and was optimistic for him that all would be well. She felt it was important to state these things despite what had transpired between them.

Dmitri read the letter over again. It felt like the closing of a book and a dagger to the gut, a feeling with which he was actually familiar. Camilla was ending things with him, and that good-for-nothing Rook had delivered the note for her... probably happily. Dmitri wondered if Rook had perhaps convinced her to break it off with him in the first place. He had threatened to do that very thing not so long ago. He'd probably volunteered to be the messenger just to make it that much easier for her. Dmitri crumpled both pages together. He wouldn't go see Rook. He'd do something entirely different.

As soon as she was herself again, the first thing Lenore wanted to do was investigate her curio, as she called it. Rook raised an eyebrow at the name but didn't divulge exactly why. Lenore had been told that it killed the second attacker, but she didn't know the full details until a few days later thanks to Eamon.

"I made a vow to always be honest with her," Eamon said.

"That doesn't require you to share horror stories," Rook said scathingly.

"I'd rather know," Lenore argued. "I need to know what I'm dealing with."

Rook said nothing to that and instead watched Lenore's face. Killing someone, even in self-defense, was not something anyone took lightly, and the first kill was always the hardest. Rook knew this all too well, and he resisted the urge to reach out to Lenore as he saw the faintest crease of regret twitch in her face. He'd address it with her later when the annoying bluster-boy wasn't around.

Once she had her wits about her again, Lenore was able to share with more clarity what she thought had happened when she activated her curio. She'd had intention to use it as a weapon, wanted to unleash the damage it could do. She held it by the hilt and, amidst panicked objections, touched the rod.

"Calm down," she scoffed. "I've tossed this thing around hundreds of times. Never once has it shocked me."

"It's possible you woke it up," Neal scolded, repressing the urge to take it from Lenore as he would a lit candle from a toddler.

"It feels the same as ever," Lenore insisted.

The gem in the pommel of the baton had begun to lighten again the day after the attack and now again looked as it always had. This, everyone unanimously agreed, meant it had recharged, which only gave rise to more questions. The biggest of these was how to recreate the effect... without killing anyone or seeking out more assassins, of course. Lenore suggested setting up a target in Kieran's room, but Neal vetoed the idea almost immediately.

"Hosting sparring matches in there is one thing—I haven't yet figured out how to apologize for the blood spilt in there—but possibly lighting his quarters on fire is something else entirely."

"Sparring matches?" said Eamon quizzically. "And who is Kieran?"

"It's a long story, one which will have to wait," Mina replied brusquely, clearly brushing Eamon off for the moment.

It had been decided not to tell Eamon about Lenore's self-defense lessons. Even Neal, who was usually Eamon's biggest advocate, could not bring himself to agree. Doing so would undoubtedly cause Eamon to want to be involved, and none of the family were about to tell him about Kieran without the Vampyre's consent. An argument could always be made that having Eamon in attendance would somehow be improper, but that reasoning would quickly fall apart. It was entirely likely that Mina just planned on putting Eamon off forever, which seemed unfeasible, but if anyone could do it, it would be her.

"Perhaps something in the courtyard?" Camilla asked.

"Again, we risk setting fire to the estate," Mina said.

"Do we know it will do that?" Lenore asked curiously.

"Best to not take the chance," Neal said.

"What if I tried using it on Lenore," Rook suggested.

Every eye turned on him as silence descended over the room. He didn't move from his perch on the arm of a sofa.

"Don't be daft," he said flatly. "I'm not actually going to, of course… not the way she did anyway. My promise will warn me ahead of time if she's in danger."

More silence. Looks were exchanged around the room.

"It might work," Camilla said finally.

Eamon made a strangled noise of disbelief. Mina and Neal were staring at one another as if they were having their own telepathic conversation.

"No, it's not worth the risk," Neal said. "We'll think of some other way to test it."

"I think Rook—" Lenore began.

"It's out of the question, young lady," Mina said, cutting her off.

Eamon looked satisfied at that, and the subject was dropped.

Dmitri eyed the woman next to him out of the corner of his eye.

She was taller than he was and somewhat thickly built, or at least that was the impression her tightly corded muscles gave. Her dark hair was braided and wound up into a bun. She had already threatened his life twice and, by the number of small throwing knives sheathed in her belt and the crossbow slung across her back, looked more than equipped to follow through. Dmitri looked around him and quickly deduced that everything about this room had been very carefully selected and arranged to incite fear. It was all very theatrical, really.

The air was stale here and smelled of damp and mold, and cold emanated from every surface. The walls were covered in a thin film of moisture, causing some kind of luminescent blue and green lichen to grow over them. The lichen cast a feeble, yellow-green and blue glow, which bled into the orange of the blazing braziers lined up along the walls. Human skulls tucked into hollows roughly gouged into the walls were eerily lit and stared malevolently ahead. How many graves in these old catacombs had been desecrated in the effort to create this macabre tableau, Dmitri didn't care to guess.

The woman next to him and the two other guards in the room all wore brass masks that completely covered their faces. The lifeless stare of the large, round lenses of the masks resembled the skulls, as they were likely meant to, though the mouths were stranger yet. The mouths were nothing more than thin, flat grates that conveyed nothing. In addition to this, each guard was dressed entirely in black leather. If Dmitri had to, he could likely take out one of the guards quickly, but he'd be hard pressed to dispatch the other two.

A door opened somewhere in the gloom beyond Dmitri's vision. He only knew it by the sound of stone scraping against stone. What emerged very nearly made Dmitri laugh aloud. The figure that stepped into the fire and lichen light was, like the guards, dressed entirely in black. Even the ragged cape looked as if it were made of bleeding darkness. Not an inch of skin showed. He or she also wore a mask, but it was far more odd. It had glassy, round, staring eyes and a long bird's beak, a plague mask reminiscent of those worn by the Old World death-speakers. The figure walked forward slowly and then settled themself down in what was clearly meant to be a throne. Thankfully, it was less dramatic than the environment around it, though Dmitri couldn't help but wonder derisively if perhaps it was made up of ancient coffins or something equally ludicrous.

After several solid minutes of heavy silence, the figure spoke, his or her voice distorted so severely it was impossible to tell if it was male or female.

"I understand you want to work for the Reaper."

"That is correct, my lord," Dmitri replied.

Dmitri was no longer so sure this was true. These people were absurd. From what he could gather from his contacts, though, The Collective, Reaper's crime syndicate, was isolated and reportedly more secure than any other. Still, the masks, the uniforms, the general melodramatic air of the organization, it was all almost too much for Dmitri. Joining them might make him into a bigger laughingstock than he already was.

"One does not choose to join The Collective. Members are chosen," the Reaper rasped.

"You would do well to choose me," Dmitri said boldly.

"Convince me."

Dmitri took a deep breath. Did he truly want to do this? If he did, there was no turning back. He thought of his shame, his anger, his lack of options… there wasn't much else to be done for it. Thus, he began his case.

"Are you sure about this?" Rook asked, not sounding very

certain himself, a rare thing indeed.

"Yes," Lenore replied too confidently. "Absolutely."

Did they really trust Rook's oath to protect her? They knew so little about the actual mechanics of bonds and even less about the curio. What if it all happened too quickly? What if Rook couldn't disengage? No, Lenore had to remind herself. That didn't line up with the data they had. Granted, it was very limited data based on the observation of one hallucinating and two dazed witnesses... no. It would be fine. Rook had less than no intention of hurting her. The test would be safe.

"If you feel the slightest—" Camilla began.

"Yes, understood!" Rook snapped. "I'm not going to try to kill your precious sister."

"I know!" Camilla shot back. "That's absolutely not what I'm worried about. Any inadvertent injuries, though nonlethal, will be difficult to hide, and Mina and Neal will have my head if they find out about this."

"You think they'd spare me?" Lenore asked, wondering what that would mean.

"Oh no, they'd kill you as well. They would just take me first."

"Why?" Lenore followed.

"Because she's the oldest," Rook interjected.

"Precisely. You must have siblings," Camilla said with a nod.

"Is that true?" Lenore asked.

Lenore had often wondered about Rook's childhood, his life before becoming a criminal, his family, and had asked on numerous occasions. Every time, he had refused to answer her, deflecting the subject into safer waters.

As if on cue, Rook replied crisply, "Let's get on with it."

Lenore was not at all surprised by the response.

"I guarantee he's the youngest," Camilla whispered

conspiratorially to Lenore.

She smiled at that and then headed over to Rook, who was looking positively grim.

"I trust you," she said, touching his arm.

He glanced at her but said nothing. With that, Lenore hitched up the hem of her skirt to expose her bare lower leg. Lenore had removed her boots and stockings to reduce the risk of any of them catching fire. Lenore may have questioned whether or not such a thing would actually happen, but she wasn't about to risk igniting herself. Camilla was on hand to act as both chaperone and medical services. They had all decided Lenore's calf would be the easiest place to hide any injuries or marks. It was also far enough away from any major organs… just in case. Rook had the curio gripped in his hand so tightly that his knuckles were white. He approached Lenore carefully.

"How are you feeling?" Camilla asked anxiously.

"Just a tingle, powderpuff," Rook said, barely keeping a growl from his voice.

From what Lenore knew, that was a good sign. Rook had told her how the oath had incapacitated him in the past when her life was in danger. She nodded at the information and stepped closer to Rook. With a flick of his wrist, he snapped the rod towards Lenore's calf. She felt nothing and looked down to see herself unscathed.

"Did you do it?" she asked, looking at Rook.

"Practice," Rook said, not meeting her eyes.

Lenore narrowed her eyes at him and scowled. "Just do it already."

"You know," Camilla began. "Perhaps if we did a one, two —"

Rook lightly tapped the rod against Lenore's calf.

"AGH!" Lenore screamed.

Camilla squealed too because Lenore had, and Rook

jumped back. Lenore looked down at her leg and saw a red mark on it.

"Are you alright?" Rook asked immediately.

"I'm fine. Sorry," Lenore explained quickly. "It surprised me more than anything."

"Did it hurt?" Camilla asked.

"Not really? A little?" Lenore replied uncertainly, rubbing the spot. It was barely tender. She looked to Rook again and asked, "Are you quite sure you're doing it right?"

"I haven't the foggiest!" Rook replied in exasperation. "All I have to go on is your fever-dream account." He then paused and said softly, "I don't want to hurt you."

"Stop playing around!" Lenore said, feeling more agitated than ever.

Rook jerked the rod towards her leg again, and this time a flash of light ignited for a split second over her flesh. Lenore cried out and leapt away from Rook. Rook, meanwhile, yelled and swore as he crumpled onto his knees. Camilla was by Lenore's side and examining the wound in a moment. Lenore's skin was red and welted and still warm to the touch. Fortunately, that seemed to be the extent of the damage. Camilla looked back to Rook, but he was already waving her away.

"I'm fine. Just leave me be," he groaned.

Camilla hesitated. She scanned Rook with her eyes but could not see any apparent injuries. Though it went against her instincts, she did as he asked and returned to Lenore.

"Is that just his vow… punishing him?" Camilla whispered to Lenore.

Lenore nodded. Camilla then headed back over to where she had been watching and grabbed a sturdy doctor's bag from the floor. From it, she drew a small pot of honey and a bandage.

"Is it still burning?" Camilla asked.

"Yes," Lenore said, trying to ignore the sting in her leg.

Camilla nodded and also drew a flask from her bag.

"I wouldn't mind a swig of that," Rook said, wiping sweat from his brow.

"It's not what you think it is. I filled it with cold water," Camilla explained.

"Unfortunate," Rook muttered.

Camilla then poured the water over Lenore's wound before placing a somewhat soggy icepack over it. Once her flesh had stopped burning, Camilla created a poultice of honey and crushed oregano with the bandages and bound Lenore's leg with it.

"I'll check on it periodically to ensure it doesn't get infected," she told Lenore.

"So what did we learn?" Lenore asked, looking at Rook.

He had recovered and was helping Camilla now. Rook recounted what he had done, starting with the second swipe. He had barely made contact, though he insisted he saw a spark, and Lenore confirmed that she had felt something.

"And after that?" Camilla asked.

"I was trying to succeed," Rook said, his voice low.

"I think that's promising," Lenore said cheerfully.

"Are you sure you're alright?" Rook asked, taking her hand in his.

Lenore smiled and nodded. She felt optimistic now and far more certain of her ability to protect herself. Even if they had only learned a little, it was a brilliant start. In addition to that, her fighting lessons would continue. Everything was looking up! Mina and Neal appeared none the wiser later that day when the whole family was gathered together again, though Lenore and Camilla kept throwing one another furtive glances.

"It'll be so quiet around here without you two," Camilla commented that evening, referring to the upcoming expedition.

If anything would divert Mina and Neal's attention, it was that.

Lenore had to admit that that was true. Half the household was leaving for who knew how long. Lenore liked to imagine they would only be gone as long as it took them to make some amazing new discovery. She was told it was going to be dangerous as well. The southern part of the continent was apparently very different from the midland where they were, but Lenore wasn't concerned any longer. She was even more excited now than she had been. They were going to a different world to live for at least a few months, and then they would dig up another one from long ago.

If you enjoyed this book, please consider leaving a review on StoryGraph, Fable, Goodreads and/or Amazon, etc. Even a single line is massively helpful. Thank you in advance for taking the time to share your thoughts.

To get more goodies from Dana, consider joining her Patreon at https://www.patreon.com/wordsbydana

You can also sign up for early updates, cover reveals, and exclusive content by joining her VIP newsletter. You can sign up for that on her website: https://www.wordsbydana.com/

# ᴀɴ Ᵽxcerpt from ɪnto the Ᵽire

*My dear Kieran,*

*Bone Port is the single most spectacular place in all of Invarnis, not that I am in any way biased... never me. You know you cannot deny it. When the waves crash against the Thunder Cliffs, is it not like being in the very midst of a mighty storm? Thankfully, without all the associated threats of being picked up and tossed by capricious winds to our deaths into that great emerald sea. Not that such things concern the likes of you and me.*

*The city proper of Bone Port is a star field of small islands and smaller sandbars, some of which disappear and reappear with the changing tides, all of which look to that slender crescent moon coast as mother. Travel between these, though possible by island bridge, is often by canoe and kayak. The sea, that green sky gently cupping each star-island, is life. Whales and fish and seal-kind teem and thrive and fly within those depths.*

*The people of my beloved home are like the coast, constantly changing with the weather and water. They are resilient and adaptable. They are a proud people, yet they are without conceit. It was because of the Bone Portis that we ever had trade with the people across the sea, though that blasted War of Light saw an end to that. Oh, but I am getting sentimental, and you had questions for me.*

*The devastation was horrific. People think they can imagine ruin because they've seen glimpses of the Char district. They have no idea. Swaths of the city were leveled in seconds as rings of gold and orange and white energy pulsed forth like deadly ripples. And from a single person! Those desperate magi lost their lives in the effort, of course, but they took as many with them as they could as they went. I am glad for my sake that I do not remember the exact site of many of those attacks, though for yours I am sorry. As I do not spend as much time underground as you do, I haven't the foggiest as to whether your friends would find any bones even if they knew where to look. How long do buried human skeletons last? You must let me know in your next letter. I imagine it must be quite a long time, based on what I've heard... at least, I assume these scholars aren't making it all up.*

*You will likely have better luck searching for their artifacts, machines and technology and the like. The buildings are just about all gone in Bone Port—you can't build great stone edifices on sand and basalt the way you can on the red clay here—so you won't find any ruins. The coves and grottoes might hold some secrets, however. Those magic-users hid somewhere during the war, and those nooks and crannies are as good a place as any, but there are places not even I could reach to get confirmation. I do know of at least one cache where you might even find some books, though I cannot speak for their condition after over a hundred years. They looked fairly safe when I left them, though.*

*Search inland for your buried treasures. If I remember correctly, that bulbous swimming contraption was found by chance after a storm. The sand is tricky in that way. It will swallow and move and regurgitate as it sees fit. Things buried in the jungle will stay put, though getting to them is a... squishy process. The skies were alight with fire and lightning back then, and many of their flying machines dove below the canopy, never to emerge again. The jungle has changed since then. Like a puddle, it has grown and stretched and shrunk over the years, sharing space with the tall grasses and surrounding marshlands.*

*Advise your friends to be wary of the creatures in those wildlands. The animals and even the insects can be as dangerous as they are beautiful... even more so in some cases. I have enclosed some old remedies my nurses always kept on hand. Just don't say from where you got them—or any of this information, for that matter—but you, of course, already knew that.*

*Come by after I close up sometime before you go. There is more I'd like to tell you... you can see through me, can't you? I know what you're thinking. I just want someone to reminisce to. Well, you'd be right. My windows are always open to you, old friend.*

*In the night,*
*Cali*

Kieran smiled as he read over the letter. She was so shameless. Though who could blame her? Certainly not him. He decided to go sooner rather than later. Whatever information she could impart was likely to be invaluable. He knew how different Bone Port was from Springhaven. The two city-states had been separated for over a hundred years, after all. Not that he had been able to experience the coast in the traditional sense, and he hadn't visited for very long—being forced to live nocturnally in a beach paradise did make one rather depressed —but even his limited knowledge told him Neal and Lenore were in for quite a surprise.

~*~

*Dana Fraedrich*

To follow Lenore and her friends into more adventures, you can purchase *Into the Fire* from anywhere that sells books. Available in ebook, print, and audio.

# Enjoy More of the Broken Gears World

### *Out of the Shadows*

**BOOK 1 OF 3**

***Pride and Prejudice* meets HG Wells with a dash of *The Hunger Games***

⚙ The beginning of Lenore's trilogy
⚙ Adventure | Light Romance | Some Fantasy Elements
⚙ Chronology: followed by *Into the Fire* and then *Across the Ice*

### *Raven's Cry*

**STANDALONE**

**A dark retelling of *Swan Lake***

⚙ Standalone
⚙ Dark Fantasy | No Romance | Fairytale Retelling
⚙ Chronology: precedes all other Broken Gears books

### *Rook's Gambit*

**STANDALONE**

***Ocean's 11* style steampunk heist**

⚙ Standalone
⚙ Heist | Light Background Romance | No Fantasy Elements
⚙ Chronology: precedes *Out of the Shadows*

### *Falcon's Favor*

**STANDALONE**

**A queer, cozy mystery romance full of food, cravings, tea, and found family**

⚙ Standalone
⚙ Cozy Mystery | Sweet Romance | No Fantasy Elements
⚙ Chronology: follows the events of *Across the Ice*

### *Death Cults and Taxes*

**ANTHOLOGY**

**For those who want more from the Broken Gears world**

⚙ Assumes you've read Lenore's trilogy, but any spoilers are mentioned at the beginning of each story
⚙ Chronology: stories take place during various points in history

# ACKNOWLEDGEMENTS

No author is an island, and no book comes to life without the touch of many people.

Firstly, thank you to God, for this creativity and passion. Thank you for the opportunities and ability to be an independent author. Thank you for courage, for support, and for love.

Chris, my incredible and ever-persevering editor, you make me a better writer. Trust me, I'm learning so much from you! Why do you think this book had fewer red marks than the last? That's your influence, though I fear some of my more American writing habits will never go away (the dreaded double preposition).

Mike, my sweet, beloved husband, you are so patient, especially as I ask you to do this... and that... and give your opinion here... and what about this? It takes a special person to support someone as demanding as I with as much grace as you do. Give it a minute. I'll probably ask something else of you in three, two, one...

Hannah, I keep telling myself to just accept that you will continue to blow my mind with your indescribable talent and so I should no longer be surprised by anything you do. And yet I still can't help but freak out when I see the marvels you create with just your hands and mind. The maps are beautiful!

To my family, thank you for always supporting me in so many countless ways. Dad, remember that ballast question I asked you a few years back in Nag's Head? That was the beginning of this book. Mum, you should know Tilly, her shop, and all the clothes would not have been the same without your influence all these years. Heather, I see you in Mina and I hope you can see why. And, Colie, I know how much you love steampunk. I hope you approve.

To my best friend, Sally, and everyone else who has the mixed fortune of being close enough to me to be included in my witter-fests. You know my process; you respect my process. Thank you for your patience and time.

Lastly, but not at all least, thank you so much to my readers.

Thank you for supporting this hopeful author. If these stories I write have a positive effect on even just one of you, that is a kind of magic unto itself.

# ABOUT THE AUTHOR

Dana Fraedrich is a three-time Kirkus Star recipient, dog lover, self- professed geek, and author of the steampunk fantasy series Broken Gears, which includes the Amazon bestseller, *Out of the Shadows*. Dana's books are full of secrets and colorful characters that examine the many shades of grey that paint the world. When she isn't busy writing or attending conventions and book festivals, she can be found co-hosting the podcast *Steam-Powered Movies*, playing D&D and video games, and exploring new interests.

Even from a young age, she enjoyed writing down the stories that she imagined in her mind. Born and raised in Virginia, she earned her BFA from Roanoke College and is now carving out her own happily ever after in Nashville, TN with her husband. Dana is always writing; more books are on the way!

If you enjoyed reading this book, please leave a review. Even it's just one line, that really helps authors.

Find Dana online at www.wordsbydana.com and sign up for her VIP Newsletter, where you can read new short stories as they're released and keep up with her adventures

Facebook: https://www.facebook.com/wordsbydana/

@danafraedrich on Bluesky, Threads, and Instagram

Follow Dana on Goodreads, BookBub, or her Amazon Author page

Or you can get goodies and support her on Patreon - https://www.patreon.com/wordsbydana - Thanks!

www.ingramcontent.com/pod-product-compliance
Lightning Source LLC
Chambersburg PA
CBHW020645110726
47901CB00001B/59

* 9 7 8 0 6 9 2 9 0 9 2 3 2 *